Words In The Wind

Book One
From the Books of the
House of Mandara

Written By
Demon L. A. Wood

ProCord Publishing
Jersey City, New Jersey

Published by ProCord Publishing, a division of Professional Coordinators, 9 Heckman Dr., Suite 1B, Jersey City, NJ 07305 • 201-435-7816
First Printing 1995, Printed and bound in the United States of America

Book cover design by ProCord Publications
Cover photograph by George Rodger, Magnum Photo Inc., 151 West 25th Street, New York, New York 10001

Library of Congress Cataloging-in-Publication Data: 40-02715

ISBN 0-9648402-1-9 (Softcover Edition)

FOREWORD

In answer to the question: "Why don't we build pyramids any more?", **Words In The Wind** was really the forth book of a series that was more concerned with what I called the lost powers of African people. The research I was doing on ancient Africa was telling me something different, so I decided to change the book's direction, and while still focusing on African Mythologies, I came to terms with their legacy of memory and imagination, which actually had not been lost at all. The proof of this still living legacy can be found today in every aspect of our lives, especially in the fact that we have survived — against all the evil that could have destroyed us. To better understand this legacy, I needed to understand its development within the annals of our African past, and it was here that I found the stories I wished to write about at last.

Even as I began, I wondered why I settled on writing fantasy, instead of historical fiction, which I hope to eventually write, but I knew that I wanted no part of the arguments from those who have written the many opposing renditions of Africa's past. Fantasy proved the necessary suit to wear, since memory and imagination had always been the African's route to success. Before the advent of writing, it took a long and secure memory to place solar events into a firmly worked calendar, especially when many of those events were many thousands of years apart; and it took an even greater imagination to survive the horrors of nature that can change a green valley into a desert, or the racial assassinations that can change the history of a people from black to white.

In this age, when the desires of youth that deal in the steady reaction to the hard facts of life, result in wildings over our moral and social codes, I find it enlightening to lose myself in the stories that only a heart has told. Fantasy is just such a vehicle, and mythology is the engine to that old car. Look what European mythology has done to leadership all over the world, where even in Latin and Arab countries — all their leaders look white and a great deal of their blood is. To this day, the myth of old English and ancient European life is so overly romanticized and sterilized that everyone believes is was the power of their weapons that killed the hundreds of thousands everywhere they went; when in truth, it was the funk of their filth and disease that killed off whole races and nations of people. The greatest of all Asian myths have been worked so firmly into our psyche, that Asians are automatically respected for their legacy of humility and wisdom, or feared because they may know one of those martial arts. Well, black people are different, and in need of internalizing their own mythologies and not the criminal mythos of white America, nor the pathos of black struggles in a white world. I want to understand the mythos that is native to us as a people, like the unity of the bodies, minds and spirits that built the great pyramids, and not the misinformation of their having been built by slaves..

Fantasy is the key to this creative mind, and when I consider the current direction of our youth or the shallow sameness of the products we produce, I am more convinced than ever that we need a little more imagination in our lives. Constant attention to the realities of racism, sexism and bigotism will not make these evils disappear, but a little imagination will take away their power from our lives. Like during the seventies when everyone wined and complained that blacks were not being properly portrayed in films, Spike came along, used his imagined and washed away those ills.

One night in a dream an old, crusty-black man came to me and asked if I'd like hear a tale. He seemed sinister at first and his name seemed a curse, until I heard him said something that I already knew and held dear. All things are illusion, a fantasy of mind for which only the strong can create or see through. Like the illusion of slavery that my people suffered, having been made weak of mind and heart. It is over, because those who knew or remembered what freedom was, could also imagine they would again be free one day, and at that time, that really was a fantasy. And tho many people today have degenerated back to that mind-set, a little imagination, a fantasy—a dream—these things will help us survive and live. Just like the pyramids that our fathers built, they appear like an illusion on the sands, like a dream some would have you believe were built by aliens from Orion. But they are real, and just like us, they are the result of the African memory and imagination that will survived through all the changing winds of time.

"The African dreams I dream and the memories in my bones are honed to the tone of a different life, and tho my blood has been away from Africa for a long time, it simmers like high-beams on the darkest of nights, yet is cool like the assurance of my African birthright."

Dedicated to the memory of
Duff Allen Nelson
Whose love of life and art will always be my inspiration

and to

My loving mother,
Lillian Novella Johnson Wood
Who prayed for me,
and proved that a mother's prayers are worth more than gold

and to

My Editor
Michele Kogon
Whose hard work was one of the blessings

BOOK ONE - PART ONE

FROM THE BOOKS OF THE HOUSE OF MANDARA

First trance words to an apprentice of the Keeper of the Blood:
"Our task is to keep our people human and to hold for them a place, by keeping within us what needs to be remembered by us, and sharing that with those in need of it. You must understand, all things in their time. For example: If when alone I strike you for what seems to be no reason, and leave you life and standing, do not bother to ask me why, and do not kill me if I am still useful to you or our people. But make sure you know the reason before we are alone again, or next time I might kill you out of hand."

"They Waited Too Long To Know"

Ebbie Farmer had been abruptly awakened from sleep every day for the last five days. This time she was being rushed from a plane, through jungle and into a waiting limousine. The sight of wildebeest and the sounds of hyenas awoke her to the fact that she was now in Africa. Ebbie looked around for the great antelopes of sable and roan; she wanted to see the good-natured elands or playful impalas. She prayed for a matriarchal elephant to come and kick the motor out of this car, but there was not even a giraffe to witness her continued abduction. Ebbie told herself that only the mean and nasty animals lived here anymore, and she turned to her captors and pleaded with them, once again, to let her go.

They had called her to the hotel to kidnap her, after being trained so well by her father to guard against this very thing from happening. Ebbie couldn't believe it, but the famous humanitarian,

Mrs. Fedora Claukens-Kylie, was somehow involved. Why, Ebbie had no idea, but she was no longer afraid. Feegarmardar had knocked all that out of her, and the drugs they gave her were making this a painless experience.

After more fitful sleeping and strange-colored dreaming, she found herself in a large magnificent hall, surrounded by Pagangenearch acolytes in dark ceremonial gowns. Hundreds of black, brown and cream-colored women were rushing about doing some chore or enjoying their various conversations. Many sat at long tables making plans, some carried papers back and forth to three elderly women sitting at a circular desk, while others worked on odd machinery or computer devices, and no one seemed to know or care who she was.

Ebbie could not recall how she had arrived here or when she had changed her clothes, and this missing memory bothered her more than the kidnaping, Feegarmardar's beating, or having been made a fool of.

"Through eyes blurred with anger, she saw an ancient woman standing before her, dressed completely in white, and bald, like all confirmed Pagangenearchs. She was older than anyone Ebbie had ever seen before. Ebbie knew this notoriously famous woman, who should be too old to still be living, and was supposed to have disappeared over half a century ago, but she wasn't sure how she knew any of this."

"I am Cleopatra Mandara a'La Hedrin," crackled the old woman's voice.

For the first time in days, Ebbie remained clearheaded and free to move about, but she kept her place as the old woman offered her what appeared to be an immense diamond with one hand, and a goblet of gold liquid with the other.

"This stone is my familiar. It is the gemstone of my people. It contains only a little magic now, but...it embodies the history of a great people, my people...your people, little sister."

Ebbie accepted the stone, a giant uncut diamond which had only become smooth over hundreds, if not thousands, of years. Its lights were brilliant and clear, and it sparkled in her hand more like light than matter. Looking at it made her dizzy. Ebbie laughed to herself, thinking she was about to be hypnotized. She looked back up at the old, fading-colored woman, and realized that it would work if she kept listening to the steady rend of the old woman's voice and continued to stare into the gem's light.

"We need you and your blood to become one with us. We would like to train you so that you, or one of your descendants, might acquire a true 'breath of wit'. What we need is a 'truthsayer', as these new acolytes choose to call it. No, you were not the first choice, nor are you the only one. Our first choice is now dead, and we will not have this happen to you or the others. That is why you are here."

The old woman then handed Ebbie the goblet and said, "This, my sister, is an ancient potion." She then let loose a hoarse chuckle. "Almost as old as I. It will not harm you—trust me. Just such a thing was used by the old blood keepers, or tribal historians [*Griots*] as they are called now, and has the power to open a place in your mind where a thing may be stored and never forgotten. It also brings to life the lives in your blood. Drink it all, and I shall begin your history lesson... In ancient times it had not been needed. When our people became human, they had great memories and easily remembered all their lives past, even their lives in other worlds and their lives as other creatures. That is why in all the oldest books written, people are said to have lived for hundreds of years. Our oldest line of blood recalls a boy, who remembered everything he saw, and everything he learned, better than all his people before him...."

▼▼▼▼▼

He remembered all the stories his keeper told, those of days without sunshine and nights without moonlight, ages without any sight or sign of other humans for times on end, which is to speak of days so alike there is nothing to tell them apart. And still, his people walked like the tall walkers, whose heads listen to the sky. He would look about the place and see the people his keeper said were "of his blood," and could not think to miss the sight of their high-stepping saunter.

His people were as tall as trees, with long necks and legs like the tall walkers, who were their friends in the bush. These friends taught them how to walk. They taught them the high scales of sound and showed them how to feed from the trees. They also taught his people their calls, and they learned to speak to this animal that was their clan relation.

From them the people learned the long neck dance, the long leg dance and the twisting dance for mating and pair bonding. The clan learned from them that tall tree tops and small bushes held special foods and medicines, and they learned to stand straight and tall and to walk with style and grace. Tho beautiful of form and movement, they were loved most because they could see and hear over great distances, and could warn the clan of any danger coming. They too were part of all the stories he knew.

This boy was an apprentice to his clan's Keeper of the Blood and could remember the names of all the blood keepers gone by. He remembered those who protected most, or protected best, or were of such a spirit that no one died of a horror during their life. The greatest of all was Cush, who lived to grow white hair upon his head and face. But on the day he died and his body was painted, his bones removed and his flesh returned to the Great Mother, the worst of all horrors came to the clan of the Tall Walkers. His people were almost completely destroyed. Only the lessons of their Keeper of the Blood had saved them. Other than being a blood keeper, there was no greater honor than to be an apprentice to one.

Even this boy had known times when a horror, or a beast, would come to run them off or eat them. He had seen his feeder eaten by the beast of many fangs, had even smelt its breath and felt the wetness of its tongue slap across his head. His sister kin had managed to rush him off with his keeper dragging others after. They knew that a beast, or one of its kin, came to the clan at least once during the length of any life. No elder that he knew had lived and not seen one. But now there were tiny slaves [*children*] enough to fill a duggi, and most would soon be old enough to eat the leaves of the berry vine and to walk the clearing alone, and none of them had seen a live beast yet.

With so long a time without the smell of danger, the keepers had traveled throughout the known clan lands. A custom for the last 2 and 10 generations, they journeyed before every fourth flowering season to find new seeds for planting and new blood for mating. Then, on a day like today, everyone gathered about the spreading waters, each taking a turn to tell the tales of what they saw or found in the lands around, and it was this boy's duty to listen and remember every word.

But today had been strange and busier than most. All the protectors of the clan wore heavy heads. Some of the strangers who had come to visit with them had not been seen all day. This was the last day of the mating dances, when those who would not be kept would have to leave, a day when all would last feast together and would be honored with one of the clan's greatest tales.

On such a day as this, it was the custom for Shhaha, the Keeper of the Blood, to be visited by all those who kept some tale to heart, which was almost everyone. Even slaves, who took to words more quickly and always had a favorite tale, paid visits to the Keeper of the Blood and his three surviving apprentices, to see which tale would be most favored for the telling. No one would have missed speaking to Shhaha today, but the strangers had not come asking for a tale, and the people of the Tall Walkers felt slighted.

The tall walkers [*clan relation*] had also stayed their distance from the duggi clearing, as if they didn't know there was a feast tonight. Not even the little walkers came into the clearing. Feeders walked about with trembling steps, upset that none had come with special herbed birds' nest, or tender new leaves, or tasty tree barks to color their soups.

As an apprentice, it was this young man's duty to keep the watch for the Keeper of the Blood, and so pinched his ear to mark himself to remember this special day and of how the tall walkers had stayed away. He saw the odd look the Keeper of the Blood wore, and knew that he also felt the strangeness.

Still, before the sun could set the clearing filled with boiling clay and stone pots, baking pits, steaming nets and distinctive color-changing bonfires. Everyone watched the new hues coming into the sky and began painting their naked bodies those colors. Using melted chalks, dyes from boiled roots and leaves, and the many paste colors made from insects or bird droppings, the people made themselves beautiful with colored patterns that would shine and glow best in a fire's light. The people of the Tall Walker Clan lived best by day, but they had also grown to love the glowing bush lights, which only came out at night. Theirs were long days, and this would be one of the longest.

As twilight gave into darkness, the strangers returned. Shhaha selected the tale of Cush, and all the clans went to the banks of the white water river. This young apprentice's keeper, Dbsha, who was going to tell the tale, started his dance. He twisted his head to make the shine twinkle within one eye, then turned his head aside for all to see his shape, and because of the deep darkness of him, his body disappeared into the night, outside the light of the moon.

Delighting in the dance of his keeper's silhouette, the boy

thought about the day when he would be a keeper, having known who his mate would be ever since his naming. The old feeders, or women as they are called, demanded their mating. He was thinking of it now, as he proudly watched his keeper change movement into color. Turning an eye to Olaah, his future mate, he smiled, knowing that she would remember every word of the tale, as well as he. He thought of Olaah as the best choice for his mate. She was born as the magical seventh infant, and was one of the highly prized slaves of Jai, from the blood of Ha, which made her almost sacred to the clan. Tho she was neither blue-black nor red-black, the common colors of the clan, she was considered "shimmering black," "true black" or "jet" [*ox stone*], the color most respected among them.

Dbsha finished his dance and rushed back over to the boy, calling him "Mah," which was a signal for Mah to begin his "echoing" of the tale. In return Mah called back, "Dbsha, my keeper," quietly like the bird which was his namesake. Then, with two words and matching body gestures, he said, "I will speak when some part goes missing, or there is a part I have not heard before. I know all the blood gone by," which meant that he knew all the clan tales and could not be fooled.

Then, as was the custom, everyone spoke the first word, the word that began language for the members of their clan. The word that was like unto a god to them. The word that would later name their god, and had more use and meaning than all other words— "Aaah!" And then Dbsha began the tale.

Some of the visiting close kin clans, like the more famous Waterhorse, the Wang, the Kangaba, the seldom seen Black Snake people, the Great Feathers, the clans of the Lion Fields and the people known as the Shittymounds, had come just to hear clan tales like the one Dbsha was telling. Such tales reminded them of who they were, and their word sharing helped them to rise above the animals. They came because they too had much to share in story, or spirit, or health, or wealth of seed and stone. Others came for feeders, or protectors to be keepers, or just to be among the people who were legend for their great stature and their dance.

Mah's people were even more renown because of the healing powers of their Keepers of the Blood. They were seldom visited by strangers because their lands were hard to reach. Situated in the Valley of the Lengths of Many Mountains, one had to cross dangerous swamp lands, desert and a great hilly plain to reach them. Those who got that far were lost to the thick jungle surrounding them, but this was considered the land of all their mothers; it was a land of plenty, and so many people tried. However, only those mated to the Tall Walkers, or their close kin clans knew the way, and now those clans and tribes came in great numbers every fourth flowering season, for visits, and mating, and the sharing of clan tales.

In the company of their close kin clan the Kangaba, there were many strangers come this season. Most were men who had come for mates. They brought to the clan the seeds of a melon vine that was plentiful in their land, the delicious fruit of which they gave to the elder women so that they might allow them mates. For the elder men and protectors, they brought sharp stones, decorative bones and many colored stones, to use or wear in their custom. Most of these strangers were very different from the Tall Walkers. They wore animal skins, and painted only their faces. They spoke many words, but were colored as if barely touched by night, and their hues were different from one to the other; yet they spoke of themselves as blood kin, tho none knew or kept a line of blood to tongue.

These men had taken to the women of the blood of Ha as well, but Shhaha had only granted one of them a mate. There were four feeders of this blood left, and they could be mated outside the clan. None of them were pleased enough by the strangers' mating dances, or their gifts, and would not have the men. Tomorrow all the visitors would have to leave, and so the men favored the women at every turn, in hopes of changing their hearts.

When the tale of Cush was done and the clans began to mingle, Mah took great delight walking among the adults and listening to them repeating his keeper's words: "...Cush was given life here in the land of Gihon...Cush was keeper and kin to all humans...Cush was a slave of Axum, first born of the Seven Sisters, born of Puutha. The Great Mother took her name from the sound her body made when she was giving birth. It was Axum who begot the first male humans and began the line of Cush...Cush was keeper of Aahes [*Min*], and Wepwa, and Itum [*Atum*], and Khenti, and...and...Pi-Lak..." which Mah was allowed to correct since he was a blood apprentice.

"The order of your naming is true, but the last male born was called Pilak or Pilak-Sha, since he was of the blood of Sha mothers," Mah deferred in words and signed his respects.

These people knew Mah as a blood apprentice and that he was considered good enough to be the next Keeper of the Blood. They treated him with respect because his nomen was Mah-Sha, signifying that he was from the line of Cush and had the right to make sure others spoke well of his blood. Someday he might be the one to honor them or their descendants by retelling this tale, since it would be his place, as it had been his keeper's right to tell it.

Mah would have liked to listen to the strangers share words about the tale, but they had no interest in word sharing. Their words were for the sister slaves of Jai alone. When the clan returned to the duggi clearing, and the feeders of Ha blood disappeared inside their duggies, the strangers disappeared as well.

The people of the Tall Walkers went to their clay pots and steaming nets and uncovered the foods they were baking or seasoning. All the slaves cleared a spot of rocks and splinters, and brushed it neat for the feeders to lay out the foods. It was then that the strangers brought the clan its first taste of flesh.

They had rushed off to a camp they had made many trees away, and returned with long sticks of cooked animals and began to rip loose the meats. All the people were curious about this new food being offered, but few wanted to try it. None of Mah's people would have dreamed of seeing a golden cat roasting over an open fire and being served up as food.

Mah hoped no black cats had been killed, because they were the blood relation to his bonded friend Odrak, another blood apprentice. Mah was confounded and put off the duty to his blood. Now he would have to memorize the exchanges between the clan keepers and the strangers, memorizing every word as they explained what this or that animal was, what came close to them in taste, and how they were stalked and caught.

Most of Mah's kin refused to eat any of the meats, even tho the strangers danced about to say its taste was good. No Tall Walker had ever eaten animal flesh before. Mah had not heard of it to happen in any of his line of blood. They considered themselves the human version of the tall walkers. It never ate animal flesh, and so Mah's people did not do so either. Mah was a little slave when insects were added to his diet, but never would he, nor any of his people, have thought to eat the flesh of a near-human creature. Besides, they had an ancient warning against it, and Shhaha often told a dreadful tale to remind them not to.

Mah thought surely these strangers knew that a few of the animals they were eating had human clans as their closest relations. Many of Mah's people were still able to mate with animals like the large firebird, or the strong, brown rambulls, or the talking, color-changing lizards. These animals were like people and meant life to the clan. Some were known to mean death as much as any horror coming, but who would eat a horror or an animal of death? The fear of taking that into oneself and then being recognized by its enemies was much too great. Also, what you ate you had to live near. Who wanted to live near a horror? And what kind of person would eat a friend? It was all too much to bear, and the Kangaba, who had brought the strangers, began to be shunned.

The strangers thought they were showing the clan a big respect, and had made a special hunting party to gain these meats. They had killed many creatures in the hopes of showing the Ha sisters how brave they were. But there began much fuss between all the people as they gathered about the roasted meats. Soon few were eating anything at all. Mah's people grumbled about the smell of the cooked flesh and the blood that dripped from it into the fires, and worse—dripped into the soil of their clearing, where slaves crawled about who might get scented by it.

The clearing became a swirl of people moving about in wonder or disgust. Since the Kangaba was a close kin clan to the Tall Walkers, they had to take the brunt of their discontent, and while everyone crowded around the meats, which had been placed next to decent foods, the looks on their faces alone demanded that the Kangaba remove them.

Meanwhile, custom demanded that those who had not been mated, and those who had mated but would be kept, stay hidden in their duggies so that no visitor would have reason to stay longer. With the people mixing hard words and looks with the Kangaba, no one was paying the strangers much attention. It was then that two of the strangers decided to take one of the Ha feeders.

Nrdoosh had stuck her head out from the duggi to see the people fussing. Two of the men pulled her from the duggi hole and tried to drag her away. Being taller than these strangers she managed to beat one man about the face. But during his raging anger he ripped her so horribly that her stomach fell open, and now she lay dying.

Nrdoosh's blood kin came rushing from the duggi, shocked and crying wildly as they rushed toward Shhaha, the

Keeper of the Blood. "Blood!" they screamed violently, which meant death was coming, or had already arrived.

The silence was thick as the elders viewed her ruined body. Her sisters were licking Nrdoosh's wounds when Mah arrived. He found the two strangers standing there, astonished by what they had done. A young protector tried to move Nrdoosh and her inners fell out. He dashed away to join the other protectors who were now dragging the strangers off, while the older mated sister screamed for Shhaha to use his magic to save the dying feeder.

Shhaha pulled on the sacks between his legs, pointed at the mated sister, then towards the hills. This was to remind Radcmada of being mated with the very kin of those who had done this terrible deed. No more words would be spoken by the clan this night, and Shhaha signed to Radcmada that she could no longer speak as one of the clan.

Shhaha took a torch from someone, looked through the dirt and then at the stars. He covered the blood with dirt before calling over a slave to check for other signs. He made the small slave walk back and forth, studying his every move, even counting the clouds of dust that moved at his feet. Shhaha shook his head and groaned while he listened to the quieting jungle around them. There were too many signs here for him to read, and those who knew him grew fearful at what they saw in his eyes.

Amidst the murmurs of mourning, protectors surrounded the strangers while the Keeper of the Blood gathered the leading elders around a small sitting fire. The others were left alone to keep the feast in the center clearing, along with strong protectors, who now acted more like spies than friends. All this was done wordlessly, since the Tall Walkers did not often use words. Like their clan relation they always seemed to know one another's thoughts and took their lead from the elders, while the strong ones protected the rest. Everywhere feeders clustered together stood women ready to attack and Shhaha had no fear of who might come near his back.

Shhaha was the first to speak, and because Mah was to inherit Shhaha's place, he was allowed to listen close to all their words. He sat quietly in the background, hardly breathing. Knowing better than to move or speak, Mah made himself nearly invisible.

"Aaah, the blood! Human blood, pouring over our

clearing. Shed it and leave the clan with nothing in hand," spoke an elder feeder.

"Aaah!, Shhaha. You carry our blood. Only you can say," spoke Mah's keeper, Dbsha.

"They eat the friends of the land," spoke the oldest man in their clan, who was now called Jerruut because he was the oldest.

"They eat death, aaah!" spoke another elder keeper.

"They now have death inside and bring death to us," spoke another.

"The strangers from the rising sun have much...Aaah, much to teach us. From them one hears and sees all manner of new things. Those from where the waters flow have stones sharp with cutting power!" spoke the Jerruut.

"Speak, Jai?" asked Shhaha of the man whose grief was the greatest among them.

"Jai did not see the stranger when blood was spilled. I do not know his heart. My heart is lost. Heal my slave, Shhaha, or the clan loses founding blood," he cried in long, thick tears.

Everyone lowered their heads in sorrow for Jai. They knew Shhaha had no power to keep the young sister with the clan. She had been ripped open as if by a beast. Moreover, it happened after sunset. They needed to prepare her for Spirit Mountain, before the rising of the sun, or her spirit would stay among them, wandering the clearing and causing trouble because of the way she died.

When next words were spoken, they were sullen and angry. "Jai does not wish Ha blood mixed with strangers come with Kangaba."

The elder sister, Radcmada, had been Jai's favorite, and she had mated the stranger called Enoc. He had proven a fair dancer and was considered the best looking of their kin. He had made friends easily during his stay and gathered much respect. It was his blood kin who had done the killing.

"You have spoken your words," grunted Shhaha. "You have shared food with them, and you wear the skin given you. It is done. Words spoken cannot be taken back. Besides, Radcmada might be rooted already. What of that?"

"Such a thing as this is unknown to us, Shhaha. What portents are here?" asked Dbsha suddenly.

They were all thinking hard, but Mah could see that

Shhaha already had his answer. He always had an answer or a story that would lead to one. Mah hoped he would have this quality when he became Keeper of the Blood.

Shhaha waited to see if the others would speak. After a short while he said, "Our clan relations knew there was something wrong with these people. Each sunrise I watch tall walkers come less and less to the clearing. Aaah!, they smelled the jungle-blood roasting over fires and feared to be next. Yet none of you paid heed or turned away from the strangers. There are evil portents here!"

All grunted and chirped or clicked their tongues in agreement and did not wonder at Shhaha's wisdom. Were not warning signs always nearby and easy to see?

Shhaha stood and began his dance of decision. In movements that were clear as words, he gave them a course to follow. The strangers would have to leave, and Radcmada would be allowed to go since she was probably rooted already. The one who had slain Nrdoosh would be kept among them, so Shhaha could learn from his blood. In the morning after all the visitors were gone, the clan would send a group of protectors to follow the strangers to their lands. If Radcmada wanted to come back, and she was not yet rooted, they would take her from these people.

The elders rose one by one and did a short, slow dance around Shhaha in agreement, while all the visitors cleared a path for them to reach the center clearing where the strangers were gathered. When Shhaha's small group reached their cooking fires, Enoc and his blood kin rose to greet them. Adra, the oldest of them, shoved Medra to the ground in front of Shhaha. It was he who had killed Nrdoosh.

Medra cried aloud as he fell to his knees and mashed his face into the dirt at Shhaha's feet. Adra began to speak and sign, saying that it was their custom for one who had spilled blood to give his to the kin of the one slain.

Shhaha's people roared against another killing. They knew these men wanted the sister slaves of Jai too much to have done this thing on purpose. The killing had not been murder, and the Tall Walkers only wanted the strangers to leave. Shhaha suggested that the flesh of killers had made them killers as well. He demanded that no more killing take place among his people, or the strangers would be driven off. The strangers did not want the Tall Walkers to take revenge on them, their being great giants compared to other humans. Adra once saw a Tall Walker cripple a man by simply shaking him, and told the others this. In tales told here by other clans, they had discovered the Tall Walkers possessed a kick that could kill, and were silent as they trembled and listened to Adra's whispers.

Neither Shhaha nor Mah understood the whispered words, but Medra did. He tried to run away, but among the crowds of clans there was nowhere for him to go. Waterhorse protectors dragged him back and his own blood kin forced him to the ground. Adra spoke more words which caused the Kangaba to fret and pace about. Then two men came over and held Medra's legs apart, while Medra pleaded wildly and screamed as if possessed.

Trying to find out what was about to happen, the clearing bristled again with the clamor of Shhaha and his people, but they stood their ground when Adra made the body signs of clan rites and called upon friendly spirits to help him. Shhaha knew the meaning of this and held his people back.

Adra began to dance around the fire. He pulled his cutting stone from the vine matting tied around his chest and shoved it between the coals. His close kin began a guttural chant that was slowly picked up by all the visitors. Someone ripped loose the animal skin tied around Medra's waist, and Mah was filled with terror as he guessed, even before Shhaha, what was about to happen.

Odrak and Bellar, the other two apprentices, dashed over to Mah and held him fast. They knew Mah would be the next Keeper of the Blood, and it was his place to know all that happened to the clan. He had to watch and remember, whether he wanted to or not.

"Blood medicine," spoke Mah, at first in whispers to the two who held him, and then in loud cries towards Shhaha.

Shhaha tried to move but was held back by his people. A blood rite had been invoked and had to be respected. Besides, a danger was in their midst, and tho a protector's first duty was to the slaves and feeders, protection was given to the Keeper of the Blood, and his apprentices, above all the rest.

Shhaha shouted for someone to bring his medicine bone. In an instant, two young protectors appeared holding a large skull of a long-dead animal that always guarded the entrance to his duggi. After placing it in front of Mah, he pulled out many small skin sacks and pottery vials, then ran the vials over to a cooking fire to heat them on the hot rocks.

The strangers chanted on as Adra returned with his hot cutting stone. Enoc held Medra's legs down with his knee and then reached over to pull Medra's pleasure stick into the air.

Here was another new thing, and the clan of the Tall Walkers cried out and began a frenzied dance. Tho they were unsure of what was to happen, they all knew something akin to a horror would soon take place. Only Mah, waiting alone by the fire and being guarded by two protectors, wept silent tears because he understood what they would do to Medra. The Tall Walkers always allowed other clans their rights and customs, but Mah wanted so much to intervene.

Their morose chanting became guttural and grew louder as everyone stepped back from the mad Medra. The members of his tribe danced around him, pissing their waters over him. Silence gripped everyone while Enoc's chanting became one long, howling and horrible chord. All of Medra's kin took turns spitting on him and kicking him, while others pissed on him still. With the language of their bodies they cursed him. Then, in one jagged motion, Adra cut loose the flesh of his dangle, leaving a sloppy mess of skin and gushing blood.

His scream silenced the crowd as they watched his blood shoot out into the dust.

"Let Puutha take him back or leave him here! He is no longer one of us!" yelled Adra to the crowd.

Following Adra's lead, the strangers covered their faces with dirt, then moved off to their sitting fire.

Shhaha had heard of such a thing as this, but had never witnessed it. Even the jungle grew silent as the clan of the Tall Walkers came near the stilled body of Medra. The feeders gawked at the blood and the loose skin that one would have called man, or pleasure stick, or hanging dangle [*old man*]. To them, he was no longer a man. He was now something different, and would probably gain some new talent with this loss, if he lived. Some wondered whether he might become a feeder. They smiled weakly to each other, hoping that something good would come of this. It was simply their way to look for the good in all things.

The protectors and keepers who gathered near could hardly stand the sight of Medra lying there in so much blood. None but the slaves could bear to look upon the empty space without turning away in shudders. The blood keepers and their apprentices grew sick from the smell of violent blood so near. Someone signed that Medra might not be able to walk because of this. Someone shouted that he would not live because of it. Others agreed, and many feeders and protectors fled. A young slave suggested that it would grow back, and his movements became the only sound in the clearing. Everyone turned to Elder Ramaa or Dbsha, who were holding Shhaha, because they could not look at him and feared what he might do.

Shhaha turned to Mah, who had just taken a vial from the fire and was heading towards him. Mah handed the hot vial to Shhaha and returned to the medicine bone to fetch other items he would need. After setting them out between Medra's legs, Mah and the other two apprentices went to a large sitting fire, retrieved torches, and began dancing and chanting around Medra's lifeless body. All the clans sat around as Shhaha went to work between Medra's legs. No one dared to move him, and were almost grateful for this chance to see Shhaha work his legendary healing powers.

After securing the seed sacks back in place, Shhaha called the names of Puutha and Axum, and then on all the keepers that came before him: "Iunet, all aaah! Iunet, come from countless ones; then Nebet, all aaah! Nebet; then BaEn, and Hafeema, and Ishaha, and Min, and Unet, and Elder Iunet, and Iunet, and Ishaha; then Shhaha, all aaah! Shhaha, then I."

Shhaha then chanted an ancient tale of how the special roots and leaves were boiled down to make the potion he poured over Medra's wound. He turned to Medra with a fright when he did not stir or moan in pain as the liquid sizzled over the open flesh. Shhaha listened for a heartbeat and found it, beating stronger than he would have expected. Knowing many medicines, he thought for a moment and recalled the thing most important for him to do.

He found the hole where the flowing liquid wasn't blood and gently pushed in a bit of waxy twig, and covered it with pinches of clean white moss. When he looked up next, he saw Mah staring back and his two other apprentices still dancing and chanting around them. Shhaha called them over and motioned for Bellar's torch. Mah looked into Shhaha's eyes and understood his teacher's plans, then motioned for Odrak to help him hold Medra down.

Shhaha laid a hand over Medra's stomach, then put the torch to the wound. His body did twitch about but he still made no sound. Suddenly, Shhaha saw Medra's spirit trying to flee, and to retaliate, he began the "dreaded moan." This chant for holding spirits fast moved his apprentices in time, and using the spilled blood, they rushed to paint the magic circles on Medra's body to confuse the spirit. After checking again for a heartbeat, Shhaha massaged [*touch of the Master Sage*] Medra's limbs to keep his spirit within with the flesh. He then dripped more of the warm liquid over the blistered skin, which he finally covered with large strips of wax leaves.

Mah brought the medicine bone over to Shhaha, who retrieved from it seven stones, each a different color, shape and size, which he placed over the seven special areas of the body. With the magic stones in place, Mah knew that the man could not be allowed to move, and must be bound and staked. He motioned for Bellar and Odrak to go into the woods to gather sticks and vine ropes.

Shhaha chanted the calls to put a spirit at ease, and then called upon the Great Mother to help him. He dug valleys under Medra's arms and legs until there were mounds of soil piled on both sides. From an animal bladder he shook loose a light coating of red powder until he had the wound completely covered, when his apprentices returned, who then tied and stake Medra to the ground.

Again Shhaha gathered his waiting council and headed for the strangers, who had taken no notice of the goings-on around them. They sat still and silent around a blazing bonfire, entranced by the changing colors of its light, and trying hard to ignore the giant protectors guarding them, who might decide at any time to take all their lives.

Shhaha rattled his many body bones while secretly pouring a powder into his hand from his wrist bones, then frightened the strangers out of their trance by instantly transforming the blazing fire into low burning coals. The only things shining brightly now were Shhaha's glaring eyes and the aura of his raging anger. He stood unmoving, towering over the strangers and looking down at them in disgust.

The strangers flung more dirt on themselves until they were covered with it. This was an act of humility for those resigned to fear, recognized and respected by all the clans. But Shhaha had his fill of these people and demanded that they leave the clearing and never again return. This order served to fill them with more dread, because now they would have to wait near the desert for the Kangaba to show them the way out of these lands.

Shhaha gave them the time it took Radcmada to decide whether to leave with her mate, Enoc. He regretted her leaving, but knew that she was rooted already and did not want the blood of these people among them. Once the strangers were out of hearing, he called to his people to finish feeding their kin. His council ordered protectors to remove the cooked meats and all that belonged to the strangers for burning.

The joy was gone from this clan sharing, but soon everyone settled into a quiet chant for Nrdoosh's passing spirit, or sat watching for signs from the mutilated stranger. Medra now belonged to Jai as his replacement for Nrdoosh, but he would forever be a slave to the clan, since he would never again be a man. After preparing Nrdoosh for her journey back to the Great Mother and removing her body from the clearing, everyone passed by Medra to say a chant, since his life or death would be part of her death and passing. They asked Nrdoosh's quiet spirit to forgive him. The feeders were fearful, saying their chants quickly and rushing on, in contrast to the protectors, who passed him as if in mourning. Some even knelt to touch his face and chest in pity, thinking better of death than of such a loss.

When the others were finished, Mah and Odrak flanked the still body of Medra and prepared to continue Shhaha's healing chants. Bellar was disappointed that Mah had not selected him, because those who stayed with the stranger tonight would be highly respected in the morning. Instead, Odrak would join Mah as Medra's protectors against some creature in the night. If all three were alive in the morning, Mah and Odrak would be considered protectors from this night on, even tho they were still only slaves.

Odrak was a few seasons older than Mah, but was visibly more frightened as the clearing grew silent around them. Even the jungle had been noisy with expectation. Slowly, it too settled, as if it understood that the apprentices chanted to save a life. Odrak looked nervously about, knowing how wandering spirits or jungle creatures waited for them to break their chant, when they would come from the jungle to mix their blood with the dust of the duggi clearing. But Mah's soft voice took away his fears soon after they had begun. To hear Mah's voice was to be reminded of the bird of many colors, the "Great Mahs." Odrak often had dreams that said Mah was this bird. He was praenomened for this bird many seasons before his proper time for naming because it had come to him one morning while still an infant. Before this time the clan had never seen the bird flying through the air, tho they always knew when it was near, because all other creatures stopped moving and turned eyes to the skies.

A giant twice the size of a fully-grown tall walker, with wings that could cover a duggi and sharp talons at each wing arch, and even sharper ones on its feet, it had a snakelike face and a beak that could surely rip a man to pieces. It always seemed to come out of nowhere, surprising the clan by suddenly hovering overhead, and unlike other birds, it sang many songs.

The Tall Walkers and their clan relations had been too quickly frightened to run away. Transfixed, even the slave's feeder could not reach him, nor call for Dbsha or protectors to help, but they soon realized the infant was in no danger. He and the bird were singing, and the sound was something clear and beautiful like a long thirst being quenched.

Without thought for their own safety, everyone moved closer and listened to their song bloom and expand without discord. At first the bird had seemed the leader of the melody, but then the slave fell into a liquid harmony, echoing each chord with flawless symmetry until they sounded like a single entity, and it was a human voice after all.

Everyone sat about to listen, and the bird allowed many hands to touch it, or to brush its iridescent wings, or feel its talons and ruffle the cloud-white fur of its legs. It had no fear. All it wanted was to sing with the little slave. Such a marvel forced Shhaha to declare this bird a breed apart from other animals, like the tall walkers; like all clan relations, it was not human, yet not quite so far away from being so.

Their singing filled the clearing until just before sunset, when the bird fluttered its wings as if to leave. Shhaha stepped over to face the bird and speak with it, hoping the bird would understand, but it had no interest in Shhaha. It played with the little slave, opening its beak and spreading its wings wide, and the horror of its long fangs and deadly talons sent new shocks through the clan. No bird they knew had teeth, and one with fangs made many faint of heart. This bird even had talons on its wings, which it could use like the fingers of a man's hand.

Gently rocking the little slave with its leg, it lifted the slave from the ground and cradled him in the crook of its wing, while it stroked the slave's head with the talons of the other. No one would have guessed it could be so, but its touch was as gentle as one would give an infant.

But its movements began to blow dust about, and tho Shhaha was still trying to talk to it, the crowd grew restless and anxious for this to end. What they had feared all along was coming true—the bird was going to take the little slave, and they all loved the bird enough to let it have its way—all except the slave's feeder. Crying, she rushed to confront the bird and fell to her knees, pleading with it to return the slave to her. After all, those born to any clan, human or animal, needed to be with that clan or they simply could not survive, no matter how beautiful their song, or their singing of it.

Shhaha roared at the bird in the voice of the golden cat, which all other life forms were sure to recognize. The bird leaped back as if to say "you dare," and the slave's feeder pleaded with Shhaha to stop his fury, while begging the bird's forgiveness. The bird hopped about on one foot, frightening many people away, yet still playfully enjoying the smiling slave.

Out of concern for the bird, and not wanting to use his voice power [*tone controls*] on it, Shhaha stood tall and pleaded with this being to calm itself. He asked if it understood his words, and the bird began to speak. It scowled over the clearing, causing protectors to run to their duggies for weapons. But Shhaha called them back, while ordering the bird to "sit!" Suddenly, to everyone's surprise, the bird stopped moving, quieted, and then nestled down into the grass.

Shhaha would swear it understood this one word of their tongue, while others would say it was the slave who had begun again to sing. Later, there would be many words between these birds and the clan of the Tall Walkers. But on that day, the bird did sit and return the slave to the ground.

Shhaha prevented the woman from retrieving the slave, saying the bird had a dangerous look, and knowing for certain that it wanted the slave. Watching it look from the sun back to the slave, he also knew the bird was now desperate to leave. There are few signs common between different tribes, except the signs for "yes" and "no." Tho they differ slightly from place to place, and for a Keeper of the Blood, from story to story, no one doubted what they meant, and so Shhaha made the sign in all the forms he knew, while saying clearly, "No!"

The bird stepped back indignantly and stared Shhaha

down. Standing its full height, it towered over the blood keeper, but Shhaha kept his place. It gazed back and forth between Shhaha, the feeder and her slave, then turned sadly towards the sun as it started its descent into darkness. Suddenly the bird let out a distressed "scowling" [*a grimacing cry or hard faced yowl*] that sounded to all like a woman's shrieking. Then to the surprise of Shhaha and everyone who watched, the slave's feeder rose and touched the bird gently, taking hold of it as if compelled to bring it some comfort.

The bird went back to hunching over the woman and even frightened Shhaha, who called for the feeder to step back from the danger. The bird did lower itself, slowly, until it could stare directly into her eyes, and yet she did not move away. It was tense and looking almost evil, with its wing talons raised over her shoulders and about her head, as if to tear her apart, while its mouth tried to form some word Shhaha was desperate to catch. The feeder cried and made the signs for singing at the rising sun, which meant the bird would be welcomed again. After rubbing her hand across its leathery cheek, she picked up the little slave and sped towards her duggi.

"MAH!!!" screamed the bird, with its wings reaching out desperately for the slave. "Mah! Mah! Mah!" it called, the sound that would become its name, and the name of the little slave, who had just earned it.

When she was gone, the bird looked over to Shhaha with all the life gone from its eyes. Twilight was almost upon them, and it made the many colors of its leathery feathers shimmer and gleam in the changing tints of light.

"We shall call you Mah, the bird of many colors, who can also speak!" said Shhaha, reaching up to the bird, his words slowly bringing the bird back to life. "Mah! The bird of beautiful colors who is now our friend!" he shouted, with even more delight at having the honor of this naming. "MAH!!! The bird who is like humans!" he screamed in the bird's own tones. The bird responded by rising to its full height, unfurling its wings into a magnificent display of light, yet resounding colors, with its hues pulsing as they sucked in all the remaining light. Then abruptly, in one swift move, it was flying towards the quickly disappearing sun.

It would be chronicled by many blood keepers, that this was the first time this bird was seen flying, if only for a short time.

With its great speed it was out of sight just before the sun fell away from the earth. But in those few moments, they all witnessed the wonderful stream of colors dancing across the sky, joined by another streak of color that twisted around it, over it and under it, until they were two whirling streams of twinkling colored lights shooting over the rim of their world.

Shhaha fell to the ground and called upon his dead kin to protect his clan and the little slave that caused this blessing to fall upon his people. His head ached with wonder and speculation as he thought about the bird, the "GREAT MAH," he clarified the name for future use. He ordered a feast to be prepared and rushed to every duggi engaging those who did such things well, dictating his needs. There would be a naming tonight for Dbsha's only surviving slave, and everyone who had heard him, knew what the name would be.

The night was made long with tale telling by Shama, who was then their Keeper of the Blood, and Shhaha, comparing their many tales of birds. They searched their memories for any appearance of this bird in legends past, but it had no blood known to them. Only the yellow firebird living down-river came close, because it was also known to speak with humans. They named Dbsha's slave "Mah" that night, and promised him a feeder from the line of Jai. The old women agreed, since there was a Ha female slave born during Mah's season. They were all happy then to listen to the little slave singing his bird-song, now that they knew what it was.

Since that day the Great Mah had become a friend to the clan of the Tall Walkers. It was never seen coming or going, and only Mah knew when it was around, but it returned every flowering season, often bringing many of its close kin. For many seasons Mah was the only one who could speak to them, but Shhaha learned enough to call them down from the sky and to make them leave when their presence was a bother.

Mah often slept with the bird and was also fed by it. He taught Odrak and Bellar its songs. Since Odrak would never allow Bellar a rest with Mah, only he and Mah could nestle within the wings of the bird and bring back its tiny oil sacks, grey odorless nodes, which when placed inside a duggi could rid it of the stale odors of many seasons' use. Most of the clan did not care for them much, but they accepted one from Mah or Odrak to show their friendship with the birds. Shhaha was only interested in their magic, since they had no smell, but claimed he had found no use for it. Others feared to open the nodes or wear its oil, as if they might lose their spirits when they lost their own scents.

Still, more Great Mahs came to sing with Mah and Odrak, always bringing them something to eat as if they were their slaves. The birds never ate anything offered nor did they harm any other creature in their land. The people knew them then as those rare beings who came from the time when the Seven Sisters walked the lands, mating with other life forms trying to create humans. These creatures came close, but considering what had happened this night, Mah knew the Great Mahs were better in many ways.

▼▼▼▼▼

By the time Mah had finished the story of his naming and had rechanted all the healing words, the sunlight had returned. To his disappointment, nothing had happened during the night to give his night watch more meaning. He listened to the still-beating heart of the stranger, and his training told him the man would live.

"How does he still live?" Odrak asked, touching the stranger and making the sign to live.

Mah also touched the man and said, "His spirit does not really want to leave," and made the sign for those who sleep.

As the sunlight moved between the trees, the duggies cautiously came to life. Slaves ran about digging up foods left during the night. Young feeders went to find purple uks to milk, while others went to dig up roots and nuts or to find fruits and greens for their stores. Protectors threw stones to see who would make the morning checks at each duggi, then formed groups to tend the planting fields. There was always food to find, animals to raid and a duggi to repair or build, which the keepers did after eating their morning meal. Shhaha had risen, and after sitting outside his sacred duggi chanting to the morning sun, he came to relieve Mah and Odrak of their duty.

"Aaah, I stay," spoke Mah, who feared missing something important to ever go to sleep on purpose.

Shhaha gave him a look that said, "I have chosen well," and sat opposite him to check on the stranger. Odrak hated to leave but was too tired to force himself to stay.

"We spoke only the words of the healing chant and the tale of my naming," spoke Mah with pride, as Odrak dragged himself away. "It is good?"

"Very good, tho it is better to speak of Great Mahs in the light of day since they are birds of sunshine."

"Tales of sunshine better at night for Odrak. Aaah! me," Mah quickly added.

Shhaha began to make fettle the wound and to replace the bloodied moss. Mah assisted him while Shhaha named each item used or described what else was needed to make the magic work.

Mah learned how to make the rich "living-poultice," which when eaten could make one who is thin, thick. It was made of mostly red tree grease and milk from vines found deep in the groves, which Shhaha and Mah collected. The grease was then boiled down with soft fish bones, yellow fungus from ironwood trees, and the stalks of black ferns that grew on the river banks. For the healthy it was not good to eat since it sat in the stomach and made movement difficult. It also made it impossible to pass water. But it kept the sick strong during the long days without solid food, and helped to retain their body fluids.

Sick and immobile for more than two moons, there were times when Medra would cry out in his sleep and make foul sounds like curses. The people feared having him among them, but it seemed that the Great Mother looked after all the clan during Medra's healing. Mah watched over him with one of the other two apprentices each night, and to everyone's surprise, not even a snake came to bother them. Mah led many nights of chanting and telling clan tales, which became the talk for many days because he knew the history of his people as far back as the legends of the Seven Sisters, and such a thing was unheard of for someone with so few seasons.

Shhaha was sure Medra would live when a clan of fierce cats came to their clearing and harmed no one. Shhaha considered this a blessing not known in all his memories. The long-tooth cats, who had not been seen for countless generations, merely rested on the hill overlooking the lake. All the Tall Walkers were nervous and feared an attack, but none ever came. The felines made a special food of some unknown animal of the deep jungle. It would be so badly mangled that not even Shhaha could tell the clan what it was, even tho it was plentiful enough for them not to look elsewhere for food.

Just when the clan went back to its normal routine, and felt the cats had come to be their friends, two cubs were born. The cats separated and five of them marched towards the mountain range, as if something had called them. Then after watching them leave, the all parted and went their separate ways.

Shhaha was so taken by the strange behavior of the dangerous cats, that he hardly noticed Medra had gotten well enough to feed himself. He still could not walk, but was able to pull himself across the clearing and into the large duggi of the keeperless slaves. Shhaha finally took no notice of him, meditating instead on the mountain range for long periods each day. He began training his apprentices more intensely and made his only duty the telling of bloodlines yet unknown to them, while making preparations for his leaving.

Shhaha asked for nothing, yet he was distant and seemed to long for something the clan could not think to give. The dry season was upon them, but there were stores of food in every variety, and still Shhaha would not be appeased. No Keeper of the Blood of Mah's clan had ever deserted them. A Keeper of the Blood was more sacred to a clan than its women and, in fact, it was more common for a Keeper of the Blood to be a woman. In these times a blood keeper often needed to be the leader of the clan, but was in truth more its prisoner, and was never allowed to leave, except to confer with blood keepers of close kin clans. To insure his staying, Shhaha, like all Keepers of the Blood, was burn-marked with the male sign and elaborately stitched across his forehead [*Star of the Circumcision*]. Anyone with such a mark found outside their clan, and also without the silver ring of passing, might be killed by those who feared such magic. His people would rather see him dead than see him leave.

No one from his clan could kill another human out of hand, and so a runner was sent to the clan of the Waterhorse to ask for protectors to come, when all else failed to keep Shhaha from carving a walking stick, an elder's final preparation for a long journey. The people cried because Shhaha would not say why he was leaving, or where he wanted to go. He spoke only to his three apprentices, and to them only of blood lines, herbal medicines, and clan tales. All Mah's free time was spent caring for Medra until he could walk, which had become Mah's only joy, since he was far too young to mate with Olaah, and if Shhaha left without passing him through the last blood trials, he might never become a Keeper of the Blood.

This anxiety went on for three moons, and it was taking Shhaha—who was old, but not feeble—much too long to make a walking stick and prepare its fighting blades. Some clan members thought it was all some terrible lesson and that Shhaha was in need of more respects. But when the Waterhorse protectors arrived, they had tales of other blood keepers preparing to leave their clan clearings. It was the middle of the rainy season, and the Tall Walkers worried more with each passing day.

The protectors who came tried to woo Shhaha from his carving and danced as best they could. Shhaha took no notice of them. But one night, during a break between the rains, while the moon was full and blue, Shhaha gathered the clan around a large fire. He changed the blaze into harmless rainbow hues, and spoke to them as if for the first time.

He began his dance of decision like never before, shaming the visiting protectors who had tried to impress him. When he finished and had the whole clearing in howls and hoots of pride, he sat on his heels and told the clan about a waking dream he had had on the day the cats left. "It is time for the Great Sharing," Shhaha spoke and signed.

Mah jumped to his feet, recalling the memory of this matter, a rare piece of their history that had yet to be completed for him, because it was a tale for telling only between elders.

"I must speak our names in the valley where the Seven Sisters gathered. There, by blood that is our own, great clan tales are shared and powerful magic is done," Shhaha declared.

These words were known to many elders, but even for Shhaha, the Great Sharing was only legend now. There was no one alive who knew the whole tale anymore. He told them that what had happened to Medra was a foretoken of the proper time, and his being healed, an assurance that his people were ready to be represented there again. Some elders agreed, because they knew the long-tooth cats were the ancient clan relation of Shhaha's line of blood. Their coming and going had to signify that Shhaha would go as well.

"I have kept the blood badly," he said, knowing that he should have been better prepared for this day. "This journey was foretold by Shama, the Keeper of the Blood before me. What happened in our clearing to Medra serves as a warning to us all. It is a portent of things to come, of magic that will be needed."

This promise of the Great Sharing was part of the blessing given to all Keepers of the Blood. It had become custom, and all knowledge and preparation for it was now washed in the mix of all his other memories. Shhaha said it was his apprentices who had awakened him to the calling more than anything else, with their retelling of the very ancient tales of Kamsa, daughter of Axum, who trained the first Keeper of the Blood, and whose descendant, Itum, had gone in search of the Great Mother, the journey that started the Great Sharing. Shhaha asked for his people's blessing and demanded that Bellar be kept behind as their new blood keeper. He promised to return, but warned that the journey would be longer than any taken by their people before. He wanted their goodwill and asked for only a hand of followers to join him.

No runner had come with this much information on why and where so many blood keepers were going. The clearing was silent except for the rush of words and signs passing between the visiting protectors, who then suddenly ran off in all directions. This news would be prized, and the runners carrying it would surely be treated to many respects from other clans.

The clearing would have been silent again if not for the emerging rustle of trees and the growing calls of the jungle. Shhaha and his apprentices were the only ones standing.

"I have chosen well in you, Mah," Shhaha said. He smiled and signaled for Mah to go to his sacred blood duggi.

Mah ran off, followed by Odrak and Bellar, and then other young protectors. Odrak made sure that only they entered the sacred ground circles, as it was forbidden for others to do so.

Mah had been chosen by Shhaha again. Odrak and Bellar would show him much respect, knowing that he was indeed well chosen. Neither Bellar nor Odrak would be sure of what to bring forth from the duggi, but they were sure Mah would. Mah laid his head upon each of their chests, a sign of welcoming respect. Then he crawled into the duggi, pulling on Odrak's leg for him to follow. Bellar stood guard in front of the small opening and chanted for Mah to choose wisely.

After lighting the small torches of the chimney nook, they held each other and jumped about. Mah was excited because Shhaha had chosen both of them to go on this journey. Since all Mah's close-blood kin were dead, except his keeper Dbsha, Mah had bonded blood with Odrak, and more. Their training to be blood keepers always kept them close, but if allowed to journey with Shhaha, they would be closer still.

Odrak was afraid because he had to go, but was overjoyed because he was pair-bonded to Mah and would not live to be without him. Odrak had no close blood kin alive within the clan anymore, and no keeper. He treasured Mah above all others. Odrak was welcomed by all the feeders, and Dbsha allowed him to sleep in his duggi with Mah, instead of the duggi of the keeperless slaves, but Mah was all the company he had ever wanted. Now even this journey would not separate them.

They settled themselves and began to carefully look about the place. They had not been inside Shhaha's duggi since their special blood conditioning [*Anti-Black Salt (Dry Acid)*] to be blood keepers, and were awed by all the beautifully patterned skins, the many polished bones of deceased elders, the vials and pots of magic powders and healing herbs, and the countless spirit sticks belonging to the blood keepers before them. Odrak started to call Mah's attention to a set of painted rambull horns, when he remembered that Mah was here to select something for the moment. This was a test of wisdom. He shadowed Mah about the room, neither of them touching anything until the needed item showed itself.

Suddenly Mah snatched up a big bundle he knew to be Shhaha's large medicine bag. He told Odrak to get the two smaller ones sitting nearby and then noticed the tops of three walking sticks. Dropping the medicine bag, he uncovered one of the sticks. The sight of it made Odrak drop the bag he was holding and come to gape at the marvel of it.

Now they knew why it had taken Shhaha so long to carve it, and as Odrak uncovered the others, they could only wonder why it had not taken him longer. The sticks were engraved with the likenesses of all their kin, from Axum and Itum to Radcmada and Mah. They were carved from the darkest ebony wood, and dyed blood yellow to make white, brown and black patches, like those of their clan relation, whose likeness was also carved in the wood.

Tied to the stick with ropes of human hair, the three fighting blades were so sharp that neither would dare touch them. One stone came to a point that extended the length of the long stick. Another laid across the side of the stick and had only one sharp side about a full hand wide. The last was very thin, but stuck out like an arm and was also fashioned to a point. At the top of the stick, they recognized the head of Puutha, with sparkling stones for eyes and woolly human hair in delicate knots surrounding her wooden head.

They quickly gathered up all the sticks to find two others that were older than the first three. One had been handled by many hands over many generations, and the other was older still, carved from a single, gigantic bone, so old, hard and dark that it too looked like wood. These last two did not have the carved figures of their kin, and their fighting ends were only worn nubs.

Mah gathered them up but found them too cumbersome to carry with the large medicine bag. Odrak suggested they leave the larger one for the clan, and took up a smaller one. He also picked up Shama's spirit stick and a few of the beautiful skins. They slid out of the duggi and ran back into the clearing, where Shhaha was still talking to his people.

The group fell silent as they approached, until Mah, with much effort, raised the long and heavy walking sticks overhead. Now the people were sure Shhaha was going to leave, and began to plead and beg at his feet, saying that it was an evil thing that he could think of leaving them. They imagined all manners of horror coming for them, because they would no longer have anyone who knew all their lines of blood, and no one who could prove that they were human. They cried that the spirits of their elders would curse them, because they would no longer have anyone who remembered them. The feeders threatened to go back to wandering the land and leave the men alone to die. Young slaves cried with all the new agitation. Protectors cursed and promised to call evil spirits to follow Shhaha on his journey. Some even cut themselves and rubbed in the blood marks, which signified that he would be considered dead among them. A mated pair tried to burn themselves in a sitting fire, saying that the Great Mother would swallow them if they had no line of blood to root them to her. They wanted to die now instead of waiting for that horror to come.

This scene went on and on, then at the first moment of calm, Shhaha took the oldest walking stick from Mah and showed his people the carving of Puutha. He first showed it to the elders, who fell back to the ground and began to eat dirt and curse themselves for having cursed him in Puutha's presence. Some said blessings to honor the beauty and skill of the work. Feeders gathered around him shouting praises for Puutha, and the blessings for being born to their sex. Keepers praised the stick and the blood that could always remember, then praised Shhaha again for having kept it so long among them.

Mah and the other apprentices were proud of Shhaha, whose patience had outlasted his people's rage. He had waited for the best moment to show off the walking sticks, and now their threats turned into paeans, even for his apprentices.

Shhaha jammed the fighting end of the oldest bone-stick into the ground, and there he let it stand. For those who had not seen it before, he told them it was the most sacred token of their clan, called a "Blood Wand," passed down through the generations so that the clan would always know the face of the mother. Then, as if on cue, Odrak pulled down from Mah a stick of Shhaha's making, and the sight of it stilled all moving tongues, filling the whole clearing with the Aaah! of secret pleasures. Shhaha could now speak in the comfortable idiom of the storyteller, and Mah could finally rest the other sticks on the ground, so that he and the other apprentices could echo after Shhaha.

"Aaah!" Shhaha pointed to the standing walking stick. "I shall leave you the Blood Wand, which must stay with our clan for all time. It has the blessings of all the blood keepers gone by. As long as it stands, your Keeper of the Blood may live. Keep it standing, and he shall return to you."

Cutting himself, he made these words a promise of blood, lending them a great magic. He could now be in two places at once, at least to his people it would seem that way. Where the blood wand stood, Shhaha would stand among them.

The protectors immediately pushed the blood wand further into the ground, not allowing even the older slaves to touch it. Shhaha promised his people one of the new sticks, which would belong to the new blood keeper, Bellar. Mah and Odrak would take the others, enabling them to carry the names and faces of all their clan with them. As they could see and recognize themselves in the sticks, so would others. Shhaha would be able to keep the clan safe, as they kept the memories of Puutha (and him) safe, with the original blood wand.

Shhaha then passed the three new sticks to his apprentices and stood with the second oldest one in the center of the clearing. While showing them off, Mah, Odrak and Bellar were careful to bring attention to the sharp stones at the fighting end. Many recognized themselves on one of the sticks, since Shhaha had included the full count of all their numbers in his carvings.

Everyone was so pleased with Shhaha that most could no longer speak forbidding words. Others still cried and said it would bring some evil upon them, but nearly all agreed that if Shhaha felt it was so important for the clan, that he should be allowed to go.

From that night on Shhaha spoke no more about his

leaving, and spoke only to his apprentices. Since Bellar had been chosen to stay and protect the clan, Shhaha needed to explain many things to him about the items in his blood duggi. This took another cycle of days [5 *days*], after which Shhaha told him that if they did not return in three rainy seasons, he should go to the clan of the Waterhorse and beg the rite of passage to become a full Keeper of the Blood. He would then have to remake the protective spell and the sacred circles surrounding the blood duggi to truly claim it for himself.

Bellar was disappointed that he had not been chosen to go along. Learning the magic of the blood duggi and the items within was only an early honor, and soon Bellar had many reasons why he should go instead of Odrak, or even Mah. Bellar grew so distraught by what he took as a slight, that one night he and Odrak got into a fight out among the tall walkers, where he got bunted in the side by an angry leader whose sleepwalking he had disturbed. Now that Bellar couldn't walk too well, he was even angrier than before. That night as Shhaha wrapped Bellar's hip in wax leaves, Bellar cursed Odrak and asked that he not have to look upon his face again.

Shhaha struck him in the face. "You will live long enough to bitterly regret those words," Shhaha warned.

The next day, Medra, who was walking better now, offered to help find the ore for the silver ring Shhaha needed to protect himself on his journey. Even without his pleasure stick, Medra was so grateful to be alive that he wanted to do something for Shhaha, who had saved him. He was constantly trying to prove himself useful to the clan. He had very few words common to the clan of the Tall Walkers, but he signed well enough to be understood and was allowed to go with the protectors to search for the ore.

On the first night of the red star, the sign Shhaha had waited for to start his journey, Medra, Dbsha and the others found silver-veined rocks in a gorge on the other side of the river. They spent two more days carrying the stones back to the clearing, where they pounded the stones and sifted the natural metal to be rid of the useless rock. They placed the smelly ore in a circular pot for Shhaha to mix with a special softening liquid, after which it would only need pounding into shape.

Medra protested against this method so much that he was chased away. He wanted badly to do this for Shhaha and fought with the others to make a silver ring his way. To have peace,

Ahhpi, the clan chief, agreed. Now they would have two rings if Medra's way worked.

Medra built himself a large pitted fire on the very hill where the giant cats had rested. He had already gathered the bones and other materials needed, and only asked the elder protectors for digging and pounding tools to work with. By the time the fire was going well, Mah and Odrak had finished with Shhaha, and went up on the hill to watch what the others were calling Medra's foolishness. As they sat, others came over and Medra began working with greater determination.

He threw in many dry bones, which he had gathered from the jungle, along with piles of oily, precharred wood to make the fire hotter. The bones made the fire crackle and spark, which served to entertain the group. Medra sat for a long while to study the silver nuggets, then after making his choices by their weight, threw them into the fire as well. Then he turned to Mah and signed that this was all for now, except that he would have to keep the fire blazing high all night. Mah and Odrak helped gather more wood, since Medra could no longer carry heavy things, then turned in for the night after wishing Medra well.

In the morning Mah found Medra surrounded by feeders watching protectors pounding a shiny, white-gray ring. Brighter than anything he'd ever seen before, it was as round as a melon and larger than a man's head. Mah found it smooth to the touch and still warm from the fire. Medra had added hair from the end-tails of tall walkers, which fanned out all around it, and included one long section of hair designed to stream down the back when worn. As the sun came into the clearing it made the ring burst with flashes of light, blinding some and frightening others, which made Medra proudest of all.

He pointed Mah in the direction of where the fire had been, and of the bones and coals Medra had used, Mah found only a great charred pit of black dust and fine, white bone ash. He saw a shiny substance clinging to the ash and gathered it up to find he was holding soft plates of silver which he could mold with his fingers. Mah threw it down, rubbing his head at the shock of this new thing, then ran toward his duggi to get his Keeper, Dbsha, who was already coming up the hill.

"What have you done?" Dbsha groaned when he saw Mah, who now had white patches in his hair.

Mah's delight disappeared when he saw the look on

Dbsha's face. And after his keeper pulled loose Mah's shoulder-length hair for him to see the white blotches, he ran back up the hill pushing through the crowd to get at Medra. Medra laughed at the sight of him, while Mah fell to his knees, pleading for Medra to tell him what was wrong, when he saw that his hands were also a pasty white.

Medra started talking but no one understood. He pointed to a pile of gray powder at his feet and signed for Mah to rub his hands in it, which he did immediately. His hands burnt a little, but he could see that all he had to do was peel the white part away. He tried to rub some powder into his hair, but Medra stopped him, saying that it would not come out. This Dbsha understood and translated to Mah. Mah ran to his duggi and didn't show himself again until after dark.

That night everyone talked about Shhaha's leaving and Medra's shining silver ring. Up to now, Medra had been barely tolerated by the others, but now they showed him more respect. Even the available feeders were smiling at him.

Mah's new feeder was trying to get him to eat when Shhaha came over, holding both Medra's ring and the yet unfinished ring by Cleesha. Mah knew no comparison to the new silver that Medra had made. Cleesha's ring was more yellow and white and still lumpy from the pounding. Medra's ring was evenly circular, smooth and clear as light. The tall walker hairs coming out of it seemed born to the metal. Seemingly alive and glowing from the lights of nearby fires, it was more beautiful than anything Mah had ever seen before. Shhaha didn't have to say a word. Mah knew which had been chosen.

In the sunlight of the next morning, the yellow-gray ring looked worse by comparison and was never completed. Medra was busy showing Cleesha how to make the silver the way his people did, and describing the things his people made, some of which had healing powers.

Shhaha would have liked to hear about those, but did not have the time. He told his people that he, Mah, Odrak, the young feeder, Keishlee, and the clan's leading protector, Ramaa, would be leaving at the next sunrise to join the Great Sharing in the Valley of Names, far off in the land where the sun wakes.

Having remembered all he could of the ancient tales of the Great Sharing, Shhaha told his apprentices they were already many generations late. "There is a thing long in need of doing," he whispered in his most secret tones. "The images I see before me are dim. Our people will not survive if one of us does not reach the Valley of Names and passes the true Test of Blood."

It was a sad night, and there were many tears and long farewells. Bellar stayed in his duggi to pout, while Odrak, Ramaa and Keishlee stayed with Shhaha to finish preparations for the journey. In order to say their parting words in private, Mah and Olaah left the clearing to spend a moment alone. Cleesha and Medra sat on the shaded hill, building fires to make more silver, and for the first time since the lost of his manhood, Medra felt forgiven for the wrong he had done these people.

2

Lorna Claukens after discovering the library's secret room: "This place is like the temples in my dreams. It is familiar to me and speaks to my soul. Let us make a baby here, Kemmenar. Let us spend many nights and days here, and then one day, our baby will tell us its secrets."

"The Many Forms of Life"

Shhaha gathered his group to leave before anyone else awakened. They could not bear more goodbyes and left quickly, carrying very little, since the land would provide. They had dried foods and water, stone tools and stick weapons, and Shhaha made them bring colorful skins, fancy feathers and healing potents; plus salt, flint and seeds, since these were the trade items between clans. As always, each male carried a full sack of various colored living stones strapped around his waist, and Keishlee carried a softened tall walker hide, large enough to cover her completely should she need to hide. Shhaha wore Medra's silver ring along with all his best bones; and they all wore the walking carry-sacks between their legs, wrapped and tied with vine strings around their waist.

Ramaa, the only real protector of the group, carried the heaviest sacks, strapped around his shoulders, arms, legs and back, and looked like bundles walking. He was very strong and never once complained, except about not having his mate to follow on this journey, instead of the thin, hard-faced Keishlee. As all could see, he missed his mate very much. Dbsha had asked for Ramaa to be one of the chosen because of his strength, but Ramaa enjoyed visiting other lands and clans and was glad to be included.

Mah and Odrak wanted the adventure this journey offered. As apprentices to the Keeper of the Blood, they would never be allowed to venture far from their duggi clearing, and once they became Keepers of the Blood, the lands of the Waterhorse would be as far as they could ever go. This might be the only time they would travel anywhere, and in the quiet of the long days walking, they looked forward to hearing the tales new clans might tell.

Keishlee hated having to leave her clearing, but when the leading elders met to decide who else would accompany Shhaha, they compared the doings of the long-tooth cats, and it was recalled by the elder mothers that one of the five who journeyed towards the mountains was a feeder like themselves. They insisted a feeder be sent along. Keishlee was chosen because she was old enough to mate and free to have any man without the mating dance. She had yet to care for any protector in that special way, and stayed in the duggi of the elder women, tho not yet a "woman" herself. She was friendly enough but distant, and had been so since her feeder died and her grieving keeper went back to the clan of the Waterhorse. But Keishlee kept to the highest form of what a Tall Walker woman should be. With the recent death of the last Axum [*honorific title in memory of the clan's founding mother*], many elder women wanted her chosen as their new leading woman, and lately that was all they talked about.

Often, as is the way with women, they fought over the rightness of this or that thing, while men fought over things. Every day Shhaha had to choose sides over an issue of blood being fought over among the women and feeders. The women were more violent than the men, and would use sticks to strike each other, or even drive one another into the river. There were many days Shhaha got wet for his trouble. Having one woman speak over all the others remained an issue of blood worth, decided by the gush of water between their legs, or the strength of their legs and hands; and Keishlee was one of the fightingest women in their clan. She fought every feeder who demanded it, in respect for their being already rooted women, while she was not.

The elder women said Keishlee was wise for a female so young, and would grow wiser still. They said this journey would bring her the respects of new clans, help the men to see the things that they did not understand, and save Shhaha from starving at the hands of other women. What they really wanted was for Keishlee to mate—if not here, than somewhere else. Those who wanted her chosen feared she might not ever mate, and then would not be worthy if selected.

Shhaha liked this idea; with Keishlee gone, this would put a stop to the bickering until her return, and the clan would be assured of some peace while he was away. He agreed that a feeder should go on this journey, a journey like no one living now knew of, through lands not journeyed since times no longer told. They would need protection from the land itself, which only a woman could provide. Only a woman, or the Keeper of the Blood, could speak directly with the Great Mother and ask for her protection against the horror that could be all of life.

Shhaha could not recall all the necessities to bring to the Great Sharing. It had been so long since one happened, his memories were clouded. One thing he did remember, which was confirmed by runners from clans of the Waterhorse and the Wang, was that the Keeper of the Blood had to bring an apprentice and his clan relation. This also made it necessary for him to bring a woman, because no man could control a tall walker as well as a woman.

A tall walker would never go far alone, and never without its mate, so he had to bring two. They all took turns riding them, or leading them along while they slept (tall walkers liked to be on their feet and often walked in sleep). They covered quite a distance during the first four days, moving constantly, since they wanted to get out of the thick jungle, which was hard crossing for giants.

The jungle yielded plenty of food for them, with its juicy bugs and roots, and the great variety of salads, greens and fruits. Bypassing the known lands to get out of the mountain range before the flowering season started, they managed to leave the jungle behind in only five cycles of days [*25 days*].

Reaching the open plains, Shhaha noticed how few habilis clans were left anywhere near. There were no real clans seen, only a few wandering about or running from some danger. Only one bothered to look them over, and none tried to hound them into service of some kind, as was their normal custom. Often his people chanted to be rid of them, tho there was really no danger, their being almost human, very small and frail, but Shhaha had noticed them lacking in the jungles. Keishlee made the mistake of calling to a habilis feeder, when the creature jumped sideways onto a tree and sprayed them with her water. Keishlee knocked her down and did not try to speak with any again.

Further off they could see fields of speckled antelope and a small human camp. Shhaha immediately recognized them as the people of Zuma, their name a wordplay on the silence of their flying clan relation, the hairpiece. This was a colorful but harmless creature found in unlimited variations, and their people separated themselves in just as many smaller groups. These timid people were everywhere in this land, and were usually from a line of nameless mothers descended from Axum. They were a peaceful and playful sort, so Shhaha and his people stopped to visit for a while.

The Zuma clearing was a rolling dale of rainbow life, fluttering upon everything the eye could see. Since Mah was really still a slave and the smallest among them, he alone entered the camp. The Zumas approached with wary looks and sniffed about. They wore wing clippings tied about their necks and fashioned over their bodies. Live hairpieces tied to silk strings decorated their hair and the short sticks they carried.

This was one of the few clans that also ate its clan relation. Everyone agreed that if they didn't, they would be too soundly smothered by them, since they came in so many sizes and could appear all at once to fill the skies and cover all the land. The tall walkers delighted in playing with the hairpieces, and romped around the clearing feeding on them as well as from the trees and bushes.

When the Zumas lost their fear of the giants and beckoned Ramaa and the others near, they saw the brilliant silver ring lying quietly around Shhaha's neck, and stood back as one to gawk at the light around him. The feeders touched him first, but soon they all were pulling him further into their clearing, where they kept a duggi- and hut-less camp.

Normally Shhaha, who always wore strings of bones around every part of his body, and was also marked with the star of the circumcision, which identified him as a Keeper of the Blood, would not have been allowed into their clearing. People feared the magic of blood keepers. He would have had to keep many lengths away, especially if the people did not have a blood keeper of their own. But seduced by the shine of the ring around his neck, the Zumas ignored all qualms, and took Shhaha for a thorough looking over.

Later the group was awed again by the artistry of the Blood Wands. Odrak posed to make himself to look like the engravings, Ramaa pretended to be the elders, Mah imitated the many slaves and called out all their names, thrilling the Zumas to have so many Tall Walkers among them, which had been brought to them on the sticks.

Shhaha learned that they were indeed the people of Zuma, a mating mixture of a fire clan and people from the far-off Lion Fields, an expansive green and peaceful valley called H'Ahar.

They traded foods with Keishlee, and Ramaa got to relieve himself with one of the two mateless feeders. This was the custom for many people, so Shhaha relieved himself with the other. It was a small clan camp, only 10 and 4 adults, with even fewer slaves to serve them.

Soon the Tall Walkers headed for the marshlands, following a route that would allow them to avoid walking the desert. Staying no more than a day or night at other Zuma camps, they soon reached the dry grasses of the desert's far side. They made good time, and were unhurt, well fed and still pleased with the journey.

Around this time Mah began having strange pains in his head, which felt like spiders' eggs were bursting inside, spreading webs of pain down his arms and legs. Shhaha gave him nut herbs to chew, and whenever they reached a lake or stream, made him stick his head under water for long spans.

Wanting to be far away from any desert, they walked for three days until they tired of snakes, insects and dying trees about them. Skulls rotting here and there told of a danger, but not a sound was heard from horrors or things that threatened human life. To be safe, they sent their clan relation ahead as lookouts, and Keishlee rubbed her scent on them so they would not get lost.

Later they ran into a wandering group of humans who looked like kin to them, but Ramaa was the first to notice they had killed a small habilis and two tiny squawks. Ramaa, who had close kin related to the larger squawks, went into a rage, and thrashed two of them with Mah's blood wand. They had not the tongue for words, and squealed all purpose grunts as they tried to flee, but Shhaha stopped them with the magic of his voice.

Ramaa threw the bodies of the habilis and squawks near a tree, alive with brightly colored snakes. He took the men who were now cowering together on the ground and dragged them over to the others. Shhaha tried to teach them the names of the creatures they had killed. Mah echoed his words, explaining in sign that these creatures were near-human and should not be used as food. He got too close to one of the older men and was almost bitten.

The man never saw Odrak coming, but everyone heard his ribs crack when Odrak kicked him in the chest. His rib bones would now be in his wind bags, and Shhaha knew that he would die in a day or two. They watched him crash to the ground, desperate for breath. Against Shhaha's protest, Ramaa proceeded to thrash the others, feeding Odrak's anger so that he would help. Together they sent those who were still able running off into the thicker woods. Shhaha wanted to help the fallen man, but Ramaa moved them on, as he listened to the sounds of unseen animals begging for the food they left.

▼▼▼▼▼

During the second moon of their journey, Keishlee and Mah awakened to a sound the others could not hear. It started during the middle of night, and just before the rise of day grew loud enough to wake the others, but then was quickly gone. Their clan relation was also disturbed by the nerve-pinching sounds, but there was no sense or sign of danger, and so they journeyed on.

One day just after high sun, their clan relation sounded a bleated warning. The others readied themselves, and soon there came the dragging thump, thump of a huge pink and green reptile with wings. It howled, and tho no sex was seen, they knew it was a distressed feeder. It had no teeth, and Keishlee approached, hoping it could not eat her. The great creature fell at her feet and spat wide nets of muck over her. Howling in pain, it rolled over to reveal its belly being eaten out, and the thing still chewing within.

Keishlee cursed at the movement in its belly, and Shhaha signed for her to prepare to leave, while trying to decide whether to go through the remaining desert or the nearby woods. Mah and Odrak quickly gathered all the rocks they could find, as Shhaha turned the blood wand blades towards the creature's belly and the hiss of snakes came out. The reptile moaned a sigh of grief and death, and then not one, but many heads came out—snakes, remotely human, with large gold and green eyes without lids, above mouths full of sharp fangs and hairless heads of more scales than skin.

Shhaha, Mah and Odrak stood their ground with stone sharpened sticks and taunted the snakes to come closer. With his packs piled on, Ramaa managed to rip a supple branch from a nearby tree and smashed to mush one that lunged his way.

The sleepy whispered screech that Keishlee and Mah had heard much too often, suddenly rang out from the desert. This time the others heard it, including the snakes, who left the dead creature, rushing towards the sound and the white sands to try and slither in. Ramaa took Odrak's blood wand and rammed the long pointed stone into the ground where one snake tried to hide.

Shhaha killed another and let the blood drip out for the other snakes to smell. It was not enough, but just then the sun hit his silver ring, moving the lights around him as if to provide a protective embrace, and the snakes stopped, blinded by the sight.

Keishlee began to hit herself in time to some steady beat. She and the others were confounded because the snakes could see. The snakes wanted to go to the cry from the desert and trying to get away from Ramaa, they clustered around a tree and hissed bold threats. Ramaa managed to kill another and watched as red blood and green ooze spat from the pieces he rashly split in two. Ramaa was sick at any killing and began to heave up dry fear.

The largest snake was kept in place by Shhaha, who was learning to use the murky moving lights of his silver ring. To add to the snakes' confusion, Keishlee and Ramaa darted about, while Mah made sounds for the snakes to feel. Odrak joined Mah, and their sounds bruised one of the creatures.

"It can hear!" Keishlee screamed, as the animal lunged, closing the distance between it and Mah, but Odrak and Ramaa were just as swift with their attack. Stabbing together they nailed the snake to the ground, and Ramaa ran his stick through its head, ripping the soft skull out from the tough skin.

This time they all stopped to heed the scream from the desert, coming to them now like a dissonant melody. Nearer. Getting nearer still, as the snakes hissed, no longer afraid to slither onto the open sands, while the humans shivered with reawakened fear.

Looking at the dead, yet still beautiful reptile, they were angry with the snakes for killing it and cursed a blood vengeance on them for feeding on its flesh. Keishlee was the first to pick up stones and hurl them out after the snakes, who were moving fast, but had not gotten very far; their bellies being full, they could hardly slither on.

Mah and Ramaa followed them with stones and sticks. Odrak reached one and flung it onto a jutting rock. Too angry now for fear, Ramaa tried to kill the snakes that turned to jab at him, but twisting away, he tumbled across the sand. Mah screamed to warn him as one came close enough to taste his flesh. He moved to help Ramaa and noticed great mounds of sand moving in lines towards them, when suddenly all movement ceased.

Cold fear became the reality here and they backed away to leave. The sand beneath Ramaa gave way to reveal a head rising up to meet him. All he saw were large, slanted, unlidded eyes before he dashed away. In front of them the fleeing snakes rose up like sentinels of stone, while steeples of falling sand blocked all the paths around them.

The sight kindled a memory for Shhaha of tales no longer told of a clan of near-human snakes. They had shapely heads with thin, fuzzy, colorless hair, and pupils one could swim in, dancing in eyes of yellow and red that made up most of the face. Their hypnotic movements reminded the humans that it was past time to flee, as a sound unheard, yet keenly felt, destroyed their will to leave. When the snakes reached a height above Ramaa, Shhaha shouted for their retreat, but no foot could move and no eye would not see.

These creatures were shades of milky green and brown, but one the color of toasted leaves spiraled its way towards them. Its face wore an almost human expression, wrapped in large folds of soft scaled skin flowing up from its back, but it was not human. Slithering along, so assured of the lack of danger here, it moved deliberately toward Shhaha, who alone struggled against the song that kept the others frozen. Slyly the fiend veiled its face, draping the cape of skin around and around itself until only a single eye and fang were visible.

Shhaha, never at a loss for words, fought desperately to speak. It was too garbled for his people to understand, but the snake creatures did and screeched "Aegypi!," their call of recognition.

Suddenly Shhaha could move again, and he jumped back a step, raising his blood wand to protect himself. In a motion too fast to see, the snake untwisted itself and the head cape billowed open behind it, then turned its head into the expanded skin, to make a sound that was clearer. "Aegypi!" it called, then turned back to Shhaha to hold him with its eyes.

For long while they were all transfixed by a floating dream within the gleaming eyes of surrounding snakes. The desert's heat rose, and its sands piled up around their feet, while the sun went down and the smaller snakes disappeared beneath.

The snake creatures only took their hypnotic eyes away from their prey in order to bite them, giving Shhaha and his people back their senses just long enough to feel it. Bitten in turn, Keishlee took it on the shoulder, the others at the upper arm, and for all except Mah, it was done rather quickly. Five of the larger, more colorful snakes surrounded him, flicking their tongues. They seemed afraid and yet attracted to him. These creatures had a keen sense of smell, and it was the scent of the Great Mahs they feared.

Mah alone carried the smell of the giant birds. He collected their oil sacks and hid them like a prize. He used their droppings to make his body paints, and he alone was unafraid to sleep within their brilliant wings, or upon the blue-white fur of their breasts. It had been many moons since Mah had painted himself, or slept upon the Great Mah feathers, but it was this bird the snakes saw when they looked at him. They hissed tones into the billows of their capes, giving each other courage. Then one of the snakes wrapped itself around Mah and laid him across the sands, while all the largest of them bit him quickly on each arm.

Later, Shhaha was only too glad to be alive. To guard against the poison he felt moving in his system, he hurried to make a potion while running from the desert. The special conditioning for blood keepers of his clan did not allow foreign elements to mix with his blood. Most poisons would have little or no effect on him, or his apprentices, as it was soon flushed from their systems. But he could see Ramaa and Keishlee were suffering as their blood began to boil.

Unfamiliar with this creature, Shhaha would not rely solely on his potion. He needed the help of the Great Mother and her all powerful magic. As part of a powerful medicine, Shhaha dug holes to bury the others, so that they would be closer to the her. Ramaa helped for awhile, but Shhaha had to bury Ramaa and Keishlee by himself, after they began to moan in agony. Trying to withstand the boiling of his own blood, Shhaha rested himself under a tree.

What Shhaha felt had to be much worse for Mah, who had been bitten many times, and was now more red-black than he had ever seen a human before. They all fought against screaming from the pain, but Mah was unconscious from it, and Shhaha knew the others would soon follow.

Distracting himself, Shhaha considered what just happened to them, by searching old tales and recalling lines from ancient chronicles, he began to understand why they had survived. He was not surprised to find each memory connected to the Great Sharing. He could see the ring of silver in his mind as past times unfolded to him. It had not been a metal ring like the one he wore, but one made of gray-white feathers, knitted together with aged water moss. The words were spoken many generations before Shhaha's birth, but the blood keeper's lips moved in front of his eyes now, retelling his tale of meeting these creatures, and how he lived to learn their name. Shhaha only now recalled saying the name to the near-human snake that threatened him. As it was so often, the memory had come when needed, even without his searching for it, forcing him to say, "Aegypi," which had saved their lives.

He wished for counsel from his elders, or from Meneliawy, the leading Keeper of the Blood of the Waterhorse clans. Meneliawy was wise and powerful, with magic in his blood that few could understand. It was an ancient blood keeper from his line, who set the rising red star as the time to start this journey. Meneliawy would remember the reason for following the star to the Valley of Names, and the snakes called Aegypi.

Shhaha did not fear death from the Aegypi bites, since they were not dead already. They might get sick for awhile, or become deformed in some way, but they would not die. Shhaha's only worry was for the magic placed upon them from the bites, and their contact with these creatures. Of this he worried a great deal, since he had plans for mixing magic of his own on this journey.

Eventually Shhaha fell asleep with the others and all ran wild in their dreams. They could see the snakes who called "Aegypi" to each other and who were a great multitude living in a vast, sandy forest. Their poison could not kill warm-blooded creatures, and their soft teeth kept them starved. Near-human, they had human kin descended from their blood, but the humans shunned the Aegypi, claiming the Fire Bird as their clan relation when they left their drying lands. Now the Aegypi were dying, counting their fewest numbers, too few to breed with any fruitility. During the night they called "Aegypi" for their human kin to return and save them from extinction.

Shhaha awoke to find himself grieving for these doomed snake creatures, who had spared their lives for the pleasure of hearing their name once more. But as his eyes adjusted to the fading light, there was no time to think of the Aegypies or their troubles. A small slave stood near him, and many wild dogs were staring him in the face. Blood dripped from their mouths, and a hungry look encased their faces.

Shhaha felt the blood wand in his hand and was about to stick it in the face of an approaching dog, when the slave ordered it away. The animal stopped, and the area filled with the howls of countless slaves and dogs. The area swarmed over with young slaves, none older than Mah or Odrak, who had been uncovered and placed against a tree. They were uncovering Keishlee when they discovered her feeder bags. Some dashed away, others jumped over her, and with calls like growls from one dog to another, they howled for the others to come and see.

They called her "Oro," which Shhaha knew was one of the Seven Sisters. From this he knew this dog tribe was human, but Shhaha had never seen a tribe or clan made entirely of slaves.

The quick touch of a naked slave told Shhaha that Mah was still unconscious and burning hot. It worried him that Mah should be with fever for so long. Mah was conditioned by the rites of the "Black Salts," and could not be poisoned except by those that killed instantly.

Shhaha tried to move, but the dogs growled, and the slave attending Mah rushed over to him bearing a small stone knife. Pounding his own chest, the slave yelled "Docga!" into Shhaha's face.

"Oro?" yelled another slave. "Oro?"

The slave backed away from Shhaha, but not before rubbing his face into the ground when he saw the feeder bags standing full from Keishlee's chest.

Slaves gathered around, pulling Keishlee from the ground, and licking the dirt from her body. Her smell drove some into orgies of touching, and made the older slaves ready for pleasures they did not understand. Others began sacred rites long lost to them from a clan they no longer knew. But their blood knew, and made their bodies perform these acts common to their kin alone.

Shhaha's people were a peaceful lot, if not made to look upon spilled blood, and he watched them honor Keishlee in their wild and various fashions. He recognized the blood of many different bird clans among the dog slaves. He watched with glee as some of them attempted building small nests or gift piles. There were even two little slaves whose blood was from a Waterhorse clan. They still walked like their people, and dug holes as if looking for water. There was blood of Zuma, Rambull, Tree-root, Tiger, and Squawker clans, whose colors Shhaha easily recognized. Slaves from Fire clan peoples ran berserk around them, making small sitting fires with the torches they carried. Few of them used words, speaking mostly in sign and jumbles of what had been words, words now lost as the they were lost. But their signing was in high form, and their meaning was clear.

As the sun set, Shhaha realized that they wanted to keep Keishlee, Mah and Odrak. He also understood that they were going to kill him. The way he sat made him look as if he had no legs, and could not run with the pack. They simply did not want to leave him here to die. They would leave Ramaa, who they feared too much to look at directly. Mah was too sick to take, yet the white patches of hair made him too interesting to leave behind.

To Odrak alone they directed their signs, and he enjoyed their attentions, especially their wild dancing. He translated all he learned back to Shhaha. They disapproved, but considered Shhaha a strange oddity and pitied him because he had no legs, leaving him untied and only guarded by their dogs. Ramaa was left in the ground, covered with extra rocks and roped to nearby trees. He was guarded heavily since he kept trying to get out and spoke angrily to them.

Shhaha saw they numbered well over five sets of hands. He tried to count them, but stopped at two sets of hands and toes, which was more than anyone needed to count. He lost track of individuals as he noticed that many were of matching pairs. The birthing of twins was yet unknown to Shhaha, and he did not recognize them as such. All of them had personalities like the dogs they followed, and who followed them—instantly violent and fighting each other for bits of food, yet lovingly warm and tender over another's hurts and wounds. The fact that Shhaha was tall even without his legs and fear of his stick kept them back. None of them had seen adult humans before and were making a thorough study of them.

A pack of black and gray dogs had taken to Odrak, and kept bringing him bits of raw meat, which made Odrak sick to look upon. It was the flesh of the creature they had stopped the Aegypi from eating. Odrak felt a great pity for this creature whose flesh was so well regarded as food.

Too weak to fight them off, Keishlee relaxed as they did their best to please her. She felt better and began to walk about the group which howled and stamped as she passed. She noticed many of the slaves were sick and starved. Bite marks and claw lines revealed the violence of living with the pack. She moved toward Ramaa, who quickly cautioned her to keep her place, as did the dogs and slaves who jumped from their resting place to growl at her intentions.

The slaves would not leave her side, and she looked tenderly at the smaller ones who continued to sniff and lick her legs. They had never lived among other humans and were almost lost to this tribe of dogs. She petted some and others came over for more. Soon some of the bigger slaves were bringing her colored stones, tiny bunches of scented twigs, and the nuts and bones they kept stored in their hair. Older slaves howled for her to come and see a leaf pile here or a nest built there for her. Keishlee became the focus of all their attentions, and soon they forgot Shhaha, who silently crept away to check on Mah's condition.

Odrak saw this and helped distract the others by joining in the mesh that surrounded Keishlee. The smell of her was strong now and it excited the dogs and slaves. Discreetly, Keishlee would wipe herself and then smear her scent under their noses, which made them run wild between the sitting fires. She sent the slaves and dogs alike into a frenzy of expectation with her every move. Even their leader, Docga, forgot himself, play fighting and biting the others.

Suddenly Shhaha's voice roared through the forest with the cry of the collard mink, his favorite call to attention. The dogs familiar with the sound ran into the thicker woods. Some slaves followed, but most were disoriented and huddled in fear near a fire, or Keishlee, or Docga.

Shhaha yowled again, and this time they all could see where the sound was coming from. Some ran towards him in mock anger, trying to intimidate him with their growls, until they became aware of his great size and long legs. For a moment the slaves stepped back in terror, but the growling and barking dogs encouraged the slaves to be brave. They formed a circle around him and Ramaa, whom Shhaha had released.

The Tall Walkers were more than giants to these slaves, but the little humans were more than brave and readied themselves for attack. Ramaa stood at Shhaha's back and entwined one leg with his. Keishlee knew the fighting stance of her clan, which signified they were prepared to suffer the sight of spilled blood.

A dog foaming at the mouth was spurred on by Docga, who called for the dog to make a leap for Ramaa.

Shhaha recalled a tale of a dog clan, its members savage and wild, with a hunger for the taste of blood. Human blood once tasted can bring on a frenzy to drive away the spirit, leaving creatures of evil seeking blood and destruction. The way Shhaha was touching him made it easy for Ramaa to get the sense of the tale without being told. He knew all would be lost if these dogs killed and ate him. At the tribe's first fit of hunger, the dogs would turn on the slaves, remembering only the taste of human flesh.

With the blood wand in hand, Ramaa ripped out the dog's innards as it flew by him in the air. One of the fierce little slaves leaped upon him, but before he could take a bite out of Ramaa's neck, Ramaa flipped him to the ground and staked him through. Shhaha disemboweled a dog on the ground in front of him before Docga and the others could strike. The sight of the dead slave and the gutted dogs brought the others to a standstill. They had never seen such a thing done so quickly.

Shhaha began a wordless chant of the memory before him demanding to be relived. It was the tale of the Red Hounds, and he hoped that some part of it would reach the blood of these slaves. A tale of true horror needed no words for its meaning to be understood, and it took hold of this dog tribe and filled them with an unknown dread.

Keishlee took this moment to go about comforting the fear-stricken slaves. They stared at Shhaha, but cried up to her to be suckled as they had been when born, especially the ones whose blood memories were still upon them.

Shhaha had been feeling a loss of his powers before he left the clearing of the Tall Walkers, but as he saw the effect of his voice-powered chant upon the little slaves, he felt his powers renewed.

"...and the hounds poured blood upon the land...mixing blood with sand...chewing bones and eating up the humans...."

Shhaha was remembering his own apprenticeship when Shama, his Keeper of the Blood, had told him that the sound of the word was what reached the spirit in blood, and not the word itself. With the proper control over all his vocal tones he could teach the blood of any living thing that could hear his voice. Shhaha spent all his life training the sounds that came out his mouth, and had developed a power his people called "voice magic." With the proper tones, Shhaha could entrance most creatures to follow his will.

The slaves of the dog clan cowed under the melody of the chant. Dogs howled, slaves cried, and others tied themselves into knots and shook. Some stared at Shhaha with lost fixation, but soon they were all calmed, taking comfort from Keishlee or Odrak. All except Docga. He was only concerned with the sticks that Shhaha and Ramaa were holding. He could see or hear nothing else. The sticks were the red-black wood of some important memory for him, and he wanted one of them. Odrak was the only one to see the look on Docga's face, while the others worried more about the rest.

Before Shhaha finished his chant, Keishlee had all the slaves clustered about her, their lost memories coming back to them with every touch. The smell of her renewed their need to be suckled close with loving care, instead of always hurting and knowing little else but fear.

Shhaha and Odrak revived Mah, who had missed all the excitement. Odrak shared every moment of it with him, while Ramaa searched for the lost and troubled Tall Walkers, calling to them from the forest.

Keishlee tried to explain to the slaves that they should go back towards the mountains and find their peoples. "Feeders cry over the loss of you," she said with her mouth and body.

This talk distracted Docga for a while, exciting him to know of others living outside the forest, who might take them in and show them what it meant to be human. He had no knowledge of anyone taller than himself. Half their tribe never lived from one rainy season to the next, a fact that made Odrak hold some of the slaves closer to him, promising to tell other clans about them so they might be found.

Keishlee wondered how they came to live alone in the forest. Docga could not tell them, but signed that he was brought here by the dogs. Some were found near human remains or being nursed by other animals. She understood that the dogs took care of them, even suckling the very young ones, feeding and protecting the rest. It was their custom to search the forest for others, who they always found, and then trained to run with the pack.

By the time Ramaa returned, so had most of the dogs, and now the slaves were frightened anew by the sight of the tall walkers and the angry growls of their dogs. Some of the slaves tried to run away, but Mah and Odrak stopped them, telling them that these were friends and kin to his people. Some of the dogs sensed the friendliness of the tall walkers and came over to play at their feet, but others kept their distance, terrified of Ramaa and his stick.

Just then Shhaha smelled fresh blood flowing and turned to see dogs eating the dead dogs and the slave who had attacked them. Ramaa saw them too and ran them off. Shhaha cursed the dogs and snatched Docga up by his knife arm, hauling him over to see close up what Ramaa was about to do.

It was one thing for nonhumans and bloodless creatures to eat each other, but human life was sacred, not something to be eaten by dogs. It was also what Shhaha had feared most for the slaves of this tribe.

Ramaa caught one of the dogs with the flesh still in his mouth. He pinned it to the ground with his knee and the blood wand stuck under its throat to keep its head in place. The dog knew better than to move.

Shhaha threw Docga to the ground in front of the whimpering animal, and in his most threatening manner, he faced the growling dogs and saw each of them die in his inner eye. All the slaves could feel the power that is the Keeper of the Blood. Even in the darkness Mah and Odrak could see the aura of his spirit reaching out to the dogs and slaves. Strange sounds came from his body, slow and deliberate, while Ramaa took the flesh from the dog's mouth and threw it to the ground in front of Shhaha.

With the blood wand blades, Shhaha staked the piece of flesh and held it out to the pack of dogs before him. Two of the dogs cautiously approached, but only one went for the bait. Before it could close its teeth upon the flesh, Shhaha had rammed the stick down its throat. The dog tried to back away but Shhaha rammed the stick further in and flipped the creature on its back. All watched as the dog choked to death. When it was dead, Shhaha raised the dog on the stick for all to see.

The dogs howled and growled in angry terror, fear and understanding. Shhaha flicked the stick and the dead dog flew into the trees. Odrak followed the lesson, and limped over to lie down in the spot where the flesh had been, pretending to be dead. Ramaa ripped a piece of flesh from the open stomach of the dead slave and threw it on top of Odrak.

Shhaha gently called the dogs over. None would move, but barked and growled with renewed frustration. With sweetness flowing from him, Shhaha called the dogs again. Now the slaves were all standing about, clutching Mah or Keishlee. Keishlee cried to herself, knowing now that the dogs were the reason some slaves never lived from one rainy season to the next, why Docga, even now, did not let go of the stone knife. She wanted to kill all the dogs, until she noticed that many of them knew the lesson, and were gentle in their ways. They sat on their hind legs watching Shhaha with their heads lowered, not a tongue or tooth showing.

Another bold dog decided to risk its life. At first she paced awhile, then tried to snatch the meat away. Shhaha was old, but he was not slow of mind or body. The dog would not see from the right side of its head for many days, if at all. It fled into the forest, howling and running from death.

The dogs understood, and turned away from Shhaha and the flesh on top of Odrak.

Docga looked up to Shhaha with tears in his eyes, then looked over at the other slaves and howled a cry full of meaning. The other slaves returned his call, turning to Keishlee and then to Odrak and Shhaha to howl and bark their submission.

One dog took this moment to try a sneak attack on Ramaa, who whopped the dog upside the face, then stood over it, ready to kill it. Docga stepped closer to him, howling even louder while trying to reach for Ramaa's stick. He turned to Shhaha, patting his chest and begging for one of the sticks. When neither Ramaa or Shhaha understood, Docga quickly knocked aside the bloody flesh from Odrak and made him sit up. He licked Odrak's face, and taking some dirt, wiped the blood from his chest. Then he snatched Odrak up and held him close and tight, until Odrak pushed him away.

To everyone's surprise, Shhaha handed Docga his blood wand and watched as the slave ran around ordering the pack of dogs. He held the blood wand to the sky, then growled up at the stars, which brought all the dogs and slaves running to him.

Ramaa kicked the dog he was guarding in its chest, then dared it to move.

The other dogs and the slaves now gathered around Docga, smelling each other and rubbing heads to shoulders, and then fell to the ground to rub each other again. Docga made another call that silenced the group. He showed the stick to the other older slaves, and tho he wanted to keep it, he slowly returned to Shhaha to give it back. He was a strong little slave, Odrak thought. The stick was heavy even for him, and he was a head and chest taller than Docga.

Handing the stick over, Docga only now saw its designs. He felt it, studying the shapes of the bodies carved there. He stared at the other forms and then up at the tall walkers. Seeing the many shapes of feeders, he tried to count them, but could not grasp the idea that there could be so many. He pointed to the carving of a newborn slave and suddenly dropped the stick at Shhaha's feet. He then fell upon the terrified dog, hugging it close while pleading with Ramaa for its life.

Ramaa waved him away. When he would not go, Ramaa kicked the slave away, and raised his stick to kill the dog. But Shhaha ordered him to stop and signed for Mah to help Docga up from the ground. The dog was in shock, but Shhaha allowed Docga to bring the dog closer to the fire, where the other slaves gathered around and made it stand.

All was stillness now. The forest was quiet enough to hear the rustle of the leaves, and when the tall walkers came a little closer, not even the dogs stirred. Shhaha was feeling drained and sat down to rest. Odrak and Mah gathered up the loose flesh and the dead slave, and began to hand dig a hole to bury him.

Docga was impressed with their digging but saw a chance to win favor with the giants. He led a few dogs over to Mah and Odrak and made them dig. Soon he had more dogs helping, and slaves to remove the loose dirt. The hole was quickly sloped down into a deep trench. By the time Keishlee had finished making body paints, the far end of the trench was deep enough for Docga to stand up in.

Keishlee gathered all the slaves around to watch as she and Odrak painted the slave's body in the custom of their people. Odrak and Ramaa gathered up the rest of their belongings which had been thrown about. Ramaa was grateful that none of the water had been spilled, and took some over for the tall walkers to drink.

Later, Odrak, Shhaha and Ramaa returned to place a finger of black paint on the slave's body. Keishlee showed the slaves how to do the same. The slave was completely covered when they placed his naked remains into the hole, which was covered swiftly, while Shhaha began a chant and dance for the dead.

None of the slaves understood what Shhaha was doing, but they had seen the wandering spirits of the dead, and Odrak helped them to understand that this was the way to give them rest. With a few more blood lessons like this, their understanding would awaken them to the humans that they were. They would understand their place in the cycle of life and realize that they were nature's spice; they could begin to shine a light into their own darkness, and, like spice to food, life would be more tasty now.

When Docga joined the dance, Shhaha felt that he might prove a worthy Keeper of the Blood for his people after all. He danced without care for the fatigue in his old bones, taking energy from the eyes of the slaves, as they returned, again and again, to the final seeding [*grave*]. The jittery nervousness Shhaha had noticed about them in the beginning was gone now. These slaves had learned an important lesson late in life. They had started out with only human blood, but they would be fully human soon.

During the days that followed, Ramaa and Mah showed the slaves how to make paints for their bodies and sturdy vine strings for hanging the many fruits they found. Shhaha showed them how to tie their hair behind their heads so that it did not always stick the eye or trip them up. Keishlee and Odrak stopped them from wallowing in their waste, and taught them to take it away from camp or showed them how to dry it with straw to use as fuel.

Ramaa made them wash in the lake, and tho he had not wanted to, he eventually had cut away their lice-infected hair. Shhaha showed them which things to eat to rid themselves of the yellow in their eyes, and taught Docga to make a poultice for the tender sores on their legs. He taught them important words for meeting other tribes and clans, and how to say the all important "Aaah!" in all its forms. He gave all the older slaves names, which they quickly understood and remembered, and asked that they name the younger ones once they could properly call the dogs to them.

Most importantly, Ramaa taught them to make the stone knife like the one Docga had found, which had allowed him to live longer than all those before him. This could be used to teach the dogs and the other animals to have some respect for them. He showed them how to cut away some of the dogs' long hair, which gave them comfort from the heat, and how to use dried straw to groom the dogs, or brush clean a place for camping.

Shhaha did not like leaving the slaves alone in the forest, but his people had stayed with them a full turn of days [*5 days*], and they had to continue their journey. When he and his people finally left the dog clan, in the place that would become their home, they were bald but clean, and talked and walked more upright. They cried and begged Shhaha to stay, but Keishlee comforted them, and made them understand that they had to leave.

Odrak had made a small version of the blood wand and presented it to Docga. It had a dog's head carved beneath the likeness of Puutha on top, and a stone blade at the bottom. Docga was overjoyed and held him for a long time, and would not let him go until Mah threatened to beat him down. Docga licked both their faces, then ran the dogs through the forest to show Shhaha's people another way past the desert.

When Mah and Odrak mounted a tall walker, all the slaves howled and ran alongside to see this sight in full. With the tiny ones strapped to the backs of large dogs, and the others running on foot, they covered much ground together. Those without their long woolly mats of hair ran ahead and were faster than the dogs.

The tall walkers saw open fields and took off at a clap, passing the dogs easily. Shhaha couldn't believe the slaves had run so fast and so far without stopping, but it was almost night-shade when they caught up to Docga, surrounded by slaves and dogs standing on cliff ledges, howling their goodbyes.

Docga pointed to the open plains, and Keishlee stopped the tall walkers to call out Aaah! in farewell. They did not really expect to see this tribe again. But Docga and the slaves on the ledging, and those still following, could be heard calling the Aaah! of abundant joy. Shhaha and Ramaa, who were out at the forest edge, stopped to reach for the sky, their way of accepting a promise to meet again.

▼▼▼▼▼

Each morning Shhaha checked the place where the sun rose against his memory of the red star the night before. They traveled along the lower edge of the sun towards a place Shhaha called the Valley of Names, a place of great wisdom, and the final home of the Seven Sisters.

They had already been many days on this open plain and were tired of the endless line of land before them. Even the tall walkers were hungry for something other than grass to eat. Whenever they came upon a bush, the Tall Walkers ate it down to a scrubby nub. The roots and barbs found here were mostly tasteless loam. Insect life was plentiful, but hardly nourishing, and had to be eaten in large quantities to keep up their strength.

The dry air took the life out of Shhaha's ring of silver. It had changed colors over the last few days and had lost all its shine. It was black now, hardly noticeable, even with the hairs flowing from it. But after four months they were finally stepping out of their clan lands, so it really wouldn't matter now, and Shhaha still loved it.

For many days they saw no other life except a lonely australopi, which they ran from, knowing how dangerous it could be. Shhaha felt sorry for it, because all its kin were gone. No female australopi had been seen since the time of Cush. Many clans had taken to killing them, and using their blood in magic, because they had the longest lives of any form of life. But they could be as evil as any beast, and would kill you just to be rid of your smell. When they saw this one, it was such a shock that it was almost upon them before they remembered the danger.

Australopi were extremely slow, and it was more like playing then running from them, but Keishlee kept stumbling and falling. Three times this happened and it left her in a trance. Everyone stopped to stare because of the rarity of it, which gave the creature lots of time to catch up. The third time she fell they picked her up with tears in her eyes. Shhaha touched her forehead with his palm. It was the touch for spirit testing, usually done to newborns, or when wandering spirits were near. He shocked her into standing when he said that someone who cared for her had just died.

She smiled up at him and said that she had been thinking about her feeder. A memory of her had just jumped before her eyes. Of course Shhaha agreed that this was why she stumbled, but Mah and Odrak knew that he bumbled on telling hard truths.

The australopi followed them for more than three cycles of days. They left it in the dust so often that it finally gave up, but soon they grew lonesome for even the sight of it on this high, barren plain. At one point they all turned around and felt they were on the top of their world. The air was cold and thin, sweeping by in whirling drafts. For many days Shhaha chanted the call of longing when the lonesomeness of the place grew unbearable to them. The few trees were bare and grew smaller than Mah. The grass was yellow and tasteless, and the tall walkers mooed to say that even the air tasted awful here. At night they had to use the heavy skins, as they were chilled by a cold they could not have imagined, and winds so hard and bitter they cut the skin like curses cut the heart.

Shhaha told tales often, trying to provide some cheer. He said it was good they had no distractions. This way they would reach their destination sooner, since it was still a long way off. The stars he charted by night were shifting and they needed to move faster in order to keep pace. And so they took this time of hunger and emptiness to run or ride the plain both day and night to be gone from here.

Off in the grayness of the land ahead they saw a great stretch of valley cut into the earth, with mountains peeking out the crack. The tall walkers could go a great many days without water, but the others were starving and dried to the bone with thirst. It was Ramaa who first caught a whiff of water flowing, and hastened their pace to reach this valley.

Shhaha had caught it too, but he also smelled something else. He told the others that a herd of waterhorses would be near, and smiled at the thought of what their numbers must be that they should come so far to live. But his smile quickly turned to a frown when he caught the smell of death around. There were water-horses near, but they were dead and putrid. Their scent was like no other, like freshwater and rich soil when alive, or filling all the land with rot when dead.

But the air soon changed and was all at once clear around them. There were many trees to see, even tall grasses and birds flying overhead. They watched insects taste the flowers on a bush, and then ate the petals, knowing they were safe. There were great juicy bugs crawling all around, which gave them quite a feast that went well with the nuts they found. Some trees bloomed with fruit, which they picked and packed, or strung around their bodies, then headed for the water, which they could hear flowing loudly, smell so distinctly, and almost taste.

Coming down from what they realized was a high mountain plain, they looked over the cliff, and gasped in awe of the great clan living below. Their village was built up along both sides of a narrow rushing stream, on land within the rip of a high escarpment.

Shhaha was looking for a way down into the glorious abundance of fruitful dark lands, when he noticed a group of women coming towards them from the peaking mountain. They were many trees away, but without tree cover they were clearly visible to the people whose eyesight was as good as any bird's.

These women wore feathers draped across their chests and down their arms. A short flap of colorful cloth hung down under the feathers in front and in back, which billowed slightly in the cool breeze blowing down the escarpment. As they came closer Ramaa could see that some were blue black like his people, but that their hair was textured differently and worn much longer.

Being that these were women, Keishlee was the first to make her way towards them, followed by all except the tall walkers, who were too busy at nearby trees.

"Aaah!" a woman greeted them, her hair catching the breeze.

Keishlee touched the woman's hair to find it unlike any she had ever seen; long and straight, and tied in thick tresses that were made more beautiful by its sheen and the brilliance of its blackness.

Two women snatched Keishlee aside and held her to the ground. Ramaa was about to interfere, but Shhaha held him back, signing to him that these women had said much to him by not noticing them, or their great difference in size.

"Aaah!" the woman repeated, this time more angrily.

Shhaha knew the meaning, tho it was the same word used by all the people Shhaha had ever known. Getting near he could see that these people were not close kin, and were of a lighter brown than he had ever heard tell. Only two were even near blue-black. It had been their long, shimmering-black hair that had deceived him. Shhaha repeated the call of unwelcome greeting, but followed with the words that begged for welcome and hospitality between friends and possible kin.

The women ordered them to sit. Odrak and Mah were the first to do so, while Shhaha removed the string of fruit from around his neck and held it out to the women. One of the women holding Keishlee came over and took the fruit, then went back to Keishlee and threw it in her lap, speaking words Keishlee could not understand.

Once the people of the Tall Walkers were seated, the women walked around the group looking them over. There were many of them, 6 more than 10. None of them carried weapons, which gave Shhaha pause, as they looked from Ramaa and the stick he carried, to Mah and Shhaha, who also carried one. The woman who had spoken to them tried to take Shhaha's stick. He gently pushed her away, and in that moment other women were suddenly upon him, jumping up to beat him about the face. Others tried to kick him between the legs when he stood, but found the spot too high up from the ground.

The sight made Ramaa and Mah laugh. They tired of

trying to befriend these women and knocked them away, demanding to be left alone, but before Ramaa could reach for another, the women jumped into a pack, each now holding a strange weapon in hand. It looked like a dead, sun-dried animal, almost as long as Odrak's arm. One of them cut Ramaa down an arm and he hit her so hard she fell clear to the escarpment ledge.

Shhaha looked down at the women with more respect. They had a weapon that did not take much strength to use. It made a cut that was smooth and sharp, and so deep that Ramaa's skin fell loose and flapped about as he cursed them, calling them his waste of water, or the rock in his entrails. These women were a fierce lot, small and wiry, with hair that covered their eyes, a thing that gave Shhaha something to fear since he could not see their souls within.

The women had no fear of these giants. They kept their weapons ready while speaking to each other about the sameness in the colors from Ramaa to Mah, who was the smallest.

Shhaha began a tale of tall walkers who died of thirst. It was a tale of sorrow and waste, and he chanted it in the way of calling spirits to him. Being so well trained, Mah and Odrak sat on their toes and began to echo the tale.

Ramaa was bleeding badly from the cut and roared for the women to leave. Keishlee slipped out of the clutch of the women holding her and jumped to her feet. She called for them to fight and demanded her blood rite for this insult to her people. She cursed them and sprayed them with her spit, but none of this did they understand, until she slipped loose her walking carrysack and pissed a hard stream of water to the ground.

Shhaha stopped his chant, surprised that Keishlee knew how to do such a thing. The strange women looked at each other and then back at Keishlee, who continued shouting at them to come forth and fight. Finally they understood, and three of the women stepped forward. One came close enough to strike Keishlee with her weapon, but the two other others shouted for her to stop, taking the weapon from her and reminding her that Keishlee was obviously a woman.

When the talk was finished, Keishlee was on the woman as soon as the others stepped back. Keishlee had no fear, she was taller and knew her own strength, and beat the woman senseless. The others shouted that the fight was not fair since Keishlee was far taller than all of them, and so two more dropped their weapons and leaped into the fight. Ramaa moved to stop the fight, but was quickly cut again on the other arm. The pain brought him to his knees, but there was no need for him to worry, the fight was hopeless. These women were weaklings for all their fierceness, and only knew how to slap and pull hair. In no time at all, Keishlee had the three women unconscious on the ground, and was kicking and chopping two others in the chest so hard, they were milking the dirt [*bleeding woman*].

No other stood forth to challenge her. Instead, they cheered and hid their weapons back into the folds of cloth they wore. Each took turns kicking one of the fallen women, then helped her up from the dirt.

Mah and Odrak did not know what to make of these strangers. They pulled up some of the grass Keishlee had soaked and rubbed it on their faces, as a talisman to guard against their being changed by contact with these people.

Another group of women were coming down from the mountain towards them. These women took a more friendly hold of Keishlee's arms and began leading her to their village.

The new women ordered Shhaha and Mah to hand over their fighting sticks, which they did, to Ramaa's surprise. One of the women snatched Ramaa up from the ground and pushed him to follow the others. Keishlee saw this and was struck silent as she realized that not all these women were so weak.

The women now behaved quite different toward Shhaha and the other men. One of them even looked after Ramaa's cuts, which had sent steady streams of blood running down his arms and legs.

Before they reached their mountain passage, Shhaha had begun a quiet chant of acceptance and peace, praising the sun and all the intelligent creatures who live on land, and those who live with fire, and those newly discovered who live in the air, like the Great Mahs. His last words brought the hurried little group to a tumbling stop. The woman who had spoken first, who was now one of the badly bruised, turned and smiled. Then asked whether they too had found intelligent creatures that lived in the air, and was greatly pleased by Shhaha's answer and Mah's promise of a tale of proof.

A woman pushed through the crowd to ask Shhaha why he had made no mention of the intelligent creatures of the water. Such a thing was yet unknown to Shhaha, or any of his clan, and they were dumbfounded. Shhaha knew that power was knowledge and so the reverse was also true. If these women had knowledge of a whole new realm [*habitat of a intelligent/civilized peoples*], then their power would be great over the land.

When they reached the passage for sliding down the escarpment, Mah and Odrak had to wait above with the tall walkers, who would not go down the steep mountain slide. The others left them their food, and Keishlee promised to return just as soon as she could find another way down.

Soon they were sliding down a steep and winding mountain-side. The women held the wide strip of material hanging from their backs under them, protecting their skin, and were quickly at the bottom. Keishlee suffered some friction burns, but Shhaha and Ramaa had the very worst time of it, tumbling down over each other in a clumsy mess.

At the bottom they were herded into a well shaded valley of straw huts, countless fruit trees, nutted palms, berry bushes, and carefully planted greens. Hearty flowers grew everywhere, and like the flowers, most of the people in the village were of colors Shhaha could not have dreamed. Not many were the eye pleasing blue-black, or the common brown-black or red-black; most were just brown like tree bark or dark brown like uk turds. Some were the colors of red earth and dark honey, or the yellow one sees in the haze of many falling leaves. The villagers had been waiting for them to come down from the mountain, and rushed them into their camp to be shown to their leaders, all of whom were women.

As Shhaha earmarked the membership of this clan, an uneasy feeling gripped him to see such a lack of men, or protectors in the village. Women of all ages were everywhere; feeders nursed out in the sun or under tall, willowy trees; young sisters ran back and forth helping older women build huts. Women prepared food in large, heavy-looking pots over small fires, in which slaves threw all sorts of things inside. Only among the slaves and the very old were there any males.

Keishlee took no notice of this, she was so taken with the women's beauty, their strength and leadership. She assumed the protectors were out running off some beast, like they did in her land, or maybe they were having a gathering of sticks, or lying in a cool duggi, or training slaves for the gathering, or any one of the many things protectors did. What she did notice was that women came to greet them, and women stood to test the strength of her odor, without even knowing her clan. Bold women indeed, since most people knew the feeders of the Tall Walker were the strongest in the land.

"Go back to where last I sat and you will still smell me there!" she had roared to her attackers during the fight. But she had not failed to see that none of the women were moved to fear by this. They had fought her better because of it, tho they had agreed afterwards that her smell was indeed everywhere. She had a moment of true pride then, and was, for once in her life, happy.

Soon they were all standing before a large hut with flat sides. Heavy colored stones hung by strings down its sides, like anchors for the roof, and it had holes for looking into the hut or for looking out from the inside. Once inside they sat Keishlee at the head of a large, still-forming group of long-haired women. They placed her near a massive rock that glistened and was embedded in the ground, while Shhaha was ordered to sit away from the women. Ramaa was forced to stand near one of the wall holes, while someone applied medicine to his wounds. They would not let Shhaha touch him.

The room was filled with talking and the scratching of their strange weapons on the ground, when a clacking began just outside the hut, and seven fully clad women entered. They were ushered in as if guarded by another group of women.

"Sonmyaa [SON-MI-AA], Shomnyaa [SHOM-NI-AA], Saamyli [SAE-MI-LI], Somaali [SO-MAA-LI], Scochaa [SCO-OK-CHAA], Shemaa [SHE-MAA] and Shaloolaa [SHA-LOO-LAA]!!!" shouted the guards.

Others joined in until the seven women were standing in front of everyone. Their voices rang through the hut and Keishlee thought this whole affair was a most pleasant sight. Enticed by their enthusiasm, she joined in with the calls of the other women.

Shhaha sat as if spellbound and wondered if Keishlee, whose enchantment with these women did not go unnoticed, knew that all the names of these feeders meant "Woman," in the sacred sense.

Suddenly Keishlee was hit by a demanding memory, and realized that these women were descendants of Caenaa [K-AE-NAA]. She remembered the tales Shhaha used to tell of the blood of Caenaa. Not having heard of them from any visiting clans, she had begun to believe that this bloodline was gone from the land. But here they were and she knew this was true, because among the descendants of Caenaa, it is always the women who rule.

The woman who first spoke to them was one of the seven, and seemed fully recovered from the fight. She clawed the air with vigor as she spoke. Seeing her now, Keishlee was glad that the fight had not been a battle of blood rite, or this woman might have clawed her face to shreds. Her name was Scochaa, and her people were called Tuk Women, which meant "women of stone."

All seven wore patches of a shiny, brightly colored leather, with patterns so identical they had to be from the skin of the same animal. From the skin of a giant snake, Keishlee thought. Another thing Keishlee began to notice was that only she smelt like a woman. She could not smell another woman in the group, only sweet herbs, heavy oils and the pungent scent of carmine dust that stood in the air like flowers just after a light rain. Keishlee tried to smell them more deeply, and some of the other women noticed. Knowing her mind, they began to laugh among themselves. Keishlee reminded herself that these women had already showed her much respect and had sat her in a place of honor, so she would not let herself feel embarrassed.

"You sit before me as an intruder to our land. What do you seek here?" spoke Scochaa, drastically changing her tone.

"We are crossing...." Shhaha tried to stand and speak but was put down by two of the women.

Shhaha was a little upset, but now he knew for certain that these women were blood descendants of Caenaa, one of the Seven Sisters. His training also told him they had too much blood from the line of Tukele, making them fighters. Their weapons told him they lived with a creature or clan relation that was instant death. He hoped these people were human.

Keishlee could see that she would have to be the spokesperson for her group. She stood and said, "I am Keishlee. KEE-I-SH'LEE. We are from the clan of the Tall Walkers. We are human and ask a courtesy through your lands. We are on a humble journey of blood with our Keeper of...."

"A Keeper!" women exclaimed and pointed to Keishlee.

Keishlee waited too long to answer, and this was an insult to Shhaha in his presence. She then spoke quickly, angry with herself for enjoying that moment of daylight dreaming. "No! No. Even the blood would not have it so," she heaped contempt upon herself. "Shhaha is our Keeper of the Blood. He keeps the blood for our clan and is respected in all our lands. He can heal with a silent chant, or talk to chicks, or call a killing boar. He is more old than you and I and has blood back deep in land and up in fires raging high...."

There was much more to the "chant of blood blessing," but the women were giving Keishlee odd looks and making nervous movements. She trailed off and stopped, wondering if they either could not understand her, or if she had forgotten something and had done the chant wrong.

Different women began talking all at once, and were understanding each other better than Keishlee could hear it all. It was obvious now that they had been showing Keishlee a great courtesy by speaking in her tongue. Every word they used now seemed somehow different, subdued and slippery to the touch. They had many more words than her people, she thought mistakenly. What she really heard were many of the same words accented differently to change their meaning.

Ramaa had gotten tired and sat down unnoticed. Now some women were trying to get him up, but even when he did, they continued to order and push him about. Keishlee laughed at the little women to herself. Ramaa might get angry with one of these creatures and pull her head off by accident.

Someone shouted for Keishlee's attention. "Woman," Keishlee understood clearly, " ... is this man creature yours? Do both of these belong to you?"

"Of course the old one is hers," laughed another and was joined by the rest.

"Even my youngest has an old one!" huffed a heavy woman who appeared only a few seasons older than Keishlee.

"Your young one must carry a well," blurted Keishlee, thinking of the possible ages of this young woman's young.

The women looked at one another not getting the joke, but when they did, one of the women standing near Ramaa pulled back his carry sack and there was a gasp from the entire group as they all looked piercingly at the long, limp flesh hanging between his legs. Ramaa made a move to snatch away her hand but the look in all their eyes told him not to. When he did finally cover himself, there was no need. Even with the weight of the few things he carried in the hanging sack, the cloth was pulled up tight between his legs, and everyone could see its great size sticking out before him. Two of the women passed out in a faint. Ramaa quickly left the hut and this time the guards only looked at him angrily. Some smiled, then turned their attentions back to the seven women, who now passed angry looks over the crowd.

"Well, are these your man creatures? You had better answer quickly and prepare yourself for the challenges I see arising around you," spoke one of the women, whose look had been secretly holding Keishlee's attention. It somehow filled her to hear this woman speak.

"You have a name?" Keishlee asked, forgetting that these women had names, that probably all the women here had names, unlike her own feeder, or many women of her clan. Without thinking, or caring what they thought, she said, "No. Ramaa belongs to...Maum. To Maum," Keishlee gave Ramaa's mate a name.

"Oh, the stinging bug," said someone Keishlee couldn't see.

"No. The sound that makes honey," spoke another.

"Do you keep him safe for her? Do you watch?" asked the woman holding Keishlee's attention.

"What is your name?" Keishlee asked the woman again.

"I am Somaali."

"No. No, I do not watch," Keishlee responded, not sure of what her answer meant.

The sensation of anxious thinking flashed about the hut, but everyone kept their eyes on the seven women. Keishlee gave most of her attention to Somaali. Remembering herself, Keishlee stood in front of Somaali, and asked that she and her people be allowed to pass through their lands. She asked for information regarding the lands around, and then demanded that Shhaha be allowed to speak to them and their people, as this would be his place as Keeper of the Blood.

The woman named Shaloolaa, whose stance and powerful appearance said that she was the leader here, agreed to allow them to pass. She ignored the mention of respects due Shhaha, and said that the men with her would have no place here without the protection of one of their women, nor would they be allowed to rest their heads here at night. Their place was on the escarpment, or across the salty river in the hutless land of the man creatures.

When Keishlee managed to get away from the other women and was bringing Shhaha some food, she found him talking to a small group of slaves, most of whom were males. They had gathered to ask him about the two men standing on the escarpment, and especially about the two large animals with them, whose necks were longer than something they called "Nelock."

Shhaha was having a good time, even tho most of the women in the village showed him no respect, but he was teaching now, and this he loved best of all. He had been trying to get someone to show him an easier way back up to the escarpment, but none of these slaves knew. So he sat to tell clan tales, and the slaves were delighted with his description of how tall walkers mated, by twisting their necks together and bringing each other bits of food to share.

Keishlee had a large leaf full of juices and morsels of strange food. It smelled delicious and Shhaha found himself hungry enough to eat almost anything. He did not think all she had brought would be enough.

Shhaha had managed to tell her after the meeting that he understood their words, but that he needed the secret to their cutting weapon. "This might be the very magic our clan might need," he had whispered, and looked at her now to see if she had been successful.

She had asked everyone about the weapon, which all the adult women carried in a pouch in the front of their hanging cloth. But no one would answer or speak about it. They would not even tell her what it was called.

Scochaa was ordered to stay with Keishlee and now acted like her guard, marking her every move and listening close to her words. They had been together all day and she had shown her many new things...things about her own body, especially her scent. The Tuk women allowed themselves to smell naturally when mating or hunting, and only allowed their scent to rise in order to keep the elder women from their fainting spells. Keishlee learned of their many foods, most of which came from the many freshwater lakes or from the green waters of the narrow river that came down from the high mountains. They also ate ground birds, tree moles, and a wide variety of snakes.

Watching the way Scochaa was looking at Shhaha, Keishlee did not want to bring Mah and Odrak down amongst these women. But Scochaa had finally agreed to show her another way up to the escarpment, and she knew Shhaha's apprentices would be anxious to be with him.

Shhaha did not want to start trouble, but found he could not stop from saying, "Scochaa," surprising the woman that he remembered her name, "...my apprentices must not be harmed in any way. I must speak with them first. No harm must come to them, no matter." He tried to make it sound less demanding, and used the tongue of her people.

His words gave her pause, and against her will, there was a little respect in the smirk she gave him.

He added, "They are probably as big as your men, but they are only slaves among my people. They may do something out of hand and we do not wish to offend anyone here."

During the stillness that followed Shhaha's words, the slaves around them clamored for Scochaa's attention. She was forced to listen while they retold the funny things they heard. All the slaves were excited and asked if Shhaha and the ones above were staying.

While they chattered, Shhaha discovered that two other groups of travelers had passed this way, and that Ramaa had taken very sick and was being tended in their medicine hut. Shhaha wanted to go to him, and it took Scochaa bearing her long weapon to stop him. He did not dare get cut by it, knowing it was the cause of Ramaa's sickness. Shhaha had helped pull Ramaa into this world, and in all his seasons, he had never known Ramaa to fall prey to any evil magic. He hated that these women possessed such magic. Forgetting himself, Shhaha gave them permission to leave. He was used to giving directions and turned away to sit with the slaves, who had quieted to a hum amidst the growing tension.

Of course Scochaa took her time leaving, but not before pulling the sister slaves out of the group and warning them not to trust Shhaha or his words.

This was a great insult. Keishlee held herself and had to slow down her racing heart before Scochaa could pull her away. Shhaha had no time to brood over this, with the slaves begging him to smile and to tell them more tales. The sister slaves sat a little further away, but listened with eyes brighter than the rest.

Keishlee was stinging from Scochaa's words and had to be coaxed along with tugs and pulls. They walked around the mountain base until the path began to run alongside the rushing green waters of a narrow river. After a short while they came to a place in the river where its banks joined, and there was a natural rock walkway across. They followed the river until it opened into a mountain cove, where the water fell into a gigantic lake from high in the cliffs. It was a spectacular sight. For a moment it took Keishlee's breath away. The water was like light come alive, clear and silver like Shhaha's silver ring had been. It foamed over like clouds comes to rest from the sky, with its spray, refreshing and sweet from the mist, filling the air with coolness and low, arching rainbows.

Keishlee continued to follow Scochaa until they stood just beside the down rushing waters. The deafening sound of its onslaught was oppressive, but called as if the water were indeed alive. Here the river began, partially surrounded by mountains, which for Keishlee was a dead end.

She was angry now and feeling very tired and wary of this woman. She was sure Scochaa only brought her here to trick her, but standing next to the thundering waters, Scochaa only smiled and leaned on the rocks. She seemed to be waiting for some-thing, which annoyed Keishlee, who turned to leave.

When she turned back, prepared for heavy blows, Scochaa was gone. Keishlee dashed about, ready to fight, or flee some danger. There was no one else around. "Soo-oc-haa!" she called, purposely mispronouncing the name. "Soo-oc-haa!" she yelled, carefully searching around, when a hand suddenly appeared from behind the fall, splashing water in her face. It was a little shocking, but Keishlee instantly felt a kinship with the room Scochaa was hiding in. She was thinking, "What a lovely secret place."

On the other side Keishlee found a large cavernous cave that echoed with the sound of the falling water and small squeaking life. Holes throughout the inner walls allowed for much light, and Keishlee could see the many paths leading up into the mountain. Scochaa was already ahead of her, laughing to herself and signalling for Keishlee to follow.

All at once Keishlee's anger was again upon her, and she called for Scochaa to stop. "You must never speak of him that way again!"

Scochaa seemed prepared for this and smiled, saying, "So he is your pleasure. He's old but healthy. No need for shame, my pretty."

Keishlee did not understand, but drew closer and more heated. "He is our Keeper of the Blood! I trust him with my life."

"He is only a man creature, and a giant beast of a thing at that. So tall, like walking trees. You are brave to lay with such a one. But then, you are so very tall as well."

Keishlee was close enough to feel and smell her breath, and knew she would have to strike this woman to force her will upon her. "YOU WILL BEG A SMILE FROM HIM!!"

"I do not know what you say."

"You will find a way to change his heart for you."

"Your mind is lost...."

Keishlee quickly set down the leaves filled with food intended for Mah and Odrak, then backhanded Scochaa across the face.

Scochaa tumbled a bit, but quickly recovered and ran up a high ledge to leaped off and knocked Keishlee to the ground. For a moment they fought each other and Scochaa seemed hardly a match, but Keishlee had to bang Scochaa's head against a rock before she begged Keishlee to stop, and agreed to do whatever she asked.

"You are powerful. I shall do what you ask if you promise to go on a raid with us," Scochaa groaned, trying to get from under Keishlee's strong arms.

"You will do what I ask, no matter!"

"No matter. No matter!" Scochaa echoed as Keishlee's hand headed for her again. After resting for a moment Scochaa continued and said, "Come with us on a raid against our enemies. They wish to kill us and our little ones. If you come with us the women here will always respect you. Tonight you could help keep us safe forever!" Scochaa pleaded.

Keishlee studied this woman, and was impressed. If she had bested a woman of her own clan, there would be no words between them for many moons. This woman considered their fight like the fly that annoys or the heat that presses too hot. Scochaa had simply shaken the dirt from her hair and kept talking.

"Yes. I will do this 'raid' with you."

"Swear it."

Keishlee realized then that this was a blood matter to these people. "Yes," she hesitated, "I swear it." She hoped it would be only small animals, but having never gone with the men, she knew not what to expect, but her real concern was for the weapon. This raid might get her hands on one, questions about which were not being answered.

Keishlee had to wait for Scochaa to recover, since she was

bruised about the face from trying to get her nails into Keishlee during the fight. There was blood in her hair, and as they continued through the mountain, Scochaa complained of pains in her back.

Keishlee knew she was moving uphill, but it was so gradual, she was surprised when she saw light breaking through the trees and bushes just outside an opening. When Mah and Odrak saw them coming they left the tall walkers and ran towards them, covering the distance with their long legs in very little time. Joyfully they entwined their arms and legs, touched heads and meshed their bodies together. They playfully counted each other's hair knots, then walked back towards their clan relation. They were so pleased to see each other, they did not notice Scochaa with her weapon drawn. She returned it to its hiding place and followed them, wondering hard about who these people were and where they came from.

▼▼▼▼▼

Feegarmardar came from a hidden room behind a wall of books. She wore the leather-film dress to let others know she was a Pagangenearch, warrior class. Others followed her from the secret room, sweaty and panting from exertion. Many others had come and gone from the room until just before sunset, but Ebbie had not seen anyone else for hours and was beginning to get hungry again.

"Food is on your mind, student," the old woman told her.

This was the fourth time the old woman had guessed her mind correctly, and it was making Ebbie very nervous.

"I've known of the Pagangenearchs for years. You know I want to continue, but you have no right to hold me here against my will."

"We paid for you."

"You what!" Ebbie tried to take this new revelation calmly.

"We have purchased you from your father," the old woman smiled. "You have no man, you have no woman, and you have no child. You have few responsibilities outside...."

"That doesn't matter!" Ebbie shouted, wanting to strike her. "My father took money for me?"

"No. No, my dear. We have paid for you with the life of two of our sisters," the old woman said flatly, hoping Ebbie would comprehend her brutal words.

Ebbie sat in silence, confronted with her own demanding memories. All her brothers and sisters were dead, each by some tragic accident. There was supposed to be a half-brother somewhere, but she was told he was retarded, unable to communicate and supposedly locked away for his own good. She remembered always thinking, fancifully, that her father was just trying to hide a strain of madness in the family.

The memories flooded her mind and scenes from the past watered her eyes. Her father had raised her like a prisoner. She never thought of him as anyone important and never believed he ever loved her. She grew up not caring. It was her mother whom she loved, and when she died, how now she wondered, all she ever wanted to know were the bloodlines of her mother's people, a study that led to an African tribe who suddenly ceased to exist. One century they were there, and the next they were gone. A life's work ended with a few paragraphs of a people known as the Tatter-Moon.

Nothing was clear to her anymore. Her father, she discovered much too late in life, was a fabulously wealthy inventor, an endangered species in North America, who had spent his entire life trying to save hers. She suddenly saw all the shady faces of all the calculated relations. There was always a boyfriend about. Early on she discovered they were paid escorts selected by her father. When she finally got free, after running away so many times, the boyfriends got better looking, but were shadier than the rest. It was just something about them, like the escorts, moments just too perfect, personalities too well researched to please. She knew she wasn't beautiful, and had become quite the brat to compensate, and yet there was always some man who lavished her with attention. She tried to think, but the visions pounded in her head like dreams set out to kill, and wanted them turned off.

"Look at me, child," spoke the old woman harshly. "Time you and I get some rest. Soon...that drink I gave you will start its work, and you will know yourself better than ever before. Rest now," she said, while ringing little bells, which Ebbie noticed for the first time.

Acolytes rushed in and stood guard, while several others left with the old woman. Another took her through a maze of halls and tunnels into another building filled with ancient Nok and Ife arts. She was led upstairs into a large bedroom done in dark woods, green fabrics and gold patterned wallpaper. But Ebbie was too tired to take much notice of decor. Her mind would have her sleep or drive her mad. As always, she chose the easy way out.

The next day, at the crack of dawn she was assisted out of bed and helped to be dressed up like some ancient royalty, then led down to a large dining hall where young men, women and Red Warrior police sat and ate, or stood guard. They sat her at a table with only women, none were dressed like Pagangenearchs, but some were already wearing the closely shaved heads of the acolytes.

Ebbie didn't really want to talk, which the others sensed and left her alone. She was coming to grips with the fact that she was going to be one of these illustrious women. Distinguished as such if only in her mind, since few people back in America even knew they existed, much less what they were about. Now Ebbie knew something about them which made her respect and fear them. They would kill to keep her, and yet all she was to them was someone to keep their history. Here she lived it. She ate it for lunch and dinner. Today she wore it, and it was changing the fabric of her world.

She knew all there was about her mother and her mother's people, but now she had a new reason to dig deeper into her African past and redo her family tree. She would add her father's family to it. She already knew many things about his people. Being here in Ethiopia gave her a better opportunity to get the rest, since his blood had come from East Africa. But she would have to continue with this mind training the old woman wanted to give her if she stayed.

"Have you had any kind of orientation?" she suddenly blurted to the women sitting across from her at the table.

"Of course. Why? Are you late?"

"Probably," Ebbie thought louder than she spoke, remembering all her dreams and still confronting the memories demanding her attention. Memories that would take her from this table, from this very room and drag her into another time and place if she closed her eyes.

She remembered the day she came to work for New York University and her meeting with the student government leaders just after being hired. There had been so many distractions on her way to that meeting. She almost missed it after being stuck in an elevator, but during that time Lorna Claukens had left the meeting. She never did get to meet Lorna for one reason or another, and now she never would. This brought tears to her eyes, which she fought fiercely, not wanting to close them and be confronted with any details.

Before she could finish her meal, she found the old woman standing behind her, silently. Not wanting to waste any time, Ebbie got up and followed her down a long colorful passage, then into a small library.

▼▼▼▼▼

Mah could not finish his meal. He was uncomfortable with the message Keishlee delivered from Shhaha. It was a warning that included these strange women. Odrak heard the danger there as well and decided to be bold. He offered Keishlee protection against this feeder and stood ready to do his duty.

Keishlee only smiled, and when Scochaa thought she understood the words she laughed aloud. "There are no feeders here, only women," she scoffed, walking around the apprentices and playing with the folds of cloth where her weapon was hidden. "This woman needs no protection from one such as you, or you," she laughed in Mah's face. "She is a good fighter and can best any man creature."

Mah pulled Odrak aside. Their time now would have to be used like the silent days of blood study, at least until some words could be heard directly from Shhaha. They would be silent until then, and would not even tell Keishlee what they had gleaned from Scochaa's few words. When they returned to the group, Scochaa led them away from the mountains, out past the trees. It was almost twilight when they reached the grassy slopes where the tall walkers could descend.

During the journey Mah and Odrak had grown close to this pair, with the feeder taking to Odrak even more than to Keishlee, now that she had less of her smell. The animals paid her little attention and often brushed her away. From Scochaa they would not allow even a touch. They could sense Mah and Odrak's tension and walked behind them, always giving Scochaa the big eye.

Once down in the rip of the land valley, they were in a huge rock gorge that trailed off to one side. There were bubbling hot springs whose vapors made breathing easier.

"It puts holes in the head," Mah tried to explain the sensation.

When they got to a grass clearing, the tall walkers stepped off to taste the nearby trees. Keishlee climbed one of the trees to show Scochaa one of the tall walker uses. Scochaa had wondered about their taste and Keishlee became furious with Scochaa's ignorance. She did not understand what a clan relation was, but Keishlee hoped that once she saw the advantage of them, there would be no more mention of tasting their flesh.

High out on one of the strong branches, she called for the tall walkers to come near. They were well rested and would enjoy being ridden for a while. They knew what she wanted and hurried to her, both trying to place themselves to her best advantage. The male received her, and holding firmly to his neck with her legs braced around his chest, Keishlee directed him toward Scochaa, who they chased around the clearing. It was all in fun, and even Scochaa had a good time. Keishlee got to show off her favorite pastime, and Scochaa got to show off her speed. She was as fast as Docga of the dog tribe, but much more agile, her body flowing into the wind instead of fighting it. Keishlee realized then that Scochaa had been false with her, and was not hurt at all. Her dashing about proved it.

Afterwards, Keishlee called her over to praise her speed. Scochaa thanked her and praised of the gracefulness of her riding creature, but complained that her enemies would be forewarned of her approach on a creature this big. "In a horde it must tear up the land," she laughed.

Mah and Odrak wanted to ride too. They dropped stones, each trying to be the first to bounce a resting stone up and catch it. Mah won the drop by snapping a stone up and into his waiting hand. Odrak called the remaining tall walker over and placed it in position for the jump. Placing himself behind the short legs and holding fast in case it bucked, he slanted his body for Mah to run up on.

Keishlee saw them choosing and told Scochaa to watch. When Mah raced up and slipped over onto the high back of the creature, Scochaa was lost for words.

"If you tell me about your weapon, I will show you how to befriend our clan relation, and how to ride," said Keishlee, trying to take advantage of the look on Scochaa's face.

Scochaa turned up a corner of her mouth in a wicked smile and said, "I already know how to ride. I am only surprised that your men know how as well."

Keishlee felt too good to let this failure upset her. She snatched Scochaa up with her and told Mah and Odrak to follow close behind. She knew the way back to the Tuk Village from the view from the escarpment, and wanted to get back before darkness was completely upon them.

The sight of the tall walkers and their riders brought all the tribe out to greet them. They called Scochaa and Keishlee by name and shouted, "Maxilia! Maxilia! Maxilia!" which Keishlee knew had something to do with a giant nest. These were very strange people, she thought, as women with weapons pushed their way through the crowd and ordered Scochaa down. Scochaa cursed the woman, who fell to the ground holding her weapon out before her.

"You see how desirable you are, pretty one. I could have this one's life, if I chose," spoke Scochaa, sliding down off the tall walker. She took the woman's weapon, then knocked her to the ground. "Sisters, put away your weapons. This woman, KEE-I-SHE-LEE, is a friend. We may have to keep her," she laughed, and smiled up at Keishlee before walking away.

Mah and Odrak slid off the back of the tall walker, stroked its long legs, and tipped up to rub its head and shoulders. The tall walker licked them with its long tongue and spoke to them as if its wordless mouthings were human words. This was all quite natural for any member of the Tall Walker clan, and neither of them thought much about the fuss these people were making.

But Mah saw the stern expression cross Keishlee's face and heard Odrak pull himself in. They had broken their silence. Since they had not used human words, it was not a serious break, but they were both too well trained to have done even this. Keishlee knew she had to get them to Shhaha as quickly as possible, before one of these women turned their harsh ways on them. She could depend on Mah to keep his silence from here on, but the only thing she was ever sure about Odrak, was his love for Mah. If he felt Mah was being threatened he might do anything.

Keishlee jumped the distance to the ground, and the women in the crowd cheered her again. She tried to get to Mah and Odrak, but some of the women got in her way. They were all trying to touch or talk to her, and as always they played with her hair, which made her smile, because she was just as fascinated with theirs.

While she was distracted, some women took hold of Mah and Odrak roughly, and led them to the large hut where they had held the meeting earlier. The sun was just going down and Keishlee remembered that the men would not be able to spend the night within the village. She broke away from the women and ran over to the hut. Two women were standing guard at the entrance and would not let her pass. They had their weapons drawn and Keishlee dared not do anything rash while Mah, Odrak, and Shhaha were inside. Three of the leaders she had met earlier were speaking to them harshly. From inside the hut, Sonmyaa gave Keishlee a grimace and then continued with her gruff words to Shhaha.

Keishlee ran to Scochaa's hut, and since there were no other women about, she rushed in. Scochaa was stripping leaves from a bush and picking over them while talking to two little slaves. There was an old man in a corner eating from a bowl, who trembled after noting her size. He then put down the bowl to stand in a corner looking at the ground.

"Sit back down, Pleg. You don't have to stand for her," huffed Scochaa.

Keishlee noticed some warmth in her voice for the old man. The little slaves paid her no attention at all, but were sent from the hut to wait near the entrance. "Your people do not call out before you enter walls, aey! Aaah!" spoke Scochaa, using the Aaah! of rudeness.

"I would like us to be friends," spoke Keishlee, approaching with both hands and arms out for entwining, forgetting that these people did not do such things.

"I think we will be," Scochaa smiled, ignoring the outstretched arms.

"If your blood can find the way, tell me—"

"No more questions about the weapon. As you say, no matter, aey!" twilight

"No matter," she agreed, trying to think of a less direct way of asking for her help. "It is getting dark now. Maybe I should take Shhaha and the other men out of the village."

"The last two just came down. Let them look around," said Scochaa, looking up from her work with a sly smile. "Let the others see them. The seed of your people might add to our pleasure."

Keishlee sat down on the soft dark earth. Its softness told her this hut was fairly new, as might be Scochaa's rank with the Tuks. As darkness settled in around them, the light of new fires gave the room a soft glow.

"How will any others see them if they are to be questioned all night?."

"Elder mothers have them in the meeting hut?"

"Yes. Yes."

"Are they sitting or standing?"

"Sit...."

"Come, sister," ordered Scochaa.

When they reached the hut, a large fire was burning out front and a smaller one inside. With Scochaa leading the way, Keishlee had no trouble getting in. Shhaha and two guards were the only ones standing. They stood near the large, glistening rock, which was veined with red, blue, black and silver ores. The guards had their weapons drawn, and everyone except the men were talking at once.

Scochaa grabbed Keishlee's hand and asked that she not be moved to violence. Here she would be killed if she attacked anyone like she had done to Scochaa in the cave, but Keishlee knew this instinctively when Shhaha did not turn to look at her. She sat behind Mah and Odrak, who were still as stones, heads lowered to the ground. She twitched when she thought she heard Mah crying, and thought suddenly that death was not really that bad.

Scochaa asked all the women to join her outside the hut. She had to strike one of the guards to stop her interference, and took her weapon, forcing the woman to wait on one knee for their return.

Keishlee paced back and forth within the hut. When no one said anything to her, she approached Shhaha and spoke directly to him without asking anything from the guards. "Your apprentices are in need of your wisdom, my Keeper of the Blood." Keishlee weighted each word carefully, making sure the other women saw that she gave honor to this man, and was, as always, humble before him. She pulled him from the clutches of one of the guards, and pointed him in the direction of Mah and Odrak. Both their faces were covered with silent tears, and still they had yet to receive words from Shhaha. They were keeping their silence well.

Keishlee stood over the four guards, making sure they saw her looking down on them. Her eyes dared them to speak or move. Only three of them had weapons now and only one had her weapon drawn. The missing weapon made a weak link between them, and she realized that Scochaa had taken away all their power when she took the one weapon out of the room. These women had been warned about her, and had decided not to take any chances.

Keishlee kept both eyes on the women while Shhaha spoke to Mah and Odrak. Shhaha was brief, but gentle and direct. No one else could hear what was said. To anyone else it might sound like wordless chanting, but Keishlee had listened all her life to this sound blood keepers made together. She knew Shhaha was providing them with every detail of the earlier meeting. Mah and Odrak would know even the number of slaves Shhaha had counted in the village, and the names of all the important persons he had met.

The name of Caenaa was said loud enough for all to hear, and it soften the guards towards them. Keishlee realized that her suspicion was correct, and wondered what kind of power it was to know which word to use to make friends of people. Shhaha spoke two more words distinctly: "Tukele blood—" and she knew it had been done on purpose, to make the guards stare at Shhaha in speechless delight.

Shhaha and his apprentices chanted quietly until the others returned, and the leaders took their places behind the glistening stone. They seated themselves on high piles of straw mats in front of Keishlee and the apprentices, and Shaloolaa was the first to speak. "We could have saved much time, my pretty, if you had told us these two belonged to you. I have wasted much time making plans for their use. This one," she pointed to Mah, "could have gained you a weapon, and I know you seek it!"

Shhaha knew the calculation that went into these words. He turned to Keishlee against his will and tried to speak to her with his eyes.

"Face the Tukshead, creature!" growled Sonmyaa.

Keishlee stood before them, remembering the fear she saw in Shhaha's eyes. They were speaking very fast again, and she had to remind herself that their words were not very different, just more quickly said. They thought Mah and Odrak were her mates. The effect of this would somehow save them but deny her the weapon. She cursed these women for not allowing Shhaha to speak. Shhaha would know the right thing to say.

She opened her mouth, having taken too long to respond already, she wanted them to know that she would speak, but in that instant she made a vow to herself: Shhaha, Odrak and Mah would be saved, no matter. No harm must come to any of them. They must get to the Great Sharing and back to their own people. Power like theirs must never be wasted, and she would stand ready to fight all of these women if it proved necessary.

"We did not come here for your weapons." Keishlee side-stepped telling a lie with the truth.

"We believe you, sister," smiled the woman Shaloolaa.

"Truth!" agreed the plump and wise-looking Shomnyaa.

The gentle-looking Somaali cut in, saying, "There is already much respect among the Tukshead for this one. Look at her, she has hair and coloring like Shaloolaa," she continued, revealing a more slippery side, "...more of it than Saamyli. There is respect for her. But, if you are false with us...."

"I give her my trust!" Shaloolaa spoke, her words striking Somaali like sharp stones. She reached over to rest a hand on Saamyli, who seemed closest to Shaloolaa and who Keishlee could not help but think of fondly.

"But she does want the knowledge of the weapon! No falsehoods!" roared the evil and sturdy Sonmyaa.

"Who does not want the knowledge?" huffed the tall and wiry Saamyli, whose hair was unusually short.

"First let us settle about these creatures," Shaloolaa spoke over the others. Pointing to Mah and Odrak she asked, "Are these your man creatures? Do you claim them?"

Keishlee did not know how to lie. "No...no," she said meekly, lowering her head. But then she remembered something and said, "But I watch over them." She told a recent truth.

Mah looked up at her with wide eyes.

"So they are mated, aey," spoke Shaloolaa.

Sonmyaa tried to speak, saying, "Too many have asked for them, and I...."

"Collecting hands full of debt, aey, Sonmyaa," smiled Scochaa, who turned an eye full of meaning toward Shaloolaa.

"If what they say is true, and I too smell it, they could give to us magic never known to our blood before," spoke the pretties one called Shemaa.

Shaloolaa stood and faced Keishlee, saying, "Our clan must come first," and gripped her about the shoulders. She was almost as tall as Keishlee, with white streaks in her hair and strong, quick arms. The move was meant as a friendly warning.

"What do you want of them?" Keishlee asked, and found it gave pause to everyone in the hut, including Shhaha, who revealed just a bit of a smile.

"We would mate with those you watch. I know something of you, and this means you will face the challenge. If you accept, then you may choose those who please you. Only you can have this power here," spoke Scochaa, taking the words from Shaloolaa's mouth.

The others were angry with her, even Shaloolaa. Shhaha hoped Keishlee would understand Scochaa's hidden meaning. He knew she had taken a great risk.

"Scochaa," Keishlee made a special effort to pronounce her name as she had heard Shhaha do, "I shall do all that you ask of me in this matter."

Mah and Odrak were stunned and almost moved to speech. Keishlee had just given her promise of blood [*sacred oath*] to this strange woman, who was one with all the others, who had earlier treated their Keeper of the Blood with such disrespect. They could not let her do this for them, even tho Shhaha had nodded his head, which meant that she had his consent. Mah felt his manhood shrink, and knew that if he looked under the folds of cloth between his legs, there would be nothing there. He was ready to kill another human tonight.

Shaloolaa's spirit seemed to take over the hut and her presence was felt by everyone. "We will give you and those with you passage. If you leave tonight, this very moment, you may go as you came. But," Shaloolaa promptly added, "if you wish to take rest and learn some secrets from our blood, and accept the challenges, there is much to learn here from such as us, by one such as you."

Shhaha was now pleased to have met these people. They were human and had a leader with great blood power. He wished to know this clan and to share clan tales. More importantly, he wanted the secret of their weapon. The portent of danger to his own people might be coming from here. But whatever danger was to come, the weapon might prove useful against it.

"I shall stay to learn," Keishlee paused, but only because of the broad smile across Shaloolaa's face, "...and to teach if wanted—or necessary," she added, thinking herself bold.

"It is done!" spoke Shaloolaa.

Keishlee's meaning was not lost to anyone. Some women

grunted to show they were piqued, but this only made Keishlee smile more. She had done the best thing for this moment, and could see it on all their faces. Shhaha raised his head and no one spoke of it, because she was finally being respected here, especially by her Keeper of the Blood. She could not wait to be alone with Shhaha, when he could confirm the pleasure in her heart. She hoped he had not suffered too much under their hands, and vowed again that he would suffer no more.

The women were preparing to leave when Scochaa called them to halt. "I shall help Keishlee with the watch tonight. She may share my hut, as a small courtesy," spoke Scochaa, trying to make it sound like a second thought, tho it was clear that she was hoping for something.

An uproar started to build, but Shaloolaa only had to raised an arm to quiet the others. "I shall help her watch this night as well," spoke Shaloolaa flatly, then left them all standing in the room.

Scochaa called for guards to help escort the men and Keishlee to her hut. Sonmyaa turned to face them, saying, "It's a long, cool night for a watch, aey, Scochaa," and then slipped out, laughing.

Keishlee grunted, "I think there is too much laughing in this place."

"My pretty, we are almost sisters now. Always give your sisters respect, and smiles," said Scochaa, also laughing.

When they were all alone in Scochaa's hut, Keishlee reached out to hold Scochaa, who was looking to do the same. Scochaa looked at her little ones sleeping with the old man and then fell to the floor with Keishlee. They began talking so fast that Keishlee recalled the moment earlier when she could not understand anything the women had said. Now she was doing it, and it was having the same effect on Mah and Odrak. Shhaha paid them no attention, since he understood everything they said.

Scochaa was saying to Keishlee, "I accepted your vow of friendship," while Keishlee held her close and said, "May you never know pain," to bless Scochaa for her help.

"But there is no time for this pleasure. I pray your creatures will work for you. What needs doing, must be done by them this night," Scochaa continued speaking in her hurried fashion.

"What would you have us do, Scochaa?" Shhaha spoke,

letting them know that he understood.

Scochaa inched over to him and ate some dirt for him to see. "This may not mean much to you, but to my sisters and to me, it means much."

"To us as well," Shhaha responded, and then gave her and Keishlee a smile.

"There is a place where long-burning wood is plentiful, and it is near, but only men may go there and gather without fighters. No fighters will help us tonight, and tho your treasures should not be left unguarded, we must build a watch-fire that must burn all night so that we may see clearly."

There was no need to say more. Mah and Odrak stood and lowered their eyes and heads to make way for her to lead them. Keishlee rose to follow, but Scochaa reminded her that she had to stay and guard the hut. Keishlee had been waiting to get a moment alone with Shhaha, and when it came, she fell slowly to her knees before him. Suddenly the weight of all that had happened fell on her, and she wanted to cry or scream. She swept up a handful of dirt and was about to eat it when Shhaha stopped her.

"We are in a new land. These people have many different customs but they are human. You, my Keishlee, are of the Tall Walker clan. I know you and your heart," he began talking very fast. He had never actually done this before, tho he had once been taught. The memories of it were upon him, and he found his highest speed was too fast for Keishlee.

He told her that he understood what they wanted. It was easy to sense that Mah had some magic about him. "It is a respect of you and the women of our clan they seek. But you are not one of the Seven Sisters, and they cannot mate with you," he laughed.

He praised her for being able to do the right thing. He confirmed for her that Scochaa could be trusted, and included Shaloolaa as one of her new friends. He revealed the power of his blood by warning her that in a fight with Sonmyaa, she would have to be careful not to be distracted, and to watch out for the whip of her hair and the speed of her hands.

Shhaha explained to her that since all humans had clan relations, there would be a powerful and dangerous creature about. The clan relation to these people would be fierce. These women were fearless, which meant that they had conquered a great horror to win this land, and had to be respected. He also told her that Shaloolaa was to be respected like a blood keeper, that she had become what the clan of the Great Feathers called a Breeder, which his people called blood counting, a thing known by all the elder women of their clan. She would be able to trust Shaloolaa to choose with some wisdom in these matters.

"Shaloolaa fears for the quality of their blood," spoke Shhaha, considering the varied sizes and colors of these people. "Only the oldest of them are tall and dark."

Shhaha's tone frightened her as he said, "You have committed yourself to a exalted ritual among these women. I am not sure why it is, but it is a matter of blood rite to them. For them, a protector can have no choice, no say, no matter. It is too important to them. Aaah! in the greatness of the blood, I say, be like the moon, my little sister, and shine your light over all the darkness. Be, of the power that is within you, like the sun and keep a light in your head. You could die here. Be aware. You have all the lessons you will need. Take heed, your power is already there in your blood," he warned, pointing to her heart, and there was power in every word, as if he were casting a spell upon her.

Keishlee agreed, asking if these people were indeed blood from the Seventh Sister, Caenaa, mixed with the blood from the sister Tukele.

Shhaha was pleased. He hugged her close, saying, "The women of our clan chose you well. I shall stand at the blood rite for your renaming. It is past time to put an end to their bickering. But we cannot stay here long, little sister. Learn all you can while we are here. These women can teach you much, but not too much, I beg," he joked.

Keishlee returned his hug and ran from the hut to check on the small fire Scochaa had burning outside. She ran around the hut looking for more firewood There was only a little, which she added and watched as it made a high blaze.

"You are not accustomed to these lands, I see," came a voice out of the darkness, startling her.

Keishlee composed herself as she watched Sonmyaa and three young women approach. They all seemed to favor her but had the look of being fully grown, tho they were much shorter.

"Have you come to challenge me so soon, Sonmyaa?"

"Not I. Not now anyway. I have come to have you meet three sisters. They would like to see your creatures up close. It is they who might wish to challenge you."

"They have no chances with me...."

"I know, my pretty," Sonmyaa smiled.

"Why do you and the others call me that?"

The three girls laughed, and one the color of dried blood took her hand and said, "Your strength is beauty to us. You are tall like the great women in the stories our mothers tell. Your movements are like the limbs of trees flowing in the gentle wind. You have a dignity in all your ways. You glow black in the light of day and shine blue at night. If you had been born here, the sisters would have named you 'Cae,' for 'pretty one.' In times past only those of Shaloolaa's blood have carried that name."

"Let them see those you watch," Sonmyaa demanded.

Now Keishlee had some idea of how long this night would be. "No. No," she said in a rush and then turned to the younger ones.

"No?" Sonmyaa huffed, "Let me by!"

Keishlee had her by her weapon's arm but sensed that Sonmyaa had let this happen. Still she held her there, refusing to let her pass. The young ones kept their place, while Sonmyaa smacked Keishlee's face when she would not let her go. It had a shocking effect, but before Keishlee could strike her back, Sonmyaa tripped her up and she snatched her arm away. More than Keishlee's face hit the dirt.

"I said, not yet, my pretty," Sonmyaa chuckled and took her company away as she left.

From the ground Keishlee could see the long braid flip up in back as Sonmyaa walked away. It had stones tied to the end of it, and she recognized the danger Shhaha had mentioned.

Keishlee sat in the dirt, hoping this would not go on all night. She ate a little dirt for her own foolishness. She had been too confident. These women had been only playing with her and now she was going to pay. She wondered how many were spying on her now, in the extreme darkness of this place. She would remember this mistake. There was more strength in their arms than she had thought, and they were as quick as their words and just as cunning.

"Ready yourself, little sister. There will be many who will test you tonight. This is our way," came Shaloolaa's voice from between dark trees. Keishlee was standing when the voice said, "You bring a gift to us."

"The silver ring?! You cannot...."

"What is that?" Shaloolaa stepped into a sudden blaze of light from the fire, which warned of a unearthly sense of timing.

"The young apprentices?" Keishlee tried to understand.

"The young man creatures. They smell of our sacred ones, you call it, clan relation. To us, she is our only master."

"The Great Mah!" Keishlee offered, remembering how deeply the women were breathing in the hut.

"You even call one of them by the sound she makes. We call her the Sun Bird of Cloud Mountain."

"Mah has had the smell from birth. He got his name from our first visit by the bird we call, Great Mah."

"He must sleep with her to acquire so much of her scent. To us this means he is greatly honored among males. He has been blessed above all others," said Shaloolaa, now facing Keishlee and standing near the hut.

"The oils of her feathers are highly prized?" whispered Shhaha from inside the hut.

Shaloolaa turned slightly away from the entrance and showed no sign of having heard his voice, but replied, "With her oil we can trade in many dangerous lands. Powerful magic it makes, and one can be invisible to one's enemies."

"Her smell is not known to anyone," Shhaha said, then quickly added, "Except by those she cares for. Her enemies need never know she is coming until she has arrived."

Shaloolaa smiled and turned it on Keishlee, still making no sign of having heard Shhaha's voice. "The wise one with you, the one you call Keeper of the Blood. I know of such teaching. I have great respect for wisdom, but man is a beast that is not fully human," she said, lowering her head as she turned towards the fire.

"You are young. To us you seem older because you are tall, broad and strong, but in your face I see you are not half my years. Be careful tonight. Take special care with those you choose. You must settle in your mind that one or both must be given at least twice, or they will not be allowed to leave. My power is not strong enough to prevent this. I will not be able to stop the raid that will befall you if you cannot make this so. This is more than breeding power. This is power more than blood."

"There is no such thing," Shhaha spoke as if to a slave who had not learned the lesson. "Nothing comes before the blood."

Shaloolaa did not respond to this, but the words were resting in back of her eyes.

"I accept all challenges, no matter," spoke Keishlee.

"So be it." Shaloolaa started to leave, but turned back just outside the darkness and said, "My pretty!" and was gone.

For the first time since darkness fell, Keishlee could see the moon rising in the sky as she waited for Scochaa's return. Guards came with their belongings, wanting to place them in the hut. They thought to be bold, but this time Keishlee was bolder, and managed to snatch all the sacks and throw them into the hut before the guards could complain.

Next came Saamyli, followed by a throng of women who paraded themselves around the fire for her. These women were all of the lighter shades that Keishlee had never seen before. Saamyli explained some of their customs, and then introduced many of the young women to her.

A woman called Tois tried Sonmyaa's leg trick, which did not work this time. Another named Demaa, and a twin called Femaa tried to double-team her, almost pushing her into the fire. Keishlee managed a side step and Femaa got some of her straight hair burned. Keishlee helped put the fire out and afterwards some of the women, including Saamyli, hugged Keishlee and thanked her for being human.

A little later another woman from this group, almost as tall as she, talked her into an insult, which Keishlee was sorry to have said afterwards. The woman took advantage of the moment and slapped Keishlee, telling her to leave their village, and then left without another word. There was little talk after that, and the others soon departed. Once again Keishlee had managed to stop anyone from entering the hut.

In the quiet that followed, the fire nearly went out because of the cool damp air. Suddenly the women called Somaali and Shemaa and their combined selections were upon her. She could tell they had been waiting for the fire to go out. Some of the women were just putting their weapons back, which gave Keishlee a chill, but she was tired and wondered how Shhaha could stay up for days on end, as he often did to train his apprentices. She looked at the fire and chanted a wish for them to leave before it went out. Not that it would matter, as she realized they would stay until it did go out.

Keishlee greeted them, growing a little afraid, but stood

her ground outside the hut's entrance. They would have to kill her to enter, she swore to herself.

Somaali introduced all the women she brought, and included definitions of their names, to take up the time left to the fire. One sister, just younger than Keishlee, shoved her hard but tried to excuse it as an accident. Tho weary, Keishlee was about to smack her face when someone shoved a piece of wood in her hand.

"I agreed to watch, but don't let the fire go out, because you don't want to wake me," warned Scochaa, a little too sweaty to have been sleeping. She had an armful of wood covered with white bark.

One of the guards in this group knocked the wood from her arms and pulled her to the side, shouting, "What have you been doing?"

"Nothing!!" Scochaa cursed and shoved the woman to the ground. "Here!" She lifted both her flaps saying, "Here, feel! Touch! Smell!"

Some of the women did.

"I wouldn't do that. I know my place," Scochaa composed herself.

Keishlee picked up some of the wood. Others came over to help, but Scochaa gently pushed them aside saying, "No, Keishlee. Let that one do it." She pointed to the guard who had knocked them away.

The woman did not hesitate and neatly placed all the wood in the fire, which blazed up high. The heat was welcomed by all since the night air was so cool. Scochaa stood with her now, and there was very little talk. Keishlee was more than delighted that Scochaa had returned, and with plenty of wood for the fire.

When they left Scochaa said, "That bunch is mostly talk. Nothing to worry about."

"Thanks, Scochaa," Keishlee smiled, glad that there would be no tension between them.

"Do you need rest?"

"I can stand a little longer," Keishlee hoped.

"Good. You will need to see Shomnyaa's force, and that of Shaloolaa's. Yes, you must see Shaloolaa's," groaned Scochaa, who then slyly added, "And my force as well."

Keishlee stared at her in surprise, mouth open. "It means so much?"

"I thought you said he was wise in the ways of blood. He has not warned you of the danger?"

Keishlee pulled Scochaa to her and rubbed their heads together, but Scochaa pushed her away, saying, "You can have no favorites. Your feelings do not count. It must be a test of blood or the might of blood rite. Think, what would you have us do? Fight amongst ourselves every time a decent creature comes a'near. No. We fight according to blood rite, which assures us of strength and power when we mate. Every mother here will fight you for her daughter, or for herself. If I had a daughter old enough, so would I."

Keishlee's head was in a whirl and she heard Mah calling, but Scochaa heard it too and shouted in a threatening voice, "Do not breach the space you have been given, man-thing."

Keishlee wanted to go to him, but dared not to, knowing already that anything he might say would only frighten her. Scochaa was stirring coals in the fire. Keishlee offered to bring more wood, but Scochaa told her there would be no need, since this wood was of a kind that would burn from now until daybreak.

"But if you wish to check the man creatures, as you should have while I slept, you may do so any time," spoke Scochaa, more to someone hidden in the darkness than to Keishlee.

Keishlee almost ran into the hut and found Mah with Odrak napping in his lap. They touched, feeling for scars or tender skin, and entwined their arms to hold each other close. Keishlee blew soft breezes into Odrak's face in the hope that he would open his eyes, which she had to see. When he did, she quickly rubbed his face and reclosed his eyes, saying, "Sleep fast and hard, and find yourself some peace."

With his eyes, Mah told Keishlee to look over at Shhaha, who sat with his back to the entrance, his eyes wide but in trance.

"They cursed him with every word," Mah spoke, but could not stop the flow of water down his face. "Insult, upon insult, upon insult, the likes of which I cannot believe my ears have heard. And to our Keeper of the Blood, to our Shhaha, whose nature is kin to all gentle things."

"Rest, Mah. Rest." Keishlee was almost moved to tears herself, her anger now fully renewed.

"They would kill him rather than let him speak. They called him a beast...a man creature and worse!" Mah stopped his tears.

Keishlee broke away, standing and saying through her teeth, "Enough. Enough!"

Mah rubbed his hand down the side of her leg, saying, "In this place, Mah and Odrak are once again like little slaves. Slaves born of you. Whatever you wish, we shall do."

Keishlee almost fell on top of him, rubbing her head against his and trying to entwine their necks, a touch that meant much to members of their clan. "You have given me new strength, Mah. I shall be able to watch better now."

Mah licked the side of her face and said, "May Olaah forgive me," he paused, then said, "I hope this tension does not make me useless to you."

Keishlee scoffed, "For such a simple thing, you shall consider it like the relief of sleep. No better than rubbing your belly in the dirt. But those I choose, I promise, shall give to you the duty of a mate."

"Maybe Olaah shall bear fruit first," Shhaha whispered.

Mah felt his heart would come out his mouth. He could not speak and tried to swallow a handful of dirt instead. Keishlee was surprised too, knowing it was true from the expression on Mah's face and the fact that Odrak, only pretending sleep now, rolled away and tried to force himself closer to the ground.

The women of their clan were adept at making sure no feeders were touched without the mating dance. Mah was still too young for the dance, but she knew that Olaah was not too young to conceive.

"Yes. Yes," Keishlee smiled. "It was a good thing. Do not worry. She is promised to you as you are to her. Who can speak against it? Take comfort, the women of our clan are a fruitful lot. Strong and blooded!" Keishlee almost roared. She wished Nrdoosh was still alive and with her. Nrdoosh was a fighter from before the time her blood flowed. She would have been a great comfort to her now. "Rest, Mah, and you too, Odrak, and know that my blood is hot for you."

Mah pulled Odrak back into his lap and laid across him to sleep. Keishlee crawled over to Shhaha and laid her head on the ground before him, paying tribute to his knowledge of Mah's secret. There was no telling the limits of Shhaha's power.

Back outside with Scochaa, she could see the night was almost half gone. She was no longer chilled by the coolness here, but burned inside from the insults to her Keeper of the Blood. She dared these women to bring her some foolishness.

Scochaa wiped Keishlee's face, making a crude comment about people who enjoyed eating dirt. Keishlee smiled at the easy way this woman brought comfort and pain. She decided to fight Shaloolaa over this woman if it became necessary. She already had an uncommon respect for Shaloolaa, but Scochaa was becoming a friend, whose truth was like all the rest of life, when living means going on, no matter.

Keishlee walked a short distance around the hut to check the clearing around them. She heard something crushing the grass and went back to see, when she heard Scochaa gasp. Keishlee was back out front in time to grab the arm of a woman about to run inside the hut. Keishlee pulled her away and struck her so hard she thought she heard the woman's jaw crack.

"You must not draw blood until the challenge!" Scochaa screamed, after flipping another woman over her back.

In that instant other women came around the sides of the tall fire. Some went immediately to check on the unconscious woman. When they were sure she was not dead, one confronted Keishlee and another confronted Scochaa.

This was the force of Shomnyaa. Each group, Keishlee realized, was larger than the last. She understood now that they were coming to her in order of rank, which for them would be in order of strength.

"You should take the challenge now!" roared the woman in front of Keishlee.

They were all standing close together and Scochaa touched Keishlee while speaking to the woman in front of her. "Get you gone," Scochaa laughed, elbowing the woman's feeder bags as she looked toward Keishlee, who had taken the hint. This was a social gathering, a time to size each other up, without fighting. To be moved to fear or violence showed a weakness on her part.

"Forgive me," Keishlee smiled, gently pushing the woman in front of her away. She knew now that she had not only to prove her strength, but her humanity and sisterhood as well. This was not an evil thing they were compelled to do, but a thing of blood rite. "I thought she might have been someone who did not know I watched."

No one laughed, but the smiles were broad and beaming. Scochaa purposely let loose a little chuckle and walked Keishlee up to Shomnyaa, who then made the introductions of the women she wanted Keishlee to consider. This time Keishlee took note of three feeders and called them out. There was almost a cheer let loose among the women. Keishlee ignored this and placed a firm hand on the chest of the woman she thought the best of these and pushed a finger into the woman's tit, just as she had seen older women of her clan do.

"This looks a bit limp for one so young." Keishlee smiled, thinking there might be some fun here after all. "Does the sun speak to these at all?" she spoke to another.

The woman pushed Keishlee's hand away, saying, "From all the pounding they've taken they should be flat as leaves, but look!" She squeezed out a stream of milk that hit Keishlee in the face.

There was laughter now and even Keishlee was pleased. The women of her clan would like this one. Good bones, some height and that odd mix of coarse and fine hair which Keishlee was growing fond of. She stopped the milk with her hand and playfully wiped it into the woman's hair, while skipping away from a blow meant for her arm.

This woman had recently given birth and was here only to test Keishlee. She could not be mated this soon, so Keishlee only smirked at her. She called out another group, which she gave less time, because they had too few words between them. She called out another and another, surprised at how well she began remembering their names. Shomnyaa called her attention to two others, while managing to get a move in that tripped her. Keishlee caught herself and surprised them all with the delicate way she regained her balance.

Before they left, Shomnyaa turned to her women, saying that this blood would be worth the fighting. She claimed she could smell the creatures sleeping within the hut. Another woman said that if they had rods like the sick one, the winners would have to carry a well, and they left laughing, repeating Keishlee's earlier joke over and over again.

When they were gone, Keishlee was all smiles. Scochaa told her that she had done well this time. Keishlee regretted not having known better when the others had shown themselves. Scochaa smiled and warned her that since she had acted like a sister with these, the others would take extra care to display themselves again during the morning meal.

"Now you will meet the best fighters of our people. They

are the best we have to offer. But be very careful, this force is not all Shaloolaa's choosing. Shaloolaa is head of the Tukshead. All the best must kneel before her and join her force," explained Scochaa.

Keishlee was surprised. She had expected to be formally confronted by Scochaa's force next.

It was still very dark, with the fire blazing only slightly less higher than before. The moon had moved over the escarpment and could not be seen. Keishlee was telling Scochaa about the women from her clan when she heard the whistle of a bird.

Scochaa knocked her to the ground and whipped out her weapon. Before Keishlee could get up, Scochaa was twirling around, sticking something into the ground. Keishlee sat up and saw all the sticks standing in the ground. Others were still coming down around her, but Scochaa caught them all and only a few were not neatly standing up next to her.

Scochaa helped Keishlee up. Keishlee was angry, but Scochaa whispered that this display was done for her alone, and that she need not be bothered by it.

Women came from every direction, reclaiming their long, thin sticks and waving to Scochaa. Keishlee could tell that most of them were guards, but they now appeared like exquisite flowers. They had untwined their hair and were dressed in the more common fashions of the village, with their feeder bags showing, and weaponless. Not all of them were the tallest women Keishlee had seen here, but all were strong and healthy, with small stout feeder bags and hard bodies. Some had beautiful stones embedded in their hair, which was mostly the same as Keishlee's. They had large eyes of black or brown, and some were the rare yellow-green or gold. Their skin colors ranged from the more common light-honey, normal to this tribe, to shades of early night, which was the most respected.

They crowded around Keishlee when someone called out, "She comes!" and they all knelt. Keishlee kept her eye on Scochaa, who was still standing, until she could see Shaloolaa step out of the darkness into the firelight. Keishlee thought surely they should kneel, but Scochaa remained standing, and so did she.

Shaloolaa was dressed in a robe which completely covered her body, and the skin of her face gleamed so blue, she looked like something poured from the night sky into a beautiful white leaf. She looked younger with her hair piled high in shapely mounds, full of shiny colored stones and bits of shells, twigs and flowers. She stood near enough to the fire to be burned, holding one of Shhaha's blood wands in her hand.

"This is a heavy thing. If you have been carrying this long your arms should be very strong," said Shaloolaa, who then threw the stick at Keishlee, knocking her over.

While Keishlee picked herself up and cleared her head, Shaloolaa bowed to her. Scochaa took Keishlee's hand and pulled her back to the ground, and they knelt together.

Everyone seemed to pause momentarily, as if waiting for Scochaa or Keishlee to say something. The moment grew longer as Keishlee had gotten the wind knocked out of her, and was taking this time to collect herself. Suddenly she could hear the beginnings of the chant of grace, the call to honor blood. Turning her head from side to side, she saw the women muttering to each other as Shhaha's voice floated from the hut.

Memories demanding to be noticed, flooded upon her, catching her up in the midst of chanting the call to honor blood aloud. Silence fell upon the group as Keishlee remembered the words to greet a visiting Keeper of the Blood. "Aaah! Aaah!," Keishlee stumbled over the word and its proper inflection for honor, "Aaah! to the one who knows the greatness of blood, and has come to this humble one. I am the dust at your feet. Move and I will be with you. Look down and I shall be there...."

Shaloolaa stared with wide eyes, her pleasure clearly drawn on her face. She ripped the robe down the front and opened it for Keishlee to look upon her nakedness. She no longer wore any of the snake skin leather. She worn no paint or decorations, no rope or twine and stood naked to the flesh.

The significance of this did not escape Keishlee. She had not really had the time to think of it or notice, but none of the women here went completely naked, as her people always did.

The other women stood and followed Shaloolaa's lead. Some ripped off their cloths or skins and threw them to the ground like Shaloolaa, others removed them more reluctantly, and carried the strips in their hands as they paraded before Keishlee and Scochaa.

Shaloolaa introduced some of the naked women, then reminded the group that she was also sworn to the "watch," and sat squarely in front of the entrance to the hut. Keishlee saw relief sweep across Scochaa's face, and the disappointment firmly planted on the faces of others. Guards stood off to the side and everyone talked like old friends until the night began to fade.

Without being taunted, or tricked, or bullied, directly or indirectly, Keishlee came to know each woman presented to her, since they all made sure to repeat their names and to mention some little detail about themselves. She also learned there were three rival factions within Shaloolaa's force, each trying to gain control over the group, and take Shaloolaa's place as leader of the Tukshead. But even with this between them, Keishlee could see and feel that they all dearly loved Shaloolaa. They respected her wisdom and followed her lead in all things. When she spoke there was no need to stop a loose tongue from catching the air. They watched over her and kept her counsel close at hand.

Keishlee learned the details of the challenge—how there would be much fighting among themselves over who was worthy to compete. Each force would have it settled before the high sun, then all would be allowed a rest. As soon as shade returned - Keishlee would make her selections. She would sit with the Tukshead on the feasting grounds and those not chosen would be free to make their challenge. Then she and her man creatures would be taken to Cloud Mountain, where they could prove the word of Shaloolaa, and show Tuk women how one sleeps with the Sun Bird. then later that night each challenge would be met.

Some of the challenges might be just for the mating comfort. Other challenges could be to prove unseen worthiness. Most of the challenges would be for breeding. Before one of the women could say it, Keishlee had already guessed that there would be those who would want the challenge to keep Mah and Odrak for themselves, and she looked for these women within the group, and spotted two.

Keishlee wondered how much difference it would make if they knew that neither Mah nor Odrak were mated, or fully grown. Either of them could be used at will by any who wanted them and could make them ready for the taking. Odrak would comply just at the hinting of it. Why was the fighting necessary?

When they were gone, Scochaa wanted to make sure Keishlee really understood all that had been said. Keishlee stopped her by saying, "Selma and Tarlane want to take them, and killing me would give them the right."

"The problem is bigger than that. Those creatures smell like our Sun Birds. You cannot know what that means to us. We do not even smell like them," Scochaa added. "But yes, Selma wants the challenge of blood rite. She says her time comes, and she wants to have one for her hut. Tarlane has hated you from the first, a strange hatred, and no one knows where it comes from. She speaks of nothing but your death."

"Tell me now about you, Scochaa."

"I shall do better than that." Scochaa stood and began a sharp rasping, "scowling" sound. At first it took all her breath, but three scowls later she was running them too fast to count.

"Pepper-Grass?" Keishlee heard Mah wake up from his dreaming. She could suddenly hear the words of her feeder at the time of Mah's naming, saying, "Each word a simple song," to describe the beauty of his voice. But her anger with Mah almost damned him in that moment. He was too loud and Scochaa surely heard him.

Still Scochaa "scowled" until it became a song. She shrieked to the trees and huts, and out into the early morning's light.

Keishlee could not look. Suddenly she could feel Mah at her back, moving like a whisper in the entrance of the hut. He was really still just a slave, and she gave herself a moment to think of him that way as he stood there awakened by Scochaa's racket. She braced herself. Nothing but the kick of a tall walker could move her now, and she doubled-eyed the font of the hut in case anyone was coming.

Women came too, lots of them. These were the masses, and Keishlee praised the sun for being early on its way. They were mostly the old, and some of these were men, but there were matches for Keishlee here, copying her walk as they came. Keishlee felt threatened, and was asking them not to come nearer, when everything stopped and she spotted a whole group of women she needed to fear. Fresh ones. Three with her seasons that were pitch in color, with brown-gray eyes.

Scochaa was still "scowling," lightly, looking slightly frightened of Mah, who stood at the entrance of the hut.

Something odd was going on, but it was something she had missed.

Without introductions, and with the women still many arms away, Keishlee called one of them out by the string of waxy flowers around her neck.

Suddenly everyone dashed eyes from Keishlee to the sky.

She looked up but there was nothing to perceive. The light of the sun was only now making things clearer to see, but the woman Keishlee called was too anxious for this scene, and she did not understand why. Only Mah had known this moment before.

The woman was bursting with some secret joy and went to reach for her. But the only touch Keishlee knew from these women was an attack, and disoriented, she knocked the woman away. The next thing she knew the woman was going after her eyes, and in no time at all they were fighting for blood, like two lizards with arms and legs for teeth.

Scochaa was silent and acting like she could not move. Abruptly she started scowling again, and this time she almost sounded like Mah, who started singing even louder, and moved out of the darkness of the hut.

Keishlee was in the middle of a terror. Others were too near her now. The kick she have given the woman was not meant to kill. Keishlee had never killed anyone. It had taken all her strength away and now she could not move. But in that instant, Keishlee was in the grips of death. A woman had jumped on her. Her legs were around Keishlee's waist, with an arm around her neck so tightly she could neither breathe or talk, while the woman's knees tried to crush the bones in Keishlee's chest.

"She has no weapon. How can she yield?" screamed Scochaa.

Others repeated these words and the woman let her breathe, but as they lay on the ground, she slipped into another hold as Keishlee lay gasping for air. When Keishlee's head had cleared, she knew better than to move. This grip, with one foot in her back and the other at the back of her head, could kill her. Death was a thing easy to sense.

Others pulled the woman away while Scochaa snatched Keishlee up and whispered all kinds of things in her ear. But from that moment on, Keishlee had eyes for her attacker alone.

A woman called, "No challenge!" Another said, "Like animals without skill...no challenge!" A third woman shook them loose, shouting, "The moment! The moment," and pointing to the sky.

Everyone fell silent and turned their heads to the sky. Now they could hear Shhaha chanting in the silence, and Keishlee saw that the women were not actually looking into, or at the sky, but listening and sensing what was in the air. Their gaze darted back and forth between themselves and Mah, who stood singing his Great Mah song without effort or thought, and they could all hear that it was a natural thing for him.

Keishlee tried to sense or see something in the air, but there was nothing there. Something was going on here she wasn't getting, and she was ready to fling herself into a curse [*body sign*]. An old woman crawled near and pulled herself up using Keishlee's legs, which gave her heart a jolt. Some of the other women jumped a little too, but quickly pulled the old woman aside, while they all stared at Scochaa and tried not to look at Mah.

Sensing his movement, Keishlee began a slow dash towards him, but Scochaa caught it, and moved to block her path. Mah stepped into the clearing and all the women began trying to do his Great Mah song, or Scochaa's scowling.

Keishlee still did not see anything, but the quickness of the passing shadows made her relax. It was only the Great Mah flying overhead. She stepped around Scochaa and laughed. Mah hastily stepped into a tall walker killing-kick position. He signed for Keishlee not to move and said, with the jolt of this new shock going through his system, "The feeder Mahs...they lay eggs here."

All the women fell flat to the ground. Mah ran to Keishlee, pulling her down to shield her, while screaming his song and "scowling," a sound that made Keishlee think of giant reptilian cats turned into birds.

Out of nowhere, huge talons appeared in her face, giant beastly things that could lift her off the ground. Then instantly they were gone. To shocked and weakened by this near attack, Mah fell off in front of her. He looked at her with amazement and said, "The Great Mah kills here," then continued singing.

"He gives us this time," Mah spoke, and the women crawled about, some going for their weapons. Others looked at Mah with shock, or disbelief, or evil in their eyes. "He says," said Mah, who saw the danger but still had to speak, "not to go near the waters. They feed their young."

Some women grunted, "We know this!" Others bowed their heads, chanting, "Sun Bird! Sun Bird!" Some snarled in disbelief, holding their weapons firm while Scochaa listened to the sky.

"Sun Bird speaks to no one!" huffed one of the few standing women.

Others tried to rise but were afraid to move. The old

woman laughed and pushed herself up against another woman, saying, "She's gone. They are all gone."

"I did not know the Great Mahs would take human life," Keishlee spoke to all of them.

"You would be such a treasure here," Scochaa almost cried to Mah. "Does he speak Sun Bird also?" she pointed to Odrak, who was hiding in the entrance of the hut.

He stepped into the light for the others to see, and from the way he set his foot down Keishlee knew he had just come out of the kick position. He stood quietly with Shhaha's arm around his shoulders, also depressed and annoyed by what he had just learnt.

Keishlee knew Mah had taught Odrak, Bellar and others the Great Mah songs. She told Scochaa so. She had never bothered to learn and now regretted it.

They other women persisted with checking the sky, and most had yet to get up from the ground. The guards ripped off their skins and shredded them to bits, throwing the remains into the fire. Some actually tried dancing a little, but Mah and Keishlee almost laughed since these people had no legs for this.

Scochaa was handling Mah with almost feminine care, sending him back to the hut, along with her two little slaves and the old man, Pleg, who had gathered at the entrance. The women eagerly renewed their presentations, while Scochaa called out their names. The first group of women were all older, but sturdy, and Keishlee got the feeling that they were here only for support, as were most of the others. The last group were all Keishlee's age and appeared not to be the blood of Tuk woman at all.

After Keishlee had seen them all, they were quickly gone. The old crippled woman pulled herself away while the sundry ones laid down to sleep. Scochaa turned to give duties and directions to several who were left, while others came back with bowls and pots for cooking, but still everyone sat and waited.

Scochaa took Keishlee into the hut and placed her on a beaten grass mat. She saw Mah and everyone else sitting up near a wall waiting for her to speak.

"Rest now, all of you," she spoke to them. Shhaha was the first to find himself a resting spot. Mah, Odrak and the old man did so after a little while. The two little sisters went just outside and sat at the entrance, fingering the dirt and doing it silently, as if they dared to do even this.

Giving Keishlee all of her attention, Scochaa said, "My

heart is bursting. This will weaken everyone."

"I do not think it is over," Keishlee said unhopefully.

"No, it is not," Scochaa laughed, seating herself close to Keishlee on the ground. "You can sleep until after we finish what must be done. This will give you some advantage. None of the others, including me...."

"I will not fight you, Scochaa," Keishlee found the words.

Scochaa paused, then touched Keishlee's arm and said, "You are like my lost sister. You are my friend." She paused again, then said, "I should not have let it come between us. You cannot take favorites, and I can tell you nothing to help you more." She let go of Keishlee and began again, "You must know by now that my force is the most deadly. And, I tell you, not because they are the best fighters, but because they will stop at nothing. My force has the power of treachery, and they are well trained. You must have some idea of the danger you face. You are not a fighter...."

Keishlee lowered her head, knowing the truth of it down in her bones.

"But you have many advantages. Many. And you are stronger than most of us here."

"I am not afraid, Scochaa. Only, I do not wish to fight my first friend."

Shhaha could not help turning in his place; of course, he was not truly sleeping. This was an important moment for Keishlee and for the entire clan of the Tuk Women. All his visions were changing. Even he was having new insights concerning old tales.

Scochaa gave Keishlee a sour, hurt look. She turned her head aside and said, "You will have to fight me! You will have to fight me, because you will have to fight my woman—how do you say, no matter. The outcome will be the same, you will be fighting me."

"Charlaa," spoke Keishlee, remembering the face of the woman who could have killed her. "Charlaa has the closeness of your heart?" She looked over to Mah and Odrak, who were sleeping arm-in-arm. Mah was holding Odrak around his waist, his head tucked under the other's chest.

"Yes, in every way. She wants them both here and no memory of you, because she knows that this is wrong. If not you, then I must fight her, or she will kill you, and then you must fight me, because I will want to taste your blood for bringing this between us. You must see how useful they could be to us. I want them here as much, but Shaloolaa is right. We must stop killing off the life around us, all the blessed creatures with the evil ones. All the women. We must find other ways to live. In the time of Shaloolaa we have learnt that the land is all around. There are many things in the world. Some very useful things...and creatures one can live with," she quickly added.

"Creatures like me," Keishlee huffed.

Scochaa gently took hold of her, and held one of Keishlee's feeder bags, which calmed Keishlee as she recalled her feeder saying, "This was a way to know another young woman. The way it hardens or the way it shakes will tell you much about her."

"You have become very close to me," Scochaa smiled. "You can sleep deeply. You will have many to help with the watch now...." Scochaa was interrupted by someone calling outside, but continued saying, "They will be here until you finish resting. They will provide for you, and your...men. The bigger one has spent his time in the medicine hut. He will be brought to you later." Scochaa gave her a sly smile. "Do not worry about him, he will be himself in another day. Explain to him later. Aaah!, don't let those two out of your sight or out of this hut until it's time. If you need anything at all, just signal to one of the elders. Few can speak your words, but all can read the body."

Keishlee wanted to say something as Scochaa headed for the entrance, but could not get the words out. Then someone else ordered Scochaa out of the hut. "Rest now. Rest. You will need all you can get," spoke Scochaa, leaving the hut.

Keishlee moved to another part of the hut and found she was without the will or the strength to keep her eyes open a moment longer.

The hut and all the surrounding land seemed unnaturally quiet and still, but soon the birds and the other sounds of nature came back to life. Mah had dozed but awoke when Odrak rose. When he opened his eyes there was a rush of air from many mouths near him. Odrak was sitting up, staring at the many faces looking in on them. He patted Mah's belly, and Mah rose to see all the eyes smiling down at them. Young women and few youths were piled outside the entrance and at both wall openings, calling Odrak and him to come over. Odrak started to go to one offering food when Shhaha's voice stopped him.

"You may not go to any of them. You cannot speak with them, or leave this hut." He pointed to the old man standing above him. "Pleg here will move the shade for you [*to do everything for someone*]. Speak to him, or to me if you need something."

Both Mah and Odrak placed themselves before Shhaha and began the chant for the rising sun. Shhaha told them there would be no lessons today, but that they should ask Pleg to clear a "window," a new word which he explained.

Pleg, too well trained in the ways of his people, did not listen to what was being said between them. Odrak had to go to him and ask him directly. Pleg then picked up a wisp of braided reeds from a pile of tools to beat away the visitors. He did not really have to hit anyone, but it was clear he took great pleasure in this.

Mah turned away from the window, saying, "All this to rub bellies!"

"If they are past the age of mating, all of...."

Shhaha stood and pulled Odrak from the window. "You think too often of relief. Is what you carry so much in need?" Shhaha smiled at him. "I know you have no fear, Odrak. But you, Mah, tell me of you?"

Mah looked over to the windows and saw them filled again. Odrak felt his nervousness and eased over to throw both arms around him. There was a gasp from the people outside, saying, "They touch. These two have feelings?!"

Mah wrapped one arm around Odrak, saying, "Blood fills my head here in the land of the Great Mahs. I want to see their eggs. I think of nothing but speaking with their young."

"Did you see the old one this morning?" Shhaha pulled Mah down beside him.

"Yes," Mah and Odrak whispered together.

"I think you have already spoken to their young," suggested Shhaha.

"I have asked, many times," replied Mah.

"Yes, and I," added Odrak, whose look told Shhaha that he had already guessed the truth.

Shhaha knew that most people ignored Odrak. They could not see the quality of his blood or the depth of his character. He worried that Odrak was not fruitful, having had many experiences with the free women of their clan, and never having produced,

Shhaha doubted that his seed knew how to fly. He had checked them both while they napped, and Mah had no anticipation; but as for Odrak, the women here were in his dreams. Shhaha could not stop smiling at him, knowing that these women thought them much older, because they were already as tall as their men.

For the first time Shhaha saw Pleg listening to them. Pleg was beside himself with disbelief because he knew no men who touched. Then people started rushing about outside which drew his attention away..

"So they lie and kill," Mah huffed, greatly disappointed.

"Always, I have told you they would be good killers, Mah, too good for them not to have done so many times," Shhaha spoke, being careful not to hurt Mah's feelings.

"They fly too fast to be seen. They could take anything for food," Odrak spoke, intending to awaken Mah to the reality of these creatures, of which he had long suspected.

"Do not speak such things, Odrak. I know they have a special place in your heart. You have buried more nodes than anyone," Mah said, his temper rising.

Suddenly there was screaming from all around the hut. People were shouting for help, and some were cursing the "man creatures" in the hut.

Shhaha pulled his apprentices to him for protection. Pleg stepped back from him, disturbed by the sight of them clutched together. Keishlee stirred in her sleep. When Pleg noticed, he ran around the room whisking the windows for the people to stop their noise.

Sonmyaa and a handful of guards broke their way into the hut, pointing fingers at Pleg and Shhaha. She made two quick hand signs and two guards left to move the crowds away.

"What is this you do here? No man creature can talk to the great Sun Bird," roared Sonmyaa.

Shhaha noticed claw marks up and down both her legs and some were still bleeding. "We call this bird the Great Mah."

Sonmyaa called for more guards. "You plot against us." She pointed an evil finger at Shhaha. "It's time we saw your blood," she roared, calling for the guards.

Mah asked Pleg for help. He begged him to wake Keishlee, but Pleg would not hear him or move. Odrak rushed over to Keishlee when the guards came in and gently rubbed his fingers down her face. Sonmyaa ordered the guards to take Shhaha's life. While they considered this, Shhaha thought to grab the blood wand Keishlee had returned to him, but Odrak watched him decide against it and shouted, "Call your name!" to Mah, knowing the word was a command to summon the birds.

As the guards went for Shhaha, Mah began to sing so loud and violently that it hurt their ears, but the pain only made them more determined to seek Shhaha's blood. Odrak ran over to block their path, knowing they would not hurt him. One of them tried to push him away and found he could not be moved.

Keishlee tried to sit up, which made Pleg so nervous, he began to loose his waters all over the hut. Some of it hit Keishlee in the face, and one of the guards screamed at him. The water fully awoke Keishlee to find the hut in an total uproar. Mah was loudly singing his bird call and guards were attacking....

Keishlee leaped from the ground to knock the guard nearest her unconscious with a back hand. Then with murder in her eyes, she went for Sonmyaa, whose weapon was drawn and pointed toward Shhaha.

The hut's roof was suddenly ripped off and wind blew dust in their faces, knocking down all the walls. A massive bird hovered in the air directly over Mah. Its talons surrounded him as if to tear him to shreds. Women fainted, and Sonmyaa screamed when the bird bent down to look at her. Mah changed the flux of his song, and the bird returned the melody. Everyone in the area was lying faced to the ground, except Sonmyaa, Keishlee, Shhaha, Odrak and Mah, who was now smiling as he sang to the bird.

The bird snatched Mah up into the air, hovering just long enough for Keishlee to see the startled look on Mah's face. When Shhaha jumped up to pull Mah back down, pleading in heartfelt Great Mah song, Keishlee was terror stricken. The bird flapped its wings, stirring up clouds of choking dust, and was gone.

Keishlee fell down in tears, pounding the dirt, while Odrak eased toward Sonmyaa, stalking her with stealth enough to go completely unnoticed. Seeing him Keishlee smiled, because now she knew whose blood he was. Odrak was born after his mother became a free woman. Her mate had died under the claws of a large black cat. Then Lodi showed up from the Oodda clan. His feeder always denied that Odrak was Lodi's seed, but had to send Lodi away to stop the talk about the death of her mate.

Keishlee broke Sonmyaa's wrist before Odrak could reach

her, and had to take the brunt of his backhand-swipe since it was too late for him to stop. Even so, she felt such pride at seeing Odrak come out of his stalker move, but now Odrak was also in terrible pain. His trying to stop in the middle of the move had pulled a muscle, and now he laid sprawled on the ground in agony.

But Keishlee could not stop here, she did not dare. She disabled the other guard, using one of Scochaa's moves. She eased up to her first, smiled to give the woman pause, then snatched her weapon and kicked her to the ground while stomping her face into the dirt.

"Keishlee! Keishlee!" pleaded Scochaa, surprised at the sight before her. Others with her were screaming for her blood. Someone Keishlee recognized said, "Cut out her heart. The Sun Bird will eat that part of the human!"

Keishlee listened without fear to Scochaa's scowl, and even smiled at the older women who scowled back. She then had a moment of the most pleasant piece of time, when she turned to place both eyes on Charlaa. She was attuned to the woman's presence and would know where to look for her from now on.

"Give me the weapon, Keishlee," Scochaa spoke nervously, standing close enough to cut her easily, or to be cut.

Before Scochaa asked again, Keishlee threw it to the ground and lowered her head. No one moved, until Scochaa ordered someone to remove the weapon.

"You want to see death?" she screamed at Keishlee, forcing her to kneel, one knee to the ground. "Ask for the death of this woman!!" she roared for all to hear and pointed at the guard, who now had no weapon.

Their was a roar of "murder" over the clearing, and Keishlee recalled that it was the same word they used for feast. She looked at the guard as she had never looked at another woman before.

"Be sure. They will kill her on a whisper!" Scochaa growled and laughed, while striking the woman's face.

Keishlee slid her hand under the woman's arm to help her up, but the woman pushed her away and knelt with her head lowered.

"Keishlee has earned the right to be called sister. She has power and does not run away. She has not come to us with creatures we cannot live with! She is MY PRETTY!! And has earned the right to look upon the weapon," Scochaa howled to the now larger crowd, then turned slowly to Keishlee, asking, "Who am I?"

Shhaha slapped himself. Holding back his tongue would leave him too weak to carry his blood wand for a while.

"Weapons," stammered Keishlee.

The following uproar renewed Keishlee's strength. Scochaa wrapped her arms around Keishlee and held her tight.

The people roared again, but then dove to the ground. Scochaa leaped to it, fearing for her life. Keishlee still had not heard it, but almost dropped to the ground herself until she spotted something moving towards her in the sky. Terror seized her, but she turned to Odrak, who she knew would be standing near, and hoped that he could speak the bird song without Mah around. This bird was too fast, she thought, trembling as it swooped down towards them.

To Keishlee's surprise, some people lifted their heads to coo and moan as they watched the bird's approach. Someone did a sort of chant, an old, tired voice that cracked off each word like someone whittling wood. Shhaha knew this chant the old, crippled woman mumbled as the chant of new blood. With it she swore to the newness of this sight, but Shhaha looked around and only saw disbelief. Even in the face of it, they could not believe it.

Keishlee feared she'd faint as it hovered overhead. She started kneeling when the bird's head spun around to look deep into her eyes. It took a another look around until it spotted Odrak. Shhaha started to get up, but the bird flashed a sparkling yellow eye towards him, and he sat back down. The bird then snatched Odrak from the ground, and the call Odrak made was not the bird's lovely song.

Keishlee realized that she had never seen the Great Mah flying in the air like other birds. This bird was still faster than any bird she knew, but she had never seen one in the air this long before. And neither had the Tuk Women.

"You must rest, Keishlee." Scochaa ate a pinch of dirt and said again to her bewildered new friend, "Rest."

"We must save them!!!" Keishlee panicked.

"If the Sun Bird wished them dead, their ruined flesh would be at your feet!" Scochaa roared back. "Rest is the thing you need."

Keishlee turned a sly eye to Shhaha, who signaled for her

to hold her tongue. He swiveled his head away and sat on the ground, while she tried to find where the center of the hut had been, but had to turned around again when she heard Shaloolaa's call. "Everyone! We must prepare for the mating feast! Go and prepare your best. There is an honored guest among us," Shaloolaa ordered, pointing to Keishlee. "Go!" she demanded.

Keishlee saw her coming and started to kneel, but Shaloolaa stopped her and rubbed the side of her face, saying, "If you must, stand your challenge even against me, but do not be afraid. Do not be afraid of any woman here. Go, and rest now."

The words pleased Keishlee so much, she closed her eyes to listen to them again in private. They were a comfort, and meant protection even from the Tukshead. Keishlee thought she might be able to sleep a little more, since there would be no one else to come attacking them. She did not know it, but Shhaha was having the best laugh in his life. He almost envied his apprentices. He chanted quietly the words of the sacred blessing, and thought of the respects he would receive from the other blood keepers once this tale was told. He closed his eyes and tried to see into the future. Tho he was too happy to see much, every fiber of his being told him that Mah and Odrak would fulfill his secret plans for this journey.

This brought back his desire to seek relief. So much talk of it had put him in need. His eyes sprang open and searched around for another eye to catch. He got one, and made himself small upon the ground, looking up from it to her. The cloth between her legs flushed a spring of wetness at the spot. He thought, "She has been ages without," and tried to think better of it, but she had already decided and was up slapping faces.

Shaloolaa had looked too hard at Keishlee for a sign. She did not want to leave her hopes with Shhaha, but as soon as Keishlee closed her eyes, she began her study of him. He was relaxed and almost smiling, and there behind the eyes—a knowledge that his two apprentices would be safe. She yanked one of the women out of her face and hurried away.

As she left, to everyone's dismay, Shaloolaa ordered the selections to continue. She pulled two guards to her side and ordered them to bring her "fast legs" [*horse (Tuk/red zebras*]. She called for the Tukshead to appear as she marched into the feast clearing, where a great many women were already gathered. Again she ordered the selections to continue, and this time fighting broke out all around her.

She stalked through the field of fighting women, slapping one to the ground and raising the arm of another. Over and over she did this until half the field was quickly cleared. There was much shouting and cursing, and all around her were their screams for blood, but of this Shaloolaa was fearless.

Her sisters of the Tukshead began to gather around her. All talking, everyone demanding and cursing this one, or speaking against her choice of that one. Shaloolaa did not speak to them until the Tukshead was whole and still.

"Do the elders prepare the feast?" Shaloolaa asked Scochaa, who quickly answered yes.

"We must keep them, Shaloolaa," commanded Saamyli, her closest friend.

"No. It will bring destruction to our people," said Shaloolaa with swift resolve.

"You say there are creatures that can destroy us?!" grunted Somaali.

"No," Shaloolaa smiled. "But, there are humans who can."

This angered many women, and Sonmyaa eased around to face her. "For my daughters, I will challenge her myself!"

Shaloolaa ordered the guards to clear a space around them. "I had expected this of you, Sonmyaa," Shaloolaa made her words a curse.

"She will challenge no one," laughed Scochaa, who gloated over Sonmyaa's broken wrist. Sonmyaa tried to kick Scochaa's leg, but could not reach it.

"You will have to fight me," Shaloolaa smiled at Sonmyaa.

"No!" Scochaa roared. "She will fight me!"

"That is not the way, Scochaa!" yelled Shaloolaa and the others agreed.

"NO! No. No matter," Scochaa huffed. "I have spoken these words as often as the sun rises. If the Tukshead is to fight each other, than I shall spill first blood. No Mother!" she stepped back from Shaloolaa. "I will not see the Tukshead raid with one another. I will not see you take a challenge from the Sisters Seven. No," she cried, then did her bird call and was surrounded by members of her force.

Guards ran from all directions to the field. Somaali's force gathered behind her and so did Sonmyaa's, which was a force of women much larger than that presented to Keishlee during the night.

"You see what it comes to," groaned Scochaa. "And this will happen even if I do not take the challenge from you. You have told me this yourself, since times before my words...."

"This is too important. You and Charlaa have traveled the lands about. You know the danger better than all others," said Shaloolaa. Her force gathered behind her now, larger than all the rest. "A test of blood rite is a sacred thing. In this matter, it alone should decide."

"You are right as always, Mother. You are our leader. But I say to you others," Scochaa turned to face the silent forces gathered all around, "did not her riding creature kick two heads to mush this very morning, and neither getting cut in the raid? These people call this creature their 'clan relation,' and they have all its knowledge. They have mastered this kick. I have seen signs of it, even in the old one. And, they know things about the Sun Birds even we do not. Is that not proof enough that they deserve our respect?"

"Charlaa and the others say she is not a fighter," huffed Shomnyaa.

Scochaa gave her a knowing smile, but turned to the others and said, "Did not those who came before them, those who had no women, did not they...."

"Yes, they continued to fight even without all their limbs, and their creatures killed two hands of our women," moaned Shaloolaa, seeing it happening again in her mind.

Another woman said, "Then the one whose head was no longer attached, called out."

This gave some of the women a shudder, as they remembered from being there, or having heard it repeated every day since it happened. Tarlane had been the one to slay him, and held the head up for all to see, when it called out three times. Everyone had been trying to get its words from her. But all Tarlane would say was that it had been a name, no more, and she held fast to the secret name, believing it would lend magic to her fighting.

"Shall we kill all the strangers who come among us? Even those who come with women of great blood?" asked Shemaa to Scochaa's and Somaali's surprise.

"This Keishlee is no fighter," snapped Somaali.

"Who does not want her walk!" roared Scochaa.

"Yes, and who would not like to stand and look down at others," smiled Shemaa.

Voices could be heard raising the raid call, "Blood Fire! Blood Fire! Blood Fire!" Scochaa whipped her weapon out and raised it high into the air. She marched up the feast clearing, pulling out women from the various forces, a majority of them Sonmyaa's and Somaali's women. She made them kneel before her with their heads almost in the dirt.

"I claim all these lives, and many more," she roared over the mass of people. "I may take these lives whenever I choose, and none may call me evil or challenge me for what I do." She raised her weapon with both hands as if to cut the pile of women into bits.

Shaloolaa screamed at her, and Scochaa turned and knelt down with the other women. She looked up at Shaloolaa, saying, "I owe my life to Charlaa and to you, only. I give it up now, if the greatness of our people can only be found in killing. Look around, all of you. Have we not lost many sisters, and not just to killing, but many have gone to be rid of us. Some go even to our enemy just to get back their own smell. I warn you now," she stood up and swept a finger around the forces. "Others are coming to our lands from all directions. Some of these will come in blood rite for their dead. And some will come for this Keishlee and her creatures, if they are not returned. Would you give up creatures like these if they were yours? Creatures one can live with! I think not."

There was a rush of voices, some coming even from the outer edges of the field. Scochaa ordered the women who were still at her feet to leave, but they continued to kneel, staring up at her with the respect and loyalty they felt for the many times she had saved or spared their lives. Their anger left them as they fought to understand her words, but they knew only that there was wisdom here.

Shomnyaa stomped over to Sonmyaa, and slyly elbowed her in the chest, while saying to Shaloolaa, "The Tukshead must never come to raiding one another. I curse anyone who says I suggested a challenge be made between us."

"Like a broken weapon, which comes to lesser and lesser use, the Tukshead must never be broken," agreed Shemaa, who turned to Somaali.

Somaali kicked up dust and stomped her feet, but said, "No weapons in the face of the Tukshead," and looked to Scochaa, who was still holding her weapon.

Scochaa put it away and a call for peace between the forces rallied around the Tukshead. The Sisters Seven each gave up their blood rite, until it reached Sonmyaa. Then there was shouting and pushing among the women as three guards marched up to the Tukshead, knelt, and begged to be heard. The Sisters Seven took their places together which formed the Tukshead, and gave the women permission to speak.

"It's a good thing to keep the Tukshead safe and true. But blood rite is due every woman. Who here has not bled?" argued Tarlane, one of the three demanding to be heard.

"Take the rite from the Tukshead, but I demand it!" shouted Tois. "There are few in our clan who can easily reach the fruit. I want to be sure that my daughters can. If we do not keep them, there is no way to be certain."

"Without raids among the Tukshead our village has grown to great numbers. The sight of our forces alone move our enemy further and further from our land. I praise the wisdom in the blood of Shaloolaa, and all the mothers before her who took the blood rite from the Tukshead. But, does not the blood rite keep us strong? Is it not the blood rite that gave us Shaloolaa's blood? It is my right, and I will have it!" screamed Charlaa. "Let the blood decide."

The sight of Mah laid splayed across the cave floor and being stroked across his chest by one of the larger adult birds sent Odrak into a raging fit. During this journey, one of his secret blood chants was that if death should take him, it should do so at the sake of saving Mah. Without fear or thought, he struck the giant bird and shouted for it to leave. He dragged Mah out of its reach and checked for signs of life, which were faint. He began the chant of wandering spirits, in order to bring Mah's spirit back to his flesh. He blew air about Mah's face and chest to clear a way for his spirit's return, while shaking Mah's arms and legs, so his spirit would remember their movements.

Mah jerked himself about.

"There!" moaned Odrak as he saw the spirit come back to Mah and put life back in his eyes. "Here!" he cried as he held Mah, kneading the muscles of his arms and legs and finishing the chant of spirits.

Odrak got Mah up, and shook him, but then stopped as he

felt the birds moving to surround them.

He clutched Mah close and wanted to run, then remembered they were in a huge cave near the top of a high mountain. The air was cold outside, but warm here among the huge birds, where their numbers seemed unreal.

Odrak felt like his waters were still flowing from him, as they had done in the air on his way here. But he was dry and losing his fear now that Mah spoke to him.

"What has happened to me? Where are we, Odrak?" Mah asked until he too saw all the birds about him. They looked at him with bright yellow or white-gray eyes, and trembled their wings as a sign of welcome.

Mah was shocked to see the great multitude of birds going about their business in the vastness of the cave. "Huitzilopochtli," Mah sang out the old greeting upon seeing his favorite bird, the one he called "My-Name," because it was she whom he owed for it. He recognized her easily by the colored patterns on her beak and legs.

The bird hurried to him and Mah fell into the nook of her wings. He sang to her of the joy he felt at finally seeing where they lived, and of seeing so many at once.

She called Odrak over and he almost flew at Mah's side. Holding his hand, he asked Mah to tell the birds to take them back. He was afraid, but he did not want to miss out on the duties required of him by the feeder clan below.

"Do not be afraid, Odrak. These are our friends."

"They are so many. I never...."

"They are people like us. Are we not many?"

"We are trapped. There is no way down from here. Look," whispered Odrak, cautiously pulling Mah away from the bird. He rushed him over to the cave's large opening, where they had to climb a mound of rocks until they could just put their heads out into the blinding sun, and the torrent of wind that hurled itself around the frozen mountain peaks.

Mah jumped back and tumbled down the rocks. Odrak dashed after him. "Do not hurt yourself now," Odrak begged, while helping him up and checking his head for injuries.

"We are like the moon from the ground with the sun in our faces," Mah said, and then walked over to the birds, who were waiting and calling to them.

Mah and My-Name spoke for a long time and most of it he did without a smile. Odrak was so afraid that his mind could no longer understand the songs he had been taught, but it was like a healed wound to hear Mah laugh again. Odrak almost fell on him in relief. He sat next to Mah and listened harder to pick up some of the conversation.

Other larger, older birds gathered around to watch and listen to Mah speak their tongue. Some reached over to turn him around with their feet. Others brushed a wing tip through his hair, and as always, Odrak was astonished at the dexterity and gentleness. They could manipulate a single feather to clear dust from his face, or use a single talon to stick and kill a large bug crawling nearby.

Mah turned to Odrak and laughed again. "They had to send their Jerruut [*eldest*] to get you. The others fly too fast. That is what took my breath away. So they sent their Jerruut for you, to make sure it did not happen again."

Odrak did not find any of this funny. "When will the old one take us back?"

Mah pointed to a young male they knew and said, "When they did not know what to do with me, Pepper-Grass took them back to look for you. He told them you were like the easy breeze, always near. He and Lizard-Eyes knew you would be there if I was there."

Some of the birds were passing Mah food, which he passed over to Odrak. Most of it was nuts from the purple mountain bush covering the lower cliffs outside. The young ones rained berries and fruits down on them, and one old bird tried to feed Odrak freshly peeled food stones [*potatoes*].

"Eat them, Odrak. You know how it pleases them to feed us," smiled Mah.

"Ask them when we can leave. No. Ask them when they will take us back."

Mah ate one of the fungus strips handed him by a young bird he knew. "Taste this, Odrak. It is so good. It makes warmth inside, and brightens up the head and eyes."

Odrak ate it quickly. It was enjoyable but he did not care. "When are they going to take us back? I do not like being up inside a mountain in the sky."

"Do not be afraid, Odrak. We are among friends. They shall take us back after all their kin has seen us. No one else has been in their citadel since the Days of Ice Covers or the Years of Dust." Mah handed him another piece of fungus. "Here, they have gathered many things for us. We must eat, and I am very hungry. They took us before the morning meal."

"Citadel, this place?" checked Odrak. "Years of Dust and Days of Ice Covers, what are they?" asked Odrak, his body making him eat against his will.

Wanting to speak to them all, Mah asked another bird and translated for Odrak. "This is the main citadel, here. The Citadel of the Highest Peak," Mah said, circling the area with his arms. "Their other kin, the ones they want us to meet, Aaah!, they are in the Citadel of the Great Land Break."

"We are far from Tuk Village, Mah. Are their kin coming here?" Odrak asked and looked cautiously towards the immense opening of the cave.

"No."

Guards came to wake Keishlee, who greeted them at the entrance. Young women placed leaves of foods before her and begged her to eat quickly. When she had finished, they took her down to a lake with all the women that had stood guard over her sleep. After soaking themselves, they rubbed lards into their skin, then dressed Keishlee in Tuk fashion, with large strips of snakeskin tied around her legs, arms, and feeder bags, and a larger piece of something just as tough, but softer, wrapped up between her legs and around her waist.

They brushed loose what hair they could with a stone covered with short quills, and gave her the paints she requested to use on what was left visible of her body. Using the liquid chalks offered, she blotched white and brown spots on her stomach, arms, legs and feet. Thinking of Mah, she wanted to streak some of it through her hair and put some on her face, but the other women frowned at this and took her paints away. As she walked out the hut, she felt alien to herself. The coverings changed the way she walked and her sense of balance.

She was rushed through the village into a large mountain-enclosed clearing. She knew where she was from the sound of the falling waters she had been shown by Scochaa. Large mats of twisted vines and leathery leaves laid atop piles of large stones, grouped in rows all over the clearing.

Keishlee was seated behind the largest mat, where she could look out over the huge field of mats that formed semicircles in front of her. Soon other women and guards came into the area, and climbed the rocky mountains around them, or stood vigil in various positions along the mountain cliffs. Masses of women and a good many men came into the clearing with herds of slaves, who carried food in large pots, leaf trays, steaming leaf sacks, human hair nets, animal bladders and vegetable gourds.

Keishlee had a strange thought come to her as some of the slaves placed foods on her mat: these women, for all their want of fighting, led a very peaceful life here. Their land was plentiful like the lands of her people. They would lose their fighting skill without the blood rite fighting among themselves. Occasions like this provided them a reason for their skill. It was not blood these women were after at all, but a way to keep the customs passed down to them by their mothers. A continuation of their way of life.

Keishlee was surprised to see that men and women walked side by side into the clearing. Slaves ran to them and clamored for the men's attention, as if they had not been seen for many moons. The men were seated a handful to each mat, while the women marched up to Keishlee to show themselves off, then each took seats next to their men or with other women.

The women were dressed in their finest fashions, unmarked cloths, fresh untorn leathers, and the most beautiful feathers she had ever seen. They almost glowed in the shadows of the trees as they came into the clearing. The old ones, who were not performing some special function, wore their hair tied up colored leather strips or flowered vine strings. Most of them wore it in thick braids filled with bits of shells or brightly colored flowers. Instead of paint on their arms and legs, they wore painted strings tied or woven into fanciful designs, making Keishlee feel dull and ordinary, small and empty inside and out. Not only had they dressed commonly but her face was bare, and she knew she could not hide her envy as they marched and spun before her.

As the voices in the clearing grew louder once filled, and the women continued their parade, Keishlee became aware of the many who were not among those selected, but who had wanted to be. When the last woman made her turn and left to be seated, Keishlee was astonished at their numbers. There were as many people here as hairs in a knot. More than half as many as the Waterhorse clans, and more than all the Tall Walker clans combined.

Keishlee felt even smaller. She was thinking of how easy it would be for these women to just kill her and take Shhaha's apprentices. They were honoring her, but she did not have time to appreciate it further. She saw a cloud of dust, and heard the whinny of bush horses trotting into the field, which reminded her of the challenges to come.

Guards ran behind Keishlee, where they formed a human wall at the base of the surrounding mountain. Behind them followed a large group of naked women, then rows of armed and plainly dressed women and behind them, the Tukshead.

Keishlee noticed that all the men in the clearing were standing as the Sisters Seven formed their standing order, with Shaloolaa, who was the tallest in the center and the other women sizing down beside her. Shaloolaa motioned for Keishlee to stand, and ordered the naked women to stand in front of Keishlee. No one had spoken aloud since they arrived, but as Shaloolaa did, her voice boomed out over the clearing from an echo created by the surrounding mountains.

Shaloolaa greeted her people and gave permission for the men to be seated. She ordered that "extras" be brought to the Tukshead and that "wine" be served. Young slaves rushed around with large bladders, pouring a dark purple liquid into bowls placed around the mats. When all the wine had been poured, Shaloolaa raised her bowl and thanked the land and the elder mothers for giving them food and life, and sisters to share them with. She drank and then so did the others.

Shemaa motioned for Keishlee to take her bowl, which she did and took a little sip. The drink was sweet and more refreshing than water. She started to drink heartily, but Shomnyaa touched her shoulder and signed for her to stop. Shaloolaa ordered the meal to begin, and then asked Keishlee to begin her selections, then the Tukshead sat as one person without any more words and ate.

Keishlee stood there for a moment unsure of how to proceed. The naked women seated themselves before her, staring at her with every possible humor. Keishlee circled the group, carefully looking them over and trying to see past their appearance into their souls. They were all young, most younger than herself, healthy and full-blooded, but their blood Keishlee could not guess or know. Which ones carried the traits most respected by this clan? Which ones came from long-lived lines and which ones were just lucky plucks?

She stood in front of them for a moment with the Tukshead at her back. She considered the strength of the men of her clan, remembering what mated women said about this one or that one, and their constant need of relief. She recalled what women had to say about Dbsha and the number of slaves he had seeded. She knew well the whispers about Odrak's blood and what he might someday be capable of, but he and Mah were still young and that was an important factor as well.

Quietly, 8 naked men were ushered up to the Tukshead. Keishlee croaked in shock to find Ramaa as one of them. With his hands bound behind him, he stood like a mountain among their men. Guards came over from the mountain base, weapons at the ready, while Shaloolaa stood to check the men over. Keishlee was once again stunned by the boldness of these women. Ramaa was a towering giant among them, and yet not a single woman looked at him with fear, or respect.

Shaloolaa forced a laugh at seeing Ramaa among the group, and told the others that he would not do. "The magic used to heal him will take his strength away. He would not be useful to any woman this day," she laughed.

Someone tried to get Keishlee's attention at the other end of the mat, and she turned to see Shhaha being seated. There were grumbles from the crowd, but she saw none of the Tukshead look at him disapprovingly. Shhaha looked up for a moment to smile at her, but quickly returned his gaze to the ground and the mat. Keishlee looked back at Shaloolaa and smiled. Now she could choose wisely. These women could do many things, but they would not be able to keep Shhaha from a decision concerning blood.

Shaloolaa ordered a replacement for Ramaa. "If any woman objects to his being seated for the feast, take him to the hut of the men," she yelled. No objections were heard except when they tried to take Ramaa away.

He fell to his knees and assured the Tukshead that he would be fit for their use of him. To Keishlee's further surprise, he asked quite meekly that he be allowed to stay, while bending low to rub his head on the shoulder of the guard trying to remove him.

There were smiles from the Tukshead and Shaloolaa agreed. The naked men were then paraded past the Tukshead to the mats of the other women, where they were taunted and jeered.

Keishlee guessed that Shhaha had managed to speak with Ramaa, and was proud of him because he honored Shhaha, their Keeper of the Blood. She hoped his duties would prove fruitful since this clan could use new blood, and his was the strongest of her clan.

Shaloolaa signed for Keishlee to continue and this time she was ready. She called for one of the taller young women to stand. She remembered how Shhaha looked over the visiting feeders and roughly grabbed the woman's arms and held them in the air. She gently squeezed her feeder bags, testing their firmness. She lightly smacked the woman on her hips, turned her around and checked for any deformity or blemish that might reveal something to her. Bending down to look at the woman's legs, she looked at Shhaha out of the corner of one eye. He had been waiting, and quickly tipped his head in approval.

Keishlee turned the woman back around and while lowering her arms said, "This one will do nicely."

A moment of wild calls and screams erupted from the clearing. Shaloolaa stood and the field went silent. "The breeding rite will be completed, I swear. Even if we have to climb the great mountain to beg the Sun Bird to bring them back. For now we need two substitutes...."

Men ran towards the guards and the two who reached them first sent the others back. They ran to the mat of the Tuks-head and knelt before Shaloolaa, their hands tucked together beneath their chins. They were Keishlee's age, and she wondered who they belonged to.

"This one shall be the creature with the signs of age in his hair, the one called Mah." Shaloolaa pointed to select the shorter man. "And you shall be the sloe-eyed one, the one called Odrak."

Mah's stand-in ran out to Keishlee's right, about five trees distant, and the other to her left. Keishlee looked hard at the woman, staring deeply into her eyes. Keishlee saw her desire for Mah and then remembered that this woman was from Shaloolaa's force.

"You may have some time with Mah," Keishlee spoke, pointing to the man on her right.

Keishlee was feeling better now. She looked over the faces again, and endeavored to recall having seen them. She only recognized a few and decided to go through them first.

Keishlee's next choice was a young woman she met

through Saamyli. She had hair like her own and was also tall and sturdy, rising almost to her chest. Recalling that Saamyli was Shaloolaa's close friend, she sent her to Odrak's stand-in at her left.

Standing over the next woman, Keishlee made her open her legs on the ground and part the long hairs. Keishlee caught the faint smell of blood and knew this young feeder must be spending time in the woman's hut. Out the corner of her eye she caught Shhaha's meaningful frown.

"There need be no time wasted with you," Keishlee spoke firmly to the young feeder who jumped up to attack her. Keishlee slapped her to the ground with one blow. Guards rushed over and stood one beside each of them. "Do you challenge me, sister?" Keishlee asked the woman once she was on her feet.

The woman huffed but walked away without another word. The guards left and Keishlee hurried through half the women. 5 of those selected were standing to her right, 6 to her left, and she thought that this was quite enough.

She looked out over the remaining women and grew tired of their faces. She disliked a certain look she found among these people, and gave a deadly leer to one feeder with it. Keishlee ordered her to leave without even checking her over. Every time she spotted the thin straight hair, the narrow hips, the flattened bottom, the bushy eyebrows or the thin lips, Shhaha coughed or cleared his throat. When she peeked over at him, he would not even look at her.

Keishlee called out the dark ones with this look, the bean-brown ones and one that was yellowish colored. She spared no time forcing them all to leave. One leaped at her and almost clawed her in the face. Rolling on top Keishlee knocked her head into the woman's mouth, and was sure even Shhaha heard the woman's teeth crack. Keishlee let her gag on her own blood for a while, then released her with a short kick to the stomach, to help her cough out the teeth.

The others fled before the guards reached them, and Keishlee returned to finish her selections, ordering the guards away. Happy cheers erupted from the clearing, and she could see that women were throwing food and small stones at the naked women that ran from the clearing back towards the village. Others went to their friends who had their wraps waiting, where they dressed and seated themselves.

Having avoided a young feeder she liked, because she

hated Sonmyaa, Keishlee was forced to remember the beautiful words the dried-blood-colored woman had said. Her hair was thick and full, and resembled water as it waves back and forth from the banks. Curls of silky hair flowed down her back and in tied trusses at the sides of her head. She also wore a small band of tiny flowers around her neck. Her green eyes upset Keishlee, and made her angry and nervous as soon as the woman stood before her. She wanted to slap her face, but turned her around roughly to find that Shhaha had not made up his mind either. Keishlee sat the woman down beside her.

Angry screams and calls rang out from the clearing. Keishlee turned around to the Tukshead, but all of the women lowered their faces and tried to eat their food.

Keishlee called out another young woman. She smelt this woman and played with her thick straight hair. She was only a head shorter than Keishlee, and looked strong even with her light brown skin. Keishlee was about to give Shhaha the corner of an eye, when a woman ran up to the Tukshead and whispered into Shaloolaa's ear.

Shaloolaa called guards over, whispered something to them and watched as they moved Shhaha back away from the mat, out of Keishlee's easy vision.

Terror tried to cease her, but Keishlee quickly selected the woman and sent her to Odrak's group.

She rejected the next six and knew from the calls out in the clearing that the people were getting upset. She heard Shhaha clatter his leg bones together and selected the next one for Mah.

Suddenly a group of women approached the Tukshead with angry looks, and they all tried to whisper to Shaloolaa. Keishlee twisted around to see but was ordered to continue her selections, while the Tukshead angrily whispered to each other and the crowd sent up disapproving calls.

Shaloolaa stood and called for silence. There were more whispers between the Tukshead and then Shaloolaa asked Keishlee to face her. "How many days do you plan on staying in our land?" Shaloolaa asked Keishlee, almost giving Shhaha a look.

Keishlee started to look over to Shhaha, but Scochaa whispered, "If you show weakness now, they will say you are not good enough to watch or choose. They will ask that we start again—with another."

"Two more days, only!" Keishlee shouted to the Tukshead

and then again out to the clearing.

A violent clatter came up against the mountain and echoed over the field. Shaloolaa called for silence and turned to Keishlee with annoyance on her face. "Then why have you selected all these young sisters? Do you plan to select again from them?" demanded Shaloolaa.

"No. No. But they should each have no more than eight apiece. I think no more than that."

"You were told that all those chosen would have to be seeded twice," huffed Shaloolaa.

"Yes."

"Do you torture your creatures, or these women?" spoke Shaloolaa with a smirk.

Keishlee did not understand what was wrong. She had yet to be touched by a man in this manner, but she listened to all the goings on between mated pairs. Of course they could do twice as many if put to it, but they were very young still and might not make enough healthy seed juice to go round. There was no sense in pushing their limits. "I can...I will select only five more...."

"Five more!" Shemaa howled.

"Two creatures for all these!" demanded Somaali.

"Yes. Yes. No more. I will not have them see more," argued Keishlee.

"More! They can not see these in two whole days!" huffed Shaloolaa.

Even Shhaha let out a little laugh. Keishlee chuckled to herself, then smiled at Shaloolaa, who was nearly in a rage.

Scochaa laughed and looked up at Keishlee, saying, "The man creatures of your people can do this?"

"No. No. They can do more. But Mah and Odrak are really only slaves. If left to it alone, in a day our men can handle more than this. This is all they want to do," Keishlee chuckled, while listening to her echo move over the clearing.

Once everyone understood what Keishlee had said, the noise subsided into grumbles of dismay. A nervous hum simmered out over the field when the Tukshead continued arguing in light whisper among themselves, but then Keishlee was ordered to continue.

She rushed through the remaining women until there were only eight left. Odrak now had ten, and Mah still had six. She had been saving this group for last, knowing that these were the ones who wanted to kill her and take Mah and Odrak for themselves.

"Charlaa," she called the woman out by name. "I give you time with Mah."

"I do not accept. I stand ready for the challenge of blood rite," shouted Charlaa, who then stepped aside and was joined by a guard at each side.

The crowd broke out in a fierce yell.

"I also want the challenge of blood rite! I want them both to remain here with women who are worthy," yelled Tarlane to even louder screams.

"Yes. The challenge of the blood," huffed Selma. She raised her arms in the air and sent the crowd into its loudest roar, shaking the mountains with their echoes.

The remaining five women were silent while the guards took the others away to prepare them for the fighting.

Keishlee called out the twins and looked them over with as much calm as she could muster. "I choose both of you, but I wish to fight you both as well," she smiled, hoping that separately she could force them to give her more respect than they did together last night. She hated the way they looked up their noses at her and wanted them broken. She suspected that they were close kin to either Scochaa or Shaloolaa, and so she also wanted their blood to mix.

The crowd went wild again and did not stop until after Keishlee rejected the next two. Only Tois was left.

"I challenge you. I will have the one with the age in his hair for myself."

"Let us fight then!" Keishlee screamed, unprepared for this. She was not sure how Mah would react to all these women. Seven or eight would probably be his limit for two days, but Tois was not going to be the seventh. "You shall be for Mah," Keishlee snapped at the woman seated beside her.

Suddenly Scochaa was by her side, and Somaali was standing in front calling order to the clearing. Guards came and took Tois away. Scochaa clapped her hands, and the sound echoed off the mountain. Women who were the friends of those chosen brought items up to lay at Keishlee's feet. Shaloolaa stood and explained, "These are gifts from the mothers of the selected ones. Some are gifts from those of us who are glad you've come to our land. You may select something you like from these, and then to honor my people, give what remains to the Sun Birds, who love all things beautiful. With these we shall beg the return of your man creatures."

"Scochaa has agreed to be your sister and to take guard of your body should you fall. She shall keep the challenge if you fail." Shaloolaa continued over the crowd's disapproval. "You, Keishlee, bring us new blood, good blood with great magic in its flow. Because we have seen the proof of this magic, we offer you that which is most powerful from our blood. We offer you the magic of our weapon, and the power of its might!" Shaloolaa shouted and silently ordered the guards to perform.

7 guards gathered in the cleared area of the field, and began a deadly dance with their weapons. Their movements were more like a march than a dance, but they twirled and spun around each other in such a way that Keishlee winced every time they moved. She was sure they would cut or kill each other, and yet they did not draw a single drop of blood. Other women threw them fruit or other objects, which the guards took turns cutting into neat pieces before they hit the ground. With frantic leaps and tumbled twirls, they ended in a pile that formed the Tukshead arch.

The impressive display made the clearing an echo-filled shutter of thunderous calls, hoots, and "scowling" shrieks. Tho Keishlee was pleasantly awed, she was confronted by a growing grief, because blood rite meant to the death, when the challenges would be met with this sharp and deadly weapon, which cut through tree branches with the same ease it cut through melons.

"Our sister protectors are the best in the land. None have more skill, and no one is as well loved by their people. Blessings to you all." Shaloolaa passed her arm over the crowd as they whooped and screamed their pleasure. Keishlee was entranced.

"We know that you are not familiar with our customs and are not prepared to make any offering of gifts to us in return." The crowd hissed at Keishlee and banged their bowls on the rocks under their mats, which woke Keishlee from her reverie. "So we shall now go to the Waters of Nelock and there prepare a weapon for you."

"Is this the moment you've been waiting for?" whispered Scochaa.

"Bring the sacrifice!" Shaloolaa commanded.

Three young male slaves were brought to the Tukshead.

Shaloolaa sent one of them away, and then ordered the two be taken to Keishlee. Since she was to gain the weapon, it was to be her choice as well for the sacrifice.

"Sacrifice" was not a word or idea in her language and Keishlee did not understand. Scochaa tried to explain it as an exchange of goods, but this did not help. Keishlee chose the slave she thought best to look at, and then followed the crying youth and the Tukshead around to the waterfall.

The wide spread of waters were in a heavy spin from the downpour off the mountain. Foam and spray were everywhere, along with the loud thump and splash of the glistening waters. Suddenly Keishlee hated being there, but was not unsure why. Everyone piled up against the waters' edge, many going down to the land bridge, so they could fill the banks of the far side.

For the first time Keishlee noticed a large reddish rock jutting out at one end of the wide pool.

Shaloolaa and other members of the Tukshead tested the water by taste, and when they were all in agreement, they motioned for the guards to take the slave. He cried loudly, and Keishlee's blood chilled at the sight of his tears. He looked up at her mournfully as a guard paused for him to give her the beaded string he wore around his neck.

The guards removed his loincloth and took him diving into the waters. Keishlee looked around nervously, searching for Shhaha, who was being forcefully guarded and held near a tree much further away. He tried to speak to them, but they would not listen. When he saw Keishlee looking at him, he stilled himself, but there was no mistaking the tears in his eyes.

Keishlee wanted to speak, but when she opened her mouth there were no words to express what she felt. She knew what was going to happen, and she knew she could not stop it. Part of her did not want to stop it. She wanted one of those weapons.

The guards tied the slave's hands to juts at the top of the rock's slated face, and swam in a rush out of the water. The slave kicked and screamed when the crowd began a loathsome murmured chant, which Keishlee refused to hear.

"Look! The Nelock comes!" someone shouted.

"A Nelock, a female of the deep!" shouted others, as rows of real Tukshead arches could be seen rising from the waters. The creature's head jumped out of the water, and it squealed horribly while focussed only on the jutting rock. The small slave twisted frantically to get away. The beast was huge and had a smell Keishlee could not endure. She would have fallen except that Scochaa was standing behind to hold her up, since the creature's nearness affected all women this way.

Keishlee angrily broke away and stumbled forward, closer to the bank. She glared at Nelock's long neck wriggling about and turned away from the huge body thrashing the waters. She saw that Shhaha no longer cried but looked at the beast with the eyes of the Keeper of the Blood. She hoped Ramaa was not in a rage from this sight and smell. He would not be as easily put off as Shhaha, but there were no other men near the waters. There was, however, the slave's feeder, who was easy to spot. She was the only silent woman in the crowd.

Keishlee was enthralled by the fact that none of these women were afraid of this beast. She did not see teeth, but knew she could fit into its long mouth easily.

The creature's screaming was a plea to stop the pain, and this brought Shhaha closer to the water's edge, and Keishlee's hands to her ears. The crowd knew this moment well and grew silent to watch more closely, but their silence was a noisy distraction to Keishlee, and a torment to Shhaha.

With blinding speed the creature whipped its neck and snapped its head towards the jutting rock. When next Keishlee looked, three spikes were embedded in the silent slave. One in his head, one in his chest and another in his groin. They were encrusted with black scales and had bloodied handles. They were the weapons, stuck firm and proven deadly.

The creature slowly stopped its screeching and looked about the crowd with large emerald eyes. They shouted "Nelock! Nelock!" over and over until the creature smiled at them, and Keishlee could see that it had no teeth.

The slave was motionless, and the Nelock no longer gave him any notice. Some of the women descended the rocks and dove into the water. Others stepped back, finally showing some fear of the creature. The swimmers untied the slave with great care, and hoistered the dead body off the rock. The creature watched their every move, suddenly looking fearful itself, as it lowered its body back into the waters, and the swimmers moved the bloody body to the shore.

The youngest ones in the crowd ran away from the banks as the body was brought over. Keishlee caught sight of the little dried-blood-colored feeder, who stood in the water and stared up at the creature. It caught sight of her and splashed water on everyone near, then slipped back into the depths. The feeder also dove into the water, and was not seen again until much later.

Women pulled Keishlee from her waking dreams and demanded she select one of the weapons. Her eyes would not let her see the slave. Instead she concentrated on the different sizes of the blades. She thought to select the largest one, but Scochaa stayed her hand. Keishlee choose the middle-size of the three and pulled it out from the dead slave's head. Its lightness amazed her and as she pulled it away, she could see and hear it cutting the skull bone with effortless ease.

Keishlee looked at the weapon in her hand and didn't even hear the women cheering her, and calling on the "Woman of Weapons" to "purify the new blade."

Scochaa pulled a small oil sack from within her robes, which Keishlee recognized as a neck node from a Great Mah. Someone handed her some netted moss, which she oiled until it dripped onto the weapon. The crusty scales fell away, revealing the slippery glitter of the weapon's pink, red and lemon-honey colors. The blade came alive and its age disappeared.

Scochaa took the weapon from Keishlee and vigorously rubbed the oil onto its sides to show her how it was done. She handed it back and ordered two women to remove the remaining weapons, while Keishlee oiled the weapon until it gave off sparks of light. She did not even notice the dead slave's renewed bleeding at her feet. Her eyes would not leave the weapon, nor the reflection of herself she saw there.

"Tuk Blade!" Scochaa shouted, holding Keishlee's weapon arm in the air. "Keishlee is now our sister. She has all our respect!" Scochaa yelled and was joined by the others shouting, "Keishlee! Keishlee!"

3

Kemmenar Sloam and Jersi Claukens speaking to friends at a party given by pledges to the Pagangenearch: Slavery was a African institution, a major form of kinship, wealth and power. All seeds sowed, and since what goes around comes back around, their descendants received what their forebears left them—slavery. Europeans drastically changed the industry and the evidence of their influence is evident everywhere. Truly black people are rarely seen any more. African descendants are mostly mud- or nut-colored, or baby shit brown, and getting lighter every generation. When was the last time you saw anyone who was truly blue-black, or even cold-black or jet?

"From Heaven and Hell Who All Must Pay"

"We should visit their kin another time." moaned Odrak, tired of begging Mah and the bird called Fresh-Rain. "We will miss the seeding feast." He looked down at the two baskets the birds had nearly finished. Large, fur-covered nests, with leather straps inside the cups for their legs and arms, and wing and leg hooks at the tops and bottoms for the birds.

"I do not want to go either, Odrak," Mah tried again to explain. He sat Odrak on the ground next to him and said, "The elders insist. You heard them talking. This is a special occasion for them. We cannot refuse."

"What if something happens to you, and I cannot wake you? What if something happens to both of us?"

The bird Fresh-Rain chirped out a mellow song and then ran his feathers through Odrak's long bushy hair. Mah smiled up at the bird and helped him tie a knot onto the basket. He stepped over to Odrak, who was sullen and disappointed with the things he had seen in this bird citadel, and said, "They are not human flesh eaters, Odrak. The elders swear this has been the way for countless generations. They eat those long, water snakes from the Red River below, and they sometimes eat the leaves from the purple nut bush. Nothing more. What is it you fear? They promised to look after us, and to bring us back to our people." Mah was suddenly unsure if this was the Odrak he knew.

As a blood apprentice, Odrak learned that one often became like the thing one ate, because of having to live like it in order to be near it. These birds he loved ate a creature that was bigger than a man, and more deadly than any creature he knew. It had a horrible smell and could kill with just a touch of its head. It had long poisonous teeth that did not quite fit into its mouth, and the birds ate or used every piece of this creature, from the prized, delicate glands of its mouth and head, to the soft bones they ground into puddings or healing paste.

Odrak did not trust them anymore. He could no longer stand the sight of them, and their nearness to Mah kept him on edge. For the first time in his life, he doubted the visions from his youth, which led to his being selected as an apprentice, and he feared that Mah would be an evil to his clan, instead of the great blood keeper he had seen in his dreams. But looking deep into Mah's eyes, he felt a shame that almost broke his heart. He shook the doubts loose and cursed the thoughts for having come.

Mah worried for Odrak. The older birds could sense feelings and none dared to touch him with Odrak looking on. They all spoke to him from a short distance away, except for Fresh-Rain, who persisted in trying to be near them both.

"Fresh-Rain says you hate the Great Mahs, Odrak. Say this is not so. Tell him this is not your heart."

"They eat the flesh of a beast," Odrak replied flatly.

"It gives them great power. It is a creature of plenty in the waters that surround us. No other creature can go near them, and no other creature may make use of them. Shhaha would say this is as it should be. Does not the Great Mother [*earth*] need us to eat in the end? Listen to them. Do you not see how they are with us? How they have always been."

"And the young ones who lied to us?"

"They have made promises of bloods never to do that again. The elders have answered us in truth about everything, and they treat us well. I trust them."

"They wish to keep you! Like all who meet you. Like those feeders below with their hard ways."

"If that were so, would they have brought you here as well? They know we are as one."

"They say this place they take us is many seasons away.

They say it is a land of great beasts."

"They said it used to be, and for them it is only a short journey. Not even half a morning's travel. We have a promise of blood for our safety. Besides, I wish to know all I can about them. I feel at peace with them Odrak, and this place is so familiar to me."

Odrak looked up at a bird who came over to listen to their words. It lowered itself so that Odrak could look into its eyes, while an older bird placed a string of long sharp teeth around Mah's neck.

"The Great Mahs are our friends, and we shall be friends with them always," Odrak said, now staring at the teeth of the water snake hanging around Mah's neck. Such a gift would be greatly prized among his people or among any people who knew of this creature's strength. It was a gift which Odrak could not disrespect. Another bird placed a necklace of the fangs around his neck, then Odrak looked over to Fresh-Rain and up at the others and sang in their tongue, "I am honored by your gift. I shall treasure it always, and I am ashamed for having shown you an ugly face."

Mah wanted to rub heads with him but before he could reach out, other birds surrounded them, stroking feather tips over their bodies, and combing their loose hair with the tiny fighter claws of their wings. All of them were singing at once.

"They want us to bathe in the lake of 'wing oil'. They say it will protect us from the hard and cold air as they fly," Mah laughed at the jealous look on Odrak's face.

My-Name came back and led them to an upper cavern where the lake of oil had been made. Many birds were already dipping themselves into the small lake, or standing around its bank to let the excess drip away. The tiny oil sacks that grew along the edges of their wings and around their necks were in great mounds everywhere.

From a lower cavern they could hear the singing lessons of the younger birds, and all the walls were decorated with a vast and varied collection of dried flowers and skins, skulls and colored stones, and burial ready bones, the likes of which Mah and Odrak only knew of from very ancient tales.

Mah got a fright at seeing these things at first. He too had wondered if they ate such creatures. But the elders had clawed themselves to bleeding to prove how against this they were. They claimed to have saved many life forms during the "dust days."

They said they prized humans because they were stronger than nature, and managed a happy life even when nature set out to destroy them. They wanted humans to survive, saying, "They were the last of life to form, and therefore completed the cycle of life."

They knew of the seven races of humans, descended from the Seven Sisters. They did not know of the Seven Sisters, but agreed that all humans were blood relations, and that a human was first seen by them in the land they called Gihon. They told them the tribes were separated during the time of ice, and that some wandered still, but that each race had survived. Mah and Odrak were impressed by their wisdom.

The apprentices removed their cloth wraps and entered the lake of oil, and one of the elders hopped over to warn them that the lake was very deep and not to venture far.

They let the oil wash over them and rubbed it into their skin, exhilarated by the way it brightened and cleaned them of their seasons of living in dirt. Odrak mentioned that he could feel it healing old cuts and bruises, and Mah noticed that along with no smell or color, it had no taste.

The oil was loosening Mah's hair, and the heavy knots he tied every rainy season to count his age were falling loose down his face. Pepper-Grass and his future mate, Black-Rock, were just coming out of the deeper oil, and on seeing this, began to peck the knots loose. Odrak went into a rage and hit the birds, knocking them away from Mah until he saw all the hair bush out around Mah's head and fall down his back. Pepper-Grass flung a wing full of oil at Odrak, and he went under from the weight of it.

An adult struck the two young birds and ordered them out of the lake. She quickly reached into the oil with one foot and pulled Odrak out, then shook him free of the pouring oil. When the elder bird put him down on the bank, Odrak sat still looking at Mah, and at all the hair bushing out around his head, covering his arms and shoulders.

"They only wanted to count my seasons," Mah grumbled, angry with Odrak for starting a fuss.

"Look at yourself. See your reflection in the oil, Mah," was all Odrak could say.

Mah did so, and was surprised at the amount of hair hanging down from his head.

Odrak went back into the lake and undid all Mah's

remaining hair knots. He knew the count as well as his own—Mah had 10 and 5 and he, 10 and 7. They could be reknotted later, but now he wanted to see Mah with his hair running down his back.

Odrak combed Mah's hair with his fingers and watched as it stretched down past his arms, soft and slick from the oil. He unknotted the old bones, root charms, and other keepsakes from the hair. Such mementos were kept by all his people and buried within their bush, but Odrak cared less for these than he did for the new sight of Mah.

Odrak washed Mah's head down to the scalp and Mah did the same for him, while chanting the call for peace, which bounced off the walls of the cavern, making the young birds dance.

Soon they were dipping and dunking each other into the oil, playing with all the new hair. Odrak found the oil a new sensation, and rubbing Mah's skin with it aroused his hunger for him. He turned Mah around to avoid looking into his eyes, but Mah reached behind and pulled him close, allowing Odrak to slip up between his legs. Odrak flung his arms around Mah's chest to nestle his face in the free flowing hair, and bit him gently on the shoulder and up around his neck. Mah shuddered as the heavy oil made every move a new sensation.

They remembered the birds in the cave, and then recalled the duty that awaited them with the feeders below. With regret, Odrak stopped tasting his enjoyment, and forced himself to recall some terrible tale. They waited for him to soften and then Mah pulled away. They rubbed themselves down again, and walked out of the lake not looking at each other.

An elder was trying to talk to them, but they did not hear as they watched Night-Sky, My-Name's feeder, come to the lake with her mate, whose name Mah had yet to translate. She told them they were now even more pleasing to the eye, and would be a great sight for their kin to see.

Lizard-Eyes and some friends brought them thick hairless skins to lay upon. Odrak and Mah spread them out and laid close, but not touching, for fear of starting something neither would be able to stop a second time. The elder stayed with them while they napped. When they awoke he asked them to oil their hair again, since they had no body fur more oil would be needed for the flight, when the cold and wind would dry them to the bone.

After they put on the new brilliantly colored loincloths given them by the birds, they returned to the birds who had finished the baskets they would ride in. An adult went to pick Mah up to place him inside, but Odrak begged him off, saying, "I will place Mah in the basket. You need only check him when I am done."

Once Mah had both arms and legs in the leather ties, a bird Odrak did not know quickly pulled on the tie ends and fastened them to the bottom edge of the basket. The bird bent down and slipped his wing hands into the top holders, then stood up and the basket fell into place on his chest. Mah was gone, and Odrak could not tell the basket apart from the bird.

Odrak ran over to check while the bird slipped each foot into bottom straps. Other birds were trying to get Odrak into his basket, but he refused until he had finished checking to make sure Mah was all right. "Can you hear me? Can you feel my breath through the air nets?" he asked, truly wary of this adventure.

Mah assured him that he was fine, and Odrak thanked the birds for making such a splendid thing. When he saw the giant birds moving towards the exit level, he realized that Shhaha would enjoy this experience more than he or Mah. These birds were more than human and did many things one could learn from. He stood for a moment and earmarked himself with the memory of the basket making, then rushed to his basket and the birds who waited to tie him in.

In the air he could see the ground below through the net between his feet. He could feel the air rushing over him, sliding off him because of the oil. Soon everything was moving too fast for him to see, and he could feel a pressure over his body, forcing him against the bird and holding him fast. Odrak felt like he would melt into the bird, as he listened to its heart begin to quicken. Heat from the bird's body warmed him, as a bitter cold tried to get at his back. He felt dreamy but unafraid, and hoped that Mah felt the same. Watching light flash by the side air nets, he wondered if this is what it would be like to ride upon the clouds. Then the pressure over him grew greater, while a low buzz rang inside his head and ears, putting him to sleep as the bird began to reach its top speed.

The Tukshead argued with Keishlee for quite a while before they would leave her decision alone. She had changed her mind about the dark, dried-blood-colored feeder, who she figured had something to do with the enormous water creature. Her name was Esa, and Keishlee no longer wanted their blood to mix. When Shhaha came over and heard the fuss, he quickly spoke his mind and none of the guards could stop him. Keishlee still did not approve of Esa, but would not go against Shhaha, and finally agreed to give the woman to Mah. But before Esa could leave to join the selected ones, Keishlee pulled the little woman close and whispered in her ear, "If I live and find that you have disrespected him in any way, I will end your days of swimming with Nelock."

The woman wanted to say something, but the look on Keishlee's face made her hold her waters tighter. She was glad to flee when Shaloolaa ordered the challenges to begin.

Keishlee took on Femaa first. They both wore only the snake leather wrappings and the bladder skin girdles. This was not a blood rite fight, and so neither had weapons. Femaa was fast and had a good slap, but Keishlee finished her with matching blows to the head and leg. They had to carry her off the field, to shouts and hoots from the crowd sitting in a semicircle around them.

Demaa took a bit longer. She managed to sidestep every backhand or sidekick Keishlee tried. Keishlee took a few punches to the face and stomach before she tripped her up. Once she was on top of Demaa there was really no more to the fight. Keishlee had her unconscious by the second blow, drew blood on the third, and the fight was stopped.

When Tois came to the field, Scochaa brought Keishlee her shiny new weapon. The sun was going down but the weapon twinkled in the light of the fires being lit. Keishlee had been given some practice time with it, and she and Scochaa fought just long enough to give her a better feel of it. This short training would be no match for the seasoned experience of any Tuk woman, but here was the test of her blood.

The weapons would lay apart on the ground between them. If Keishlee could stop her from getting to it first, she might have a better chance. Scochaa and Somaali each held a leg between them, and then pulled it back for the fight to begin.

Keishlee tried to smack Tois in the face with one hand, in the hopes of shocking her into a bend so that she could smack her with the other, but Tois bolted and was on top of her before Keishlee knew what hit her. Tois had planned it just right, and was in arm's reach of her darker weapon. Desperate for her life, Keishlee grabbed Tois by the throat and brought her down on the other side. They tumbled for a while, Tois mercilessly clawing

Keishlee's arm, but this blood was not enough to stop the fight. Keishlee flew into a rage and got on top, pounding Tois about the face. Tois knocked her off with a knee to her side, scrambling to get close to the weapons. The crowd screamed and yelled for blood. A few threw small pebbles, which Scochaa had told Keishlee would happen. Keishlee leaped on Tois's back, but Tois was stronger than Keishlee had imagined, and got to her feet with Keishlee still attached. Keishlee slipped down, but was tripped up, and now Tois was slapping her face with back and forward hands. Keishlee was sorry all her hair was not tied back tightly like these women. The age knots gave Tois a sturdy grip to pound Keishlee into the dirt. Tois slipped out of Keishlee's grip and dragged her across the ground towards the weapons. Keishlee heard her hair rip as she caught hold to Tois' leg and brought her down on top of her. Tois reached for the weapon and got it, but Keishlee managed to kick her in the face and jump over the swinging blade to roll close to her own. Keishlee got the weapon in hand just in time to block a chop to her neck as she sat there on the ground. She saw the wild look go into Tois' face, and then she felt the fragility, knowing without being told that the younger weapon could destroy the older one. She braced herself as Tois jumped back and then came in swinging. Keishlee crawled and rolled until she could leap up from the ground. Suddenly, Tois was a black eagle coming for the kill. Keishlee fought to remember Odrak's catlike moves, and in an attempt to slice Tois' throat, she hit and cut Tois's blade hand. The shock gave Keishlee enough time to jab the weapon into Tois' lower rib. As she watched Tois fall to the ground, more in shock than pain, all Keishlee could think about was the young slave who had died for her to have this weapon. In one quick sideswipe, Keishlee cut off the tips of both feeder bags, along with some of Tois's face. The body fell and blood splashed up over her. She had never killed a human before, but she knew it would be too easy to do so again. There was a new smell in the air that filled her with pride. It was her own, and she loved it.

Scochaa rushed over and insisted Keishlee be given the rest period, while both Selma and Tarlane argued with her over the killing. Tois had only asked for seeding and so the fight should have been stopped after the serious hand wound.

Scochaa ordered them away, because it was Keishlee's right to simply wound or kill any of her challengers. After all, they had challenged her and not she them. Keishlee was exhilarated and wanted the challenges to continue. She stood her ground and argued with Tarlane, who spit at her. Scochaa had to drag Keishlee to one side of the field in order to stop the blows that started between them.

"The next two are deadly. You will appreciate the little rest you get," Scochaa smiled at her. "Take care with Selma. She fights with blade in either hand. She is stronger than you, so do not let her grip you or you will be lost. You have only two advantages with her, the length of your arms and legs. Use them well."

Keishlee placed Scochaa's palm on her forehead and thanked her for "coming out human," a high blessing from one woman to another. Two women brought her drinks, one of wine and the other of sweet water. When the water bladder hit her mouth, she was surprised at the extent of her thirst. She did not drink this much when they came down from the escarpment. The bladder was large but still she wanted more. She could actually feel the water going to parts of her body she never thought needed it. Scochaa only allowed her a small sip of the wine, which refreshed her more than the water, and quickly numbed the pain she felt trying to take over her body.

A guard came over and handed Keishlee Tois' weapon and laid her own down beside her. She explained that the weapon now belonged to her, as did Tois's hut and a time with any one of the creatures from the men's hut.

Women started walking around her throwing small rocks or flower petals. Scochaa started to tell her what this meant, but Keishlee stopped her, asking only for the proper reply. She licked the blood of her wounds for the gift of the rocks and threw the rocks at the women who had rained petals on her. She could see women doing the same to Tarlane and Selma, who sat in their separate camps taking advice from the different women around them.

One of the medicine women came over and put salves on Keishlee's wounds and listened to her heart. She laughed and brushed Keishlee off as she left with the women taking away Tois' body parts.

Quietly, Keishlee began the chant of peace while thinking about her keeper. He had taught her the Tall Walker killing kick, and she smiled at the memory of him saying that it was her duty to learn it as a member of their clan. This kept them strong in the face of a horror coming. It had taken her a long time to learn since she did not care about such things, but in the end he told her she did it better than many men. Later, it kept other women from wanting to fight her over some small thing. She hoped now she would get the chance to use it.

"It was good you killed Tois, Keishlee. She would not have settled for the sight of your blood. You did the right thing," spoke Scochaa.

Keishlee did not reply but she had sensed it was well done. More importantly, she knew killing a real enemy would please these people, and prove herself worthy to them. She looked over at Selma and Tarlane and found no hesitation inside herself. Especially with Tarlane, whose blood she wanted more than all the others. Something about the way the woman looked at her, those unyielding, malignant glares made Keishlee hate this woman, and whenever she was near, Keishlee remembered a woman who dared to throw waste water into her feeder's face. The memory came whenever Tarlane was near, and tears swelled her eyes as she heard her feeder's call.

When the time came, and Selma was standing before her on the sticky field, Keishlee could sense the power of this woman filling the distance between them. The signal was given and Keishlee felt the woman's strength coming for her. She jumped back in time to throw the woman off and kicked her square in the face. This did not bother Selma at all. She took hold to Keishlee's leg on the back stroke, and flipped her up in the air. Keishlee rolled away, thinking Selma would go for her weapon, but was kicked again across the field. As Selma came to stomp her, Keishlee whirled around and knocked Selma flat on her back, but Keishlee did not want to be that close; she needed time to shake the new pains from her body. Selma took her time getting up. She had no fear of Keishlee running to her weapon. She marched over and Keishlee kicked her leg and almost sent her down. Keishlee went to slap her face when the woman leaped and grabbed Keishlee by the throat, slamming her to the ground. Selma was slow and single minded and pounded on Keishlee with delight. Keishlee could hardly breathe, but she felt the blood drip from her nose and mouth and snatched herself up into a protective knot. She managed to kick Selma in the face a couple of times with the heel of her foot. She broke loose and crawled away to catch her breath, but there was no time. Selma was middle-height, stocky and broad-chested with huge, square shoulders. She stomped Keishlee in the gut and what little air she had was gone. Keishlee bolted and was on her knees, her body taking over, back kicking Selma in the leg. Selma cursed and screamed, but even with her now fractured leg, she limped toward Keishlee, who was still on her knees catching her breath. Keishlee resisted the nearness and her own desperation to go for her weapon. Instead she sidestepped Selma, who fell and got a knee in the face. Selma cursed and swore to feed Keishlee's guts to some creature. Selma forgot her pain and charged. Keishlee saw a rhinoess coming but could not think of any creature to beat it. She ran backwards, and sidestepped, but still got caught by her hair from behind. Keishlee elbowed until Selma let go and did not stop back kicking until Selma was out of reach. Keishlee turned and almost ran into one of the women carrying torches to light the field. She doubled back and hoped she had gotten the count right. Then after a short run forward, Selma made her leap and Keishlee braced herself and kicked. She heard the jaw crack and the collar bones snap and knew she had gotten it just right. The crowd screamed, but it was not the distasteful roar of blood she heard after killing Tois. She limped tiredly over to her weapon, retrieved it and plunged it into Selma's chest. The ease of it woke her up, and she turned directly into Tarlane's face, who was being held back by two guards standing near enough to touch.

Scochaa was by her side, almost holding her up, but Keishlee could not take her eyes off Tarlane. Inside her head voices screamed at her to kill this woman, which suddenly made Keishlee ashamed. She pulled away from Scochaa and the other women so that their blood lust would leave her.

The guards ordered Tarlane to run around the field during Keishlee's rest period, to help even the fight.

"Those who would cut you later in the dark will not think of it now. Selma was old, but she was a killer. She was fighting for many women here," Scochaa grinned, truly pleased. "I have wanted to see that since our time in the cave. I started that fight just to see it. I knew it was there, and that it was deadly!" whispered Scochaa.

"I am thankful to have been kept, and grateful to my feeder for choosing my keeper," Keishlee managed to drag out the words. All she wanted was time to lay still and breathe.

"What is that—a keeper?" asked Scochaa.

Keishlee tried to explain but Scochaa knew none of the words. There were no such ideas to her people, since the slaves belonged to all the women, and only the female slaves were really kept.

In the time Keishlee had, all she could think about was her keeper, Pison. She had never thanked him for the lessons or the time he took to train her. Other young slaves brought their keepers ibex horns that could be found near the green mountains, but not Keishlee. She had ignored the gift giving and now felt loathing for her selfishness. He had saved her life just now, and she made another promise to herself, that when she returned she would make the journey to the clan of the Waterhorse, and bring him the horns from a solid brown or white ibex, even if she had to kill it herself. She would beg his forgiveness, and if he were still without a mate, she would find a suitable one for him.

She stopped caring for anyone after her feeder died, but now she regretted it. She almost cried thinking of how distant and uncaring she had been to her keeper, when he too was dying of grief. Shhaha had to send him away in order to save him, and she had not even cared enough to dance for him at his leaving. She, one of the best dancers in the clan, almost as good as a man, they said. She had to fight four women who had wanted him, for this insult to him. Still, he loved her, and had many visitors ask after her when they came. She would make it up to him once she returned.

Keishlee got a good long rest. They hardly gave her any water this time, but she had her fill of wine, which she needed to help her with the pain.

Scochaa warned her that Tarlane was next in line to be the woman of weapons. She had fast legs but only used her upper body in a fight. Tarlane would go for her weapon right away. The best chance Keishlee had was to stop her from reaching it, or to get hers first, and do that trick she had used to cut Tois' hand.

Keishlee laughed, remembering that move had been an accident. She shrugged it off when Scochaa wanted to know what was on her mind, but told her she would do her best.

"You have another advantage," Scochaa smiled. "Tarlane knows she is better. That can often make one rush to the end when the middle is where they need to be."

Scochaa and two others squeezed her muscles and stretched her arms and legs. They made her run just a bit to make sure she had the energy for a good fight, and then walked her to a freshly cleared field.

Tarlane came over and pushed Scochaa aside, then called out over the noisy regrouping field. "Sisters! Sisters!! You've all wanted to know about the three words spoken from the severed head. Even now you come to me and ask, as if my death should come and the knowledge die with me. Fools!!!" she screamed, "I have told some bits and pieces, and others less. I will tell it all now because I want this woman to know. Aey, Aaah! The three words were a name, remember sisters. Well, that name was KEISHLEE! The head of the dead creature said KEISHLEE! He called for you! Now come, so I can send you to him!!!"

Keishlee pulled Scochaa to her and asked, "What does she mean?"

Tarlane hit Keishlee in the chest and put her out of arms's reach. "A giant beast I killed, a moon before tonight. A 'Water-horse' man creature, he said!" Tarlane shouted. "From your land, I think. He even had the look of you. I wear his bones, see," she snarled, and shoved an arm toward Keishlee that was strung with human teeth.

Suddenly the torches were blinding and the sound of the crowd, deafening. Keishlee remembered falling and what Shhaha had said. Why had she doubted? Shhaha was never wrong. He knew the blood signs better than anyone. That is why Pison had stayed on her mind when confronted with this woman. That is why they hated each other from the first.

Keishlee back-smacked her but was stopped by Somaali, who made them stand their places for the starting signal.

"I did not know," Scochaa turned to her as she positioned herself for the signal. "No one here could have known."

Keishlee almost spit at Scochaa. She no longer felt tired or pained. Her vision was clear, even to the darkened corners of the field, and all she could see was this woman dead before her.

The signal was given and Keishlee hit Tarlane so hard she knocked the woman off balance. She snatched up her weapon and started zinging the air, throwing flashes of light into the field. The crowd backed away as the torch bearers ran out of reach of the swinging weapon. Tarlane was sliding around in the dirt, avoiding the weapon with great skill. She managed a jump flip and a back hand that knocked Keishlee's weapon away. But before she could retrieve her own, Keishlee was on top of her, ripping out mounds of hair and pounding Tarlane into the dirt. Tarlane twisted and had a hand full of Keishlee's hair by the roots. She flipped Keishlee on the ground twice, stomped her in the gut several times, then kicked her in the face. Keishlee tripped her and clawed and managed to get Tarlane's face. She could taste the blood as it jumped up on her. She stood and kicked her in the jaw but the kick was not well placed. Tarlane back flipped but reversed herself to elbow Keishlee's stomach. Keishlee spit blood and fell to her knees. Tarlane kicked her in the chest and shoulder, knocking her to the ground, and then went for her weapon.

Keishlee crawled to get hers but was stopped by a swift kick to the side and a slice on her arm. Another swing almost got her in the face, but Tarlane stopped to kick a torch bearer away, slicing her face to warn off the others. Keishlee was cut across her back as she ran. She tumbled and twisted around, with weapon in hand, just in time to stop the onslaught of Tarlane's thrashes. Keishlee held her place and got to her feet, after slicing Tarlane across both legs. Keishlee rolled across the dirt and came running and swinging toward the limping Tarlane. Their blades struck together so hard their echoes drowned out the other women's screams. Keishlee felt the weapons chip and then suddenly, the blades locked. The crowd was roaring full force now, even the men screamed for blood. Keishlee slid around and kicked Tarlane up and down the field, with the point of her weapon almost pushed into Tarlane's face. Keishlee used all her strength to push the locked weapons over and around Tarlane's head, then jumped up and turned around to back kick Tarlane in the face. While flying in the air, the women cheered her now that they knew what a Tall Walker was. It was a blow that would have killed Tarlane had she been there, but she had gotten up and was yelling for someone to throw her a weapon. Keishlee punched her in the face, the force of which brought Keishlee down on top of her. Crazed, Tarlane tried to take a bite out of her cheek and Keishlee clawed and gouged at her eyes. Tarlane managed to push her off but Keishlee kicked her in the side and chest. Keishlee gave herself distance to make her killer kick, but someone had thrown a weapon onto the field and this gave her pause. She heard Scochaa scream something and looked over just in time to catch the flying blade. Tarlane was picking her weapon off the ground when Keishlee made the first hack at her neck. It came off with a second stroke, and her body took three steps before it fell to the ground, convulsing, the hand still trying to find the weapon.

Tarlane's head rolled away and Keishlee watched her body

die. When the false strength left her, Keishlee fell to the ground with her weapon in hand.

▼▼▼▼▼

Mah was already out of his basket when they sat Odrak down. They were on a terrace between two high mountain peaks. It only took Odrak a little while to come around. Mah snatched him up and held him close, feeling him all over to make sure he was all right. After he climbed out of the basket, Mah took him to the edge of the terrace wall to look at the landscape far below.

"Do these birds ever walk the land?" asked Odrak, upon seeing the distance they were from the ground.

"No. Almost never. They say it is harder then to get into the sky. As long as they stay in the air, they can forge their own currents."

Odrak did not understand and changed the subject, saying, "You cannot see any land here. Nothing but dense jungle."

Mah took him to the other side of the cliffs where they could look down upon earth, and flocks of land birds gathered on the other side of a deep stream. They could see clearly in the light of late day, which had been sunset when they left.

"Let us visit with their kin and get this over with," huffed Odrak, looking for the entrance to the mountain.

"Prepare yourself, Odrak. I hope you are very hungry."

Inside the mountain citadel, they found My-Name and Fresh-Rain waiting for them. Larger, older birds lined the entrance, and touched them with their wings or gently clawed through their hair as they were led deeper into the cave. After a short while Mah could not walk any more and felt like all his strength had left him; his bones felt stringy and bending to break. One of the older birds was there to catch him as he fell into the crook of his wing. Odrak was about to complain, but he too could no longer stand and fell into the wing of another bird.

Both were sleeping hard by the time they were taken to quarters reserved for the very young birds. Young birds were still arriving, followed by older birds who had watched over their flight. This cavern held many huge resting pallets, made of beautiful large feathers. Each pallet was a different color, with feathers sewn onto mounds of tiny twigs and fresh straw. Each mound was trimmed with matching colored gems, held in place by a thick black tar, making the pallets sparkle in the reflected light off the gray-white walls of the cave.

They laid Odrak and Mah in separate pallets next to other sleeping birds, but Odrak stirred and Fresh-Rain moved him in with Mah. No human except these would know, and they were too fast asleep to hear, but Fresh-Rain and other birds were laughing and making jokes about their time spent with the humans, while My-Name made introductions to the others. A parade of birds passed by to see and touch them, or feel their hair. So much hair it covered both their upper bodies, and they looked like two small black trees.

Lizard-Eyes uncovered their faces for the others to see. Pepper-Grass cried that he wished to be human and to have the pleasures these two knew. He, like all the young birds, could not mate or hunt for many seasons yet, and he was already older than Odrak. What was needed would not be fully grown for some time yet. He teased his nest companions because they were only black on their faces, or around their eyes, and they had no long hair to oil.

Night-Sky carefully removed their loin cloths. He punctured some of the nodes under his neck with his beak, and let the oil drip down on them. My-Name smoothed it over their dust-dry bodies, singing to the others about Mah's first song.

The oil brought back their blue black hues, and the birds chirped joyfully to see them sparkle like the jewels surrounding the pallet. They were delighted to see creatures who were as beautiful as night, shining and glittering as they lay on the white feathered pallets like black stars in a bright sky.

Some of the smallest birds pulled their pallets closer and laid down to sleep near them. Adult birds paraded by to view them, and laid down items they had made for them to wear. Items made from their very precious feathers, which were never allowed to fall to the ground. Brilliantly colored feathers that brought out all the other birds to see, as they were fashioned into matching necklaces and two cloaks, collared with white fur and trimmed with the teeth of the water snake.

Nuts, fruits, edible leaves, and roots were gathered in baskets and placed around them. Elders had to stop younger birds from adding to the piles. There was already more here than any 10 humans could eat in a full turn of days.

Regrets rang out when one set of elders told the others that they had to be returned at sunrise. Some insisted they be kept longer, until they were told about the promise given to Odrak. The parade began again, as those who had seen wanted a second look, since there would be no time for them to be known by all.

The Great Mahs considered themselves overseers for the world they knew was round and mostly made of water. They had tried to speak to humans, or show them where they lived since they were first spotted walking upright across the land. But all of them had died when brought to one of their citadels. These two were a great pleasure to see, and hearing that they could sing their songs had most of the birds sitting around to await their awakening, to hear this for themselves.

The idea of humans as intelligent as themselves gave them peace of mind. They hoped these creatures would grow to be like them, and help to nurse the planet back to good health, which only they knew was sick at the time. A planet they had seen grow sick and nearly die twice, because nature was a wild and beastly thing, whose only saving grace was that she forced the stronger to survive, thereby growing stronger with what remained. The Great Mahs took care of all forms of life, and knew that these humans, who were gentle creatures, would do the same, and then feed themselves back to the planet when they died, since they could not. Yes, the idea of humans living on the land who thought as they did was a blessing to them, and to these two they would show their gratitude.

▼▼▼▼▼

Keishlee awoke to find the moonlight shining from behind the mountains. Scochaa sat by her side along with some of her force. The feast clearing was quiet and empty.

"How do you feel?" Scochaa asked, glad to see Keishlee's eyes open at last.

"Only Charlaa is left, right? I will continue the challenge," replied Keishlee.

"Not tonight," spoke Scochaa in a low voice.

"But we can stay no longer than two more days and...."

"It is well," Scochaa averted her eyes but continued, "It can be done after your watches have been returned. Listen, the clearing is empty. No one argued against this delay, and," she paused, "Charlaa was the first to suggest it." Scochaa was happy to impress this upon her.

"Really. She wants fresh blood is all," said Keishlee.

"Would you have the easy kill?" demanded another woman.

Keishlee sat up, pulling the aches from her back into her head. She stretched her legs to keep the muscles from tightening and looked around for the woman who spoke.

"You have killed three this night. No one would want more than that. All in a single night, and from the same sister," spoke Esa. "The women are filled with respect for you, having thought you might be an easy kill."

"Our sisters are festive tonight and wish a topping to their thrills," spoke another woman. "Even the young ones seek a blood rite test tonight. They hope to prove their worth—to you."

"Yes. Even the ancient one cheers you," spoke another. "She crawls around and retells every move you made."

"Yes, truth! Your kills were hard won," blurted a woman. "At moonrise they formed a raiding party. Tonight our blood is hot enough to destroy our enemy, utterly," she cursed.

"The women of our village await words from you," Scochaa said, turning serious. "Only if you have the strength, and would raid with us, we will ride this night. If you can ride and take the lead, all will follow your orders this night."

Keishlee looked at all the faces about her and found friendship there. This moment gave her such pleasure, because for once she wanted the friendship of someone. But she could not smile or touch them with comfort. Her heart ached, and she began to cry over the memory and lost of her keeper Pison, whose seed gave her life, and whose help had saved it.

Some of the women understood and turned away to let her grieve in peace. Scochaa held her close for a little while.

"All this is no matter," Keishlee sniffed and broke away. She was angry again, and the blood lust renewed itself. She looked out to the field in the hopes of seeing Tarlane's body. She remembered the kill clearly, and raged within herself for not having had the strength to hack the body to bits.

"I will gladly raid with you," Keishlee produced a smile that was chilling in its effect. Scochaa signaled two women who ran off. Keishlee then asked, "Who is Tarlane's feeder?"

Once they understood, Scochaa and the others laughed, and Scochaa said, "Tarlane fed no one but herself. Her mother," which was a word Keishlee knew, but was reserved for someone sacred, "...was Sarai, who was killed in a raid. Her mother is Zorai, blood sister to Saamyli."

With the hope gone of killing Tarlane again through her mother, Keishlee said, "Who is your mother, Scochaa?" pronouncing the word with the reverence she had been taught.

There was a rush of words from the women and one of them rushed to Scochaa's side. She kissed Scochaa's cheek, a thing Keishlee had never seen before, and it startled her; making her to slip a little away.

"You have my blood in trust," spoke the woman, kissing Scochaa's cheek again.

Others touched or kissed Scochaa and repeated the words. Scochaa had said nothing to bring favor upon herself, which Keishlee did not understand until she found out that Shaloolaa was her mother. She gripped Scochaa about the shoulders and held her tight. Keishlee had acquired a great respect for Shaloolaa, and now loved this woman who had been born of Shaloolaa's blood. She rubbed their heads together and found her mouth watering to try this kiss.

Scochaa gently pushed her off, saying, "You will fight Charlaa next, and then you will no longer love me, as I will no longer love you," she hissed and marched off towards the village.

The other women took Keishlee's hands and tried to comfort her, but Keishlee was shocked and stunned to shame. The women led her from the field, following Scochaa back to the village. All Keishlee could think about was how she could breach this break coming between her and the first friend she had ever made in life.

The village was a tumult of excitement and good cheer. They greeted Scochaa and the others as "the women with Keishlee!" The guards rushed forward, each pushing Scochaa about on purpose. They brought one knee to the ground before Keishlee and rolled praises off their tongues. They praised her form, her beauty, her stature, her strength and might, the blood of the women of her village, the strength of her hair, her sense of timing, her special kick, and took special effort to praise even higher her mother's blood.

Tears were in her eyes as Shaloolaa and the rest of the Tukshead approached. They rode short, wide bush horses and were already armed for the raid. Other women on bush horses rode in behind, yelling curses to their enemies and blessings to the blood of Keishlee. They helped her mount a horse and showed her the hair-ropes to control its movements. She pushed them away and wrapped her arms around the creature's neck and spoke to it with sounds she knew the horse would understand. She clenched the free hair of its mane and received a weapon. She knew it was her own when they were all raised to the sky and only hers shone bright. Here she found a new exhilaration.

Shaloolaa called silence to the noisy gathering, as young sisters, slaves and old women offered Keishlee leaves of food, bowls of wine and drink, which she ate and drank with lust.

"The force of Shomnyaa shall lead the way. With luck we shall reach the land of our enemy before the moon is at its peak. Keishlee, if you can over take their lead once the raid call is sounded, then you shall be our 'Dido' and all your orders shall be obeyed. Come, let us ride," spoke Shaloolaa.

Someone helped tie Keishlee's weapon to her back and the horse bolted from a hard slap to its rear. Guards ran along behind, and Shomnyaa's calls led the way.

When they got past the mountains, the moon was bright and she caught sight of Scochaa riding next to Charlaa. She wanted to be near her, but thought better of it and rode up behind Saamyli, near the front of the raid pack.

Saamyli, an expert rider, gave Keishlee a firm slap on the back. "Do not let others see that long face or some of the women shall lose heart for the fight," she said keeping pace with Keishlee. "You ride well. You have ridden a wag before?" Saamyli asked.

"Yes, a few times. There is a striped kin to these in our lands, but they do not have this beautiful mane," Keishlee smiled but could not stop from looking back for Scochaa.

Saamyli steadied her hand under Keishlee's horse's ear, and they began to run in time. She smiled over to Keishlee and said, "You cannot separate those two. Tried and failed has been the rule."

"I only wish to be her friend. Both their friends, if I can," Keishlee sighed.

"Then you must let Charlaa kill you," Saamyli laughed and sped up her horse.

Keishlee rode behind Saamyli, looking into the beautiful shadows of their lands. The river turned wide in places but followed them over every hill and around every turn. There were mountains everywhere here, and it made the lands dark and mysterious, yet luscious and cool during this season of sun [*summer*]. Keishlee was falling in love with the place. She felt awakened here and that made her feel new all over. She decided to give herself over to what she knew she loved, riding, and began sending her horse faster and faster, until she caught the feel of the horse's optimum speed.

Others tried to catch up or pass her, cheering her on. She passed all but the leaders of Shomnyaa's force, and then slowed it down. She realized that they had given her the fastest wag. Even the other horses favored it, and once caught, never tried hard to pass her up again. On occasion she felt the near slice of the weapon strapped to her back, attempting to cut into her skin. But she did not care, riding had been her only love. Dancing was a gift her body already knew, but riding gave her more pleasure than she thought anything else ever could. But now she found herself distracted from even this pleasure, by thoughts of what pleasures awaited her entwined to the life of a friend.

Her thoughts strayed back to Charlaa and Scochaa, who were as close as Mah and Odrak. Far closer than she had ever been to anyone, except her feeder. She almost cried again thinking of Pison, her keeper. To stop the flow she took note of their direction and sped out pass the others.

"RULE HERE!!!" they shouted as they approached a small clearing of fires and lazy trees. "RULE HERE, SISTERS!!"

Keishlee tore off from the pack, dust billowing up over her legs and trying to get in her eyes. They did not just let her lead. She had to push hard to get more from the creature, but her wag was strong, and left them many trees behind.

Something fell out of a tree and almost hit her. It clawed at her leg, and she was sure they came here to kill wild cats. She struck at something in the shadow of a tree and the horse bolted. Holding tightly to the horse's mane was all that saved her from falling off and into the onrush of hairy beast coming up from behind.

She got her weapon, slashed out, and something screamed like a giant squawk. Keishlee saw its eyes and a cold fear gripped her. These were human size australopies, about as tall as a young Tuk woman. The large eyes and fanged teeth in an almost human face were just more corruptions on such deformed and lumpy bodies.

Running hunched over or swing-knuckling the ground,

they bit her wag and it bleated in pain and dashed forward. Keishlee ripped her weapon through as much flesh as she could find and still they came for her.

Soon the camp was a thunder of stomping hooves, screams and squawkish cries, and the calls of women to light fires. Keishlee saw some of the brave women jump from their horses with only their torches swinging. Others rode in to protect them, slicing off arms and legs, as the creatures came at them from all directions.

Keishlee rode over and stabbed her blade into the eye of a creature about to take hold of a woman's hair, now loose and flying free from the hard ride.

Keishlee choked on the smell of death that was everywhere here. Even the trees smelled of disease, and Keishlee cut their branches as well as the creatures, while stomping them into the ground with her wag.

She turned an eye to an area being well lit from the moon, and was not surprised to see Shaloolaa in the midst of the fighting, slicing and chopping at the dim-witted beast, from a horse already covered in blood. Some of the blood was from wounds received by the beasts as they tried to eat the horse where it stood. Saamyli was nearby, cursing the creatures as she struck them down with ease.

Keishlee found herself smiling, as her body found a way to rid itself of all its frustrations. She was proud to be here. There was not a woman among them who cowered or turned away from the attacks. The young and the old fought as bravely as anyone would to save their home.

Keishlee spotted some creatures about to leap from a tree down on Saamyli. She hurried her horse over and cut its arm off just before it reached her. But another was now on Saamyli's back, and Shaloolaa was too busy to intercede.

Keishlee pulled them both down, falling hard as the creature turned on her. Keishlee had her weapon in its chest before it saw the weapon move. She backed away as it tried to claw her, then yanked her weapon out to strike another leaping from a tree.

Keishlee looked around and saw that there were still many of them, and that some of them were indeed near-human men, covered with so much filth and dirt they were indistinguishable from the creatures they emulated. They began to keep their distance now, as the power and slaughter of the Tuk women became clear to them. Keishlee looked back at Saamyli still lying on the ground, and saw the quick stream of blood rushing from her neck.

"Blood!!" she screamed, not knowing what else to say. "Assistance for blood that pours!"

Two women on horseback were by her side, leaping to Saamyli's aid. Taking leather pieces from their legs they wrapped them around Saamyli's neck and tied others tighter around her arms. Together they carried her to a nearby tree and stood their ground to shield her.

Keishlee cut a smaller beast in half that tried to come near, and the others backed away in fear. There was fighting all around her, and the closest thing to memory she had of such a thing was a fight between a clan of boars and a tribe of attacking plains lions. Keishlee wanted to use the tactics she remembered and called other women over to explain.

While fighting off those that came too near, they formed small orderly lines in the midst of the riot. Other women watched their backs as the front line charged forward, plunging their weapons into the creatures, then running away as the second line came up to do the same. Keishlee remembered that the boars ran away after startling the lions with their fierceness, which made the lions miss the ones coming from the side. Using this tact, the women eventually surrounded the creatures, slicing them to bits. This was done in small groups at first, but others rushed over to make new lines, or retrieve weapons for the others to quicken the pace of the formation. They attacked like this back and forth across the clearing, leaving nothing that moved as they moved on.

The creatures were fast, strong, and hard to put down. They fought without limbs and their bites were mortal wounds. Many simply fed themselves at the women's throats. Occasionally their lines were broken by creatures attacking from the trees. For these, Scochaa's and Shaloolaa's force of strong weapon fighters were best. Shaloolaa ordered the lines of women to keep their place, as she and others ran between the lines, tearing through the flying horrors.

Keishlee screamed when she saw one of the man creatures ripping the insides out of a fallen woman. When it began to eat the gore, she fell on it with a vengeance and cut it down to twitching nubs. Two other creatures attacked her and one even held her weapon until its fingers were cut free. Another struck her and was coming for her throat when the front line of her formation rescued her. After they had removed its arms and legs, she was given the final pleasure of removing its head.

With so many of the creatures dead, low sobs could be heard now, and the crying of small slaves. Keishlee was trying to find them when she heard the roar of a real australopi. It had surprised a woman, and had her dangling by an arm with her throat torn out. Some of the women moved into old formations and were about to attack the creature, when Keishlee noticed the beast was dragging another woman. A woman fully rooted [*ready to give birth*], and alive.

"Stop!!" Keishlee screamed and pointed to the woman being dragged across the ground.

There were important things to remember about this creature. Australopi were near-human and could understand some things; they were wild and unpredictable, and this one moved as tho it had some speed, but Keishlee took the chance.

She let her weapon fall to the ground where the great beast could see it. The other women screamed at her, but she ordered them to hold their places. Scochaa and Charlaa took places at her side, ready to fall into the plan.

As Keishlee slowly walked up to the creature, Scochaa and Charlaa circled their way around to get behind it. Others helped to scare off or kill the creatures that got in their way, and they watched Keishlee edge closer to the large beast, making signs with her body and hands, telling the creature that she would exchange herself for the woman it carried. It threw off the dead woman into a nearby group, who were knocked down and fell upon by other creatures.

Keishlee kept her eye contact with the creature. Its large eyes shone brightly in the moonlight, while its fur ruffled in the cool night breeze. It growled and hissed at her, while it shook the leg of the mother to be, who screamed.

"Remember. You must cut out the heart of this creature or it will not die by force," she shouted, not looking at Scochaa or Charlaa, who were almost near enough to strike.

The women who had gone on this raid before screamed out "DIDO!!" to praise her for this news. They were remembering those lost to the fierceness of this creature, who'd had all its limbs removed at one time or another. It had either run off or run them off, and was always found again, intact, and leading a new band of these hated creatures.

Distracting the creature with words and signs, Keishlee

was now almost close enough for the creature to claw her face. It dropped the leg it held and kicked the woman free. Someone dashed towards her. Keishlee screamed to try and stop her, but this creature was faster than any Keishlee had ever heard of, and ripped the woman's arm off before Keishlee, Scochaa or Charlaa could get to her. But while the woman was falling to the ground, soon to be dead, Scochaa and Charlaa were upon the australopi. Once again, hacking the creature to pieces and screaming, "THIS TIME YOU DIE! YOU DIE, BEAST!! DIE, BEAST!!! DIE!!!!"

Still the beast managed to claw Charlaa with its feet and to knock another woman down. The remaining creatures in this group charged, and Scochaa had to stop and contend with the new onslaught, protecting Charlaa's back and regretting only that someone else would get to rip its heart out.

At the death cry of the old australopi, its seeds lost heart and were running away, dragging body parts as they left. The women cursed and some ran after them but were called back. Keishlee returned to look for the sounds of crying slaves, along with the women who would not leave their Dido unprotected.

She found a small female slave, of maybe 2 season cycles. She was tied naked to a tree and above her hung the half eaten body of another.

The food Keishlee had eaten earlier forced its way out of her mouth. She cried and screamed and fell on her knees, pulling up the grass. She jumped up and looked around for more of the creatures, hoping to find another one to kill. Out of frustration she started hacking away at the branches of the tree, and to her joy, an ugly creature fell out.

Guards still on their horses rode up to assist her, but Keishlee ordered them to hold their places, asking only that they not let it get away. Other women surrounded the creature as it looked for a place to run. Keishlee cut it when it moved to get away, and then dropped her weapon to give it courage. The other women took this as a signal to circle behind the creature but she called them off, demanding to take it by herself. This creature would have harder bones, but she managed a kick to bring a large human down.

They all heard something crack as she struck its head, but the creature did not fall. Instead of killing it, she had only crippled it, and it came for her. Keishlee sidestepped, managing to stomp the joint of its leg, breaking it as the creature clawed her down the back, ripping loose the girdle of snake leather around her chest. The beast clawed the air and ground trying to get up. Another woman shouted for her to finish, and Keishlee went for her weapon. Another woman was about to stab the creature when Keishlee turned to shout her down. "If you kill it, I shall kill you!" she roared and watched her back away.

Keishlee chopped off the creature's good arm and then dragged the screaming beast over to the now silent slave. She held the creature's face up to the slave, who looked upon the creature with teary eyes and began to scream.

"This little sister is human," spoke Keishlee as she cut the little slave free.

Another woman went to cut the slave, and Keishlee knocked her to the ground. Shomnyaa stopped Keishlee from rising and ordered her to let someone kill the little sister, saying, "She is part beast and therefore, not fully human."

Somaali came over and agreed, but reminded Shomnyaa that Keishlee was Dido of the raid, and her word was to be obeyed. They called Shaloolaa over who was tending Saamyli. She and Scochaa ran over to see what the problem was and both looked at Keishlee with shock. They agreed with Shomnyaa that the beast seed should be killed.

A woman pushed Shomnyaa's hand aside and helped Keishlee to her feet. To her surprise she found that it was Charlaa.

"This slave is human. And I will not kill harmless, blameless humans!" Keishlee shouted for all to hear.

The area was being cleared of the creatures, while others gathered around the tree where Keishlee stood, arguing with Scochaa over the life of the slave. Shaloolaa asked for proof, and some of the women recalled what the slave had done. Keishlee reminded them that the slave had not shown fear towards her, and only cried as slaves often did when being treated badly. She thought the proof was obvious: the slave's body was hairless even tho she was only brown, but more importantly she explained, "Only humans cry with tears. If that is not proof of a human spirit, what is?" The others could only stammer and look away.

"See her now. She listens and tries to understand. Is that not human?" Keishlee reached out to the little slave, who had tottered to her and was clinging to her leg. "No. I will not have you kill this one." Keishlee held the slave close.

Scochaa walked off in a huff as the arguing threatened to

continue, but Shaloolaa called for quiet and said, "In the past we kept these lives for the sacrifice alone. Then their blood began to mix with the blood of our people—and there are those creatures and women which are known to me. During this generation, we kill all we find. But you are the Dido, and we will all obey," she paused to make sure she had everyone's attention. "We shall build a hut away from our village for these little ones to grow. When the little sisters begin to bleed, if they are still human, we shall offer them the blood rite to keep their lives. The man creatures take their chances at the sacrifice. But all who show clear signs of having beast blood may be killed on the spot. How do you say, Keishlee, no matter? No matter!"

All were silent as they watched Keishlee, and then the slaves come out from their hiding places. There were not many, but Keishlee dreaded any of their deaths. Some came directly to her, having sensed that she would protect them over the others. The ones that came towards her knuckling the ground, she cut down herself.

The moon was falling by the time the Tuk Women had cleared the land of the all the dead creatures. Riders took the pieces to the Red River, and threw them in to feed the deadly water snake, which was the sacred food of the Sun Birds.

Keishlee heard the words of Shhaha ringing in her ears, "Life and Death are the slaves of the land." She smiled as she sat by the river chopping up the animal remains along with the human ones, keeping a sharp eye on the older male slaves to see which ones would try to steal a piece for food.

To Keishlee's comfort, she discovered that only the Tukshead and a small number of women did not want the slaves. Before they were led away from the clearing, all had been claimed by someone and given names, except for the male slaves, who sat apart from the little sisters and even kept their distance from each other. Keishlee looked out over their numbers and counted 10 and 8. She wondered how long they would live. Some of them might not live through the night, if Scochaa or Somaali caught them looking back to the clearing with that longing in their eyes.

Keishlee resigned herself to their fate. The Tuk Women had to do what was necessary to protect their blood. Saamyli had told her there were many of these beasts in these lands. They had been running from them for generations, until they discovered the Tuk Blade, and the oil that hid their scents.

The thought of lands filled with these creatures sickened her soul. She saw again the half-eaten bodies of slaves hanging from trees, and the bodies of rooted women killed for the food inside them. Shaloolaa said they ate even every seed, and their filth laid waste to the land. "When they finish with a place, nothing grows there anymore." As further proof of their destruction, she asked that Keishlee consider the great escarpment they had crossed. Keishlee shuddered, remembering the total isolation found there, regretting now that they had not killed the australopi they had found.

Keishlee was the "Dido" and so the women brought her word of all the goings on. Saamyli had been badly cut and had lost a lot of blood. Women were already carrying her back to the village. They had found other young women, some now insane because of the abuse they had suffered at the hands of the beasts. Keishlee had no choice but to order them put to death. Shaloolaa told her it would be a comfort and a rest, and looking at their faces, separated from their bodies and their pain, she saw them return to the peace they had once known. Those who were left she ordered taken back to the village, along with the three they found that were rooted. These were women they had believed were dead, and everyone praised Keishlee and called her "Cae Dido," to honor her.

When all was done and they were back at Tuk Village, the sky was still dark and the night fires continued to burn. Slaves were awake, tending cooking pots with the old women, and for the first time Keishlee saw the real men of the village. Not many, as compared to the women, but each sat cross-legged, awaiting his woman to dismount and welcome her home. The men sat with damp cloths, small oil flasks, and other things the women might need, then followed them out to the Green River where they all went to bathe.

For the first time on this journey, Keishlee felt lonesome. It was the lonesomeness she had grown accustomed to, but now it was different. She felt alone and lonely, and its weight burdened her.

The village was unusually quiet, as the couples and groups went about in their silent satisfaction. Even the old women, who were always grumpy here, happily prepared foods for the returned fighters. As Keishlee walked about, not knowing what to do, she came upon the large hut of the men.

Instead of the leathery leaves and straw, this hut was built of sturdy wood, and was square instead of round. It had small square windows, and it had a wooden "door," which also had a small window. Guards sat outside playing a game with sticks and stones and greeted Keishlee as she passed.

"Keishlee. Keishlee," she heard the familiar voice of Ramaa. He was crouched at one of the windows, beckoning her near.

The guards did not seem to notice or care, and she went to greet him, glad to have someone to talk to.

"Tell me what has happened," he begged.

"Have you been here since the feast?" Keishlee asked.

"Yes. Tho I thought there would be some pleasure for me after," Ramaa huffed. "We 'extras' have been placed under guard until the 'seeding.' Taken away, even from the feast. They fed me here, with these who are not protectors, and who will never be men. They have not a hand of words between them, and do not touch or try to speak. This is all I know. Tell me how things are for you."

"So much has happened to me here," she almost cried.

Ramaa stuck his hand out to her and rubbed at the cuts and bruises on her face. "I see you are much changed. You should speak with Shhaha. There are wandering spirits about this place, maybe you are being seized by souls."

Keishlee let her head fall into his hand and he could feel the tears as they slipped through his fingers. "Rider of the winds," he moaned, calling her by what her name meant, "...what ache have you inside that brings your soul to me?"

"Pison is dead," she said, fighting her tears.

"How so? This day? Is that why you are covered with blood?" Ramaa began to roar as he saw the blood.

"Is the creature hungry?" one of the guards came around to ask. Keishlee checked with Ramaa, and then called to one of the elders to bring food.

"One of the women here. He journeyed with his Keeper of the Blood, as we do. They have all been slain."

Ramaa broke a piece of wood from the window. He started to break another but Keishlee stopped him, saying, "I have taken vengeance this day. I have slain a feeder among them," Keishlee spoke with regret.

"Not so!" Ramaa cried. "Shhaha knows? There are

respects. Leave here. You must speak to Shhaha, now."

"He knows."

"Go from here. You must seek him out in private and ask him to perform the rite of angry spirits passing."

Keishlee watched the stunned and sorrowful look on Ramaa's face turn to stone against her. He withdrew his hand, and she knew he would say no more. She left him standing at the window without the proper words for leaving, but only because she could not think of them now.

She would seek Shhaha out, but not now. She was sick of her own smell and the stiffness of the dried blood and guts upon her. She searched out one of the guards to take her to the "woman of supplies." She was sure the woman would be Saamyli, and that would bring her Shaloolaa as well. No one asked to see Shaloolaa unless it was important village business. But Keishlee wanted to see her. It would be like seeing Scochaa.

The guard took her inside the hut. It was filled with people tending Saamyli and others talking to Shaloolaa. Everyone stopped to greet her, and Shaloolaa asked her to sit near even tho they were already clean.

"Why have you not bathed? You must rest. We have to journey to the breeding grounds of the Sun Birds tomorrow."

"I would like to have clean skins to wear and fresh...."

Two women left the hut without having to be asked. She could over hear them asking one of the guards outside to bring "fresh leathers, oils and a girdle for the woman Keishlee. Bring them to the white waters."

"Come," one of the two returned and reached for her hand.

Keishlee followed them to the lake and found out their names were Adah and Zama. Keishlee was glad for this distraction from her thoughts. They talked about their first kills, and Zama suggested she find a friend to sleep with to avoid bad dreams. Keishlee remembered Ramaa's words and knew now what he meant. She was considering going to Shhaha and did not pick up on the thing being offered.

Adah had helped unstrap Keishlee and was cleaning her with handfuls of dirt when another offer came. Keishlee did not know what to say. A nervous reaction forced her to pull the woman down and rub their heads together. Keishlee loved the feel of the long straight hair on her face.

Adah undressed and led her into the waters, which were still full of other people, both men and women, washing each other and playing. Zama left, and suddenly Keishlee felt shy about being so close to someone she did not know, but had to admit that this was why she had gone to seek Shaloolaa.

Later, as she looked out the window at the sky beginning to lighten, and laid back, running her fingers through Adah's hair, she regretted never having joined in any women's play. She had never slept close to anyone except her mother, and the warmth of Adah's body was a titillating solace. She laid there clutching Adah, tighter and tighter. She wanted to reawaken her, or pull her close enough to make them one. But it was no good, she had worn Adah out, and their bodies could not be kneaded together. This time she did the kiss, and it felt delicious.

She suddenly thought about Ramaa's words and thought yes, she was very much changed. A new being altogether, and looking forward to the future, which was remarkable all by itself, considering she never thought past the moment at hand. But now she could talk to Shhaha. Something inside had fallen into place, and she felt whole and in time with the world around her. Once again she heard the crack of silence strike the air. The Great Mahs were flying and all life held its breath for their passing. This was the only land she knew where the birds did not chirp and the cocks never crowed at dawn. The rising sun brought peace and silence to this land, and it found a resting place in Keishlee's heart as she finally fell asleep.

▼▼▼▼▼

"I am quickly losing my appreciation for these sections of your stories," grunted Ebbie Farmer to both the women sitting in front of her. "It's bad enough how you describe it, but what's in these books is filthy."

"I agree," grunted Michael Blackamoor, a young fledgling Red Warrior, and also an American. "You want us to believe that in them days, everybody was a faggot."

"Of course not," crackled the voice of Cleopatra Mandara-a'La Hedrin.

Feegarmardar smiled at Ebbie, then introduced herself as the Assistant Regent Ambassador and Special Agent to Ethiopia. She said, "You Americans always pick out the juicy sex bits of any story. What say you, Mageeta Sparrow?"

Mageeta looked about the room and nodded to everyone. She smiled over to Feegarmardar and said, "Fee-gar-mar-dar, in Japan we understand there is great difference between the male and female. It is only natural for them to enjoy their own company more. In doing so, they may find special attractions for each other."

"Oh come on!" grunted Michael. "I'm starting to feel like I'm in a training camp for queers. Even after I finish those god-damn exercises in camp, they want us to do all kinds of touchy-feely things. They've even started asking us to kiss each other! I can't get with that!"

"You American men are such manly creatures," joked Feegarmardar as she opened her shimmy to reveal a magnificent body encased in a yellow film-dress.

"We of the Pagangenearch do not wish any of you to become homosexual. Have no fear, Michael. They will never ask you to take another man unto yourself to bed. If the Pagangenearchs want anything, they want people to breed, to flourish and be plentiful throughout the universe. What is the sacred act?" Cleopatra asked Ebbie.

"Childbirth, conceived with respect to the blood alone," replied Ebbie and Mageeta simultaneously.

"What is the sacred condition?" Cleopatra asked Michael.

"Nurturing," Michael replied sourly.

"And preparing the inheritance to pass down the knowledge and its power, child! Leaving something so that those who follow need not start all over again," roared Feegarmardar at Michael, as she jumped from her seat to stand before him.

All he could see was the wealth he knew she possessed and the beauty of her body, but he managed to say, "While loving his people and himself, and respecting all forms of life."

"Who are the Red Warriors?" Cleopatra asked him.

"Men, in service to the blood of life!" he spoke this time, wanting to impress Feegarmardar. "But, a faggot I am not, and you are hot to trot...."

Feegarmardar snatched him up across the table and held him there by his collar. "How can we trust you with the blood we save, if you refuse to love it if it comes in the form of a man?" Michael made no reply and she continued, "You child, are a product of the eighties generation. Young Black Americans about to become, once again, African Americans, who fell into the coffins left by the killing off of homosexuals. You wore their clothes, spoke their language and took their jobs, and you discovered some of their power. But the best thing you came up with was rap music. A simply monotonous ego feed, often performed with stolen music. The best thing they did was dance. Great dancing," she joked.

"If you had gained any true power, or developed some of your own, your music would have rallied you to brotherhood, and creation. But no! What did you do?" she asked, finally letting him go. "You killed each other at concerts, and destroyed three hundred generations of African genes with drugs. You gave yourselves up to prison armies to be used against your own people. You created a ruling class of lawyers, who created and manipulated the private war market, and that wasn't even the lowest level," she snapped.

"I ain't with all that. I was never that interested...." Michael tried to recover himself.

"That is because you are a bureaucratic punk, a ninny and a dunce head. Rap was easy, and it gave black youth a hope they had never had before. They fought at concerts just because it was so easy, and they saw no reason to be denied. All they needed was that break, get some notice. It made them try for something and tho many did not make it, the attempt gave them strength and fortified their will to try again, or for something else. Guess what? Your parents are some of the ones who made it at something else," smirked Feegarmardar.

"Give me a break already," he huffed and turned away.

"If only I could. I would love to rip your tight little ass in two. Giver me a Rasta, anytime—especially one not into music. But you have a true, near pure strain of Spanish-African Moor blood running through your veins, and the sisters want it, and by the blood of Ras Tafari, they will have it. Even if I have to give myself to you to get it," she smiled sweetly at him, totally confusing him now.

"Hold your tongue, woman," the old woman snapped at Feegarmardar as she was about to speak again.

"Yes, Blood Mother." Feegarmardar humbled herself and bowed to the old woman with reverence. It was like seeing a lioness turned into a lamb.

Cleopatra only needed to eye her students to get their full

attention. She asked, "What is the Pagangenearch?"

"A sisterhood in service to human life," answered Mageeta and Ebbie together.

"Praise, not withstanding," joked Feegarmardar who then proceeded to leave the room, ordering Ebbie to follow.

At the door Ebbie turned to Michael and said, "And you're having wet dreams over her. I told you she was a royal bitch."

Out in the hall Feegarmardar smiled at Ebbie for her nerve, and then praised her for having taken her vows to the sisterhood already. She held Ebbie's hand and suggested that her father, Rockmon Farmer, was in some kind of trouble, but would only say that he was in good health and was now under the protection of the Red Warriors, and living at his home outside Addis Ababa.

Ebbie tried not to worry, but owning the patents for the new cloner-solar wave guns had even the United States after him under one ruse or another. He stayed in hiding these days, working on new inventions that he hoped might bring power and wealth to the new East African nations.

"They think his new toy is the key to producing real teleportation devices. A device like that could change the face of our world, woman. It would save countless resources. It has been on the secret agenda of many great houses," Feegarmardar whispered as a group of acolytes passed.

"They just don't want this discovery in the hands of wild African countries."

Feegarmardar swung her around and had to stop herself from slapping Ebbie's face. "You must first become a truthsayer for our people, then you can tell us something of the future. Then you may tell us our blood is too wild. But now you must be able to understand and process simple information like this to a useful conclusion, not just a critical one."

"I know Wind Limited is in control of most of northern Africa, and why. They have brought great wealth to the continent with their new inventions, or rather, rediscoveries. Especially the film-dress material; every country demands it. The Big Seven want it, and it's only produced...."

"Here! Overnight, we have become a great nation again, and they crowd our borders for entry. Every exile begs reentry. Conservationists all over the world are in love with us, because we have created a product that helps restore the land. A building constructed of this material feeds the earth it sits on, and Abyssinia is feeding the world again," Feegarmardar spoke with relished pride.

"Also," Ebbie smiled and said, "having taken every woman out of the Sudan has finally ended the civil war, lending notoriety to the sisterhood and a base to finally deal with the Egyptians. Ethiopia has the powerful new disrupter guns, which can turn a man, or anything else made of water, into dust. The ancient weapon that turned Lot's wife into salt."

"Yes, very good," Feegarmardar smiled. "Such power."

"When words and prayers fail, enough power will always garner some respect. The nuclear groupies thought they would survive a total holocaust. To hell with the rest of us. But this weapon is assured to produce a totally dead planet. Even the film-dress material cannot block its rays. If Wind Limited adds teleportation to their arsenal, nothing will be able to stop them," smiled Ebbie. "How go the talks in Cairo?"

"Soon we shall have a United Africa. They wanted to stall, but the UAR threatened to withdraw from the talks, and it seems they are seriously considering doing an under-the-table deal."

"They will turn their backs while the UAR takes, by force if necessary, all South Africa?" asked Ebbie.

"Better than that," Feegarmardar smiled as they reached the glass doors to the barber's quarters. "They have already agreed to block out all news of it as well, and even to help arm us. Just for another peek at the weapon."

"Another murder, and another chance to steal it."

Feegarmardar laughed and squeezed Ebbie's hand. "We are new at this. We must play some more and learn how the game is played best. Oh, did I tell you, I finally got to meet the mysterious Ms. Lord, the female 007 of Holland. She was trying to kill one of the leading technicians of Oshima Tong, she had personally murdered three of the British scientist already. I had to relieve her of her spine. I wanted them to think an alien predator had done it."

Later when Ebbie returned to the others, she avoided their eyes. She did not want to see the stares and be reminded that she was now bald, and would be so for many years. She hated the way she looked, and thought it overly dramatic for them to insist this of her. But she had the film dress now, which she would never have been able to afford on her own. She felt stronger already, and thought, she too might be able to pick Michael up out of his chair, and he was over six feet tall. The thought coerced a smile from her, but his smirk made her angry, and she turned to Cleopatra, asking if she had missed much.

Mah and Odrak were having the exhilaration of a lifetime, free falling from the mountain top along the steep pitch of the southern face. The birds never failed to catch them and place them back together on the mountain. Odrak even dared to have them drop him from the sky and catch him midway to the ground. The birds were always careful to float them along without jerking them about, and soon Mah and Odrak were fearless in the midst of this dangerous play. Fresh-Rain said it was great exercise for the young birds, and that flying slowly was an exciting mystery for them.

The adults did not like their being seen so freely flying, but all creatures knew to stay themselves during their arrival to a citadel. The Great Mahs, having survived the time of ice and the days of dust, refused to have anything moving about when they came to a stop from one of their long flights. And they listened to the earth with their special hearing, and even after many generations were still angry with the worms for their constant moving about. The elders explained that is why they teach the other birds to eat them, as punishment for their lack of respect.

The young birds stopped their play, knowing that soon Mah and Odrak would weaken from the long journey and would need to rest. They were taken inside the mountain, down deep into the galley chambers, where feeder birds prepared the giant water snakes to feed the younger birds. Molting birds barely taller than Mah, with white eyes and clawless wings, were kept inside the mountain for many seasons before they would be allowed to make the long journey. Mah and Odrak sang to them, but they were too young to understand. The infant birds huddled close and tried to feed Mah and Odrak, imitating the older birds, who were feeding them.

Mah and Odrak fell asleep within the wings of adult birds even as they were being fed. The elders took them to the resting chamber and laid them down together in the smooth, stone-cupped containers, filled with clean, dry skins. A large bird, who had come back with them from the massive land break, and who Mah called Fox-Rabbit, poured oil over their bone-dry bodies. The oil was sucked up like a sponge, and an elder told the others that these two could not be flown long distance again for a long time. Another bird rubbed the oil over their faces and into their hair, and then My-Name covered them with one of the large feathered cloaks.

When Keishlee awoke, she found Adah gone. She quickly dressed and stepped out of the hut to find Shhaha sitting outside the entrance. She sat down beside him, greeted him properly and humbled herself before him.

"You have learned to make friends?" Shhaha inquired.

Keishlee held his arm tight, rubbed his leg bones and noticed that his silver ring was once again bright and shiny. Shhaha told her that Shebeth, Zama's feeder, had rubbed it clean with an oil cloth. She knew then that Shhaha also knew who her new friend was.

He wanted to know why she had avoided the rite of angry spirits passing. "Life is a gift, which is why the young are slaves to the old." He started to reprimand her with a hard tale, but could see that she had heard the tale before. "There are many spirits who walk this land come night. These people do not bury their dead. What they do may be more useful, but they need to learn respect for the spirits of all things," he spoke while caressing her oiled hair.

"Does Pison wander?" she hesitated to ask.

Shhaha lowered his head and Keishlee could see the tears forming in his eyes. She remembered that his feeder had been a close kin to a blood keeper in Pison's Waterhorse clan.

"Bilahoway was old and filled with blood magic. Meneliawy, the slave of his blood, has gone back to the Great Mother. I could not speak with them, but others have told me that some bones remain."

Keishlee quickly recalled the strings of teeth on Tarlane's neck and arms. "Is my spirit in danger?" she asked.

"It is good that you have taken your sleep during the light of day. No spirit has power to walk in sunshine. It is the moon that brings them from the Great Mother, and the night that gives them power to be seen."

"Teach me what I must do," she begged.

Shhaha set about to teach her the chant for the rite of angry spirits passing. He explained that the tone of the chant was more important than the words. "This chant has to be whispered. Your tongue should taste the air as the words take flight. Also, it has to be done at moonrise, when there rises a light breeze around you."

Before he left, he told her that Ramaa was becoming affected by all the wandering spirits here. When last Shhaha had seen him, Ramaa complained of cold flashes and hot spots on his skin. Shhaha was going to him now. Being an old man, he was allowed to move about freely.

When he got to the large hut of the men, medicine women were inside giving Ramaa an herb wine. He sat between two of them as they looked over his naked body for signs of ill health.

"It is a spirit problem," Shhaha told the women.

"Watch over him, and we shall return with the bones of our dead," said the woman called Swaahali. Her look and movements told Shhaha that he was respected here.

They left the hut and the other men gathered around, staring at Ramaa, who was only sick of heart. Shhaha made his way between them and comforted Ramaa. Ramaa clung to him and begged for the magic that would relieve him from his agony.

He had put the hut in a fit last night, dancing and chanting the call for the dead. Ramaa tried to get some of the other men to join him, explaining that he needed their help to speak with the Great Mother, but none of them understood. They were all terrified of him, and many of them had no words, or would not speak them. Afraid to cause more trouble with the spirits, Ramaa would not push them to it, and cried and chanted for all the village to hear, because he was too afraid to close either eye and sleep.

Shhaha offered him more of the wine, which he discovered from a taste included a powerful medicine. It was the same medicine they used to heal others from the cuts of their weapons, mixed with the wine to make it stronger.

It was not offered to a man here lightly. The other men knew this and gathered around in the hopes of getting a sip. Shhaha offered Ramaa another drink, and wondered if Swaahali had left the full bowl on purpose.

Ramaa was hot and sweating from sitting on his heels all night, but Shhaha knew this was mostly fear and tension from lack of sleep. Not wanting to insult the power of the spirits while they slept, he said nothing more to Ramaa. He stood and took hold of one of the naked men, forcing him to move in a close circle around Ramaa. Once the man continued to move without being forced, Shhaha showed him how to move his feet in a dance that would call to the Great Mother. Two guards, who were always present outside this hut, opened the door and looked inside, but made no comment. It was forbidden for any woman, other than the women of medicine or someone bringing food, to enter the hut of the men, and so Shhaha was free to do as he pleased with them.

Once the man was doing the dance properly, Shhaha started another and then another, until he had five men dancing in a circle around Ramaa. Already Ramaa was happy. This was something he knew. He meekly looked up at Shhaha and thanked him with his eyes. Soon Shhaha's voice became the only presence in the room and the dancers moved by his will alone. The other Tuk men recognized something in Shhaha that filled them like a warning, and fear forced an appreciation of the dance upon them. But Shhaha smote them with curses and would not let them dance with the others.

They cowed together to one side of the hut, and pushed themselves to say the words Shhaha ordered them to speak. "Spirits be not angry," he said repeatedly, until they had the sound he wanted.

Ramaa folded his legs, one on top of the other, then lowered himself to the ground to begin the chant for angry spirits passing.

Swaahali and her medicine women returned, and on seeing the men dancing around Ramaa, she dropped a leaf bag of bones right in front of him and the dancers.

Ramaa let out a groan. Shhaha ordered the dancers not to stop and had to push some of them back into the moving circle. Ramaa continued his chanting while Shhaha walked over to Swaahali, smiling. He was thinking that she did just as he would have, and yet she does not know our ways. Ramaa would say the Great Mother snatched the bones from her and brought them near, and Shhaha would not be able to disagree.

Shhaha asked Swaahali with his eyes not to stop the dancing, and she surprised him again, by ordering her two women to sit one on either side of Ramaa. Then she sprinkled a little dirt over the bones, which was a nice touch, Shhaha told himself, and fixed it in his memory. He was glad this woman knew enough not to disturb the bones once they lay still upon the ground. He worried that Ramaa might not accept the medicine she offered, then it would not take, and he would be much harder to cure.

"You have my respects, as Keeper of the Blood for your tribe," Shhaha said in the formal manner. With his eyes closed,

Shhaha listened for the slightest change in the tone of Ramaa's chant. There was none. Ramaa would accept her magic, and be himself soon.

Keishlee took the strings of bones from Scochaa and sat down to eat the food given her. Adah had come back from her morning chores, followed by her little male slave, who she had taken to the hut of the sacred offerings [*Treasure Room/Waiting Room*] the night before. There were many women here now, and she found herself overwhelmed with their presence.

They were combing out her loose hair, it being knotted and tangled from the fighting, and were showing Keishlee how to make tresses. They tied it up from the roots to the end with painted strings and tiny bits of shells. They wanted to look their best, because they would soon go to the mountain of the Sun Birds to beg for the return of Mah and Odrak. The Sun Birds were the only creatures these women feared, and they wanted to be near Keishlee, who had no fear of them.

They were starting to take out her hair knots when a woman came running over to them. She was too excited to speak and pulled on Scochaa's and Charlaa's arms for them to follow. Adah and Keishlee ran to her hut and retrieved their weapons, then ran into other groups of women running towards the feast clearing.

Along the way Keishlee noticed that all the men went into hiding. The village appeared once again to be filled only with women. Even the slaves disappeared into their huts, which continued to look empty even tho Keishlee was sure those inside were looking from their windows.

Before Keishlee reached the clearing she saw what had so frightened the young woman: birds hovering and gliding in the air like the white vultures of Kurru clan. "It is Great Mahs," she whispered, knowing no other bird as big. The sight stunned her, knowing without doubt that she had never seen them flying or gliding in the air like other birds.

The Tuk Women had never seen it either. She overheard others saying that something must be very wrong for them to allow themselves to be seen like this. As she reached the clearing most of the women were lying on the ground, almost breaking their necks trying to see the birds above. Keishlee heard someone say, "Only Shaloolaa and the elders have lived to see such a sight."

Keishlee continued to move into the clearing, following close behind Scochaa and her force of women, who began their scowling call. Keishlee saw many women dive to the ground, but none of the birds moved in a threatening manner. The other members of the Tukshead rushed into the clearing where most of the women laid down or stilled themselves where they stood, but Shaloolaa walked boldly up to Scochaa, signing for her to speculate about what the birds might want. Scochaa had no idea and continued to scowl, silently ordering her women to do the same.

Moving to some unheard call, the field went suddenly silent. Women leaped to the ground. Keishlee lowered herself to one knee, because this time she heard the low ras-ras, ras-ras of leathery wings, and the quiet knocking das-han, das-han, of a large heart quickly coming down from the sky. Keishlee looked up and around. She felt the quickness of the breeze dash overhead but never saw the bird. Adah fell down beside her, frightened because the birds never came this close to the ground except to kill.

Shaloolaa, Keishlee and Scochaa were the only ones standing. Once again Scochaa began her "scowling" cry, and managed to change it slowly, but smoothly, into the song she had heard Mah sing. It was sweetness to Keishlee's ears and she cursed herself for not having learned the song when Mah had offered to teach it.

Suddenly Shaloolaa turned to the crowd and signed for everyone to lay flat on the ground. Scochaa did so, and signed for her women to submit. It was a hard thing for them to do, since the greatest challenge they could face was to dare to stand or move while the Great Mahs flew.

Adah pulled Keishlee down on her stomach when she saw a bird glide down the face of the mountain. Keishlee looked up again and saw another, larger bird coming from behind the mountain down into the clearing. There was no mistaking Odrak, holding onto the bird's legs.

Keishlee started to move but heard the unmistakable "scowl" of a real bird which told her not to dare. The very volume of it was like a slap over all her flesh. She let her body fall and pushed her face into the ground. Scochaa could be heard scowling again through the grass. The bird scowled back and then sang a little.

Keishlee heard Odrak jump to the ground and looked up at him. He said, "No one should move or speak!"

The bird sang to Odrak, and they spoke together as if

saying farewells, and then Odrak signed for it to leave. When the bird flapped its wings it was like a storm on the ground, but it quickly died as the bird vanished from sight. Another bird came over the mountain, scowled and scowled until Mah jumped down from its legs. He too ordered everyone to be still, and then sang to the bird before it left.

The village of the Tuk women was only full of light during high sun. Being located in the valley between a high escarpment and even higher mountains, it was always shaded. But suddenly an even heavier shadow came over the clearing. Keishlee blinked to clear her eyes, and found the sky was dark with Great Mahs, slowing coming down from the sky. Keishlee liked the birds, but this was a horror to her. She could hear women screaming in their minds, some weeping openly and chewing the grass and dirt out of panic and fear.

The birds were lowering something over Mah and Odrak, which fell over their shoulders and billowed in the swirling breeze around them. She heard both Mah and Odrak singing, as a wind blew over her that threatened to lift her from the ground. There was a quick whiplash sound of synchronized wings, and the field became a chaos of flying wind and women.

Keishlee found herself in a sitting position when the clearing was silent and the air was calm again. She could see that all the women were pulling themselves together, while Mah and Odrak stood calmly looking into the sky with sad and somber eyes.

She scanned the area to find all the birds gone. She ran over to Mah and Odrak, but stopped as she saw the new things they were wearing. The capes covered their bodies and fell out over the ground. Each was constructed of glistening, brightly hued leathery feathers that changed colors as one looked or moved about. It was the full shading of their land that allowed them to be seen at all, but even here they were bright and glaring, making her look away to clear her eyes.

Others were gathered around them now, and Keishlee saw one of the women she had chosen for Odrak, fall to her knees, ripping loose her hanging cloth. Before anyone could think of what to say or do, she was lying naked before Odrak.

Scochaa had to hold the others back, while Odrak threw off his cape and hefted his loin cloth, asking, "Now?"

His eager readiness made the woman squirm over the grass, moaning with expectation and dreaming of becoming a bird.

Keishlee took his hand and led him away from the group, almost dragging Mah after them. Guards followed but stayed a good distance away to give them privacy, and also because they were afraid of the two man creatures now.

"What have they done to you? To you both?" she looked them over and realized that they were somehow physically changed. Their colors were richer and brighter. Their skin gleamed in the light. The fullness of their hair now surrounded their faces and fell in thick crinkles down their shoulders into the cloaks. Their eyes were so bright and clear the whites glowed. "I see you are both quite ready for the relief offered you here," Keishlee smirked, but was glad to see that they were more than willing.

"I am breathless when I think of all I have to say," spoke Mah, glad and excited to see her.

"You are much changed as well, Keishlee," smiled Odrak, feeling warmth and tenderness in her touch.

Keishlee pulled them tightly to her, and for a moment they rubbed heads, entwined arms and legs, squeezed toes together, played with each other's hair, licked each other's faces and tried to entwine their necks. Both Mah and Odrak were happy to be back on the land, but were even happier to be once again in human arms.

"You are much changed," Mah said, after letting the others go.

Keishlee hoped she could do it as well as she did during the early morning, but she did not care how it came out, and kissed them each on the cheek.

Both Mah and Odrak rubbed the spot in amazement, and touched their fingers to their lips, storing the memory of how this thing was done. They each took one of Keishlee's cheeks and did the kiss in return. They were making a mushy mess of her face when Shaloolaa came up and pushed them aside.

"Enough," she ordered and stepped away for Keishlee to follow, holding out a hand to let Mah and Odrak know not to. "Are they the same ones?" Shaloolaa asked, truly concerned. Keishlee nodded, and then Shaloolaa looked at the two and said, "The guards will be busy all day. I almost regret your coming now," but looked at Keishlee with a smiled. "There will be so much jealousy. We have all worked hard to make gifts to bring to the great Sun Birds, and today they brought us two covered in gifts from them. Do you feel the burden of what this means?"

"I only hope the seeds laid here will help your people grow stronger," Keishlee spoke frankly, feeling the pride and power of her position. She almost wished she could do the selections over.

Keishlee turned around to see the field covered with women trying to get a look at the cape in Scochaa's hands. It pulled light to it from all directions, and when sunlight hit it, parts of it and everything behind it seemed to disappear.

Shaloolaa spotted it too, and marched over and snatched it up. "Here, this belongs to your man creature." She quickly gathered it up and passed it over to Keishlee, who flung it backwards to Odrak and signed for him to hide it. Mah caught the signal and removed his cape, folding the outside in and letting it fall over his arm. Odrak fumbled a bit at first but did the same.

Stunned, they all stared at Mah and Odrak now. Keishlee signaled for them to come stand beside her, while Shaloolaa called her people to order, which was a bit out of place since there was not a sound coming from the clearing.

"Guards come!" Shaloolaa spoke unnecessarily loud. "Take them to the seeding huts. Have Swaahali see them first," she spoke to the guards that came to her call. Having gotten their orders, they gathered around Mah and Odrak, and for the first time, the guards waited for them to move of their own accord. "The chosen may wait outside on the itching pallet. Keishlee shall decide your allotted times. Saamyli is better now, and will be able to track the shadows for you, as I know you wish her to. I say the seeding is now begun."

Shaloolaa took hold of Scochaa's arm and resolved to leave when someone shouted, "There is a challenge yet undone!"

A roar of voices picked up the call. Wild shouts and mixed words flew in all directions, and Keishlee saw a sadness cross over Shaloolaa's face. Charlaa stepped forward, awaiting permission to speak. Keishlee was overjoyed to see Shhaha sneaking his way towards her, the only man in the clearing. He was an ancient thing to these people, and no one seemed to notice or care that this giant carried his blood wand.

Shhaha was careful to avoid notice, and did not come close to any member of the Tukshead. He circled around and got next to Keishlee and managed to say, "I must speak with my apprentices," loud enough for Mah and Odrak also to hear.

Shaloolaa turned an angry look on Scochaa and signaled

Charlaa from behind to speak.

"No one can deny you your pleasure, my sisters," Charlaa raised both her arms in the air, signalling them to listen closely. "I have challenged and it has been accepted. Nothing can change that. But, the challenge is best by fire light and the seeding best in the light of day. Would you wait another day to begin your tomorrows?"

The hum of the field dwindled to a total silence, then quickly became a roar of "Nos!!," mixed with grumbles of discontent. Mah and Odrak inched up closer to Keishlee and Shhaha, and the guards marched out around them.

"Sisters," Shaloolaa turned to her people. "Make the feast clearing ready for the Challenge, which shall begin at sunfall," she ordered and left the clearing followed by Scochaa and the rest of the Tukshead.

The guards tried to move Mah and Odrak, who were not ready to leave. They were unwilling to use force, and tho they were many, they looked to Keishlee for assistance. She asked that they wait a moment, while she spoke in private to her people. As they stepped aside and Keishlee could see the field clearing of its mob, there remained Charlaa, standing alone and looking at her with many words behind her eyes.

"What has happened, Shhaha?" asked Keishlee, pulling her people off to one side.

"I have seen the bones of this tribe. I know them. I have seen a thing for them that yet may be. It is a thing full of blood to the clan of the Tall Walkers as well," Shhaha said, trying to hide the desperation he felt. "Killing may be the way of these people, but you must spill no more blood, and you must not let this woman take your life."

"What do you say!?" questioned Mah, in shock with what he could read between Shhaha's words.

"You have taken human life?" snapped Odrak at her.

"She has slain three feeders in the same night she has covered herself in near-human blood."

Keishlee was now full of shame for the pride she had begun to feel for her new self.

"Rider of the winds, not you. Near-human and human life as well," cried Mah, trying to whisper.

"I had no choice," spoke Keishlee, near to tears.

"How can such a thing be necessary to be done?" moaned Odrak, now ashamed of her, as he thought of her covered with blood. "No matter these women. We are your protectors," he continued, wanting her to feel her insult to his pride.

"Say no more," Keishlee cried.

Mah took hold of Odrak's arm, saying, "Keishlee, my heart is a knot of pain. Shhaha, let us leave here now, or the blood of those slain will be upon us."

Shhaha slowly raised his hand and brought silence to them all. "It is done, but there could be worse to come. You can destroy these people, and ours, with your death, or hers." He looked over to Charlaa. "Mind you, there is no way for you to taste her blood unless she gives it to you, and then they will kill her when you will not. Your death or hers, no matter. I see the same vision."

Keishlee could not hold her tears any longer. She moved to fall into Shhaha's arms, but he stepped back. The move shocked her to standing and stillness. She wiped her face and turned to see Charlaa still standing there. A guard came over who was more determined and said, "Sister, they wait."

Keishlee looked at Mah and Odrak and pulled herself together. She pulled them close and said, "I will always be a Tall Walker, but some of what I have learned here helped to fill my blood. Now, go with these guards and I will follow." Keishlee softened the demand in her voice, then turned to Shhaha and asked him to look after them with her eyes. She watched them leave, then turned to face Charlaa.

Charlaa came over slowly, smiling and looking deeply into Keishlee's eyes. Keishlee was relieved to see her own struggle somewhere else. They sat down and their hands came together as if by some unseen force. They sat quietly for a while staring at the ground. When the tension lessened, Charlaa let go her hands and said, "Shaloolaa teaches us that women are like flowers. With you this is very much so, and I have watched you bloom among us."

Keishlee smiled at these wonderful words. This was exactly how she felt, and the words instantly endeared this woman to her.

"We have a woman, Swaahali, who we call our woman of medicine. You understand this I am told, because they say the old one with you has some of her magic," Charlaa continued in her solemn voice, but Keishlee almost cracked a laugh at her understatement. "Swaahali often says that visions come to her of things yet undone. If only I had such power, maybe I would make fewer blunders. I only want to say that I hold you and your people in high esteem."

"Your people are not ready to have creatures like Mah and Odrak loose among you," Keishlee spoke without thinking, but knew the words were true.

"I know this now," Charlaa grunted. "But the challenge cannot be withdrawn. The forces would gather together and kill us both."

"An insult to the blood of the tribe," huffed Keishlee.

"An insult to all that my people have become. Even I will not have that," Charlaa huffed back, also angry at the situation she put them both in.

"I hold Scochaa close to my heart. Because of her, you have a place there also," Keishlee changed the subject, having decided, like Shhaha, to leave what may to what would be.

"I admit my jealousy of you," Charlaa humbled herself. "See what blunders I fall prey to. I have known Scochaa all my life. Nothing can take her from me." She paused to look deeply at Keishlee. When she was sure no one else was listening, she said, "She has a man, a creature one can live with, if one could live in a tree. But he is beautiful, and is as rich in color as you."

Soon they were sharing confidences and laughing and telling each other about their lives. Keishlee found out that Shhaha had found relief with one of the women here, and that Sonmyaa's fighting hand was permanently crippled. This meant that she would soon be removed from the Tukshead, which is what really brought Keishlee into Charlaa's favor. Keishlee explained to her the business about the dead head calling her name, but forgot that these women held a keeper in small regard and would not understand her anger. Keishlee changed the subject and told her the story of how Mah had been named, which was a great prize to Charlaa, and she thanked Keishlee for the tale. Keishlee was telling her about the women of her clan as they were heading out of the clearing, when Charlaa begged her to find a way to let her ride one of her clan relations.

"I will do this myself," Keishlee said with pride.

"No," Charlaa took hold of her as they came into the shadows of the trees. "Once we are back in the village, you may not speak to me again, nor I to you. They will think we plot together in favor of ourselves. The forces will surely kill both of us then."

"Will this time be understood?" Keishlee wondered.

"Yes," Charlaa smiled wickedly, "I always take some time with the woman before my challenge to her begins. I usually feel the need to tell her I am sorry that I must kill her," she laughed, before leaving Keishlee standing there alone.

▼▼▼▼▼

It was just after high sun. It was hot, and yet everyone was still at their chores. Keishlee walked up to the large wooden platform centered in a small clearing. On both sides sat two fresh green windowless huts, with straw doors attached, and tall palms to give them shade. When the women on the platform saw her, they called the guards to come from the huts. They did so quickly, each bending one knee to the ground before her. One of the guards from each group called out for Mah and Odrak, who stood in the entrances awaiting some word.

Keishlee told the guards she wanted to inspect the huts, and called Mah over to follow her inside Odrak's hut. Once they were alone they pulled Keishlee to them and each spoke at once, trying to tell her something of their stay with the Great Mahs. Keishlee hushed them quickly, letting them know that they should speak to her later of this. They assured her they would do all that she asked.

"Do this for yourselves, young protectors. You are free to choose among them. They have already been prepared into two groups."

"Yes, we see," smirked Odrak. "Why has Mah fewer than I, when he can lay all as well as I?" he tried to whisper.

"Do not mind that. I do not think they will refuse either of you. I have never seen two protectors so much desired. And both still so young yet," she smiled at them. "Keep each one with you as you choose, but a woman will come who you must respect, almost as much as Shhaha. She gives you rest and a moment for yourself, then she will return to tell you it is time to begin again. Keep in mind, it is your seed they want, so do not bury it in the ground. Also, each one must be relieved and seeded twice, so save some for tomorrow."

Mah and Odrak paid little attention to the details, and she could see that they were in a hurry to start.

"Look, Keishlee. They feed us like the Great Mahs," Mah

laughed as he pulled her towards the back walls where the women had prepared trays, and bowls, and leaves of foods.

"Shhaha says we are to eat these before and after each woman," Odrak held up a bowl that had only one item in it. "It is something from the salty waters here." Odrak took a bite and offered the rest to Keishlee.

"Yes. Shhaha and the woman, Swaahali, say it will give us plenty seed for all," said Mah, picking something else out of the pile. "I have all of these in my hut as well. And this," Mah sprinkled a tiny pinch of something into a clear bowl of water, "...Swaahali says will keep the pleasure stick from falling, if we should lose our strength. She says it is called the 'Disiac'," he laughed, and sat the bowl down without drinking it.

"So much food," Keishlee spoke, feeling her own hunger.

"Take it away," Odrak insisted. "I am sick at the sight of food."

Mah pulled him close and said, "The Great Mahs would not let our bellies rest. I look at this feast here and tire."

Keishlee noticed smoke billowing up around her and out a smoke hole in the roof. "What burns so sweetly?"

"Yes, that is a prize," smiled Odrak as he went over near the door and brought back a bowl of thick, slowly burning sticks. "They call them incense. Mah's hut has a different smell inside."

There was a call at the door which gave them pause before they thought to call back. It opened and Saamyli stepped inside, holding the wrappings at her neck. "Shaloolaa has begun the seeding, sister Keishlee. You must know these young ones who wait are wet and grow impatient, and the itchy pallet only makes it worse," her voice rasped, and Keishlee could see she was still in pain.

"Say no more, Saamyli. I come," Keishlee hurried to the door. "Come, Mah, both of you remember, it is your seed they want."

She walked over to Mah's hut, peeked inside and closed the door behind him. Standing in front of the women she said, "I have given the man creatures the order in which you are to be seen. There must be no fighting," she demanded, and to her surprise, there was not even a grumble. But she saw some of the hard looks they gave one another, and remembered their hard ways and said, "You must give my people a little respect. They are not accustomed to less."

One of the freshly dressed women jumped up from the low platform, and holding her covered breast tightly, said, "Think we know not the gentle way with man creatures who are not animals or beast? We all have mothers here," she huffed as if she had been insulted.

"Give them some subtlety they may use to increase the pleasure," rasped Saamyli.

Keishlee felt stupid for not realizing this, and thought to herself, "We are all sisters here." Then she turned to them and demonstrated with her arms. "I used to have a mother too, and I have been told there are many different ways with men. The best thing you can do to comfort a man from our clan, the clan of the Tall Walkers, is to touch him in a way that some part of your body entwines with his. These two will find great pleasure with you, if you hold them close when you take them. Do not ride them like the women of Hairpiece clans. They will want to hold you close, and feel your warmth all the while it is done. Let them see your pleasure bowl first, and let them put a hand to it. They will want to know for certain that you are wet and wanting. Also, try this thing you call a kiss on them. They would enjoy that greatly, if you teach them how it is properly done."

"We now claim the watch!" announced the guards, who made it known they had been waiting for this moment, and were tired of standing about. Some sat down right away.

Keishlee had forgotten they were there, and their voices startled her. One of them pushed her aside, but lowered one knee briefly out of respect. She ordered two other guards to the huts with body signals and they called at the doors.

Keishlee backed away to move herself out of the clearing. She watched Odrak wait until after Mah made his selection. He pretended to be remembering something, to allow Mah time to choose, then bowed his head to her as he had seen other men here do. He stepped aside and followed her into the hut, then closed the door. Odrak used the same ruse, but walked by her side and opened the door for her as they went in.

Keishlee let herself fall behind a tree, exhausted and starving, but found herself thinking not of food or rest, but of Adah. She picked herself up and watched other women bringing food and wine to the guards. Keishlee counted the guards and found them 20 and 7. She smiled, knowing Mah and Odrak would be well protected, then she left in search of Adah.

▼▼▼▼▼

Michael Elliot was fuming. He had wanted the old bat to continue with the "Legend Of Maat's Rising," but it was past curfew. Now he would have to suffer the torture of seeing the acolytes on maintenance duty in these corridors. He cursed his mother for making him come to this place, but he was smart enough to know he needed this training, all of it. Africa was always a dangerous place to live, but now it was deadly beyond all imagining. If his father had failed to get him accepted, he would likely be dead now, all because his father took a high profile job at Wind Limited in South Africa.

He turned the corner and said goodbye to Ebbie Farmer and Mageeta Sparrow, as they headed in the opposite direction towards the women's dorm. He looked closely after Mageeta, who he thought was an odd looking creature, a black and Japanese mixture of lust and studied charm. He continued down the corridor, hoping this once he might avoid seeing the black film dresses of the acolytes. He had 90 more days of abstinence left, and all the physical exams to pass, before he could get out of these nondescript sheets he had to wear in public. He knew once these women got a look at his great body, the outline of his big dick, and the way he walked, he'd be able to make up for all the lost time.

He smiled at himself, thrilled with his new awareness with respect to smells, how important they were to memory storage, and in developing a hypersense about one's own good health. The body told the brain everything and even sent it samples, each with its own smell. If he paid close attention, he could catch that smell and know all that went on within. But he turned a corner and as usual, all he caught were smells and memories of juicy wet-hot pussy. Hairy ones, with deep dark cherry fillings, and bald ones with dark chocolate lips. It tired him down to his bones thinking about the tiny sealed up twats that he could not have for another 90 days. And yet his mind never ceased thinking about the small normal ones that smelled of stingy spices, or the fully opened ones, busted out all over and always dripping in preparation for more, more. He wanted a whore so bad.

He leaned against a wall for a moment to calm himself, breathing deeply to clear his frustration away. He had his eyes closed when they sneaked up on him. As he sprung to attention in the attitude of service, he promised himself to train harder. One day he wanted to be able to walk down a long corridor like this, and not be seen as prey.

"Aey, look what we got here!" smirked the country's only female Puerto Rican, Janice Elray. She moved toward his crotch saying, "Bet'cha ya like to give me some," but being careful not to actually touch him, as was the rule.

"Who was Kafur Al-Ikshidi?" snapped one of the acolyte troopers.

Michael nodded quickly to jerk the information into place. "A black eunuch who became a Lord of Egypt."

"What is the Golden Preypet Tool?" asked the beautiful and wicked Janice, a novice acolyte.

Michael did the nod again, saying afterwards as calmly as he could, "I don't know, but maybe you refer to King Prempeh and the Golden Stool of the Ashanti."

"Which is the deadliest kick?" asked an oriental acolyte.

"The one that kills," he smirked, tired of all the formalities. "May I have the corridor, sisters?"

One of the acolyte troopers looked around and snatched down the top of her film dress, revealing large fat breasts. "Wouldn't you rather have some of these," she laughed, and jingled them in his face.

The young woman introduced herself to Mah as Tanzaa, and no sooner did he sit was she upon him. She did not even bother to remove her hanging cloth, only the under girdles and some of the leather straps. It was over for him rather quickly since he had been holding himself back for so long. She was moist and fresh smelling like the Great Mahs, and she held him close after she sat down on top of him. The effect was a quick release for him and for her, which she had the moment he entered her, and he upon the first stroke.

She continued to press him close and the freshness of her breath excited him. He bit her tenderly across her chest as his keeper had told him to do, and felt himself grow stiff again inside her folds. He could not stop himself from moaning to her softly, but she stopped and stared down at him, and all he could see was her pain. She removed herself and fell flat on the mat beside him, weeping quietly.

Mah felt a panic rush up his spine. It bolted him up to sit beside her, when he realized he did not know what to do, or how to touch a member of this tribe. He whispered that she should forgive his inexperience and allow him to try again.

She flung herself around him so that he could not see beyond her pretty face. She ran her fingers through his loose hair and began playing with the feathers around his neck. "Some are saying these are the feathers of the great Sun Bird," she said as she fell back to the ground, holding herself so as not to let the seed escape. "You have filled me to bursting. I shall have to leave soon."

Mah brushed the feathered ring around his neck and shoulders. Pride returned to his face with the memory of the other gifts he and Odrak had hidden behind the mountains, away from the village. "They are the feathers, but the bird you speak of is called Great Mah."

"It is true, you speak to them and are understood?"

"I knew their songs before I knew the tongues of humans." Mah smiled and ran his hand up and down her arm. "Why must you go?"

"I think my flesh is torn. Your seed escapes me," she moaned, looking down at him.

"Can I help?"

"Yes, call Saamyli to come to me."

Mah retied his loin cloth and rushed to the door, a thing still strange to him, but he opened it. The women on the platform started to agitate and guards came over to quiet them. Not seeing Saamyli right away he stepped outside. Two guards ran over to him and pushed him back. He nodded his head and told them that Saamyli was needed. One of them marched from the clearing, calling for her to come. The clearing suddenly overflowed with women trying to see what was going on. Mah could see Odrak standing in the entrance of his hut, fully naked with even his feathered necklace removed. A woman was trying to pull him back. Two guards went over and ordered him inside, but he would not leave until Mah signaled that he was all right.

Odrak closed the door and the woman he was with knocked him to the ground. He sat there fuming with anger but did not speak. She smiled and returned to the mat and laid down, ordering him to come to her. He did but would not touch or look at her.

She caressed him saying, "Now, there is peace between us. You have hurt me, and now I have hurt you."

Odrak wondered whether Mah was having as difficult a time as he. "Is this the way of your people? To promise relief and then not to give it? Is that what they do to Mah?"

She did not understand nor did she care. She pulled him to her and this time forced him on his back. He was surprised at her strength, but he knew he could hurt her if he tried. He wanted the noise outside to quiet down. It made him worry over Mah. He wished they could have shared a hut together.

"This time you are not to move, I say," she ordered. "I will hold you close, but wait until I say!"

Odrak did not like this woman and forced the name Olouvaa from his mind. He wished he was not so ready for her to take him, but his pleasure stick would not soften. Even when she argued with him and struck him about the face, he found his body would have the relief she offered, no matter.

He laid still while she finally got him inside. He wanted her closer, but found he enjoyed the look of pain on her face. He had never seen it on a woman's face at a time like this and thought it suiting for such hateful people. He moved a little and it made her screech and clench her teeth. She hit him hard in his chest, and he could not believe a young feeder could be as mean as this. He tried to separate himself from the pleasure in his loins, but not thinking of it only made it sweeter. She was tighter than any woman he had ever known, wet and sweet smelling like Mah. Before he could stop it, her warmth brought forth his seed. He cried out and twitched about from the pleasure he felt running up into her. He tried to pull her close but the pace of her movement increased his flow, turning his hot thrills to tasty chills. He had to bite his own arm to stop this pleasure, thinking now only of Mah to give the moment meaning. He felt her grip him around in pulses that threatened to start the flow anew. He had to admit he enjoyed this sensation alone, but as she was about to fall on him in the grips of her own relief, he pulled himself out of her roughly and slipped out from under her.

She screamed and cursed him, kicked him and called him a beast, which he did not mind. He was done with her and still not satisfied. He would await another and hope she would be of a gentler sort. He watched her gather her wraps and dash out of the hut, smiling at her leaving and at the guards who came to see what the fuss was about. He got up to speak with them, but they ordered him to keep his place, so he returned to the mat, and then stared down at the blood and seed mixed together in a little puddle.

▼▼▼▼▼

"Come, Keishlee," Adah pulled her close and then led her to the Swaahali's medicine hut. "Everywhere one goes in the village today there is trouble and fuss."

Keishlee agreed, having received many rude looks and threatening gestures. "I just want us to go somewhere alone. Come with me."

"You must see Swaahali. She wishes to speak with you first. It should not take long. Your man of medicine is with her, and he wishes you there as well."

The shadows had returned to the land, and Keishlee was exhausted without her midday rest. She stepped into the hut to find many women and guards there. Shhaha was with Swaahali and another medicine woman, tending a young woman Keishlee recognized as one of the selected. Shaloolaa and most of the Tukshead sat off to one side.

Swaahali noticed her weariness and offered her the bowl she had been drinking from. It was a rich smelling brew with tiny bits of leaf and herbs stewing in green water. Keishlee drank it when she saw that Shhaha had a bowl of it as well.

Swaahali crawled around to sit where all could see her. Having more power than Shaloolaa in her medicine hut, she ordered the guards to leave, then called her medicine women over and asked that she take the sick woman, and go to the seeding huts to tend the others who might need her.

Shomnyaa and Somaali were a bit put out and started to speak angry words, but Shaloolaa motioned them to keep their places. She and Swaahali looked at each other, and tho their colors were different, Keishlee knew they shared close blood. These two could speak without words, and this put a stillness in the air that took away Keishlee's weariness.

Swaahali lowered her eyes and said, "There use to be a custom among our women when we lived in the desert lands of Caenaa's birth, of mixing the blood of seeding pairs in a bowl of soft carrara stone. It is said that the medicine women of those days could look at the mixing blood, after being touched with fire, and tell the futures of the seeding pairs. The magic of this has been lost to our people, but it has been kept alive among Keishlee's people."

Everyone looked at Keishlee and wanted to speak. Swaahali laid her hand on Keishlee's leg and smiled at her as if to say, "Do not take offense," and said, "Keishlee has never been seeded."

"You have no daughters?" huffed Shaloolaa and Somaali. "What a marvel you are," said Shaloolaa alone.

Swaahali continued to smile at Keishlee, saying, "A woman can only acquire her full strength from the Great Mother once she herself becomes a mother. They marvel at you now, unseeded, thinking of what you shall be after."

"What is it you called us here to say, Swaahali?" asked Somaali.

"Keishlee knows not this blood magic, and I read only bones. No other in our village has proof of this power—but there is one here who has gained my respect, and who...."

"I know what you would say, Swaahali. I also feel we might be making a mistake mixing their blood with ours. It might have been better to let them go their way then to bring their magic among us," spoke Shaloolaa.

"Yes, I must agree," huffed Shemaa. "The thought of favor with the great Sun Bird has brought madness to our women."

"Even the little ones kept themselves from midday rest," whispered Shomnyaa.

"They will have finished all their storage of wine before the night comes to relieve us from the day," spoke Shaloolaa. "They argue between themselves over deeds they have to drag back from memory, and they fight each other for places with the other man creature of your village."

"New challenges come to the Tukshead even now," grunted Somaali as she saw three women approach the guards outside.

Swaahali said, "The women of Tuk village will abide by the words of the Tukshead, as long as the Tukshead keeps the respect of their words. You cannot stop the seeding as it has begun, but we could use this power of blood to know what is to come. I say we use it. The bones of our great leaders are damp in a dry bag."

All the Tuk women in the room were jolted by these

words. Even Keishlee shook, having sensed her meaning.

"Our ancestors cry to us of some near danger," Shaloolaa directed her words to Keishlee.

"I have tried all day to see this danger, but I cannot see the full vision without drinking the poison for the blood trance, and I have none as you know," continued Swaahali.

Shomnyaa was beside herself with worry. "It is a journey of more than five days to the field of black crowns."

"The trance takes too long, besides the journey," huffed Swaahali.

"Who is it that has this power to read the blood?" asked Sonmyaa, getting to the point they were all avoiding.

"The women would have to be cut by this person," said Somaali, angry and knowing the answer.

Keishlee rested her hand on Shhaha's leg and he inched up closer to her. She was wide awake again and looking at the empty bowl and wanting more. It had thoroughly restored her strength.

"I can draw the blood, he only...."

Somaali jumped up from her place screaming, "No man creature may perform magic on our people. You yourself keep the skull of Caenaa as a reminder of how she died. Is this not why our land became a desert, and all men known as beast? You would have this happen to our people here?" Somaali roared at Swaahali, who could only lower her head for having made the suggestion.

"Swaahali, this is our most sacred service to our people. To keep them from this danger. This is why we do not share the land, or keep a mate to ourselves alone. Keishlee, I would become sacrifice if it would help my people, or save them from some horror, but this I cannot do," Shaloolaa spoke, feeling the weight of her position. She signaled to the Tukshead and all of them left the room.

A young apprentice to Swaahali, who had gone unnoticed, came over and wrapped her arms around the older women. "It was good you sent the younger Somaali, and all the guards from the hut," she said, trying to comfort Swaahali, "Her mother may hold her tongue, for she has respect of you, but the younger would have you challenged."

"I know," moaned Swaahali in despair. She turned to Shhaha with a terrified and lost expression, saying, "Do not take offense, Shhaha. I grant you already know the tale of Caenaa.

Well, this is what has become of her daughters."

"May I speak as I would to my own?" he asked, looking at her and then over to her apprentice.

"My name is Shemaa. Swaahali has the promise of my blood. If she has respect for you, I am like the dust at your feet. Speak as you would."

"You did not tell me you had such a sacred thing as Caenaa's skull. With such a thing...."

"True, it has magic," Swaahali interrupted, "but its magic is dangerous. Many who have used it in the past have been driven to madness by their visions. I don't dare use it, and I cannot let you see it or touch it."

Shhaha turned away and fixed his eyes on something deep inside, his face like cloth being held against the wind.

Adah had been hissing from outside for Keishlee to come, but she did not dare move without word from Shhaha. He was deep within his power now. This was the look they said he could kill with. To her people it was to curse yourself to move about in his presence now. If she were running from some danger and came upon him in this state, she would stop and be still until he told her to go, or the danger got her. She knew these two women were truly of the blood [*Blood Keepers*], when they too kept still as stones.

The fuss made by Odrak's first woman gave him a touting from Saamyli. She ordered him to be more considerate with the others, since most of them would be seeding for the first time. He was an apprentice to the Keeper of the Blood, and knew this from the blood they left behind. It had unnerved him, since he was too young to mate, and had been no feeder's first relief.

He had checked himself while with the second one, to find she too dropped blood on him. He almost lost all desire for her. To wear blood spots meant someone close had died. But she had been gentle with him. She had even showed him how to do the kiss, which drove him quite crazy when she did this on his lips. He had rolled on top of her and listened to every sound from her body and took control of her pleasure.

Soon he was doing so again with this one, whose name was Nuba. She had insisted on him entering from behind, while she was on her knees. This was his favorite position, with her feeder bags hanging down away from him, where he could hold and squeeze them, instead of them hanging in his face, where he lay in dread of her milk getting in his eyes.

Her name he would always remember. She had a sweet musty smell, and was black like his people, with a slight blue sheen. She wore her hair in many small braids that fell off her back, each one threaded with colored strings and tiny fresh berries, which he nibbled while they laid together.

Unlike the others when finished, she stayed and dressed in front of him, saying, "I shall have to fight to keep your seed. Every sister in the village is jealous of me now."

"Swaahali says that all of the selected ones will be protected when we leave."

"That will only be for a short time. I wish you could stay. You two man creatures are not like any of the creatures of our village."

She noticed he did not like being called a creature and pulled him close, running her fingers across his long shapely lips. She did not believe that men were human, but she hoped that he might be, and offered to eat his food. She told him her helping to eat the food would be a sign to the others that she had been pleased. When he brought her one of the leaves of fruit chunks and nut meats, she told him that she would need three more to show how great her pleasure had been.

"Teach me how to speak to the great Sun Birds," she asked, dipping pieces of her food into the juice bowl he had brought for her to drink.

"I do not think I can," he stumbled over the words. "Mah teaches me still. When I hear his voice, or one of the birds, I can remember how to make the sounds. Without that, sometimes I cannot find the voice."

"It sounds so strange. Like the language of a people with many tongues in their mouths."

She had explained the sound perfectly, and it brought the call to "stop" to his tongue, the call he was most familiar with, since he was always telling them to stop feeding him. Her eyes never left his mouth as he made the call a few more times, and then he did the one for "human," which pleased her greatly, and she set about to excite him over again.

To his surprise, she did not want him to enter her, she only wanted to play with it. She insisted he save himself for the others. He rubbed their heads together, while feeling the hot juices thicken between her legs. He begged and fell out on the dirt, still and quiet so that she might take him any way she chose, but she said her sisters would need him, and that she would not be greedy with her time.

Before she left, she had eaten four leaves of food, which was quite a lot. Saamyli had to come to the door for her, and she looked on them with more cheer than he had seen from her all day. Nuba ran her fingers through the knotting of his long hair, then gathered up all the empty leaves. Saamyli stepped aside, and Nuba stood in the door for a while, fanning herself with the moist leaves. She smiled back at him and then threw the leaves in front of the entrance and left. Odrak noticed that some of the women on the platform smiled, and slid themselves closer to his side. The guards who came to clean the hut after her could see for the first time that he was happy as well.

Ramaa stood in the entrance to the men's hut hoping that the woman with the heavy trusses down her back would win the fight. He thought it was stupid for these women to fight over him like this, but he did feel honored by it. Guards stood around them in a circle and would not let them pass until this fight was over. It was to be the last, and the woman called Nuba had beaten 10 and 2 women with great ease. He was sure his mate could beat them all, but this Nuba gave him pause for her strength and her beauty.

The other men in the hut were jealous of him now and angry that these fights were keeping them from their pleasure. Ramaa had to give one of them a good thrashing, before they all stopped spitting on him. When it was over, most of them cowered in a corner and left him the best view of the fight. Some of them, the ones Shhaha had taught the dance, had earned his friendship. Most had few words, and none of them had names that were actually words. But they stood next to Ramaa cheering and howling, this being a familiar sight to them.

A stepping jump kick, which Ramaa had never seen the likes of, put an end to the fighting. The guards put the women in order, and lined them up outside the hut. They called Ramaa out, along with the other seven naked "extras," and lined them up in front of their respective groups.

Outside the wooden hut, Ramaa was relieved to be standing his full height again. But then he had a shock that almost canceled his excitement. There was a long line of women in front of him. He looked over to see the 3 or 4 women walking away with the other extras, and was now jealous of them.

"The two others that came with you have almost ten each. You are more than twice their size. We are not too many?" asked the woman Nuba, who was at the head of the group.

Ramaa was speechless. He could not relieve so many women. At least, not in only two days.

"I can see we are too many. Well, may you find strength, but if not, we have a gift that may help. I say come now, you are mine for a time."

▼▼▼▼▼

Mah sat and recalled the names of the women he had spent time with so far. There was Tanzaa, who had gotten sick and had to be taken away; and Mabaasa, whose coloring reminded him of Olaah. She had taken great pleasure with him, and stayed to eat a bowl of fish soup and 3 leaves of food. He laughed now, having thought her sloppy when she threw the leaves and the bowl against the hut. But his next woman, Rhaapta, had explained this before she left. She had also shown him much pleasure. Having had much less experience with feeders than Odrak, he was glad when they took the time to tell him something he did that added to their pleasure. When she left, and added her two bowls and one large leaf tray to the pile outside the hut, Mah felt he had finally gotten the kiss done right and looked forward to trying it again.

He waited until after the guards left to have a taste of the mysterious red powder. Shhaha had laughed at seeing the powder, saying that he had not seen any since he was a slave. He acted like it was unimportant, but Mah caught him pinching some into one of his hollow bones, which told him that it was a source of some magic.

He put a little water in a bowl and pinched in some of the powder and stirred with his finger. He had been told to use only a little, but the water did not even change color, so he added another and another, until the water was a light brown, and then he drank it down.

"Is she your slave?" Ramaa asked Nuba when they entered her hut.

"What is that? I've heard the woman Keishlee use this for the little ones. What does it mean?"

"The one who comes to serve," Ramaa replied.

"Is that what they do?" she smiled at Ramaa. "Is that what a little sister is to you?"

"Does she not do all that you ask? Does she think other than what you say until her blood memories return?"

"I understand blood memories, but it is I who serve her. I must tell her everything she needs to know to live."

"What you tell her is in service to you and your people. How else can she become a member of your tribe?"

Nuba smiled and called her daughter over and introduced Ramaa. "Put this face to memory, daughter. Remember he is now forbidden you and your sister. How do you like this one?"

"He is much too big, mother," she said, and looked up at Ramaa with a harsh glance.

Her mother kissed her before she ran from the hut. Nuba offered Ramaa some food, but he refused and tried to lay her down next to him. She twisted herself loose and kicked him in the arm. Ramaa smiled up at her, not wanting her to think she had hurt him. "Why are your people so rude? Have you no kindness in you? Has the Great Mother deformed your hearts?" he snapped.

She stood her ground and stared down at him, a little sorry to have spoiled the mood. "I guess we shall see which one of us is the beast," she tried to make it a joke as she looked over at the unrolled mat on the ground. She smiled and walked to the back of the hut, removed her hanging cloth and then the weapon from its folds.

Ramaa jumped to his feet, saying, "You expect some pleasure when you threaten me?"

She smiled and stood the weapon up near one of the windows. "If you go near it, a guard who is watching will rush in here and cut you to pieces. They watch all the huts visited by a man creature. No creature must lay his hands on it."

"I do not want your weapon," he said flatly.

"I just wanted you to know a thing."

Ramaa remembered the pain of his sickness more than the pain of the cuts. He did not want to ever see another weapon.

"Come," she whispered and sat down at his feet, beckoning him to follow. "Do not let our harsh ways upset you. We are human as I think even you might be."

Ramaa laughed aloud and sat down facing her. This was a joke to him. All people knew that the clan of the Tall Walkers were the first humans. His clan was human before the clan of the Waterhorse, and even tho they have greater numbers, they gave respects to his clan over all others.

She pushed herself on top of him and began removing her straps, unwrapping her waist girdle and slipping it out from under her. She was like the others here, smelling more like flowers than a woman, but it was tantalizing, and as she sat back down, her softness and warmth seemed to go right through him. She pulled off her chest girdle, and Ramaa came erect and slapped up against her back. She looked down at him, pulling on her thick tresses, and said, "They say the woman Keishlee told the selected ones to be gentle with the man creatures of her village. I think you may have to be gentle with me instead."

With his long arms Ramaa pulled her up closer to his face, but she slid herself down from his chest, slowly letting it make the room it would need. She gasped for a moment and almost removed him, but Ramaa held her close, as gently as one would hold a newborn. He had yet to see or know of the kiss and when she did so to his chest, bracing herself there, it so thrilled him he twitched and snapped up into her.

"Don't make me scream, creature," she groaned, all her muscles pulled tight and tense. "If I scream too loudly, they will have reason to interrupt us."

It was taking Odrak longer and longer to give each woman the seeding they required, but it was no less enjoyable. He remembered what Swaahali had said about the red powder, and as he could feel the rapid clutching and pulsing, he forced out the seed juice, telling himself that he would try this disiac before the next one.

She fell on him, fully satisfied but obviously glad that he had finished moving about within her. She slipped off and laid next to him, asking him to bring her food, and beginning the round of questioning he had started to grow weary of.

They all had asked about the wide scar down his chest to his stomach, which could be seen clearly now that he was so clean, and they all wanted to know how to sing the songs of the Sun

Birds. The one after Nuba, whose name was Tanga, wanted to try on the feathered necklace, and talked and talked about the colors and beauty of the feathered cape. Next came Fezza, who he would also remember. She had been hot inside and gave him twice the relief in the time it took to get this present one. She ate five leaves of food, and still hardly let him speak. She talked nonstop about the magic she would have with her tribe if his seeding took root. She dreamed of being like Shaloolaa and having her place at the center of the Tukshead, since the magic he received from the birds would now surely come into her and make her taller. Then came Ghat, who was the perfect choice after Fezza, because she hardly spoke at all. But she was nothing to lay with. Odrak felt like he was forcing himself on her. She made no sound or move, nor showed any sign that she enjoyed this thing they did together. But she was a delight to the eye, and smelled even sweeter than Mah. Then came Mycee and the woman Arba, who was with him now. Both were the color of Mah's Olaah, but neither would ever be tall. Mycee had light brown eyes and thick juicy lips which he enjoyed using the kiss on. She was wet with thick juices that did not rub off as easily as the others. Arba was light brown, and hot like Fezza, with almost no hair between her legs. He was playing with it now, as he had wanted to do before they started. This was a delight to him, never having seen one like this except on very young slaves. His hands could not adjust to the feel of her nearly hairless folds. He rubbed his face on her and sniffed, and licked until she pulled him up on her again.

Adah finished putting together the long tresses on the other side of Keishlee's head. Keishlee thought they felt glorious, and made her feel stronger somehow. She wanted to do the rest of her hair but feared taking out all her age knots. She told Adah she had 20 and 4 of them, and that if she removed them, they would have to be put back or the women of her clan would think ill of her.

They finished the small meal Adah prepared, and Keishlee stretched out to be given a rub down before her final challenge. She had dreaded this moment coming, but nothing had stood in its way and so she readied herself. When the time came, a group of guards and many women gathered around the hut to bring them to the feast clearing. Keishlee went to them, but Adah refused to go, saying she could not watch, reminding her that Charlaa was the next best fighter in the village. Only Scochaa stood a chance of beating her.

As Mah brought Carthaa into the hut he was too nervous to wait for her to undress. He paced about the room, looking down at himself and feeling a strange kind of pain all over. It was painful for his pleasure stick to be inactive. Sitting with Femaa and Assyria earlier had been like torture, even tho he had patiently waited for them to take him twice. He was losing patience now, and hoping that this feeder would not be new to seeding. He wanted her to want more than the others.

He dared to touch her without her asking for it. He felt on the verge of pinning her to the ground and plunging himself into her. With all the calm he could gather he rolled on top of her and hoped she would not scream. He tried the kiss but was too nervous and knew it showed. It was a pleasure to find her less tight than the others, and more accepting of his movements, which were quickly becoming deep thrusts that he wanted to drive out her other side. He was having strange urges, and wished that he could go on undisturbed, by her or anyone for the rest of the night. All he wanted to do was feel the pleasure of her enclosing him, her body sucking him in deeper, and then squeezing his throbs so that he would not burst open within her. Wetter and wetter she became. The way she moved under him gave him a new thrill, and when she wrapped her legs around his waist she cried louder than all the others, as he finally got all of himself inside. He feared he might actually hurt her, but he could not stop. He gripped her tightly around both arms, covered her small mouth with his, and made sure she could not move. He began to pound upon her as if to drive her into the ground. She clawed his back and he continued to grind, hoping she did not want him to stop. He looked at her, and all he saw was wild abandonment, but he did not know what that was. She did not scream too loudly, she only moaned and tossed her head about, so he continued to pump himself up into her. When he heard Saamyli call at the door, it angered him and he cursed, feeling he had been cheated of some of his time. He knew he had to release his seed, which would pain him because he did not want to stop. Saamyli opened the door and he let himself go, hoping this time it would bring him some relief.

Odrak had dozed off during the long rest period and was awakened by Saamyli's call at the door. He once again retied his loin cloth, and put back on the feathered necklace. He went to the dwindling spread of foods and took a tiny pinch of the red power as Shhaha had suggested. He mixed it with a little water in his mouth, swallowed and hoped it would do as Swaahali had told him. He was beginning to feel the strain of having such hard desires.

There were only five of the women left on the platform, and for the second time, he and Mah were making their selection together. He smiled over to Mah, but lost his grin at the sight of Mah's loin cloth sticking out in front of him, and the manic look about his eyes. It would have been more like Mah to have waited for him to choose this time, but Mah hardly looked at the woman he grabbed and rushed into the hut. He did not look at Odrak at all.

Odrak stood there in silence for a moment, not noticing that twilight was almost upon them. Something was wrong with Mah, but what it was, and what to do about it, Odrak could not think. As the door closed he saw the guards grinning and Saamyli's look of embarrassment. He overheard one of the guards say something about Swaahali and wondered if she was in the hut as well.

When next he looked at the women on the platform, they were all standing and looking at him angrily. Odrak snatched one and led her to the hut. He paced about while she spoke to him and undressed. He was not listening to her, he was trying desperately to hear something, anything from outside the hut.

"You seem worried over the other creature. You would think you were human," she said and the insult brought his attention back to her. "Don't worry about him. He'll be all right once the effects of the great horn wear off. A rest in the hill waters, and he'll be fine."

"What are you taking about?" he asked, coming closer to her. He did not understand her words.

She looked about the hut until she found the small bowl of red powder and held it out to him. "This," she smiled. "He has probably taken too much, is all. It is harmless except to the woman he lays with," she laughed. "Here, try some. You must need some by now."

Odrak took the bowl from her and looked at her severely,

knowing that he had already taken some. He put it back in its place and took her by the shoulders roughly, asking, "Can you take me to him? Is it allowed?"

"If the guards will let us."

Odrak had her quickly out the door where he confronted guards sitting on the platform. No one else was around.

"Where have the others gone?" he asked.

"The final challenge takes place. They go to watch," one of the guards huffed and tried to back him into the hut.

"We wish to see the others," spoke the woman with Odrak. "Maybe we can all go and watch the challenge as well. It is past time for a break from our sitting."

The guards looked at each other and agreed silently. Odrak almost ran over to the hut. The guards signaled to one another and those near the door let Odrak and the woman in.

When they entered, Odrak was so frightened by what he saw he pulled the woman in after him and quickly closed the door. He hoped that none of the guards had seen. Mah had the feeder pinned to the ground with a hand over her mouth, and the position they were in did not look good or natural. Odrak rushed to Mah and pulled him off the feeder, while the woman with him went to tend the other. Odrak had to pull Mah to the ground and pin him there, until he came down from the fury that had taken his mind and body.

Mah looked up at him, and the shame he felt turned his head away. He broke loose from Odrak and begged the woman to forgive him. Mah was so disturbed that he could not see that the feeder was only a little shaken and not angry at all. She was laughing but trying her best to hide it.

Mah slammed himself into Odrak, clutching and holding him tight to his chest. Mah began pleading with Odrak to forgive him as well, and suddenly found Odrak's nearness disorienting, and a greater temptation than the new woman. He released his hold on Odrak and wrapped his arms around himself, hoping to stop the rushes up his spine, but nothing seemed to help.

"Mah, you must calm yourself." Odrak gave him a shake, making Mah's whole body quake.

"Do not touch him. He will be able to fight off the disiac better if there is no one touching him," said the woman who had come with Odrak.

"Touching makes the drug stronger," said the feeder Mah had attacked.

Odrak pulled Mah's arms apart and stepped away. They waited for a while, and Mah's breathing slowed. He had never seen Mah like this. He had never seen anyone like this, and thought how true it was for these women to think of men as beasts. The protectors of his clan would have attacked Mah, had they discovered him like this.

"I am so ashamed. I thought I was fine until we removed our cloths and she took me."

"This challenge is about to begin, Mah," Odrak spoke harshly, now worried about what Shhaha had told them earlier.

"Oh yes. I had wanted to speak with you about that. I have thought of a way to stop it. We must speak with Fresh-Rain or Pepper-Grass, before the fast ones are out of the citadel. Only they can do what has to be done."

"Twilight is almost upon us, Mah. They will be gone from this land soon."

"Come, let us hurry. No, do not help me up. I will take care." He turned to the women who had come over and asked, "Can you take us out of sight from the others?"

Odrak could see that Mah was still trembling, and that even with the sadness on his face, he still carried a painful throbbing of readiness between his legs. For a moment Odrak thought, how terrible, anyone could just take him in this condition. While Mah tried to dress himself, Odrak looked at the lovely face of the woman he had been with, and wondered what he would have found if she had also taken this powder.

Keishlee was stunned by the speed of this woman. Sometimes she moved more like the wind than something made of flesh and blood. Keishlee could barely see the blows coming. At other times the woman was like a hopper, and just when she thought she had timed it right, the woman had gone in another direction. Keishlee would land a good kick and send the woman flying, but as soon as she had recovered herself, Charlaa would have her by the hair, pounding her face into the ground.

Keishlee began to feel helpless. She had no real desire to fight Charlaa, and yet the fight had gone on longer than any of the others already. Charlaa already had two very good opportunities to take her life, and never once went for her weapon. The delay made the crowd eager for blood, anybody's blood. They shouted, but not for either of them, just for their blood. Even the guards were hostile with them, shoving each of them back into the fight whenever one got knocked too far away. Keishlee hardly had time to catch her breath. She could feel the eye that had been swollen, swelling up again. The tresses Adah had fixed were a great help. They gave her leverage against Charlaa every time she took hold of one, but they were heavy and the pain of solid punches threatened to take her head off.

Keishlee tried to land another good kick, but ended up almost twisting her ankle. She fell hard to the ground and clenched herself to stop the pain of a muscle in her back. She didn't have the strength to move, and choked on the blood dripping down her throat. She prepared herself to accept the death that had to come. The crowd was screaming "favors" like a curse, and ordering Charlaa to make the kill.

From the corner of a tearful eye, she knew Charlaa now had her weapon in hand. She could hear Shhaha's words ringing in her ears and see the awful look of Swaahali's warning that this must not happen. She hadn't wanted to fight, but once it began, she had given it all she could. Her pride had even got the best of her when she got knuckles in her eye. She fought hard until she got the upper hand, but it was lost so quickly, she was convinced that Charlaa had let it happen.

Suddenly she could see or hear nothing and the field around her moved out of time. She could feel something sharp sticking in her stomach, and she knew that Charlaa had plunged her blade through her. She remembered the stories her feeder used to tell, about spirits going back to the Great Mother, by way of the nearest mountain. It was said they did this because the mountains were like the Great Mother's feeder bags, and there the spirits could be nursed anew, in preparation for life among the dead. She knew this was true now, because she felt like a spirit, rising and floating above the ground, as darkness pressed in upon her body and her mind.

Nuba, the elder, had felt the strength of Ramaa, and had been so pleased by him that she could not think of him as less than human. Just as she wanted him to, he had managed to take her in a way that forced her to respect him without feeling threatened by him. He was gentle and tender with his affections, and yet could selfishly enjoy himself once he had her wanting more. Before they were finished, she liked him enough to warn him about the dangers of his being at the feast clearing, but the challenge between Charlaa and Keishlee had already started, and he was determined to go.

"You might kill a few, you might even kill many, but all would be lost since you are out numbered, and our weapons make us invincible. Besides, the Tukshead has been meeting all day to stop new challenges. There is even a whisper that Swaahali has pulled out the sacred icon, which I will not speak more of, except to say that a great danger must be facing our people because of the new blood come among us."

These fears had set the village into a frenzy of fresh agitation and Nuba did not want to let him go. Not because she wanted to keep him for herself, but because she wanted to save his life. She was proud of the strength of her sisters, but one of the others might not be able to keep him from the feast clearing. When her words had failed to stop him, she stood near the entrance, dressed and ready to put her weapon into action, if she had to.

"If this Charlaa is as good as you say, and you have respect for Keishlee, why then do you not try to stop this thing? Why should Keishlee have to die? You people are...."

"Ramaa!! I give you my respect, and I have not done so with any man creature. If Charlaa takes Keishlee's life there may be a chance to save others still, but if you go and break out among our people, you'll find blood there to reckon with."

Ramaa did not have to look at the scars that would now and forever be on both his arms. It was a horror to imagine these women gone mad with such a weapon in hand. They had cut him with smiles on their faces. He blinked the thought away and sat back down, cursing the weapons that gave them this power over his people and, he thought, over many people.

"The people of the Waterhorse clan will come to avenge their slain Keeper of the Blood. Such a one is sacred to our clans, and all will die for him."

"That is a thing for another time," she said plainly.

"How could your people do such a thing!" he roared and jumped to his feet to remind her that he was a giant to her people. But he ended looking foolish since he had to pull his head out of another hole he made in her roof.

Nuba feared he might totally destroy her hut, but said simply, "Ramaa, let me tell you a thing. There was a time when fighting was not known to us, and for many generations the women of our clan were chased from one land to another. We were always a clan of women, who kept the men among us in few numbers. The other clans did not approve of us. They hunted us, ruined our daughters, and took our human men away. From place to place we ran, and everywhere we went the life we found was less and less human. Those who lived joined with another clan of women with our customs, but these women taught us to fight."

"The blood of the Seventh Sister, Tukele," Ramaa spoke, remembering a tale told by Shhaha and the name of Nuba's village.

"You know of the Seven Sisters?!" Nuba asked.

"It is sacred to all those that are human, is it not?"

Nuba's eyes watered, but she did not move from the entrance. Demanding memory was trying to speak to her, but she had not been trained to listen. She could sense some of the turmoil brewing around her. It was like being lost in a flood, or having to trust walking in a deep desert in the middle of a sand storm. She was suddenly frightened, and had to remind herself of how she had earned her weapon: on the night of her first raid, when she got to see for the first time the beast that had chased her people for generations.

She wanted to go to him, to comfort him, and to receive comfort. She called her daughter inside and held her against her leg, more determined now that nothing should move around her. She knew now why the other women had stopped waiting and went to see Swaahali. They must have felt it too: Swaahali, doing magic.

Shhaha watched everything Swaahali did and told himself that he could not have done better. The honor and pride he felt at being allowed see the skull of Caenaa was overwhelming. He could not imagine the faces of the other blood keepers, when and if he lived to tell this tale.

He had chanted to help her go into her trance, but the hut was soon surrounded. He remembered the warning she gave him about doing anything in this hut that could be taken for magic. "Any woman who sees would be free to cut you down," she had said over and over, to impress upon him the lack of power, even among the Tukshead, to save him.

He saw the signs of strong blood magic in her. She was lost to them all now. The crushed bones and herbs, mixed with her own blood inside the now covered skull of Caenaa, had worked its magic without the special potions he carried hidden in his bones. Her eyes rolled and turned inward. She would be safe, if the spirits of her people were deep in the land, and her power was great enough to reach them.

It was a long time before she made another move or sound, then her tongue shot out as if it alone were trying to speak. The women outside began to back away from the windows and the door. He had never invoked the spirit words in front of others, and did not remember that he too had looked like this. She was deep in trance and speaking to the spirits now. Her tongue shot forward again, obvious to anyone that it was longer than it should be. It flapped against her face and chin, filling the room with a slip-slap sound that made many women call her name out of fear.

He had seen his teacher, Shama, go visit the Great Mother many times, and he had always come back more human than he left, but the deed took a score of seasons from his life and showed in his appearance. Having lost so many of his own apprentices to some horror, he had not dared to cut short his life, and had not taken this journey.

Her eyes began to roll and spin in their sockets, as her skin was sucked to the bone. It then swelled, and crinkled and swayed, as if blown by hard winds. Shhaha let his tears fall, knowing that it was indeed the skull of Caenaa, only a relic linked to life when it was new could have such magic.

The women were screaming outside the hut, calling for the Tukshead to appear and tame her, or kill her, or bring her out of this trance that had taken away her mind. Shhaha wanted to act, knowing that power like this allowed wandering spirits to take the weaker minds gathered near. If only he could comfort these people with his chants. If only Mah and Odrak were here. They might let them speak. He chanted silently to himself, hoping that it would reach those in need.

The tongue slapped about more wildly than before. This time there was the word, "ka'bal'la." He had known the word would come, when he saw all the liquid leave her face. He began to respect her power, bowing and swaying gently as he was moved by her magic. He could feel his hair come alive, as he saw hers do.

He gave some regret to his own death, as he knew they would kill him for sure, even if they did not fear her enough to do so to her. But he would not be able to stop his chanting, or stop from going into tongues as the deep spirits she had made contact with demanded to know who he was, and why, since he knew how to speak to them, he did not do so with some deference. The spirits pinched him and threatened to make his bowels move. His head was shaking uncontrollably, and it was all he could do to stop from dancing about.

He closed his eyes to the changing colors of her aura as he saw the spirits come to greet and take her. He tried to close his eyes and mind to the screams of the spirits demanding he speak. They were all around him, and his silence angered them, and they shook sticks loose from the hut.

Women screamed now and tore down the walls of the hut in order to see. He felt their warmth and then the heat of torch fires near his flesh, but he could not stop himself from beginning the chant of passing into darkness. He proceeded into the blood-calling chant, and felt the sharp edge of a Tuk blade cut into his flesh. He could not scream from the pain, or even take note of who had done it, or what was going on around them. He was locked into the haze world of the prevision, where he waited to be judged by the ancient spirits, before going on to meet the Great Mother.

Shaloolaa ordered the guards to seize the women slashing Shhaha on his arms and neck. The medicine hut was coming down around them, as the rest of the Tukshead appeared. Their personal guards were having to protect them from their own women, as everyone demanded that the magic of Swaahali be stopped.

Shaloolaa had to fight her senses and the skin from crawling up her back. She saw Swaahali and then Shhaha convulse and thrash about. There was chaos all around her, and her inner sense of time told her night had come upon them too quickly. Her control was waning with these women. In this moment, if her enemies had been less afraid, she could easily have been dead by now. But all the Tukshead kept to her orders, and held the other women back.

It had been a wise move to have the walls of the medicine hut destroyed. The women who had not seen the start of this would not take his chanting as magic, if he were not inside the hut.

Glad for a distraction, Shaloolaa ordered the women who had attacked Shhaha to kneel. Whatever this was about, peace and quiet had to be restored, and then maybe she could think of what to do.

She could see too clearly that Swaahali was lost to some other world, even her flesh was not her own. Who could say her power was not the greater, and that what Shhaha did was nothing, and what she did was all?

"Slay them!" ordered Scochaa, coming towards her mother. "They have wasted blood in the medicine hut, and they have done so with one Swaahali uses to assist her magic!"

Shaloolaa wanted to fall on both knees before her daughter, her best friend, her most wise and loyal servant. The scene started to quiet and Shaloolaa tried to put on a smile, a sign of power to her people when done facing danger. She gave the smile to Scochaa, who had seized upon the thing coming to focus in her mind, and yet left Shaloolaa to rule over her people still. Shaloolaa whipped out her weapon and stepped back from the kneeling women.

"He was using his magic in the medicine hut!" screamed one of the women at her feet, now hugging the ground.

"True! He spoke magic words!" shouted another.

"The hut is no more!" Shaloolaa spoke to the quieting crowd. "It is Swaahali's magic that is in power here. Look at her! Who can not see her power?"

Some were still crying and screeching in fear, but others started suggesting that what had just happened in the feast clearing might also be Swaahali's magic.

Shaloolaa ordered the women at her feet to be removed. "Swaahali shall decide their fate, once she returns to us!"

"It was Swaahali the eldest to last call upon the magic of the skull, and she never returned!" a women cried.

Some peace was coming back to her village, and tho most still cowered on the ground and held each other close, they tried to cope with all that was happening to them. "Then, we shall do as we have done in the past!" Shaloolaa shouted and signaled for the Tukshead to join her.

As they came over, Shaloolaa looked around carefully. It was the center of the village and darkness was upon them. Women brought torches to light fires as they calmed themselves, and all looked upon Swaahali and Shhaha, who were transfixed where they sat, and looked like stones with monsters inside, trying to break free.

The madness that threatened to take her people had passed, and she could feel their embarrassment at having lost all control. Her people were strong and brave, and she was proud to be their leader. She watched the apprentice medicine women move the others away and begin drawing the circles in the ground around Swaahali; to keep her magic confined.

They would contribute everything strange this day to her magic now, and all would wait, days if they had to, for Swaahali to return, or to fall dead before them. Only then would they think on their own again.

When Odrak and Mah had returned from the escarpment, they had gone back to the seeding huts with the two women. Mah was still feeling the effects of the great horn, and would not be touched. It took all his control to stay calm, and he feared what he might do left alone with the feeder, Mabezi.

On the way back to the clearing, Odrak insisted that the women find some way for them to share a hut together. This way he could make sure that Mah didn't hurt himself, or anyone else. The truth was the drug was beginning to take its effect on him as well, and he didn't want to be alone with this woman he was quietly growing fond of.

At first the women objected, but only because they knew the guards would not allow it, and they feared losing their place or their seeding rights if they refused to obey. Odrak threatened not to return and to take Mah with him if they did not find a way. When they neared the seeding huts and found no one there, the women rushed them inside Mah's hut and hoped that the guards would not check on them for a while.

It was a good walk from the escarpment to this side of the village, far away from the main huts. During that time, the four of them got very friendly with each other. Zambe liked both Odrak and Mah, and shared food with them as they sat down to rest. She spoke of how unusual it was to see man creatures who could stomach each other's company.

"You two seem to like each other," smiled Zambe.

Mabezi huffed in disbelief and even tho both Mah and

Odrak laughed at them, she said, "All men are part beast, and at any moment, one might turn around and eat you. You two seem different to us, but one of you is sure to kill the other one day, and for no good reason."

Mah was glad he had some control of himself. He signaled Odrak to be still as he saw him dig his toes into the ground. Mabezi did not know what she was saying. She did not know his people and had no knowledge of their ways. He smiled at her as if she were a young slave who knew no better. She was definitely totally unaware that Mah had just saved her face from a kick, which Odrak could do well sitting on his heels. Odrak turned away from her in disgust, for her insult to Mah and his people. Zambe felt his pain, and pulled him close, while trying to speak to Mabezi with her eyes.

Mabezi was only interested in getting back to where they left off, and did not see that her words had destroyed their friendship. She positioned herself out of Odrak's view and removed her wraps. She stroked Mah's pleasure stick, which he could not believe had stayed erect all this time.

Looking at them, Odrak wondered when the drug would start affecting that part of his body, and had purposely stayed near Zambe's touch. He wanted to forget Mabezi's words and to be rid of the sight of her. He began to fondle Zambe's feeder bags, but because of his anger nothing happened, until he was naked and she was lying on top of him.

Mabezi had moved Mah to the other side of the hut, making room for them against the wall. She had refrained from touching him too much, even now. He seemed in control, but the panic that glittered behind his eyes blinded her to the sleeping anger there.

Odrak and Zambe were already riding each other, each rolling back and forth over the mat trying to take control. Mabezi took Mah by the shoulders and pulled him to her. Mah shuddered and fell into her arms, surprised at the pleasure that even she could bring by just laying both hands on him. He managed to control himself and lay still, as she climbed on top and took him.

Odrak was moaning with delight. He did not feel any different really, but the thrill he got between his legs was much greater, and to his surprise, he felt like he could hold himself back from releasing his seed just as easily as he could let it go. He felt pinched and squeezed by her as he felt himself swell within her, entering through all the narrow spaces of her channel. Zambe gasped and held him to stillness, adjusting herself to what was different about this new pleasure; squeezing and rubbing and moving over him to see which things she liked.

Odrak heard Mah cry out, and looked over to see him on the ground, with Mabezi riding him in the fullness of her own delight. He could see that Mah was trying to hold himself back, but he was still enjoying himself. Mah felt Odrak's eyes on him and was ashamed that he lay with this woman who had insulted them. He could not look at Odrak and this made him fight back his own pleasure even more. Somehow he found the strength to roll free of her.

Odrak saw it and the pleasure of it made him stroke his body up and down into Zambe, harder and harder until she screamed. He forced her to him, revealing his true strength as he rolled on top of her and forgot the others in the room.

Now Mah's eyes were on him, and Odrak knew it and would not look, but softened himself over Zambe, whispering to her that he was human and not a beast. She already believed it, and held him close, painfully forcing more of him into her, waiting now for this to be finished.

Mah called to him, and the pleasure of it made Odrak release his seed. He stopped holding Zambe but stayed in her until Mah called to him again. He withdrew from Zambe, slowly, and went to Mah, not looking at him but glad that Mabezi sat alone, brooding and angry.

Odrak sat down on his heels in front of him and pulled Mah to his chest. "Nothing she says is true, Odrak. We shall love each other forever. I give my blood to you in this."

"Then you should have let me kill her, for she tries to curse us with her words!"

Zambe came over and sat next to them with tears forming in her eyes, saying over and over again that she believed them both to be human. Mabezi huffed and cursed them and stormed out of the hut. The three of them sat quietly for a while holding each other, not speaking, yet understanding how each other felt. Mah had complete control of himself now and sat on the ground with his head resting on Odrak's knees. He could feel the hardness of Odrak's pleasure stick sticking up between his legs, but felt a flush of real relief, as he could feel that his own was not.

"I have never really believed that all human men were

gone from the world. I have heard whispers that others, including the daughter of Shaloolaa, has found one. I wish you two could stay," she said, and found herself hoping that Charlaa would take Keishlee's life.

Suddenly, they realized the door was open and that no one had come in. In that same instant, an unnatural darkness fell, and there was no light to see each other clearly. For the first time they began to notice the total silence around them. They stumbled around for their loincloths and feathered necklaces, and waited for Zambe to dress. They looked around, but there were no guards or anyone else about and Zambe said, "The seeding huts always have guards near. This is one of the places women come to fight."

As they were walking, both Mah and Odrak fell to their knees, Mah crying out in pain, "Shhaha is in danger."

"I can feel it, too. I sense him strongly," Odrak spoke from the ground, frightening Zambe.

"I can hear him call, Odrak. He needs us."

Mah took Zambe's hand and started running towards the main village. Zambe told them to follow as she broke loose and took the lead. They were surprised at her speed and might have been able to pass her, but it was dark, and they could hardly see until they neared the first cluster of huts.

"Shhaha is the old one with you?" she asked, stopping at the edge of the village. "He has such magic that he can speak to you from far away?"

Odrak was the first to reach her and pointed to the center of the village. "He is there somewhere."

"He is with the woman, Swaahali. She has blood magic and is with him," Mah spoke in a panic. He had never heard Shhaha in his head before like this.

"He has such magic," Zambe snapped at them.

"Yes, of course. He is our Keeper of the Blood," Mah replied.

"No man creature may perform magic in our village. It means death to them who try."

Odrak snatched her around. "You must lead us to the woman Swaahali. Mah says Shhaha is with her. We must go to him, now!"

She looked at them closely for a moment and then explained why they could not run through her village. "It is not permitted, but there is the quick-step. You may do the quick-step," Zambe spoke and then showed them how to do it.

They did not get very far. Guards ran towards them and pulled Zambe aside. As they got nearer, Mah relaxed when he saw that all the members of the Tukshead were with them. Shaloolaa signaled for them to come forward.

They were taken to the meeting hut where others were already gathered. In silence, Mah and Odrak agreed to break free of these women, if they refused to give Shhaha to them.

"He calls," Mah moaned, unable to stop the words.

"He makes magic in our village!" some women shouted.

Shaloolaa silently ordered guards to remove those women who spoke. There was a moment of cursing, and arguing, and some struggle, but the women were removed and Shaloolaa waited for silence before she spoke again.

But Odrak spoke first, saying, "You must take us to Shhaha, our Keeper of the Blood, or we will be forced...."

"Do not speak again in my presence without my permission, or you will die is what you will do!" Shaloolaa roared in a way that snapped both Mah and Odrak to silence. "Bring in the other man creature," she ordered to the guards.

Ramaa was dragged in. His hands were tied to his ankles and thick leaves were tied around his head and eyes. They sat him up close to the Tukshead and Saamyli removed the head bindings. Ramaa's eyes caught sight of Mah and Odrak right away, and it was obvious that he was glad to see them.

Shaloolaa ordered everyone to sit, but Mah and Odrak would not move. Shaloolaa continued to stand and looked at them as if she might pull a weapon out and kill them, but she squeezed out a smile and said, "I have watched you two very closely whenever you have been near. You," she pointed to Odrak, "...and he might be human," she continued over the rising disturbance in the room. "Between you two I have seen affection and caring, intelligence and consideration, which I have never seen in man creatures before. I know you watch over him," she insisted, pointing at Odrak, "...and would gladly give your life to save him," then signaled to guards who surrounded them before Odrak could move. They had their weapons out, and one of them was at Mah's throat. Odrak fell to the ground and began to eat handfuls of dirt for Shaloolaa to see. "That is not necessary. All I wish of you is silence and answers to my questions. Sit!"

As soon as the guards stepped clear, Odrak pulled Mah down to him, keeping his eyes on the guards as he sat. He put the face of the woman, who had touched Mah's skin with her weapon to memory. He had never planned to take a life before, not even of the smallest creature, but in his eyes anyone could see that he was planning her death.

Still holding on to Mah, he turned back to face the Tukshead and tried not to let his blood boil out his ears.

"Something happens now that affects the blood of all my people. Your coming here may be looked upon by our daughters' daughters as a blessing, or a curse. Our woman of medicine journeys to see the Great Mother, and she has taken your...your," she fought with words she found impossible to say, "...your man creature with her. They are in trance together and cannot be touched. Nothing shall happen to either of them, until they are dead from this, or come back to us," she said, coming closer to Mah. "Both of you have spread your seed among us, and are as one with us now. If you know of a way, without the use of magic, to help them, or for the Great Mahs to help them, it would be wise for you to do so now."

Mah sighed in relief, and looked at Odrak with eyes that spoke a secret language between them. Knowing that Shhaha was not in any physical danger made their hearts beat softer. "Yes," Odrak spoke to Mah. "Yes. The chant of the sacred journey would be best."

"A chant is all that is needed," Mah spoke to Shaloolaa, distracting her from the thoughts she had of words being missed between them. He chose his words carefully and said, "We have many chants, but this one should do. It is a journey they are on?"

Odrak was relaxed now, and could feel the anxiety and distress that abounded in the hut. It was all around the village, he thought. "A journey to see the Great Mother you said," Odrak spoke to Shaloolaa.

"Yes." She looked at Odrak suspiciously, then turned to Mah and asked, "Is this a thing of magic?" and her tone impressed upon him the seriousness of the question.

Odrak could now hear sounds outside the hut, it grew so quiet within. Something dangerous was in these words, and it had the smell of death. He slid a hand over to Mah and forced him to hold it a particular way. It was a move they had practiced many times that would allow Odrak to throw Mah clear of danger. They had discovered it by accident, fleeing an attack from a crackhorn rambull. He would rub the rambull scar on his chest as the signal to make their moves.

"Magic?" Mah spoke the word slowly. "Magic is all about the land and the life upon it," he spoke, knowing his next words might bring him to a bloody death.

"But is it blood magic?" asked Sonmyaa holding her broken wrist.

"It is good for the spirit. All our people may chant the ancient words given to us by the 'nameless mothers'," Mah spoke the words no longer looking at Shaloolaa, but trying to sense the movement of the guards.

"Aaah!" Somaali whispered. "You creatures know of the women of no name? The Nameless Mothers?"

"Aey, Aaah! If only one would come to us now," said Shemaa, looking at Mah and Odrak with amazement.

"Yes," moaned Scochaa, "It was one of these who led our mothers here and told them we would be safe in this land." She turned back to Mah, saying, "This knowledge is common among your people?"

Not giving Mah a chance to respond, Sonmyaa asked, "Then this chanting is some magic good only for a man creature?"

Shomnyaa huffed, "No. If your women gave it to you, and all the other man creatures of your village use it, then it cannot be magic at all. No woman would give man creatures something of power over her and her daughters."

"Yes. Magic cannot be something used by all," agreed Somaali and Shemaa.

"We will permit this thing you call a chant," spoke Shaloolaa.

"Can we go to him?" asked Mah, feeling Odrak release his hand and finally relaxing.

"No. I do not think it wise," she spoke, almost smiling at Mah. "You two will stay here with the other man creature." Then she whispered something to the rest of the Tukshead.

Mah looked at all their faces in the hope of discovering some sign of their words, but noticed tears in the eyes of the one called Scochaa, and turned away. He saw another woman in the hut with tears in her eyes and remembered seeing her with Keishlee. He hated what had to be done to her, especially since she had helped to make Keishlee more human, but he told himself it was for the best and pushed all regret away.

Shaloolaa turned back to them and said, "We Tuk women keep our words true. You may pass through our lands and leave us. There need be no more challenges, and I say the seeding is finished if all the women have been seen. You may leave as soon as Swaahali releases the one you call Shhaha."

"What of Keishlee?" spoke the woman called Adah.

"You dare to interrupt the Tukshead?" huffed a guard, now standing over her.

"Yes. I dare! For the life of Keishlee. She must be given back to the cycle," Adah snapped back and stood with one knee lowered towards the Tukshead.

"Anything for the life of a woman!" rang the hut with this single demand.

"Woman to woman! Within her body the cycle of life!" came the echo chant from the Tukshead. The first thing truly chant-like that Mah and Odrak had heard from them.

Odrak turned to Mah in surprise and pleasure and said in chant together, "The blood of woman is the life of all the land!"

"Give her back to the cycle, and the land will be fruitful there!" The hut trembled with all their voices, but the eyes of the women turned to Mah and Odrak in shock and disbelief.

The Tukshead and the other women gathered around them, looking down with wide eyes and opened, airless mouths. Shaloolaa broke the silence and stepped before them, motioning for them to stand. She stared at their faces in the persistent silence, until her eyes were almost filled with water. She embraced them quickly, but firmly and full of warmth. She ordered Scochaa to hand over her weapon, which she did with some reluctance, but then turned a small smile to Odrak and Mah that dried her eyes.

Shaloolaa turned then to Adah and motioned her forward, saying, "We believe Keishlee," and then she turned back to Mah and Odrak and continued, "...and Charlaa are dead to us, or they are subject to Swaahali's magic. Even their bodies have been taken by the wind, so there is nothing I can offer to you my daughter, or to you, Adah, except the weapons they earned among us. I shall give Keishlee's to you later, Adah, and then to send her on the long journey, you may use it instead."

She lowered her head, making some resolution to herself,

then looked down at Mah and Odrak and said, "You who have come among us, continue to be a marvel to us. You have honored us with this knowledge of the sacred words, and I believe you have taught us how to say them as it should be done. Such a thing requires respect, and a deed in return of equal worth. I have no gift to offer you as great as those already given you by the great Sun Birds, except our weapon, which you may never possess." Then after warning everyone to stand back and cover their eyes, she used all her strength to mash the weapon on the large glistening stone that stood between them.

When Mah and Odrak opened their eyes again, they could see that the entire weapon was now a pile of thin splinters and shiny shards upon the ground. Shaloolaa signaled her people to leave the hut, and then without another word, the Tukshead was gone, only five guards, Ramaa, and Adah remained. She asked one of the guards for permission to speak to Mah and Odrak. When it was agreed, the guards left to place themselves by the windows and the entrance.

"I made a promise of blood to Keishlee," she began and almost cried. Mah could hardly bear to look at her and would have turned away if not for Odrak, who began to wipe his face as if he were removing tears. "She asked me to look after you both, if she failed in her challenge. I do this gladly. If you are in need of me, you may demand to speak to me from any woman here. My name is Adah."

"We know of you," spoke Odrak, trying to distract her as she looked up from her grief. "Your touch helped to make Keishlee more human."

She almost smiled, but then lowered her eyes and said, "I would ask a thing of you. Her belongings should go back to the sisters of her village, since there is no sister here to share them with us. But of her belongings there are two small strings of bones she wore around her ankles when first she arrived. I would ask these of you as a friend to her. To my people this...."

Mah turned away. He could not bear her pain or Ramaa's sobs, who he had forgotten was in the hut. He could not look at either of them in their grief, and wanted to run away. It was obvious she cared for Keishlee, but he knew Odrak would not let him speak freely to her. They had even agreed not to speak to Ramaa about it, and now that the Tuk Women were going to let them go, Odrak would not have anything change that.

"You may have them. We have a similar custom. Keep them and think of her while you live." Odrak lowered his head so she would not see his face. He was thinking that if he told a lie it might not kill him after all. But keeping to the truth without the lie was still a better feeling.

When she was gone Odrak gave Mah a little shake to remind him of the guards watching them. But he heard the low moans of Ramaa trying to whisper the chant of gentle spirits passing, and could not resist a glance. He was sorry to find Ramaa looking directly at him, and calling with his eyes for him to come and comfort him. Odrak hoped the pain building in his head would not kill him, and he turned away from Ramaa, shutting him out of his mind.

Mah did not dare look at Ramaa. He stared at Odrak with meanness and said, "We should collect the bits of the weapon left us," pulling Odrak towards the rock. "Yes," Mah spoke with an idea in his head. "We shall put them in a pile before us, while we chant the Call to Return."

Odrak realized at once that this would be a better chant than the words of the sacred journey. He could detect no sign that the guards were aware they were going to change the chant, and he was glad they were paying no attention to them, because from the careful way Mah was arranging the broken pieces of the Tuk blade, he knew Mah was intent to try some magic with them.

After making sure they had all the pieces in one pile, which they placed between them, they sat close to the ground and began the chant as they did all the powerful blood chants of their people. As they would begin any chant of magic:

> *"Great Mother, now one with all earth, Spirit*
> *be your fame. To you they come. When blood is done*
> *with flesh, and withers in the earth...."*

Ramaa gasped as he heard the words of a chant forsaken to all but the Keeper of the Blood. He was not sure what this magic would be, and worse, he was afraid that they might not be able to do it properly. He stopped his tears, his moaning and his chanting, and twisted himself so that his face lay in the dirt. Silently he chanted now. A chant intended to take away his fears.

Mah and Odrak noticed the new silence from Ramaa and his twisting about, but they had started the powerful chant, and would see it through.

> *"...With unfinished days before the journey ends. Having made for us a way, for all things needed to be said. Keep them not for selfishness, but empower their hearts; for yours was a promise of life, that the journey may be known, that the journeyer return home, as long as blood flows. Aaah!"*

Over and over they repeated the chant, then remembered that Swaahali was with Shhaha and included her without saying her name. Soon the chant was spinning, and the words were gone. Mah and Odrak were now in perfect mental sync and began to move their bodies in time with the tones. They needed to create a special form of energy between them, a thing that could wrap itself around spirits and draw them near.

They rocked until their bodies were like long reeds being flicked back and forth. Mah was first to put his arms into the flow, then Odrak followed and began to lay his hands on pieces of the broken weapon. Soon they added the tinkling clatter of the shards to their chanting, and the thing was being done by both Mah and Odrak, as if being done by one.

Ramaa had dozed off and was awakened by one of the guards cutting his bonds. He turned to find Odrak and Mah still at their chanting, which had become a sitting dance and song.

"They will soon be sacred to the clan," he said, almost loud enough for the others to hear, but did not really care. Mah and Odrak looked like Shama and Shhaha, when Shhaha took over the rites and became Keeper of the Blood. They were making a fierce magic together. He sat up and turned to face the guards, and hoped they would not see what these two really did. He stood as she ordered him to do, and then he saw the one called Scochaa and remembered that Keishlee was dead.

"Swaahali has returned to her people. She has words for all the village and wants you and them to come to her." Scochaa pointed to Mah and Odrak, saying, "They do not hear or see us. Stop them from what they do."

Ramaa looked at Mah and Odrak and a thought filled him with dread. "Shhaha is dead among you," he spoke and looked at Scochaa threateningly.

"No. He and Swaahali are well, and both remember who

they are," she smiled.

Ramaa did not understand anything she said, but had heard the "no" and was furious with her. "Then why have you not let him come to them. That is who they call. That is who they protect with their...with this," Ramaa turned to Mah and Odrak, stuttering with the near fatal mistake in his mouth.

"He comes," spoke another woman coming into the hut. "He is here."

As she said the words, Shhaha stepped into the hut and Mah and Odrak stopped and turned to him. They nodded to him, then lowered their arms as if they were great weights. They were both in terrible pain.

The action had been too profound for these women not to see the magic here. They had looked like wind-blown trees, but were hard and heavy as stones when the women tried to stop them. No sound would they hear. No pain had they felt. But the women knew Scochaa would settle all arguments in only one way now that Charlaa was gone, and she was ready to leave.

Shhaha asked for a moment to speak alone with Mah and Odrak. Some of the women started to complain then, but Scochaa ordered everyone out of the hut, giving Shhaha permission to speak with them, but only in her presence.

Shhaha knelt down beside them. He rubbed his head against each of them, first separately, and then together. He sat close to the ground, smiling and feeling good about the wisdom that led him to choose these two as apprentices.

"My blood shall always be at your service."

"No. No. Do not say such a thing. We are not worthy. We are the dust at your feet, move...." both Mah and Odrak tried to object. They wanted to move their arms around him, but the pain was unbearable.

"You have saved my life. And the life of Swaahali," he whispered in the low tones that only blood keepers would hear. "She, whose name shall be great in the land. Come, she has much to say to you both, and to her people. I know you must be pained and weary, but come, find the strength to walk by my side to greet her."

Shhaha had offered them the greatest of his "humble blessings." One tried never to walk in the same path as the Keeper of the Blood, and one never walked in front of him. But above all else, one never walked in step with him by his side. To do so was to say that he or she was his equal, and everyone knew there were none.

As painful as it was, they stood and slowly walked out beside him. He slowed his pace to cover the difficulty of their steps, and they headed for the village clearing where the medicine hut used to stand.

When Swaahali came out of her trance, she had been drenched in all the various wastes of her body. Her skin and wraps were soaked with bloody sweat. Tears, slobber and goo ran down her face from her eyes, nose and mouth. She had emptied her belly, bladder and intestines completely, and sat in streams of urine and thick gobs of muck and manure. Shhaha had sat with the same mire around him, but he did not awaken or rise until Swaahali called him. This had been agreed between them, and it settled the worries of the Tuk women. Swaahali's power was seen as the stronger here, and all who had planned his death, now did not care about him at all.

Shhaha would not allow the contents of his bones to be ruined, so only Swaahali was fully dipped into the lake, but the medicine women and their apprentices cleaned him more thoroughly than he would have himself. Walking next to his own apprentices, he felt like himself again.

Swaahali sat upon a beautifully twined mat of soft leaves atop freshly turned soil. She was dressed in her most sacred wraps, and had around her all the articles a medicine woman would be known by. Many were the same tools and familiars used by a Keeper of the Blood. Mah and Odrak would find no trace of the awful smell that had been created here. There was no sign of the blood that had poured down Shhaha's back, or the muck that the ground had become. Swaahali was aglow with her power and her bright eyes assured them of it.

The throng parted to accept them, and Scochaa led them to a place at the head of the crowd, directly in front of Swaahali. Scochaa took her place sitting behind Swaahali with the rest of the Tukshead. Mah and Odrak sat one to either side of Shhaha and waited for Swaahali to speak.

Swaahali opened her eyes and the clearing grew silent. Nothing moved except the invisible energy around her. She looked over her people and tried to see every face, to remember every name, and her look made them feel she knew their fears, their hopes and dreams. "The Great Mother is proud of her people, all her people," she smiled, and signaled for Shhaha to be recognized.

"This one, my sisters, is called Shhaha. Know him, and know also that he and his people are human. He is to be respected."

Of course this caused a little disturbance, but all knew better than to actually speak aloud while the medicine woman spoke of her trance revelations. To assure complete silence, Shaloolaa signaled guards, who began to make their way around the people, bearing their weapons and warning the women that to speak would cost them their lives.

The people looked on from their nearby huts, from the trees, and from the hilly land mounds as Swaahali signaled, and Shhaha returned to his place. She signaled for Mah and Odrak to stand but Shhaha had to assist them. To the shock of all, she walked over to them and greeted them with hugs and kisses, and then lowered one knee to them.

"You, Mah, who has the wise and pure blood of the great nameless daughters descended from the line of Axum, I give you my respects. And, to you also Odrak, of the mixed blood of Axum/Oro, from the line of the daughter Kkuh, I give to you my respects. I know what you two together have done for Shhaha, and for me. My blood shall always be at your service."

Slowly Swaahali took her place back in front of the Tukshead. All the women were in a consternation over man creatures being honored this way among them, but Shaloolaa sat stonefaced, and so none would speak, move or turn away.

Shhaha helped Odrak and Mah to sit. Their muscles had begun to tighten and knot. It took all their strength and control to move, and yet the only sign of the pain was the stream of tears flowing down their faces.

Thinking that they were crying because of the honor given them, the young women they had been with also cried. Swaahali placed the palm of her hand to her forehead and, using a power new to her, she silently called the selected women forward from the crowd. The crowd began to mumble and hoot, as room was made for them around Mah and Odrak. Everyone could see that it was Swaahali calling them, and they began touching their own faces in surprise and wonder.

"Sisters," Swaahali spoke to them all after the women were seated. "We are in need of this new blood among us. Because of the seeding, I have seen a great people spreading out across the land. I know the Tukshead has stopped the seeding in fear of our people being overwhelmed by new magic. I say it should continue, but that these people must be free to leave as soon as it is done. There is a thing needing to be done that is for them alone to do. What they do shall help to save our world. They shall be always remembered among us, but they must be allowed to leave. Everywhere shall we be in this world, my sisters. But, a 'change' shall be forced upon us. Our ways and this land shall be destroyed...."

Suddenly the Tukshead crawled around her and made the signs to beg for her silence. The people were speaking among themselves, and even the guards were so disturbed by her last words that they made no move to stop them. "We shall 'survive' this horror that shall come to us...." Swaahali tried to continue, but the Tukshead began standing around her, trying to get her to come away from here and the crowd, which was closing in on her.

Finally Swaahali kept silent and looked away from the Tukshead and her people to the ground. Shaloolaa spoke to her ear alone and then addressed the crowd. "This is a matter for discussion among the Tukshead. We must see clearly. We must plan," she said quickly and then left the clearing with the Tukshead and Swaahali, surrounded by guards. Scochaa and Shomnyaa were left behind to handle the crowd.

Scochaa and Shomnyaa called their forces around them, while the crowd was ordered back to their huts. Scochaa assigned selected guards to look after Mah and Odrak, ordering them back to the seeding huts until word should come from Shaloolaa or herself. Women were called together to rebuild the medicine hut, and Scochaa and Shomnyaa repeatedly assured everyone that the Tukshead would do what was best.

Shhaha began to realize that the Great Mother was reaching out to all her people. Just like his people had received the shocking portent of a great horror coming, these people might now be saved by a different warning.

Scochaa followed the women leading Mah and Odrak back to the seeding huts, while she watched other women come and lead Shhaha and Ramaa away. Nearing the huts, two guards came and ordered her back to the meeting hut, but before she left, she looked around and found Zambe's eyes asking to be chosen, and so Scochaa put her in charge over the other selected women.

Before entering the seeding huts, Zambe took it upon herself to interrupt the group. She asked that the guards allow some of the women to take Mah and Odrak to the hill waters. All could see that both Mah and Odrak could hardly walk, so the guards did not complain.

A guard led Zambe and six others off and up a rock side. Soon they were crossing a small cliff-side stream, over hot rocky land that led to a small lake of steamy warm waters.

Once they were naked, the women pulled Mah and Odrak down into the waters. Zambe and Carthaa were the first to remove their own wraps to join them, but soon the others followed and began rubbing and scooping the warm waters over them. Odrak wanted to sleep here until the next full moon, but could not rest with these women surrounding him and rubbing all over him and Mah, but he was too sore and tired to move or complain, so he chanted to himself in the hopes that they would go away.

Mah and Odrak fell asleep, while the women sat around comparing their experiences. Nuba, Fezza, Mycee and Zambe, who had laid with Odrak, agreed that he was human by proof of his gentleness, his ability to use many words and the pleasure they felt deep inside at his touch. They wished he could stay among them, and Mycee joked that she would challenge any woman in blood rite to keep him with her. They laughed because he would be the first young man creature ever to be kept alone for one woman in a hut. They pushed her in the water, saying that she was not strong enough to keep him all to herself.

Tanzaa, Carthaa and Mabaasa had varying opinions. Tanzaa believed Mah to be human since his pleasure stick was not covered like other man creatures. Carthaa wasn't sure if that meant he was human, but agreed that his touch was made worse by its thickness and the strange way it looked. Mabaasa loved him already, and told the others she would earn her weapon just so she could journey after him, and bring him back. The others thought that was an honor-filled thing to do, and suggested that they might go with her.

Zambe told Carthaa that Mah was under the effects of the great horn Swaahali makes, and that he had taken too much. This put a new light on her face, and they all laughed. They all hoped to be rooted and to give the clan new blood. They knew this would be the best honor of all, and might even get them into Shaloolaa's force, once they were all trained and bloodied by the raid. They made promises to the moon to stay close to each other because of what they shared, and swore to protect each other during their rooting, and not to be jealous if the seed of one of them did not take.

When the moon was falling, they pulled Mah and Odrak from the waters and let them dry. They rubbed them down with the oil they carried and waxed them over with dry skins. Zambe was telling them she was sure these two were human, because she had seen them care for one another. When she told them what happened in the hut with Mabezi, they all made promises to the moon again, saying that they would never say such things around them. Zambe assured them that Mah and Odrak were different from all the man creatures in their village and pointed out the difference of their pleasure sticks. Then she described the affection she had seen between them. The other women refused to believe it.

Tanzaa reminded them that neither Mah nor Odrak had shown any sign of missing Keishlee, who had gained their respect. Zambe agreed and did not know what to say about that, but said, "In the meeting hut, a village protector held her blade to his throat," Zambe pointed to Mah, "and you should have seen the look on Odrak's face. A look that is sure to curse the woman in some way."

They could not believe it and accused Zambe of trying to win false favor for them. Nuba suggested that they see for themselves and asked that they change places to see what the one they did not know was like.

"They will be too weak to provide seed after today. They will need the 'disiac,'" Zambe smiled knowingly. "Once you take him, and are sure that he is under the disiac and lost in his own lust, give that one some harsh word about the other."

Carthaa grunted and said, "No man creature gives up the lust of the disiac."

Zambe only smiled and said, "If they are but common creatures like all others, then nothing you say or do shall matter. I think they have a heart between them, and will shun you. I think Odrak might even strike you, so be careful with him," and patted his chest while he slept.

Zambe then told them the item she had saved for last. "Do the Sun Birds ever fly after the sun has set?"

"Have you become silly from your lust?!" grunted Nuba.

"You know they only have their wings while the sun is shining. They turn into snakes at night," huffed Carthaa.

Zambe stopped them and said, "Well, I have seen it. I

have stood next to them. I have even touched their wings, and I swear, darkness was upon us. If you cannot believe me, then ask Mabezi, who hates me now too much to lie for me."

A guard called coming up the rock side. The women were in too big a hurry to discover the truth of Zambe's word and did not wait for the guards to help. They carried Mah and Odrak down themselves.

The other women were gone when they reached the huts, and the guards informed them that the seeding would continue after sunrise. The women surprised the guards again when they did not leave, and instead laid themselves out over the itchy pallet. While guards were putting the men inside their huts, Zambe, Nuba, Carthaa, Mycee, Tanzaa, Fezza and Mabaasa kissed each other, and made promises to the moon to keep one eye open, to help protect Mah and Odrak during the night.

Zambe was the first up and sat on the platform watching the light of the sun take over the sky. Having lived here all her life, she was accustomed to the warning stillness and was able to sit motionless until the birds began to sing again. This meant the great Sun Birds had finished their morning feast and now all other creatures could move about.

Mabezi was the first of the others to return. She gave the others evil looks and asked the changing guards whether these women had been properly watched during the night. A guard who was leaving smacked her to the ground for having suggested that she had not done her duty. Mabezi brushed it off and went to sit, but the seven women on the platform made her stand and gave her sour stares.

By the time Saamyli arrived, all the selected women were present except two who had decided not to return. Zambe and her friends cheered, and the old women started coming into the clearing with large leaves of food and bladders of water. Zambe and Carthaa woke Odrak and Mah, and they were seated at the entrance to the huts and given food to eat.

Both Odrak and Mah felt much better and stretched their bodies out into the clearing to get some of the light. The women removed the old food from the hut and fed it to the little ones as they started running through the clearing. Saamyli appeared tired and looked like she had not gotten any sleep. Her neck was still bothering her but she could speak much better.

That morning all the women came by with their whispers of Swaahali's trance. They spoke of Swaahali's new powers and how she seemed to understand what was wanted before it was asked. They whispered of how the one called Shhaha had been badly cut before the trance and how Swaahali had healed him.

After they had eaten, Saamyli agreed to let Odrak spend some time with Mah. They greeted each other as usual by grabbing hands together and enfolding their fingers, but this time they also rubbed cheeks together, a custom used more between mates. They had always been close enough to do this greeting, but Mah already had a chosen mate, Olaah, and this greeting had been something to save for her, especially since he had already given his heart and the pleasures of his body away to Odrak. In the village of the Tuk Women, they realized they had truly passed a blood trial that gave meaning to their titles as protectors. They had passed into the third stage of life where they were free to live and do as they pleased.

They sat in total silence for a long time, trying to give each other some peace of heart. Their heads were filled to bursting with all the sights and sounds, the names and smells, the colors of the land and those of the women, and all the new things learned about the Great Mahs. These details would make this time a tale they might be called upon to tell, many, many times; and still, there was this Great Sharing yet to do.

Mah broke the silence between them with a look, as they shared the weight of still more knowledge, which Shhaha would pour on them from his trance with Swaahali. They looked at each other with quick flashes, running the rivers of details within them through their minds. Odrak smiled at himself and then passed it over Mah. He felt his own pride for being able to remember all he had ever been told, or shown, or tasted, or known, or touched.

They swore a promise of blood and ate dirt trying to outdo one another. They retied each other's hair knots, each adding a new one even tho the next rainy season was a long way off. This time the hair knots were tied so that they could be seen clearly, and they were put in neat rows from the front to the back, with all the side hairs pulled back to do the last knot. They stood and looked at each other, liking that they had done their hair identically, leaving the longest hairs in back still hanging past their shoulders.

It made them more like one person, tho they knew they were very different to look at. Mah was a head smaller, with round muscles, small ears and large eyes. His lips were full and fleshy but sat small and round upon his smooth clear face. His skin was soft and had the sheen that said he would never grow hair on his body. His face always caught the eye, with its high cheekbones spreading down under his eyes and around to his ears, giving him the look of always smiling.

Odrak was narrow and cat-like, with long hard muscles that ran down his belly to his legs, then up his long arms. His eyes were little almonds, hidden by shapely brows and long lashes. Both had the eyes of jet common to their people, but his lips were narrow shapely things that stretched out across his face when he smiled. He had large ears and the keenest sense of hearing in his clan. His hands and feet were also large, and he had long hairs under his arms, which meant he would also grow hair on his chin someday.

They were sitting together in silence when the old women and young slaves came in to bring more food. It reminded them of the seeding, and they looked at each other knowing they were not up to doing even one. As they watched the women come and go they eyed each item until they spotted the small yellow gourd that would contain the red powder.

"It's a bone," said Mah.

"Swaahali called it 'red horn,'" Odrak spoke, running through his memory of all the creatures he knew that had dark-colored bone horns.

"They have a wealth with this alone," Mah suggested. "Many would trade food for this during the dry or rainy seasons with so little else to do."

"Then we would have to kill all the men who would come here to ruin our women," snapped an elder who had overheard.

Mah started to ask a question when she gave him a knowing look and then left. He looked around his hut and saw all the fresh foods and drinks, and felt his hunger rise up in him again, but not the pleasure stick between his legs. He lifted his loin cloth and wondered if it would work today at all.

There was a call from the open door. They were surprised to see Ramaa standing there with a dark brown woman. Mah and Odrak started to rush over to greet him, but the woman signaled for them to stop. She offered Ramaa the hut and he bowed down to enter, but before she could close the door, the look on his face drastically changed.

"They say you are to be given to these women outside," Ramaa said and looked them over very carefully. He had to stand half bent because these huts had nowhere near the height he needed. "I have had to be all night with women. I am only now finished and have come to tell you about a gift."

"The disiac," Odrak smiled and started to come forward.

"You know of this?" Ramaa huffed, looking hard at them.

Mah hid his smiling face in shame while Odrak said, "I hope you did not take as much as Mah. These women will run you off and call you a beast."

Ramaa almost smiled, but said, "Yes. They try, but are too small and tight. It is they who go running off, screaming and leaving blood on you where it should never be seen." He stopped and looked at them sternly. "Is that the blood you wait for? Is this how you show your respects?"

Mah saw the angry look now and was on his way to him. He thought Ramaa was upset because they had not greeted him properly. Odrak stopped him with a swing of his arm, saying, "We greet you, Ramaa, but I see it is not well with you."

"Have you both been so changed by these people, that you care not for your own any more?"

"Are we not glad to see you?" asked Mah, once again stepping up to him, but knowing there was danger here.

"Have I missed the rains? I see no blood on your arms or legs. Or on yours!" Ramaa shouted to Odrak. He looked down at them and the surprised looks on their faces. He pissed some water on the ground before them and left the hut.

Mah rushed to dig up the dirt and cover the spot. "I will not be able to go through with this, Odrak. We should have told him."

Odrak rubbed their heads together, saying, "Not until we are gone from here. Let us leave here first."

Saamyli came into the hut soon after and announced that the seeding was to begin, and Odrak had to return to his hut with one of the women.

▼▼▼▼▼

It had taken all his strength to confront Mah and Odrak about their disrespect of the dead. He still couldn't believe they had worn no blood for her; Keishlee was distant and cold, but she was human and their kin. He had never known anyone to refuse to wear it. Even Shhaha waited for him to mourn with; following him from hut to hut as the women took him and passed him around, like a meal that might never be finished. When he was put out of the last hut, because the disiac had worn off and he was no longer useful, he saw Shhaha with two sets of fresh blood marks on each leg. With one of his own fingers, Ramaa broke the skin and rubbed in the stains. They sat together and quietly chanted for Keishlee, and as always, Shhaha shed a little water from his eyes and rubbed it into the dirt to let the Great Mother know that she was loved by her people.

It was then that Nuba came and greeted them in the custom of her people, squeezing her feeder bags together under the hanging cloth she wore. She brought Ramaa his skins, and while he covered himself, said that she would take him to sit in the hill waters before his body stiffened and he got the crippling pain between his legs.

Ramaa didn't know what she meant and refused to move from under the tree with Shhaha. But Shhaha gave him leave to go, telling him that he should do as the woman asked, or be sorry later. Shhaha told Nuba that Ramaa was mated and had four young slaves yet to teach. Ramaa didn't understand how or why those words softened her, but they did. She became more considerate, and there was respect in the way she spoke to him. Instead of telling the women who approached that he was no longer useful to them, she told them that she "watched." She said this to enough women so that even now, others no longer bothered him, and he was truly grateful.

They had passed the clearing where the women sat atop a wooden pallet. They were the most eye-pleasing creatures he had seen here, and he remembered that these were the ones they called the selected, who would put Mah and Odrak through what he had been. He saw the numbers of them, and felt sorry for the young protectors. He still had the little sack he'd made of the disiac, which he collected from the huts he'd gone to during the night. He had thought of it as a gift at first, but thought of it now as a way for these women to use him against his will. Still, he thought they might find it useful and had asked Nuba if he could speak with them.

He regretted having taken the time. His body had begun to stiffen, and now that he was climbing up a cliff side, he could feel a fire stirring in his groin. Nuba heard him gasp from the pain and told him the waters would help. When they were near enough for her to point them out, Ramaa ran as best he could and jumped in.

Nuba was laughing like a slave who has just learned how. She teased him about running like the feathered and wingless croup. Ramaa knew which bird she meant, and it was nothing to be proud of. He wanted to pull her into the water with him, but the pain ran all through his body. He dared to move at all, and was glad to see her removing her wraps to join him.

With the sun shining down on them, the hot, soothing water started to work on him quickly. Ramaa felt his lack of sleep as the last of the disiac was washed away. He could feel it coming out of his pores. It had stopped clouding his mind, and he found himself worrying whether he would still be able to seed male slaves, believing that the disiac had made this a clan of women.

He slid further into the waters until they reached his mouth and as he fell off to sleep, he saw other women coming up the rock side, calling to Nuba.

▼▼▼▼▼

The Tukshead had been in the meeting hut all night with Swaahali. Shhaha was glad for her, because she needed calm heads to share words concerning her journey to the Great Mother. He knew the pain of what she suffered with all the blood memories, and the new powers it had given her.

Recalling the journey they had made, he could see the wide dark road, where each elder of his line of blood came out of the shadows to greet him, floating upon a vast, murky river of blood that merged into the road. Multitudes greeted him with only a touch, and a flash of light from their eyes revealed the lessons of their lives. The weight of this abundance would have destroyed lesser minds, but Shhaha knew where and how to store the knowledge. Swaahali did not, and Shhaha knew not the easy way to give her assistance. By the time he caught up to her, she was in a furious rage over having the world she knew destroyed. It was only the things she thought she knew tumbling down around her.

Shhaha remembered trying to cross the road, but every attempt to swim the river of blood made the road and all his kin disappear, to find himself in a place devoid of life, with all his knowledge flying in the air above him, emptied and alone. But he knew he was not alone, and called upon the spirits of his elders. He reached for them, and they were there to anchor him ashore.

Knowing the answer now, he shouted for Swaahali to reach out, and there came upon her someone that she knew. A white faced woman with pink and slanted eyes, a darkly bloodied mouth and hair the color of his skin. This woman showed her to another, who had the ways of blood within her touch, and now Swaahali knew them too, and could move through knowledge in their proper time and place, no longer lost.

Their journeys became the meetings of old friends, who retold the uncounted tales he already knew. There were new revelations too, and the proof to guesses he had made. Like the hideous beasts, far from being human, that sprang up out of the darkness like monsters he could not get away from, in a river filled only with close blood kin, but he would touch them too.

When they reached the lines of nameless women from whom all life had come, Swaahali suffered again under the weight of what she thought she knew, now strapped to her like a giant unwieldy tree she was forced to carry.

To Shhaha's disappointment, the nameless ones were not all human. Some were such ghastly creatures he refused to believe had ever lived. But theirs was a time when all life could be mated upon itself, and so his blood relations moved in the line, creatures from races now lost in time, and in the flash that he got to see their faces, there was everything in life to find. From the beast of many fangs, who was a masterly fiend, to the majestic Great Mahs, who colored the scene, each had their turn to greet him, and there were no words to mind.

Swaahali was first to reach the Great Mother, who was only the night reaching out to touch her. From a distance Shhaha watched as the Great Mother enveloped her, and began to drive her mad. At her feet lay the life of a man, swimming in a lifeless circle but surrounded by the energies of light. And then the circle grew larger and larger, filling with the blood from the river in which Shhaha stood.

Swaahali began to bleed, and it dripped from her legs onto the ball of swirling life. Then Shhaha began to hear the call. It had a sweet and sour taste, and it touched him more closely than a hand. The Great Mother suddenly had eyes, that turned to him and he was affected, no longer moving on the river road. The darkness, which was the Great Mother, parted her legs, and between them there was something like the sun; small, barely making any difference to the darkness of her form. It shot an arm of light into her, and from her came a light that streamed out past the road.

The chanting could be heard louder now, and he knew who and what it was. It was the chant for the returning journeyer, and it began to give the Great Mother form. Soon she had lips and a smile, and was distracted by her changing form and she let Swaahali go. Instantly, Swaahali stood next to him, and they watched as the Great Mother grew fascinated by the chant. She started to dance, then he and Swaahali could move of their own accord. Suddenly, the weapon of the Tuk women was sticking out of the lives at her feet. It had no handle, but the Great Mother took it up and became a woman. Blood poured down from her hand onto the ball of life, which then became women and men. She took the weapon and cut an opening into the night, and then threw the opening onto the river of blood flowing between them. She smiled, and the opening grew larger and exploded into light. Shhaha reached for Swaahali, and together they jumped into the opening in the night.

He remembered everything again when he looked up into Swaahali's eyes. She had just come from the meeting hut and looked weary, but willing to go on. There were guards all around her who stopped anyone from approaching. Swaahali sat down next to him, greeting him in the way of his people. Nothing she would do now would surprise him. The Great Mother had actually touched her, she might know all things now.

He tried to greet her in the way of her people, but it brought laughs from her and the guards. Feeling silly, he stopped and chuckled at himself.

"I could use your assistance and your wealth of training with blood," she said, motioning for him not to speak. "But you cannot stay even another sunrise. You must finish your journey and prepare both Mah and Odrak for the Test of Blood. You have been holding too much back from them. Tell them all they need to know. Forgive the disrespect there is in my voice. I hold you in high esteem above all others. I say to you, good journey, and may you keep good time. Farewell," she said and looked up with hard eyes to face the guards, who were looking down on her with disgust.

They abruptly turned away, and Shhaha could see the life

of this woman before him. She was already a prisoner to her people, both treasure and curse upon them. She would be worse off than he, and spend the rest of her life trapped by their needs. The sacred skull of Caenaa would drive this tribe to warring among themselves, but only after her death, which was now going to be many generations away. Her nearness to him gave him these visions, but he lost track of them thinking of her power joined with his at the Great Sharing.

"There you will find those who would destroy the Great Mother. But there are those like you, whose foresight will help to save all. You must get there with your apprentices. Do not allow others to delay you again. Use the power of your voice if you must, or fill that bag with deadly salts of which you trust, but nothing must stop you from reaching the Great Sharing. Nothing...I still think you should give them some warning." Again she stopped him from speaking, "But I know you will follow your own mind, which is probably the wisest thing to do. I will look over you and yours in my dreams. I grow stronger with every breath, but I am only human," she said in such a way that it gave Shhaha a fright.

A human was the highest form of life. What she suggested gave him cause to fear. Her words said so many things, he doubted whether she understood herself, yet et looking deep into her eyes he saw the control, and the swelling of tears that said she was still human.

"I must look for strength in the things that I can understand. There I will find what is human resting between all that we can love and hate," she said to him now with a smile. "You know the answers to all those questions wanting to leap off your tongue. I will be safe here. My people do what they feel they must, and still they try to understand. They have not killed me already," she laughed to Shhaha's dismay, "...and this speaks well of them. They are not animals who run and hide, or cower in the face of what they fear. They stand up to it, strong and brave, and like humans, want from it what can be useful to them."

Shhaha found himself understanding against his will. He wished these women respected him more. He had the power to comfort her, but he knew that he, and no man from here on, would be allowed to touch her. She would be more sacred than the skull soon. He offered her a silent chant of blessing and watched her go on her way, surrounded now by guards, as she would always be, who one day would be women and men, some the descendants of

Mah and Odrak.

He sat quietly chanting for a long time. He tried to call forth another prevision, but could not concentrate. He was about to leave when a group of guards came to get him. They took him to a hut which looked freshly made. It smelled of wax leaves and new twine, and was tall enough for him to stand up in, and filled only with his people's belongings.

Scochaa came in and told him that he was to make ready to leave. She was still angry and hurt, and treated him roughly, but she had cut both her legs and wore two sets of blood marks to honor the dead, which pleased him since this was the custom of his people, and her doing it honored them all.

▼▼▼▼▼

Odrak couldn't believe the disiac had worked so well. He had gotten through his time with all the women and even managed to have three new ones he hadn't seen before. He sat with Zambe, who had come in after Demaa, which signaled the end of the seeding. They laughed together, because he had struck Mabaasa and Carthaa for their unkind words about Mah. He had rushed through their seeding and cursed them when they left, and now he felt ashamed, since it had all been a test to see if his love for Mah were true.

Odrak held her close, having heard that Mah had done the same, but he had to be told sooner, because he would not let the rest of the women touch him. He had so depressed himself that he had to eat more of the disiac to make himself useful again, and still he refused to lay with Mabezi ever again.

Zambe did not tell him that Mabezi made such a fuss, Saamyli had to use guards to hold Mah down. The women were all teasing Mabezi now, saying that Mah had not given his seed to her, and she would not be rooted come the next season of sun.

Zambe held Odrak, and they laughed while eating the little bits of food that were left. Odrak thought the disiac might come in handy for trading when they were once again on their journey, and she helped to make a small sack from the used leaves outside the door. It was already dark by this time and soon guards came to take him and Mah to the hill waters. Zambe, Carthaa, Nuba and Mabaasa came along, while the others were taken to Swaahali, who had asked to see them. After a gentle rub down, the guards informed everyone that the man creatures would be leaving. Zambe and Nuba then kissed Mah and Odrak to say farewell, which angered the guards, who called them "silly odors" and sent them all from the cliffs.

Mah and Odrak were taken to a new hut at the far end of the village, away from the high escarpment. They were glad to see all their belongings neatly packed, and Mah and Odrak sat quietly recalling the last few days.

When the leaders of Scochaa's force came without her, it was a strange sight, but no one knew where she was. They had come to tell them that they would be awakened early and shown the best way out of their lands. They placed themselves around the hut and lit fires. In the light they could see that Shhaha and Ramaa were fast asleep, and were excited to be finally leaving this place, but their bodies were worn out from the day, and so they joined Shhaha and his dreaming.

The sun had not even begun to light the sky when the guards came to wake them. Ramaa and Shhaha were already dressed and covered with their packs for the journey. Mah began strapping the water sacks to his arms while the guards left the hut. Odrak let out a little scream, and Mah turned to see the blood marks on both Shhaha and Ramaa's legs. Ramaa turned from them in disbelief, and was about to leave the hut when Odrak and Mah fell upon Shhaha, wiping and licking the blood clean from his legs.

Odrak did not see the first blow as Ramaa kicked Mah to the ground, but he did not bother to look as he leaped from the dirt, wrapping his body around Ramaa and violently knocking their heads together. They slid down a wall of the hut, striking each other. Guards entered the hut to see Odrak and Ramaa trying to set each other up for a kick.

Shhaha had been studying the look on Mah's face, and when he understood, he ordered Ramaa and Odrak to stop. He pretended anger and ordered them not to speak. Mah rushed over and wiped the last traces of blood off Shhaha's legs, and went back to his packing. While he was strapping the bundled feathered cape onto his back, he accidentally touched Ramaa, who slapped his hand away with a look that threatened his life. Odrak stepped over and the heat of his body flushed out his nose. He was about to piss his water on the ground before Ramaa, when Shhaha voiced a tone of warning. Ramaa stopped himself and smiled at both Odrak and Mah, showing them all his teeth, an act reserved for enemies.

As they made themselves ready to leave, Shhaha asked

where his tall walkers had been taken. They had been resting outside the hut during the night, and he hoped they had not wandered too far away. The guards told them that they were chased on ahead, along another route which did not take them over the mountain pass.

Along the way, no one spoke except the guards, who were in a hurry to return to their village before the sun came. They feared losing their lives to the Great Mahs, who dared all to move about during this time of day. Just before the sun came up, the women spotted the resting tall walkers. They were well away from the village, and the women pointed them in the direction they should go to avoid the higher mountains. They warned them to stay away from the deeper jungle that spread off to the right, then ran away so fast they were out of sight before Ramaa and Odrak could remove their packs to begin their fight again.

Mah tried to speak but neither would listen, until Shhaha struck both of them. Mah smiled as he realized that Shhaha was still a strong man. He had knocked Ramaa to the ground and had Odrak gasping for breath by the throat.

"These women have a thing which they do to show great affection between each other. It was passed down by their elders, who used it to survive desert crossings, when water was the most precious thing one could give another. To do this thing they call a kiss, is to give blessings to the water which gives you life. It is like saying I am glad you are alive and mean to keep you so," spoke Shhaha as he kissed his apprentices. Mah and Odrak held him close before falling on their knees before him.

Ramaa was like a torch ready for the pyre. His anger threatened to be unleashed even at Shhaha, who stood in front of him and smiled, then gave him leave to speak.

"How can you honor these two, even with the blessing of another people, when they are a disgrace to their own. I cannot believe they have come to this, but...."

"If you cannot believe it, then you should not, Ramaa," Shhaha snarled and brought him to silence. "These two shall be remembered among our people as great blood keepers. They love their people even more than you, who shame them by striking them down in the face of strangers, and without warning, like an animal," Shhaha cursed him and brought him to his knees in shame. Ramaa could only mutter.

Shhaha turned to Mah and Odrak and asked, "Do the birds

fly near enough to hear?"

"They need not," said Odrak getting to his feet.

"They will hear us while we are still anywhere in their land," Mah said and pulled Odrak to his side. They began their song as the sun was just coming over the far hills.

Shhaha signaled Ramaa to silence, then waited for a moment to make sure Ramaa would hear him. "Keishlee is still alive," he said, then turned to await the arrival of the birds.

As they always do, one appeared out of nowhere hovering overhead, its wings spread wide, blocking out the sky. Only Mah and Odrak were standing as the bird sang back to them, and then as suddenly as she came, she was gone.

"Is this true?" Ramaa asked, now frightened for the blood keepers. Of course it was. Mah was the pride of his people, and he and Odrak were apprentices to the great Shhaha, who everyone agreed was the strongest blood keeper in the land. All the tribes came to ask a vision of him. Would Shhaha fail to see blood spoiling among them? Ramaa could not look at them as he asked them to forgive him. He wished he could have thought of something to get around the weapons of the Tuk Women.

Suddenly he felt Odrak standing in front of him and without a word, Ramaa pushed out his chest and asked for Odrak to give him the killer kick. He knew Odrak could do it well, but held his neck forward, so it would snap back harder and bring him a quicker death.

"All I ask is that you swear blood to Mah, and that you never, ever lay hard hands on him again. Never!" Odrak shouted.

"I have no faith. I am not to be trusted. I have already sworn blood to keep you all safe, and yet I have brought shame to you, myself and my people. Kill me. Take my life. It is all that I deserve," Ramaa cried and positioned himself again for the blow.

Shhaha pulled Odrak to the side and brought Ramaa to his feet. He held Mah to his belly and then released him, saying, "They needed you and me to wear the blood marks, to convince these people of their deaths with our grieving."

"We are sorry for having to bring you pain, Ramaa," Mah offered. "We did not want to deceive you."

"Yes," Odrak huffed, but continued to look hard at Ramaa. He was still waiting for the promise of blood.

"I give my blood to you, Mah, and to you also, Odrak. I

shall not think evil things of you again. If I fail you this time, may the Great Mother take me with a horror."

Mah and Odrak shouted him down and begged that he retract the curse upon himself, but Shhaha warned them that it was done and there was nothing to change it. Words can never be taken back. He chanted over them so that their words would not be misused by evil spirits resting nearby, and then pulled loose the bundle on Mah's back to show Ramaa the feathered cape he had asked about during the night.

As it rolled out before him, he realized why the guards had been fighting over who would get to lay it down. Touching it, he felt honored, as he was dazzled by its beauty and the vibrantly shifting colors.

"Old-Tree comes!" Odrak shouted, pointing to a dot flying in and out of the freshly lit sky.

"I think it's his mate this time," Mah suggested. "Yes. It's Wind-Chime, and she has Keishlee."

All names were just words. Usually words with more than a single meaning. Odrak meant "the last drop," and was named so because at his naming, all his close kin in the clan were dead. He was indeed the last of the blood of his line. Ramaa meant a "bull of great power," and he had been given his name for showing great strength from the time he was a little slave, but Ramaa could not figure out what "wind chime" meant.

"I shall show you," spoke Mah, as he reached up to help Charlaa down from the claws of another giant bird. As he looked at her, he almost laughed, thinking how fat the birds had made her. Odrak assisted Keishlee and then turned to speak with the birds, who each handed Mah and Odrak the large leather sacks of gifts they had hidden. Shhaha and Ramaa then rushed to greet Keishlee and Charlaa. Ramaa made sure to wipe the blood clean from his legs before touching them. Mah and Odrak sang again with the birds, laughing and playing with their chest fur while the birds played with their now neatly-knotted hair. Mah called them down and placed the kiss upon each of their beaks. Odrak did the same and sang goodbyes to them as they made ready to leave.

Once the birds were gone and Mah and Odrak returned to the others, Mah saw Charlaa stand and begin to speak solemn words, but he stopped her, and asked that she not continue her blood rite challenge with Keishlee.

"I do not wish it," she smiled at him. "I wish to offer you

the blood of my life, as you say. You have saved Keishlee and myself from useless deaths."

"You have also saved us from a death of abundance, as well," Keishlee groaned and rubbed her plump belly.

"Yes. Yes. That too," laughed Charlaa. "'Eat' is a human word they all know."

Mah and Odrak broke out laughing and agreed that they had indeed overfed Charlaa, who had tied her hanging cloth up under her belly as if to hold herself in. They could not believe she had gotten so big so fast. Keishlee laughed privately, but agreed and described all the foods they were forced to eat. Mah and Odrak laughed and agreed that they could not be long with the birds without bursting.

"It is the only human word they care to learn, besides 'food', 'more food,' and 'hungry?'" Odrak laughed.

"Listen to me," Charlaa interrupted their laughter and rested a hand on Mah and Odrak. "What you have done shall be remembered among my people as a blessing. Shaloolaa is much older than she appears, and Scochaa is the only one among us worthy to stand in the center of the Tukshead, even if she does not have the height. But she hates the fighting among us, and it is only I who keep her with us. She has probably gone from the village already. Our people need her wisdom and only I know where to go to bring her back."

"What you say is true already, Charlaa," spoke Shhaha. "You should go to her, because she grieves for you."

"I shall leave you then. But Keishlee, you should have the weapon. It is yours by rite and honor. These lands are filled with man creatures who are truly beasts. It will prove very useful to you."

"But I dare not go back to the village," spoke Keishlee.

"No need. I go to a secret place where Scochaa finds comfort. If you come, than you can say your farewells, as one should to a friend," she spoke, pulling Keishlee close. She turned to the others and said, "They showed you out of the village without a word, I know. You had no woman with you, and it is a disgrace to us to give thought to a man leaving our village, or even to say farewell to him."

Shhaha thought about his last moments with Swaahali, remembering that she had dared to do just that.

Charlaa stood up and readied herself to leave. After she had kissed the others and was about to do so with Odrak, he held her arms and said, "I would ask a thing of you."

Charlaa dropped to one knee and said, "Whatever it is, even to my own death, you may ask."

"First, may I come with you? There is a woman from your village I must speak to."

"You must not go back to the village, but yes, you may come with us."

Mah stood up and tried to speak, but Odrak held his hand and signaled for him not to ask. Then a moment of fright took hold of Odrak, and he pulled Mah around to him and said, "I shall return if I am only pieces. I shall not leave you with my memory alone."

Mah quieted him by holding him close and then striking him firmly on the chest to bring back his courage. He sat back on the ground with his legs folded and told Odrak that he would not move until he returned.

It was done, Shhaha thought, and all without his say. They had truly come into their stage of life when they would be protectors. They did not seek the word of others to decide what to do for themselves. They were going to be bold and brave, the qualities a protector needed. They had powerful blood between them, and Shhaha would give them this time.

"Go now," Shhaha ordered, feeling more like himself. "Hurry back. We must be gone from here before nightfall," he said, being glad for this moment alone with Mah. There were so many things he had to tell him, and things he knew Mah wanted to tell him in return. He looked over to the large sacks the birds had left and found himself suddenly unable to hold back his curiosity. Ramaa saw him staring and brought one of the bags to him. After opening it they could only marvel at the contents that fell out on the ground.

"What is this? What is that?" they asked Mah, bringing each item to his face, so that he could keep his words to Odrak. "Wind chimes?" Ramaa roared as he heard the ringing of tiny objects he held up to the air. Each time the gentle wind passed through it, or Ramaa moved, it made a sound that ran up his spine, and Ramaa yelled "wind chimes!" and was so proud he had been smart enough to figure it out.

▼▼▼▼▼

Seeing Keishlee from a long way off, the tall walkers ran up to greet her. She was so glad to see them. She gave them hugs and brushed their thick skins. She pulled herself up on the female and then pulled Charlaa up with her. Odrak managed to get on the other by climbing up a tree. Once they reached the base of a tree-covered slope, they dismounted and left the tall walkers and went off into the woods.

They went up into a mountain, climbing steep rock sides and crawling through passages that were not made by humans. Having seen the Great Mah mountain citadel, Charlaa suggested that this place had been one also. Odrak disagreed, telling her about the other mountain citadel and explaining that they were both much higher from the ground than this mountain was high. He also reminded her of the height in their caves, which were vast in comparison to these tight places.

Both Charlaa and Keishlee were happy to share their experience with someone who believed the stories they told of the Great Mahs. Charlaa was sure her people would never believe it, and had planned to keep the knowledge of it to herself and Scochaa, who might also believe. Charlaa was still in shock over being in the feast clearing one moment, then waking up in the mountain citadel the next, with two big birds trying to feed her.

"I have never been so afraid," Charlaa sighed as she pointed to the light coming through a hole from an upper level. "I thought Keishlee and I had managed to kill each other, and had returned to the Great Mother. My people believe she sends the Sun Birds—the Great Mahs," she corrected herself, "to bring her people to her."

"There was a bird I recognized," Keishlee smiled. "It was bigger than I remember. She was trying to say 'My-Name,' but could not make the sounds. Then she called out 'Mah' and 'Odrak', over and over and then said, 'eat.' After that, I knew we were not dead," she laughed.

They reached a spot were Charlaa asked them to wait and be very quiet. She made them promise not to move unless they heard her scream out the bird call common to her people, which would be their signal to climb back down and leave, stopping for no one, not even for her or Scochaa.

Charlaa then turned into a long dark passage. She didn't

have to feel along the walls to remember her way in the total darkness. She even remembered the spots where the trap holes were, and jumped over each of them without a second thought. When light allowed her to see the inner room, she could see the weapon that had been placed across the stone rise. She laughed at herself, thinking of how simple and obvious the trap appeared, but she remembered those who had fallen for it.

Charlaa dived into the cave and called out the secret word between them, "Thunder!" It was the name they had given to the sound of the lighting storm, which they could watch from the high mountain window here. Charlaa smiled, looking up at the window and still believing the Great Mahs had used this place once.

Scochaa was in shock, gasping for air and control of her weapon's arm. With wide eyes and tears beginning to stream down her face, she covered them and fell to the floor. "Take my life. It is yours, for I am mad. You have surprised and confounded me to blindness. I am useless to my people. Kill me," she cried with her hands still covering her eyes.

"Would you really have stayed here and starved yourself?"

Scochaa peeked through her fingers, and still seeing the face and form of Charlaa, let her hands fall to the stone floor where her weapon lay.

"Well, you have probably chipped that good weapon. Let us go change it for a new one and dirty it so none will know."

Scochaa fell on her, striking out at her with all her might, cursing and crying. She pulled her close and brushed back her coarse but well oiled hair, and then kissed her face. They sat holding each other, Scochaa still not believing but not wanting to let go. Charlaa holding even tighter, because Scochaa was true to her word, and was here where they had promised each other they would be, since they were little sisters fighting over the right to carry the extra weapons, to this their ancient hiding place.

"Too many women know about this place now," Charlaa said, gently pushing Scochaa around and into one arm. "We should find another."

"When the lighting hits this room, it makes the weapons sing and that makes them stronger. This shall always be their hiding place." Scochaa backed away and looked at Charlaa with dismay and wonder. "It is you. How is it that you are alive? Has Swaahali become so powerful that she can now bring back the dead? And make them fat as well?"

"When we return, then I shall tell you all," Charlaa laughed, and stood holding Scochaa's hands.

"This is only a vision, then. Swaahali sends you to ease the pain in my heart," Scochaa cried, and sat on the floor.

Charlaa pulled her up again and held her close, squeezing the breath out of her. "I am real. I am alive because I have yet to die. Stay here," she directed, and quickly left the small inner cave to fetch Odrak and Keishlee.

When they returned, Charlaa silently placed Keishlee and Odrak in a corner and told Scochaa that someone was coming up after them. Scochaa prepared the weapon trap, and then she and Charlaa readied themselves, one on each side of the entrance. It was a good wait, but the sounds of jumping soon started, and they counted, to know how many were approaching. Seven women were coming, the number of an attack force.

A woman in guard dress ran into the room, heading for the weapon. Charlaa knocked her to the ground. Another woman came in, and Scochaa quickly had her against the wall under the window, threatening the others that she would die if all their weapons were not piled up in the center of the room.

The women reluctantly complied and gathered together in a group, away from the weapons on the stone floor. Charlaa released the woman and kicked her into the group while taking hold of the weapon used as bait for this trap.

Odrak's eyes were afire, and he could not stop himself from moving toward the woman Charlaa had kicked. Charlaa signaled him to stop, but he didn't and went up to the woman and turned her around. Scochaa ordered the others not to move and called Keishlee over. Charlaa went over to Odrak and held him back with one hand and threatened him with her eyes.

"This is what I would ask of you, Charlaa. Is your word true and lasting?" Odrak asked, trying to control himself.

Charlaa slightly bent one knee and said, "Do you dare?! My word is like the blood that flows through me. I guard against all that move here. All but Scochaa will I kill out of hand for you!" she roared at Odrak.

Scochaa snapped a look at Keishlee. "This place is within the lands claimed by the Tuk Women. Our ways will be obeyed even here."

Keishlee gave Odrak and the woman a careful look. She smiled over to Charlaa and ordered Odrak to be calm. He relaxed his stance and stepped back from the woman while Charlaa kept her place.

"I demand respect for Odrak. It is not the custom for our people to suffer less. This woman has offended Odrak deeply, and he demands a show of respect from her, or the right to force it from her," Keishlee spoke, knowing what Odrak wanted from this woman.

"You may speak, Odrak," Charlaa said, using his name instead of "man creature," which showed her respect for him.

Odrak walked around to face the kneeling woman. "You have threatened the life of all I hold dear. You have put a weapon to the throat of the pride of my people. You have cursed Mah, and I will not live and remember it with ease. You will come back to face him, and eat full hands of dirt before him. Only then can I let you live, or allow myself to walk by his side and call myself his friend."

All the women started laughing, especially the one he was talking to. Odrak wanted to kick her in the face, but Keishlee's look told him not to move.

"So. You both are alive," spoke the woman, smirking over to Charlaa and then up at Keishlee.

"The challenge is then unfinished," huffed another.

"Silence!" Scochaa roared. She thought for a moment, then said, "The challenge was properly fought, but Swaahali's magic has changed all things. There will be no more blood rites to the death, unless it is to recover the honor of the dead, and then only by those deserving to do so," she spoke through her teeth.

"Then why have we not been told this by Swaahali, or the Tukshead?" asked another woman.

Scochaa smacked her hard and the woman fell to one side. "You call me a liar?" she growled. No one said anything for a while, but then Scochaa called Keishlee over to face the women. "Keishlee shall stand for the challenge of blood."

"No!" Odrak yelled.

"Within our lands it is the only way," Charlaa tried to break it to him gently.

"No!" he continued to yell.

Keishlee signaled for him to be silent. She said, "I will

gladly force her to it for you, Odrak. There would be no shame."

The woman laughed and said, "You will have to kill me, woman, and I do not think you can."

Charlaa reached down and pulled back the woman's head by her hair tresses, saying, "I know you well, Mycee, and I have taught her some things especially good for one who fights like you, horse woman."

Keishlee laughed, remembering how the Tuk women learned and trained for fighting, by choosing a method known to a good fighting animal. Keishlee had learned the best defense and attack for this method easily, since she was already accustomed to riding animals and knew their ways. "Now you have insulted me as well. I think I would like nothing better than to see you eat dirt and kneeling at my feet."

Mycee started to rise but Charlaa knocked her back down, laughed and said, "This is how it should be."

"No! Keishlee, I beg you. My blood is Mah's. I wish no woman to fight for me. It is bad enough to have one fight over me, but to have one fight for me as well does not bring me comfort, only shame. Charlaa. Scochaa," Odrak pleaded.

Scochaa signaled Charlaa and the others to silence. She swung her weapon to point it up at the wall window, saying, "The land beyond the trees of this mountain sits outside the rites of my people. In the lands outside this valley, I have had to fight many men who are stronger than any here, and who do not know our ways. Will you step outside our lands and do this, Mycee? Are you wet enough to serve as water?"

This time the woman jumped to her feet and spit on the floor near Keishlee. "I shall kill him!" she screamed, and then spit on the ground near Scochaa. "I shall kill him!! Then I shall challenge you, Scochaa. We need a new woman of weapons. You are always full of complaints against our ways. We should be rid of you, and I shall have your place!"

"This proves interesting," Charlaa snorted and grinned over to Scochaa. "Then it's settled?"

"It is settled!" Scochaa laughed and spread the spit over the hard rock floor with her foot. "Now," she barked at the other women, "why have you come sneaking up here?"

"Swaahali sent us to get you. She said you would be here. She said to tell you, 'get your kisses and then come back to where you belong'," spoke one of the women.

"Why are there seven of you then?" snapped Charlaa.

"She made her come," replied another, referring to Mycee.

"Yes," agreed some of the others, now looking up at Keishlee and Charlaa strangely.

Scochaa ordered the women out of the inner cave and asked them to wait outside by the trees. She waited for them to leave and then greeted Keishlee, falling into a clutch and holding her close. Scochaa begged her forgiveness for being cold to her, and Keishlee thanked her for being her friend. She greeted Odrak and thanked him, knowing now that he and Mah had been responsible for saving Charlaa.

As they were leaving, Charlaa held Scochaa around her waist and waited for the others to leave. Then she unfastened her hanging cloth and piles of small waxy balls fell out. Scochaa almost knocked her over trying to get to them. "Sun oil!" she whispered and without thinking, stuffed one of the nodes into the folds of her hanging cloth.

"We have more than enough to last many generations," Charlaa smiled as she continued to pull the little balls out from the pockets and folds of her cloth. Scochaa ran into the corridor and returned with a large fur bag. Charlaa was still removing the nodes she had stuffed all through her leathers and hidden in her hair. When Scochaa was sure she had them all, the fur bag was almost full and heavy. She said, "We must pay for these. They are too great to accept as a gift. Let us ride to the spice tree forest and kill a few beasts to offer to the salty red waters."

"No. I have Keishlee to thank for these. The sun birds, or Great Mahs as they wish to be known, do not like them taken. One of them might have killed me if not for Keishlee. I have promised her weapons for her, and her...."

"A deserving woman may have as many as she can carry. What she does with them after is her own affair," Scochaa warned Charlaa not to speak. "She shall have five of them. It is almost a cheat, I know," she said, feeling the solid mass of nodes through the fur bag, "but I do not think she would want more than that—for now," Scochaa smiled and pulled Charlaa to her. "If she returns, she may always have more if she wishes—to give to the other women of her village."

She turned a little serious as they walked into the dark corridor and said, "There are many things I must tell you, Charlaa. The village is much changed."

As they walked through the corridor, remembering to jump the dark pits, Scochaa slipped a handful of weapons out from a secret hiding place between the corridor walls. She wrapped them together in another fur sack, then slipped it into Charlaa's hand, asking that she not argue with her about it.

Charlaa squeezed her hand and said, "I hope you have considered them all. Even the biggest one is also human. They are deserving."

"I have picked out all big ones this time. Keishlee can learn the difference the weight makes with her long arms. She has told me the women of her village come bigger than she, and I give these to Keishlee and those women," Scochaa snapped.

Outside, Scochaa was glad to see Keishlee's tall walkers, and Charlaa made her way around them so that the others could not see the fur sack. Charlaa quickly handed it over to Keishlee and asked that she not look inside until they were well away from the Tuk lands. Keishlee promised and they all proceeded towards the hills.

Charlaa picked a spot for the fight away from Shhaha and the others. Scochaa made both Odrak and Mycee promise to forget their differences once the fight was won. She had to strike Mycee, who demanded that it be a fight of blood rite, but even the other women shouted her down since she was fighting a man creature, whose blood they did not consider worthy of any rite, but whose seed they thought might contain some special magic. Her killing him might destroy that magic, and none of them wanted that.

Odrak asked her again to submit, but Mycee ignored him and attacked him before he was ready. Keishlee smiled at their opening tussle. It would be natural to underestimate the people of the Tall Walkers. Her people were mild mannered. They were gentle and slow to anger, and filled with a desire to reason. As Odrak began to seriously defend himself, she had no doubt that he would win the fight. The strength in his arms came as a real surprise to these women, and especially to Mycee. Yet none of them realized that he was only a slave among his own people. Keishlee laughed, thinking how threatened they would have felt if Ramaa were attacking them. He was strong enough to rip their heads off.

Scochaa had to pull Odrak off the woman, as he screamed at her to submit. For the second time Keishlee had to gasp at the speed and sturdy placement of Scochaa's moves. She would be a deadly foe if crossed, and had Odrak trying to catch his breath from the chest blow she dealt him.

Mycee still refused to face Mah and humble herself, but this time she made it clear that she had never believed Odrak's words. She thought it was all a plan to ambush her, because she had been among those who attacked the journeyers from the clan of the Waterhorse. Keishlee went to her and pissed her waters on the ground. They splashed up into Mycee's face and she rolled away and cursed, while Keishlee told her that she and her people were not animals who attack without warning.

"The people of the Waterhorse clan are not ours to avenge. Their people will come for you," Keishlee said. She cursed Mycee back and swore that she would not bear another insult from her, then she tried to get Odrak to leave.

Odrak refused, and this time he went to the woman with tears in his eyes, "It would be abhorrent to me to take the life of another human. Aaah! but I think that *you* are not human. I will kill you if you do not do as I say."

Something in Odrak's face began to convince her, even after Scochaa laughed and said, "We here are all your sisters. Do you think we would let an outsider kill you without just cause?" she asked, stepping between her and Odrak. "Only another sister can do that," she laughed and smacked the woman hard across the face.

The woman thought for a moment, then dropped one knee for Scochaa, and then turned and reluctantly dropped another for Odrak. She agreed to make the peace between them, and returned with him to Mah. Scochaa and Charlaa followed, after sending the others back to the village.

Alone among the giant man creatures, Mycee made a big display of her humility for Mah. She heartily ate two full hands of dirt, some of which came out with worms, but she ate the dirt as she found it. Mah chastised Odrak for making her go through with this. He knew she had only been doing her duty, but she agreed that she need never have touched his skin with the blade, especially since he had yet to drink the wine that would protect him against the sickness of the weapon.

"The slightest cut would have made you deathly ill," she moaned with regret.

Mycee smiled at them both, hardly believing that human men had come upon them at last. She asked to see Odrak and Mah embrace, and when they rushed to it, she cursed herself for not having asked to challenge Keishlee for seeding.

"I am glad to call you human. I am happy to know they still exist," she said happily, gently touching them both.

As Scochaa and Charlaa were getting ready for the long run back, Mah remembered Adah and the look on her face. He called Odrak over, and they reminded Keishlee of Adah's grief, and told her about the ankle bones they had given her.

Keishlee was frantic, screaming at Mah and Odrak for having extended their deception to her. She was about to strike them both when Shhaha and Ramaa explained that they too had not been told. They believed now that Mah and Odrak had done the best thing. Too much was happening in the village. Someone might have given it away with a look or a word. Ramaa had to agree to this, saying, "The woman, Nuba, who watched me. She is the sly one. She might have guessed."

"Yes," agreed Scochaa.

Scochaa tried to comfort Keishlee, who now wanted to return to the village to speak with Adah. Shhaha and all the others refused. "We have delayed our journey long enough!" Shhaha roared, feeling the words of Swaahali weigh on him. "Prepare to leave now," he ordered her, using the tones needed to force her to obey and think no more of leaving.

Keishlee retrieved her packs from Mah and Odrak and cried, because she had nothing more to offer Adah than her old ankle bones, and that she had nothing to offer the Tuk women for all that they had taught her. It hurt her deeply that she had forgotten Adah, and now could only think of her grieving, and her being still alive and gone without a word.

Sensing Keishlee's thoughts, Odrak unwrapped the large bundle he had begun to put on his back. He flung it open and the cape of the Great Mah feathers glittered out into the bright sunshine. "Give this to the Tuk Women. I have often thought of seeing Shaloolaa wear it. It drags all around me as I walk. I do not really like to wear it, and besides, we have the other," said Odrak, forcing it into Keishlee hands.

Mah came over with other gifts. One was a long string of sharp teeth that was also decorated with bits of smooth and shiny colored shells. "Give this to your friend, Adah. She can wear it around her neck and...."

"The Sun Birds gave you this?" spoke Scochaa, choking on

the words. "It is the teeth of the deadliest creature in these lands. Even if we could kill it, it is the sacred food of the Sun Birds, and it is death to harm them. The Sun Birds only allow us to cross the waters they feed in because we offer the dead to feed this monster. None may cross the waters, or go nearer to her home in the mountains without making this offering."

"A woman who wears these teeth among our village shall be more respected than, Shaloolaa," spoke Mycee, who stopped to look again at the cape. "Well, maybe not over the one who wears this," she said touching the cape again and finding its edges also lined with the teeth.

"You have been a friend to us as well, Scochaa." Odrak handed her a plain set of the long string of teeth and then handed a smaller set to Charlaa.

"Would you like a tooth, Mycee?" Mah asked.

Mycee snatched it up without looking, and hid it in the folds of her hanging cloth. She clutched the spot where it rested and fell at Mah's feet to eat another bit of earth.

Keishlee lowered her eyes and refused to take the mesmerizing cape, but Odrak insisted that she give it to the others as a gift for Shaloolaa. Keishlee petted the feathers, treasuring the touch. The sight of it was "fabulous," she thought, smiling, finally understanding the word one of the birds had spoken to her. She folded it up and handed it to Scochaa, thanking her and Charlaa again for the gift they had made to her, the contents of which she already knew.

Charlaa made Mycee give her promise of blood not to tell the others and then said, "It is a terrible thing we do allowing strangers in this land of many dangers. All are sure to die here without it, and the blessings of the Great Mother. It is a small kindness in the face of this, the greatest of all gifts come to us."

"Your people shall always be welcomed among us, Keishlee. Send a woman with all who would come to meet us, and give her only a chip of the weapon, and she shall walk among us as one of our own. Over this I pour my blood," said Scochaa, cutting herself with an edge of her weapon, making the promise of blood in the custom of the Tall Walkers.

Keishlee held her for a moment, hoping that they would see each other again, and telling Scochaa to give Adah her regrets for not being able to say farewell in person. Then they went their separate ways. Mah and Odrak looked after them until they were out of sight, glad that they were finally gone from Tuk Village, and the women with the deadly weapons. There were those they would think of later on the journey, but for now the sight of hutless hills, and nothing but open land was a relief to all their senses. They gathered the rest of their belongings and after strapping them to each other's backs, ran to catch up with the tall walkers, who were once again leading them towards the rising sun.

"Dialectics of Sex Revisited" by Cleopatra Mandara a'La Hedrin: ...Gods like the ones we have today were not created until after the ego became genetic to human life. It was not conceivable without humans first being able to separate themselves from the other forms of life; thereby allowing for the belief that humans were "special" or "supreme." Ancient humans lived, acted and often ate like their animal familiars. [...] Even their first gods were not Gods as we think of them today. They were the living essence of great ideas, or great ancestors who had lived, or were still alive; becoming deities, demigods, [...] any thing of power or powerful possibilities, like fire, wind, water and the Great Mother: earth; [...] and their powers were only divisible by sex or not at all [...] The acknowledgement of ego receptives stimulated a desire for higher and higher hierarchical degrees of human identification. Also a wider diversification of allowable concepts, behaviors and diet [...] Sacrifices were given in trade for deity services and were always served at a feast for the people, or eaten by the deity alone [...] Our Gods today, especially the concept of the **one** God, is what appeared after the smoke cleared on the battlefield between all the supreme egoist of our times....

"When Knowing Is The Price"

Shhaha and his companions did all their traveling by day, up and down rolling hills that were squeezed between dense forest jungle and high purplish-red mountains. Occasionally, they entered the jungle where the dark forest opened up, and gathered fruits, nuts, melons, juice canes, berries, vegetable greens, roots, edible bush and ground foods. But always they were attacked by the bloodthirsty creatures one might have mistaken as human.

These were the beasts Keishlee had already seen and slaughtered, but as they got further and further from Tuk Village, the creatures appeared more human, their hirsute bodies were better formed and they stood erect when they attacked, or carried weapons and made sounds more like speech.

Ramaa hated killing them, and often tried to speak with them, but hungering for flesh, they never stopped to listen to his words. Shhaha called them the "curse of mating too close," because they were the proof that at one time humans had mated with beasts.

Keishlee taught her people how to use the Tuk blade, and they killed these creatures whenever they attacked, never letting even the smaller ones escape, because Shhaha and Keishlee considered them a menace to all other life. Mah and Odrak would have given the young ones to the fire, which was their way to separate the part that was human, from the part that was ruined or beast, but there was no time. If they stayed too long, more always came, and never were they satisfied with what they might be eating already.

Having no stomach for these endless battles, the Tall Walkers spent most of their time on the grassy trail that ran downhill from the mountains, like a giant path cut out from the jungle, stretching down the land like a road going their way. But the jungle was always near, sometimes closer than they would have liked, at other times almost out of sight in deep, mysterious grabens.

Often they spotted of a group of animals traveling carefully along the tunnel of land, eating the grass and shrubs. They munched right up to the edge of the jungle, where the growth tried to reclaim the hilly land. Sometimes Ramaa would spot a man creature hidden along the jungle's edge, and watch it easily snatch up an animal that wandered away from the herd, or was caught in a growing tangle. It surprised Ramaa, because he expected the munching creatures to be extremely heavy, since their tracks were so deep and plentiful.

Mah wanted to help this peaceful, munching creature, but Shhaha said it was the least intelligent animal he had ever seen. The herd did nothing all day but eat. If not for the grass in front of them, their teeth might not have pulled them along. Occasionally the females allowed themselves to be bullied into mating, and even this was done without joy; and none of them protected their young, or took notice when a man creature took one.

Shhaha said, "We must let the man creatures have them. It may be other humans we save. As they grow accustomed to the taste of this creature, maybe they will think less of humans as food."

After many days, Shhaha began to see a figure reappearing off in the distance. At first they all kept a day's run behind. It was a solitary figure, dressed in long robes, who they thought might be related to the munching creatures, but after the Tuk women, they were leery of strangers and did not want to be trapped by unpleasant company.

Odrak wanted to meet this person, hoping he might be as peaceful as his clan relation, only not as stupid. Keishlee agreed with Shhaha, and did not want to spend time with anyone related to this dumb animal. But the stranger was never seen with the constantly chewing creatures, and since Shhaha did not think it was a Blood Keeper making the journey to the Great Sharing, they kept their distance.

Days passed when this person was not seen, and they worried that the stranger had been attacked by the man creatures. Then the figure would appear again, but was always out of hearing, more than a full day ahead. Keishlee and Odrak took turns running after the wanderer, but the figure always floated out of sight over the next hill or turn of land, or into the forest, and never responded to their calls.

After many more nights, Shhaha saw the stars that said they were headed in the right direction. They were traveling faster, since the tall walkers liked this peaceful land, and the jungle's bounty of food always within their reach. Odrak and Ramaa knew it was because Shhaha had quickened their pace.

Shhaha assured them they would reach the Valley of Names before the next rains. He said the call of the Great Sharing came clear to him now, and soon even they would hear it, like a heart beating, and each beat saying, "Come."

The jungle's water vines and tree saps provided them with liquid until they came upon fresh water streams flowing down from the mountains, or out from the forest into ravines. Keishlee took to washing herself in water whenever she could, and cleaned the snake leather wrappings given her by the Scochaa, which she now wore all the time, and looked more like a Tuk woman everyday.

All of them wore the sharp teeth of the water snake, except Shhaha, who said it made them look like this creature's clan relation. Mah and Odrak knew he would never wear animal bones next to the bones of his elders, which was the common sign of his power. He especially did not want anything touching his silver ring, or the tall walker tail hairs hanging from it, which brought their clan relation closer to him at night.

But he did not ignore the bones; on the contrary, they

became an active study for him. He spent every night grounding them into a fine powder as he sat with Mah and Odrak, sharing the tales of his trance with Swaahali, and they, their visit with the Great Mahs.

Keishlee and Ramaa sat and listened to the fantastic tales, in awe of Shhaha's helplessness as he moved along the road leading to the Great Mother, and his descriptions of the faces that came to him out of the river of blood. Mah's and Odrak's Great Mah tales would not have been believed at all, if not for Keishlee and her standing witness to the contents of their mountain citadel.

One night, Mah was telling Shhaha about the land break, and how the birds had watched it happen from the sky. He was explaining that it took countless generations, and that their land was no longer connected anywhere to the land these Great Mahs lived upon. Ramaa balked at the tale. Ramaa had never doubted blood keepers, but this night he accused Mah of mixing up the facts. Odrak repeated the bird song and translated the words, but Ramaa refused to believe that something could rip the Great Mother the way they said. He went laughing around the fire, shouting that Mah had begun to lose his memory, and that he was only 10 and 5 knots, and that one of the knots had been tied much too soon.

Suddenly a voice, clear and distinct, said, "He speaks the truth."

Everyone jumped for their weapons and snatched torches from the sitting fire. Ramaa and Keishlee searched, but found nothing. They called, and demanded a response, but no one answered. For a long time they waited, without reward, forcing Ramaa to keep both eyes open during his watch that night. Only the howls and screams of the mating curses could be heard, but he knew the one who spoke was still watching them.

For days they kept an eye open for the lone stranger. At night they talked in whispers, and held a nose and ear to the wind for human smells and sounds, but there was nothing.

Mah and Odrak took to telling the Great Mah tales even during the day. Keishlee complained that they had already told stories for three cycles of days, with no story repeated, but had spent less than two days with the Birds.

"For the birds, a single flutter of sound may contain an entire tale," explained Odrak. "I am still changing their tongue into our words. I am only now understanding all the parts that make the stories whole."

"Adding things you think they said," Ramaa huffed, while paying close attention to the nervous tall walkers.

Mah sang a high toned melody, that was done as easily as one would take a breath. Odrak soured his face and said, "You see. Mah has just counted the times you thought you saw the wandering stranger today. In the 'pitch,' yes, in the pitch of his voice, there is the description of the time of day. In the melody, there is the stranger's color and dress, and the look upon your face. The last tones are always about the sun, its position, and the angle of its light."

"So much?" Keishlee asked, walking alongside a tall walker, and not really understanding a word Odrak said.

"For Great Mahs, every description includes the position of the sun, the angle of light and the direction of the wind. We know these things from the colors they use. The Great Mahs know of a great many colors," spoke Mah.

"Mah always uses the expression on the face and what one wears when speaking of humans. Sometimes I get confused," offered Odrak.

Shhaha had to slow down to think, while the others walked on ahead. He was disappointed with himself for not having learned more of this bird's language. From the few things he could say, he knew the sun was a constant preoccupation with the Great Mahs. To include the wind as well, that meant they knew the movement of the clouds, and possibly their shape, color and size, and whether they meant to rain, or storm. A language like that could say much with few words, and make it easier to remember more things.

As he caught up to the others he understood why his early vision of Mah as a great blood keeper would hold true. Mah would never forget anything. He would always have room for his memories. He would not have to spend his elder time fighting off the madness, that often takes a very old Keeper of the Blood. The "madness of memories" his people called it, which is the reason all blood keepers die talking. They are always trying to let some of the memories out.

Shhaha wanted to ask Mah to teach him more of the Great Mah songs, but as he reached for him, he knew he was too old, or rather, too filled to take on such a task. Odrak saw the move, but Shhaha quickly reached up and fingered his own hair knots, wondering if the palm oil of the Tuk women could loosen the mounds of knots piled atop his head. There were 4 sets of 20, and 9. A thing of great pride to him and all his people, but they weighed on him like the packs Ramaa carried.

"The beast creatures have stopped following us, I think," Keishlee said to Ramaa.

"For six days I have not heard them rustling the bushes," replied Ramaa as he slipped down from a tall walker.

"He sleep walks already?" asked Mah.

"They do so sooner these days," Keishlee replied.

"And we walk well into the night before sleep even begins to come," added Odrak.

Suddenly the tall walkers awoke and began calling. "They see a danger, Shhaha," Keishlee called to the others, then turned to speak with the tall walkers. "They say the land moves," Keishlee stammered, not sure she understood.

"They say the land comes," Shhaha corrected her.

The tall walkers stopped to look about. Mah and Odrak ran to the forest edge and climbed a tall tree, while Ramaa and Keishlee calmed the tall walkers. Shhaha stood guard over Mah's and Odrak's discarded packs, noting the direction the tall walkers wanted to go, then looking for pathways through the forest, which the tall walkers might not mind. He could feel a rumble starting under his feet, but he listened carefully for the sounds of man creatures, who might sneak up on them at any time.

"There is a wide run of land beyond this forest!" Odrak shouted from the top of a tree.

"It comes this way," shouted Mah. "Moving fast, and some of it has horns. It is the munching creatures!"

"Yes. Yes, it is a great many of them," shouted Odrak, climbing down. "They are moving fast this way."

"They are very far away, but will be here soon at the speed they travel," called Mah.

"Ramaa!" shouted Odrak as he jumped down the rest of the way from the tree. "Keishlee! Bring the tall walkers!"

"They do not want to enter the forest," Ramaa called Keishlee to come and help.

"They block our way?" Shhaha asked Odrak. "There is no way around them?"

"The land is wide and open in all directions further on.

But it is covered by the munching creature, everywhere the eye can see. You cannot see the land beneath. They are everywhere! And they come this way, to this narrow strip of land."

"We must make our way through these tall trees," Shhaha ordered. "Come down, Mah!"

Ramaa ordered the tall walkers into the forest. Mah came down to help, and they managed to get them in under the trees. Further into the woods, they could see wide openings, but the land grew dark and lacked ground cover or bush, since no sun got through these trees, which were the tallest trees they had ever seen.

After checking to make sure there were no man creatures around, Shhaha and Keishlee signaled for the tall walkers to continue further into the woods, while the sound of the coming stampede became so loud, it sounded more like lightning striking. Then suddenly, the light was dimmed even further by the massive herd passing their sections of trees.

The munching creatures were taller than Mah and Odrak, and many of these did have high standing horns and dark red and black hides. The thunder they made was deafening, and Odrak often looked up through the trees to see if a storm had actually come their way. Their only voice was the thundering sound of their feet trampling over the grassy land. Some of them were pushed into the forest, and part way up the slope. Others ran atop one another, as the faster ones made the slower ones disappear beneath the charging mass.

Shhaha and his people backed further into the forest, covering their ears from the pain of this sound. The animals plowed over the grassy path and through the forest edge, knocking down small trees and upturning the earth. Animals that couldn't keep up were trampled and killed, or ran deeper into the forest, where they continued to move with the herd.

Shhaha began to feel a presence around him, ominous and enclosing. Peeking at Mah standing next to him, he could see that Mah felt it too. They turned around together and Mah went for the weapon tied to his back.

Shhaha made the signs that called for strangers to speak. "Are you human?" he asked, as he would of any stranger.

Some of them had stick weapons. Others carried long, thick reeds, which they held in their mouths. Shhaha felt the danger coming more from those, and noticed that these men were holding to a deep breath. He motioned for his people to keep their place, as one of the men stepped forward.

His skin, like the others with him, was like the darkest part of night, with an oily, dark brown sheen from a recent sweaty run. His eyes were bright and honey brown, and he stared as tho he could see through Shhaha. His hair fell around his head in heaps of dirty curls, in thick swirls of black, brown and yellow. He looked back and forth from Shhaha to Mah, and smiled as he touched the skin of Mah's face. Odrak had his weapon out and was starting to move when a voice said, "Be still, and let them know you!"

Shhaha did not have to look. He had echoed the sound of that voice in his head for many days now. He knew every inflection it could make, and had known it was a tongue of many words. The strangers were looking at the figure with smiles and remembrances. He watched as they all fell to the ground and rubbed their faces into the dirt. This was something Shhaha knew. Whoever this person was, who was a woman, was also someone to respect and fear.

Off in the distance, near a tree as wide as a waterhorse, stood a figure covered from head to foot in yellow and purple robes, trimmed with odd designs. The long sleeves were pulled back, and Shhaha could see arms covered with strings of bones, and fingers strapped with fangs for claws.

Shhaha bent his legs under him, and then folded his body to the ground with his arms crossed at his chest. Mah had seen Shhaha do this whenever they were visited by the great Keeper of the Blood, Meneliawy, of the Waterhorse clan, who was now dead at the hands of the Tuk women.

Ramaa and Keishlee sat on their heels. Odrak waited for some sign from Shhaha or Mah. But Mah could not take his eyes off the figure removing its head cloth. Odrak and Mah could see now that it was a woman, almost as old as Shhaha, with wrinkled brown skin lying close to the bones of her face. Her hair, like arms of knotted rope, danced about her head as she moved, and her eyes transfixed all who dared to look into their chilly, gray stillness.

Something about her forced Odrak to sit on his heels. He tried to pull Mah down with him, since no one else dared to stand in her presence, but Mah was like stone and would not be moved. Mah stared at the woman and it seemed that he fought her with his eyes. His arm jerked away and he struck his thigh, muttering and spitting on himself.

Shhaha pulled himself back up using his blood wand and gave Mah a frightful look. Clenching their weapons, Keishlee and Ramaa poised themselves for attack. Odrak cursed the woman, and held his weapon out as a warning. Shhaha asked Odrak to be still, as he realized that the woman and Mah were entranced together.

Some of the strangers looked up from the ground, alarmed and mumbling a sound that rose up from them like a muted thrashing, but they would not move more than their heads and eyes, or raise their voices above a whisper.

Ramaa noted their fear, but could see that these were strong and intelligent people. He wanted to strike, but only watched as the woman crept forward, her body lurching as if moving outside her will, each step not of her own countenance. As she passed, Ramaa saw a drop of blood dribble from her mouth. He tried to look away, but knew for certain now that he could not move of his own accord.

Odrak alone managed to struggle, using all his strength to raise the light weapon. He wanted to cut down this stranger that was attacking Mah from within, but as she passed and waved a hand over Keishlee's face, Odrak watched in horror as Keishlee tumbled slowly to the ground.

The gray-eyed woman closed her eyes and rushed past Shhaha, but before Odrak could strike her, she shot both arms out towards him, and a force of whirling winds took him. Helpless, he watched himself flying through bushes, while his weapon cut down small branches just before he hit a tree.

He recovered quickly, and tried to get his weapon when he saw the woman fondling Mah, but someone twisted his arm, and others pounced on him and pinned him to the ground. Another man stood over him, threatening him with a short reed in his mouth. Then they dragged him over to the woman and threw him near Mah, who was now on his knees and looking exhausted.

"I mean you no harm," she spoke to them, and waved a hand over the clearing. "But you," she spoke to Mah, "you are something different come to life. You interest me."

Mah strained to gather his strength, but managed to bow his head to her and say, "Why...how...why do you attack me so? What have you done to me?" He searched himself, as if looking for something that might be just under the skin.

"You," she said reaching for Mah, and then turned to

Odrak, who struggled to get free of his captors. "I will not touch him," she smiled to assure Odrak. "If not for your teacher, I would have killed you and the others, and taken this one with me." She pointed to Shhaha and then Mah.

Odrak kicked one of the men holding him and broke his arm, forcing a splinter of bone to rip through his skin. The man screamed, while the others fought to restrain Odrak. The man with the short reed returned with his cheeks puffed out like overfilled bladders. Just then the woman shouted something Odrak did not understand, and the men immediately let him go.

Odrak cautiously approached the woman, reaching first for Mah to pull him aside, and then for Shhaha, who seemed stopped in time.

The woman spoke to Shhaha, and he opened his eyes and stepped in place, surprised to find himself still standing. He was about to use his voice on the woman when she humbled herself, and even ate dirt for him; a very tiny bit, which she rubbed on her tongue with a finger. "Blood Keeper, you have my respects," she intoned with the veneration due the words, then stood to faced Mah and smiled as if delighted, but paced about trying to make up her mind about him.

Odrak pulled Mah away again, and asked the woman, "Why have you come here?"

"SHE WHO HAS NO NAME GOES WHERE SHE PLEASES!!!" the woman declared and snapped her fingers.

The men lying on the ground all began to stand, mumbling words up to her with downcast eyes. This time Mah pulled Odrak behind him, and took his place in front of the woman. He threw her a covered glance, then stared deep into her eyes. "Are you human?" he asked, trying to keep the respected form.

"Yes, I am human, and I know that you are because you have asked," she replied in the correct form. "And you are right to fear me. Never let anyone do what I have tried to do. Now you know how to stop it, as your teacher has known for generations," she continued speaking to Mah, but was giving Shhaha wondering looks. She turned to Odrak and said, "Guard him better," then turned to Shhaha saying, "This one interests me," indicating Mah. "He may survive the testing. It is good you have ears to hear the call of the Great Sharing. Few can do it without the stone."

Ramaa was helping Keishlee up when the woman came over and touched her face and smiled. Before Keishlee could react, the woman flicked her wrist and produced a shard that filled the palm of her hand. Keishlee's eyes lit up at the sight of a piece of the Tuk blade. "You have been greatly honored, woman. You have my respects." The old woman looked at the weapon on the ground, and then eyed the one in Ramaa's hand.

Ramaa gave her a dirty look, and moved Keishlee back a step. The woman laughed, and dared to reach up and feel the muscles in Ramaa's arms and belly. She then turned back to Shhaha and said, "These ones, are Kamituians, and are human," pointing to the strangers. "If you are going to the Temples of Light, go by way of their village, then pass through the lands of the Hoteps and Obies. They will not know your words, but all shall be human and give you respect."

She lifted her hood back over her head and left them with the clatter of the herd returning to their ears, as if this moment had happened in a dream. When the noise filled the forest again, she was gone.

Shhaha had to shout to call his people around him, and together they joined the strangers, who were beckoning them to follow. Only then did Odrak noticed the two protectors fighting over his weapon. He wanted to retrieve it, but the noise of the stampede was too painful, forcing him to rush away with the others.

The village of the strangers was sprawled out over a large rock- and pebble-covered clearing, where many people gathered around deep sitting fires. Everyone seemed calm, but all were yelling at each other as if they had not left the noise of the charging herd behind. Women were making things with slivers of reeds, or stringing together large square teeth. The men, who were in greater numbers, weaved mats and the skirts they wore from strips of the red and black hides, then stretched and dried them in the smoke from their sitting fires. They also cooked flesh, and everyone was eating it.

Shhaha always noted the type of enclosures people built, but he didn't see any. From the looks of the people they appeared to be a close kin clan, with the look of having lived in one place for many generations, each member closely favoring the other. But if they built no enclosures, then they must be a wandering tribe, whose colors and shapes should be more varied than he saw here.

They took a liking to the tall walkers. They gathered around and encouraged each other to touch or speak with them. Shhaha's silver ring got some attention from them, but all the men and young protectors wore circles of bones in holes along the outer edge of their ears. When someone pointed out Shhaha's ring to them, they would fling their hair aside to show off their rings, and shake their heads to make the bones clack together with a light pop. All Shhaha saw were their diseased and rotting lobes. Some had ears that were nearly falling off.

Mingling among the people, Mah and Odrak were already learning their words, shouting them back and forth, which appeared to be the custom here. They asked about everything they saw, and Odrak ran back to tell Shhaha whenever he learned some important word or sign among them. These people knew that both Mah and Odrak were young; even tho they were as tall as their men, they treated them like slaves. The young ones swelled to a crowd around Mah and Odrak, but they respectfully kept their distance, making no move to touch either of them, which put Ramaa's mind at ease.

Keishlee was glad these people paid her little attention. She found herself thinking only of Odrak's weapon, and how soon they would give it back to him, or when Odrak would make a move to take it. One thing was for certain: she would never allow it to stay with these people. If she had to, she would get it back herself, no matter how badly Odrak might take offense to her doing so.

Ramaa thought not of these people, but of Shhaha and his apprentices. Shhaha had been deep in thought since the old woman left. All the way here he had only spoken to Mah and Odrak, only sparing the time to sign back to Keishlee to say that everything was all right, and to confirm that these people were human. He was getting a pain in his head from traveling with his blood keepers. He could not go from terror to peace within himself as quickly as they did. On this long journey it grew more and more difficult adjusting to strangers and strange ways, whereas his blood keepers seemed able to make themselves at home anywhere after a time. Ramaa and all his people were mild mannered as does, but a Keeper of the Blood could kill quickly, and it was hard to understand how Shhaha knew he need not have attacked this woman, with her coming upon them in such a way. Ramaa was convinced of her wealth of blood magic, but Shhaha had great magic as well, and yet he hardly ever used it.

Laughing off the memory of her word and voice power, he recalled a time when Shhaha had taken him and other young protectors out to gather ground foods, when a clan of large lizards came to attack and eat them. Shhaha had nothing to fear because he was far too tall for them to swallow, but he stopped the protectors from running away, and lined them up with his back to the creatures while he chanted. The lizards came closer and closer, but looked around as if they no longer saw the young protectors, some of who could not control their waters because of their fear. Shhaha had Ramaa and others chanting and dancing before they realized the creatures had gone. There were other things Shhaha did or was known to do that demanded respect, and Ramaa would not think twice about giving his life to save Shhaha. He was offended by this woman's treatment of him, and even the freedom with which these people gave themselves to speak to him, all of which Shhaha was allowing.

And then there were his apprentices. Mah and Odrak were causing him much worry. Odrak was rash and quick to anger where Mah was concerned. He was too protective of Mah, and might become more of a hindrance than a help. Ramaa had taken the time to look back when they left the forest's edge, and saw these people make use of the long reeds as weapons. They blew air into the reeds, and the fallen animals that tried to get up, moved no more. If not for the old woman, and maybe something Shhaha had done, these people could have killed them, without their ever having seen the danger. They would have done so if Odrak had struck the woman.

Mah on the other hand was always thoughtful, but Ramaa wished they had left him behind. Mah was overappreciated from birth, and now everywhere they went people picked him out for one reason or another. He was just too different, especially with those white streaks on both sides of his head. He made them all stand out, when all they wanted was to be on their way. Ramaa shook away his anger, hoping these people were not going to keep them longer than they wanted to stay, and especially not because of either Mah or Odrak.

Shhaha and Ramaa were placed among a group of their men. They were brought food and drink by strong young protectors, who tried to talk to them, but only Shhaha understood some of their words. They appeared to have few body signs, but could actually feel the need of their attentions.

Shhaha sat in silence as he ate, remembering every look, tone and move of "She Who Has No Name." He searched through the new blood memories received from his trance with Swaahali, looking for the name of this woman, who had subtly warned him that they would meet again. Of course she was a Blood Keeper, one of the truly sacred kind, and older than his dreams. He knew it when he saw the black bones strung around her arms, melted away by time, and in the gray, unnatural eyes, in ruin by overuse and her sheer force of will to keep them alive. She had to be nearly blind. Shhaha had locked her out the instant he saw her, but she took him to a place inside herself, where she hid from him with ease.

He wanted to comfort Mah, and was angry with himself for not having taught him the power of enclosures beyond the simple building of physical walls. Mah and Odrak were young still, and he wondered now how he had dared to think of taking them on this journey. He always saved the more difficult training for last and knew they were not prepared, but the journey and the Test of Blood was an absolute necessity now. Yet, how was he to know a Nameless Mother still existed?

He threw the bone of food to the ground, cursing and spitting as he suddenly realized he was eating nut gruel mixed with animal fat. "Animal flesh!" he cursed, and continued to spit the taste out of his mouth.

Keishlee had already sat down her bone, while Ramaa continued to eat, engrossed in his own thoughts, but Shhaha did not notice either of them as he searched his memories for this woman's name. His powers were strong, and he knew he could stand up to anything she might do. After all, he came from a long line of blood, mixed and well planted by 45 generations of humans, whose blood magic was renowned in their world. Her blood would still include beasts, and would be mated close by necessity and therefore weaker by default. But she would have raw, natural energy to command, and some of nature to control by will alone. She would not have to spend the time to mix and match her magic, and like the speed of the Tuk Women, she could overcome him with her force alone. He needed her name to know which line of blood she possessed. It might prove to be his only leverage against her, especially if she tried to force Mah to some test. He would not have her discover the power Mah had yet to learn himself. He had other plans for Mah, and Odrak.

Suddenly, scenes of men murdering Mah, then visions of Odrak's familiar near humans burning in a pyre, and the madness of life rushed in on him. Every word she used had been well placed. He was being reminded of his duty, but his head ached with trying to recall some memory of the dreaded Test of Blood, which came like tiny drops of rain upon the desert. He needed more. He had to have Mah and Odrak prepared before the night was upon them. Just as Swaahali had said, there was no time to spare; no more forms of harm or inconsiderate care could befall his people again. He could no longer even leave Mah's protection to Odrak alone. While he still had time and life, his apprentices would fulfill the vision he had seen long ago, which came now more clearly to him here.

Odrak had learned enough to get the elder men to understand that his people did not eat flesh of any kind. They had seen Shhaha throw away his food bone and had taken offense. Odrak did not understand the look on Shhaha's face, but was surprised that he had even taken it. The entire clearing smelled of cooked or raw flesh, and he had no doubt that it would be mixed in everything served here. Odrak got the men to understand that Shhaha did not mean to offend, but that their offering had offended him.

The men then did a very strange thing. They took turns smacking each other across the face. They bent their bodies from side to side and shook their heads, letting the bone dangles hanging from their ears clack together like speech.

A man called Uurxi, who had the clearest skin Odrak had ever seen, explained to Mah and Odrak that they regarded Shhaha with the same respect as "She," who Mah knew was the strange old woman. He ordered some of the young protectors about, who began to climb vines and search through bushes. Mah then pulled Odrak aside and pointed to the sight in the surrounding trees.

"Nesters!" Mah purred, pointing to the enclosures built into the massive trees. Some were simple, open canopies and walkways, tied together with vines and covered by layers of leaves. Others, whose contents could not be seen, were like huge hives built of twigs, leaf strings and light-colored moss. They were built into all the surrounding trees, and the trees were as tall as mountains, with their tops sticking up into the clouds. Only the branches of the trees that surrounded the clearing had been removed, leaving an opening for just enough sunlight to provide a twilight haze.

Odrak was about to run to Shhaha to point all this out, but Shhaha was already standing, having discovered it for himself, and was in awe of the sight.

Young protectors entered the clearing with arms full of fruits and vegetables. Uurxi made a whistling sound while pointing to Shhaha, and they ran to him and made a show of their offerings. Shhaha returned their respects, and Mah was pleased to see that they offered him only fresh foods, from which he selected for Ramaa and Keishlee. They waited for Shhaha to sit back down and eat, and then they offered food to Mah and Odrak.

Uurxi and the adults left Mah and Odrak with a group of older protectors, and they ate together and tried to understand each other's words. Younger ones gathered around, but sat in a cluster about a tree away.

To Odrak's relief and pleasure, the two who had been fighting over his weapon returned, still carrying it between them. Each held the butt of the handle as if they were glued to it. Both their hands were bloodied, and they had serious cuts on their legs and arms, causing them to suffer from the weapon's poison.

Mah turned to Shhaha and smiled, since he had already begun to make potents and was mixing medicine salves. He had one of the strangers hold a flask of cleaning liquid over a sitting fire, and Keishlee sat near with the long gourd of Tuk wine, ready to do as he commanded.

Mah and Odrak rose to greet the two protectors, but one of them pushed Odrak away. Mah held Odrak back, while listening to other protectors explain that Odrak had lost the weapon, and that it was no longer his. Mah understood, but tried to warn them, saying, "The weapon will make you sick, and it belongs to Odrak. You should not try to keep it."

One of them smiled quite broadly and said something that even Odrak had no trouble understanding: Mah had no say, because the weapon never belonged to him, but Odrak could fight them for the weapon if he wanted it back.

Odrak barked the call of the black cat, which meant he was ready to fight. He ordered the two to drop the weapon and fight him one or together, here and now.

Mah knew they had to get the weapon back, but he did not want Odrak to take advantage of them, since they were already weak from the poison. Mah touched each of them, placing the palm of his hand across their beating hearts, a sign of warm respects, but they did not understand, and one of them smacked Mah in the face.

Shhaha and a large group were approaching when the hand made its way across Mah's face. He ordered Odrak to be still, but Odrak wasn't going to listen. He slipped in front of Mah and back kicked the protector, breaking his leg. Before the young man could hit the ground, Odrak snatched up the weapon and had the other one by the hair before Mah could stop him.

Shhaha howled and filled Odrak's head with pain. Odrak let out a tortured scream, dropping the weapon and frightening everyone as he crumpled to the ground. It was something worse than what the old woman had done, and Mah was dumbfounded because he had not known Shhaha could do such a thing.

People surrounded them, and Shhaha could see reed weapons being prepared, but he kept his calm and slipped the nervous protector out from under Odrak. He whispered a healing chant over him and slowly rubbed his face. Instantly the young man was entranced and silent. As Shhaha suspected, these people could feel and see the aura of his power even better than his own people did. The clearing was silent except for Odrak's moans and Shhaha's call to Keishlee for help.

Mah knew Shhaha could make wordless calls to his ear, and back at Tuk Village, he learned that Shhaha could touch his thoughts, but this was something new. Shhaha had done something even worse to Odrak than the old woman had done to him, and he was still alive. A serious lesson had begun.

Mah stepped in close to the injured protector and took in his smell, a thickly sweet aroma, like a full basket of mixed roots and herbs. He turned to Shhaha and attended his every move, reacting to him as if they were of one mind and body, flowing into action and reaction like two made one.

As always, Mah had the flask in his hand without his needing to ask, and Shhaha dripped drops over the man's wounds, while Mah took the moss poultice from Keishlee and rubbed the liquid into his cuts. After Shhaha had braced the broken leg, he took a gourd from Keishlee of another potent, red and steaming, and pulled back the thick curls of hair. Without having to be told, and not fearing the heat, Mah scooped up a small portion and rubbed it over the diseased ear. The youth let out a small whimper, and the crowd uttered a tender coo, as they realized that Shhaha had set himself to healing a thing they thought a necessity in their lives.

Soon everyone was kneeling around Shhaha, calling for him to rid them of the disease of green fur and sores that would eventually breach their faces and cover their necks. Only the oldest ones had it badly, but all the males wearing bone rings had some form of it. Shhaha pointed out the different types of bones to Mah. After assuring the men that they would be returned, he removed the bone rings and placed them in a gourd of cleaning fluid. Once Mah realized there would not be enough fluid, he went off to make more.

The young protectors who had been treated already followed Mah and gave him assistance with their supplies. They had large, heavy clay jars that were hard as stone, and made more perfectly than those of his people. They helped him empty and clean one, and then filled it with water, which Ramaa poured from a massive jar, amazing them all with his strength.

Mah stirred in the sacks of powders Shhaha had given him, one of which he knew was the grindings of the snake teeth. He asked Ramaa to see to Odrak, and gave him a bone of water for Odrak to drink.

The water bubbled and swirled quickly inside the pot. It had a new smell to it now, which stung the nose more harshly then before, but Mah knew it had been made more powerful by the way it brightened the inside of the pot. This was a common external medicine used by all his people, which had been cloudy-colored and burned painfully when put to open wounds. It was sparkling clear now, and after breaking his skin with a pine needle, he found it less painful, but it sizzled over the cut even more than before.

Mah poured some into bladders to save for later use, and then into the jars and gourds filled with the men's bone dangles. Shhaha used the cleaning fluid to wipe off the red salve he'd put on all their ears, and was so relieved not to hear them screaming. Their ears dried quickly and Mah used the fat end of the pine needle to scoop out their earwax, which he rubbed over the cleaned sores for added protection.

Keishlee had been trying to get Odrak to his feet, when Ramaa came over and threw water in his face, then yanked him from the ground over to a tree. Just then a slave appeared from inside a hollow in the tree. He ran over to the forgotten weapon and carefully picked it up, then brought it over and propped it up beside Odrak. He stumbled into Ramaa, and then dashed back into the tree hollow without a word. Keishlee and Ramaa looked for him in the hollow, but the next time they saw him, the slave was walking above them across a branch, where he disappeared into a large tree nest.

Ramaa laughed at the scene, but then started shaking Odrak again. Keishlee tried to stop him, but he pushed her away and struck Odrak. "Trying to get us killed!" he growled once Odrak opened his eyes. Odrak just bowed his head and squeezed his lips tight. "You are too close to Mah, always. Keep a distance!"

"No!" Odrak spoke with his eyes.

"Keep a distance, or I will take him...."

Keishlee gasped at the terrible threat and struck Ramaa hard enough to knock him against the tree. She stomped off to find Shhaha, cursing Ramaa as she left.

"Even if he lets you, I will kill you."

Ramaa laughed and yanked Odrak up by his throat and held him against the tree. "You are like a rooting feeder looking - out for threats, which need only be a look for you."

"Leave me alone," Odrak tried to speak against Ramaa's choking him. Recalling Shhaha's latest warning to him, he forced Ramaa's hand away, and after falling some distance to the ground, said, "You are right. I have moved too quickly to attack. Lately I cannot bear others touching him. I must learn to protect him better," Odrak said, recalling the very words of the strange woman.

"Will you be this bad once you and he are mated apart?" Ramaa joked, coming down from his anger. "Keep some distance. All attacks do not come from close up." He motioned towards two men with long reeds. "Some attacks may come from many trees away." Ramaa signaled above them at the many look-outs posted in the distant trees.

Odrak was still trying to clear his head and sat back on the ground, angry with himself for needing discipline. He could still feel the pain of Shhaha's thoughts, like hard body blows. His words, "You will get him killed!" were ringing in his ears like torture. He wanted to cry as he spotted Mah and remembered Mabezi's words.

He heard Shhaha calling again, but this time there was no pain. He looked at Shhaha and Mah tending groups of kneeling men, and heard him say that he was loved, but did not see Shhaha's lips move, nor did Shhaha look in his direction. Odrak started to stand as he watched Ramaa leave, but a voice like tender caresses suggested that he sit and rest.

Shhaha was using a powerful magic on him. Magic that compelled and demanded, like the blood memories that could shoot in and out of focus before he realized what his body was being forced to do. A list of duties flooded his mind. He waited until the orders stopped, then picked up his weapon and went to get them done.

Shhaha and Mah finished with the last of the men. Shhaha double checked a few of them, but some ears could not be saved, so he cut them behind their ears to stop the pain. They already had something for the headaches.

The few women in the clearing had been standing around for some time, not speaking or moving much. When Shhaha and Mah moved off, they rushed around the clearing checking the men, making loud slapping sounds with their palms against their naked end-mounds. As the women became more excited and bent to slap themselves, a man crawled near and took a sniff, licked his lips and clapped his hands to his thighs. Women came out of the trees making this lusty sound, and the men responded with lapping, sensual body smacking sounds of their own.

Some of the women that gathered together, began arguing among themselves. Some of the elder men came near and sat at their feet, awaiting some word. The women spoke in whispers, and moved around like runners, in total contrast to the loud talk and quiet movements of the men.

The women approached Shhaha smiling and looking determined. Some even tried to copy the high-step, ambling gait of the clan of the Tall Walkers. The three eldest men, including the one called Uurxi, crawled along the ground at their feet.

An elder woman meekly signaled Keishlee over, and made a great show of asking if Shhaha was still useful between his legs. Keishlee understood the looks and gestures. She turned to Shhaha, who signaled for her to speak the truth, which she did in words and signs. Two women came forward and removed the skins that were carelessly roped or hanging from their bodies. They squeezed, rubbed and touched themselves in such a way that it was obvious what they wanted. They stuck fingers into themselves and gave Shhaha their hands to smell.

Shhaha was about to speak when Ramaa stepped over and offered himself instead. He went to touch one of the women and

Shhaha ordered him to be still, saying, "If you touch her without her asking, they will use their weapons on you."

Ramaa looked around to see every reed in the clearing pointing in his direction. Even women were ready to blow through reeds at him. Those without weapons sat close together on the ground, staring hard at him. Ramaa backed away as he listened to the women gently refuse him.

A group of men crawled close together and made a bench of their bodies. Uurxi gave Shhaha another look and reached up to touch his chest. After feeling Shhaha over, he called more men over to make the bench longer. Uurxi then slipped into the hole their bodies made and looked up at Mah with a smile.

Mah choked on his breath as he figured out what they intended. Shhaha was put off as well and wanted to refuse, but looked about the clearing, considering what would grow if his seed took root. From the small number of slaves and the general look of these people, new blood was needed here.

He called Odrak over and offered him and Mah to them, telling them that their seed would prove more fruitful. "Old seeds are not often found."

The women took the offer like an insult, and refused with indignant looks, saying something about "uprooting small trees with ease."

The clearing went back to normal, with the men checking each other's ears while others tended the food and continued to cut and skin dead animals. Shhaha thought about it a moment longer and then agreed, but limited the task to just one. When he was understood, the women argued among themselves again. A woman was finally selected by a leading elder mother, and then was placed across the backs of the men with her legs sticking up in the air.

Shhaha didn't know what to do. Keishlee walked away and Mah left with Odrak. Ramaa went in search of the tall walkers and Shhaha was left alone with this strange sight.

Getting comfort and relief from available free women of other tribes and clans was expected, almost necessary. It was an act of hospitality and the offer showed good manners. But this scene was unthinkable to him. He planned to give her his seed quickly, so that he could prepare Mah and Odrak for when next they would meet the woman with no name.

Shhaha looked the woman over very carefully when she

reached up for him. He slipped a finger into one of the many disiac-filled bones tied to his legs, and then stalled to give the disiac time to work, by slowly removing his packs off his back, and the walking carry sack from between his legs. But there was no need for him to stall long. The disiac worked quickly and savagely when taken dry into the mouth. He could feel Mah and Odrak looking at him. He had kept his thoughts linked to theirs, so they heard his silent scream and wondered what he feared. Shhaha broke his contact with their minds, then turned off his self control to satisfy the thing that throbbed under his loin cloth.

▼▼▼▼▼

Odrak had borrowed enough skins to build a tent between two small trees. Many of the younger protectors tried to be helpful until Mah came over and they all backed away. Odrak's body language had told them too, so he smiled at them, glad that he was finally getting some respect. But he lost his smile while looking into the eyes of a slightly older protector. Here was someone who didn't catch the hint, and with him, others—staring, judging and setting down marks before they were scored, and counting him out.

Ignoring the protector, Odrak gently pulled Mah closer to the tent, telling him with the firmness of his touch that he wanted him to hold still. He tied the loose ends of Mah's loin cloth up between his legs, as Shhaha had instructed him to, then after doing the same to his own, he kissed Mah on the cheek and licked his face. Mah tried to hold him close, but Odrak said, "Finish preparing the enclosure. Shhaha wants it ready for a blood trance."

Mah was surprised. Odrak was very protective of all the responsibilities of his apprenticeship, whether it be personal or duty. Making ready a special enclosure for the Keeper of the Blood was his guarded province, one of the few things Mah had yet to do. Pride made his face swell, and he chuckled and grinned as he asked some of the young protectors to help him finish staking the tent.

Odrak searched the faces of everyone he saw. He made a study of these people, how they only looked him in the face when he was close up, and how they always sensed his coming near. This was something he was good at, sizing people up. Shhaha had told him this was his greatest talent, and that he could always trust Odrak's opinion of others. Odrak had the ability to see into people's hearts, and so he set about to find some friends. Those older protectors who were set against him were all following him, and against so many he would need some friends.

He spotted a group of worthy protectors who also did not like the ones following him. He spoke to one of them whose hair was more like his own, except that it was loose and trailing down his back in bushy waves. He offered Odrak a bite of a large piece of meat. Shhaha would not approve, but Odrak chanted silently and slipped off a piece. He rubbed it into the dirt and ate it quickly before they could take offense. Trying not to taste it as it went down, he wondered how long it would be before his stomach forced it back up, but he was determined to make at least one friend here.

There were five of them and they greeted Odrak by touching his face and feeling its contours. None of them paid any attention to the lusty cries and whimpers coming from the center of the clearing, tho they talked about it in great detail. They made guesses about Shhaha's weight and height, his size and length, and they counted his strokes.

Counting with them, Odrak learned to count the numbers between 10 and 20, for which his people had no names. When they reached twenty, one of them would throw a small stone into a pile that was building up in the circle between them. Once Odrak learned how to call the numbers, he threw the next pebble, and Kangar told Odrak his name.

Odrak knew he was not supposed to look, since no one else did. The young protectors did this counting like a special game among them, with young slaves were running back and forth between other counting groups, sharing the numbers they had reached. Odrak could barely hear the slosh-slap-a-lack of Shhaha and the woman. The adults who were not in counting groups began to talk even louder or held loud conversations as a distraction, and Odrak could see that some of the protectors were losing count.

Odrak sat and stopped the protector called Umboi from throwing his stone too soon. Kangar hadn't lost count, and signed for Odrak to throw the next one. When the pile of stones had passed the count of fingers and toes, there was an exhausted breath of something thrilling in the air. Kangar was breathing hard and they all patting the ground, as if they could not stand to keep the count in their heads any longer.

Suddenly women were sliding down vines or running

across the clearing from holes in the massive trees. Some women were slapping their hands together and making a clicking sound with their mouths. Odrak and Kangar were the only ones still keeping the count in their group, while the others kept those away who tried to distract them by yelling in their ears. The woman with Shhaha screamed, and then an elder called to the groups just before Odrak could drop the next stone.

Kangar gave Odrak a winning look while Umboi counted the pile of stones. Kangar said the word Odrak remembered for 10 and 4, but Odrak counted 10 and 8. Umboi and the others smiled and called out the name for 50 and 2 stones. Kangar then clapped his hands in the air to call the elders over.

Odrak turned to see Shhaha rising from the woman. She was crying loudly now, and threw her body about like someone in mourning. She had to be restrained and carried out of the clearing, up into a tree. Other women ran around the tree, screaming as if they too had some pain, but clapped their hands together as if for some joy.

Umboi and the others guarded their collection of stones like a bird would its eggs, while men and protectors walked Uurxi around the clearing so that all could see the seed that had spilled onto his face. The women disappeared into the trees, their voices clacking in a torrent of confused sounds. Men brought food and drinks for Shhaha and tried to get him to rest, while the elders called his name, repeating it between themselves as a promise to keep the fruit of his seed safe.

After Uurxi was taken around the clearing and everyone had seen him, he made his rounds among the anxious counting groups. When a group had the number wrong, he threw the stones at them, and they sat quietly with their ears covered while he shouted insults and pelted them. Two other groups, whose counts were 51 and 9, and 52 and 3, were brought over to Umboi, who smiled up at Uurxi and called out 52 and 14, but Umboi pointed to Odrak, who then called out 52 and 18.

Uurxi stepped back and gasped. He did a little dance and reached into the folds of his skins to pull out a handful of slimy black stones. The groups jumped around, screaming and surrounded Uurxi. Even Mah came over and tried to see what the items were. Protectors pushed through, calling out a list of names, which Odrak could tell was a line of blood.

The protector who had given Odrak evil looks stepped out

from the crowd and threw his stones at Odrak. He was older and more broad-chested, but Odrak was glad for the larger target.

Uurxi screamed something at the protector, but Mah could tell that it was not a curse. Two men appeared, blocking Uurxi from speaking to the protector and giving everyone in the crowd evil looks. Odrak sensed the blood ties between these men and the protector, but both favored the protector so much it was hard to tell which one was his keeper.

A hand snatched Kangar aside as the crowd grew silent. Kangar yelled something to Uurxi, who shouted, and this time Odrak was sure it was a curse. Uurxi called out 52 and 18, and the whole gathering gasped. He repeated it until the men stepped back, and momentarily awed, the angry protector dropped his clutch of stones. Uurxi rubbed Odrak down one arm and gave him three oddly shaped stones with growth on them, and then gave the angry protector, Kangar, and the 4 youths with him, one apiece.

Kangar received the gift as if it was precious and rubbed it against his face, before meticulously storing it down in front of his girdle of skins. The angry protector gathered his friends around him, and then reached down into his skins and pulled out four more stones. He showed them to the others, yelling, "FIVE! FIVE!" which he repeated to the two men standing behind him. "FIVE!!" they bragged and pointed fingers at Uurxi.

Odrak kept still while Uurxi argued with the protector, who was unduly set on being angry over the count. Umboi and Kangar pulled Odrak over and both took turns shouting to him, but it was more than he could understand. He searched the clearing looking for Shhaha, whom he realized had foreseen something here, and had had Odrak tie up his loincloth. Odrak was relieved when he caught sight of Mah and called him over.

"Umboi says if you give him or Kangar the 'spice,'...yes, the 'spice seed,' either will fight for you," spoke Mah, while pulling something out from his hair.

Uurxi howled and snatched up Mah's arm. He had whatever it was before Odrak could get away from Umboi, who was prepared to hold him back. Uurxi ran around showing the others what he'd taken from Mah, sniggering and tapping hands together with the other men. Uurxi then hurried back and hunched himself at Mah's feet. He held the black stones out to Mah, pointing to the cuts and marks that looked like bites, and cried over them.

He gave the precious stones back to Mah and ran over to

one of the gigantic trees and pointed to it. He held himself there, stroking the tree as if it were alive, and talked to it as if it could hear. He ran back to Mah and pointed at the seeds in his hand and touched each one of them gently, holding up the large unmarked one and rubbing it over his face. He placed it back in Mah's hand with great care, and there was no doubt that these seeds were sacred.

Suddenly a stone struck the side of Mah's head and he yelped from the shock of it. It was a small stone, but all eyes turned to Odrak, who was flushed with anger. Uurxi and Kangar flung themselves at Odrak, being careful to point out to him that he still had the spice seeds in his hand, and his weapon strapped to his side. The two men moved in front of the angry protector and Odrak was sure who threw the stone. The men were calling Odrak forward, but Uurxi and Kangar would not let him go.

Odrak could hear Umboi begging Mah for the smallest of the three seeds. Odrak tried to calm himself, but his blood boiled and he could not speak words. He felt the hot stare coming from Ramaa, who had just stepped out of the dark forest into the light of the clearing. Odrak turned to Mah, who held the stones out to him and motioned for Odrak to put them down into his loin cloth.

"No!" Odrak managed to shout, and then quickly calmed himself. He pulled Mah to him saying, "No. You cannot fight this one. He insulted me first."

Odrak was taken back by the furious look on Mah's face. His large eyes were narrowed slits, and his smiling face, a grimace of evil intent. Mah turned away from Odrak, raising the stones in the air and calling for someone to assist him. "Is there no one here who will guard them for me?" he asked.

Everyone was looking back and forth between Mah, Odrak, the protector and the two men guarding him. But the stones in Mah's hand were too much for these people to resist, and soon slaves, young and old protectors, and even grown men rushed to Mah and held out their hands to receive the seeds.

Other men lined up behind their keeps, looking from them to the angry protector and his keepers. Some men pulled aside their keeps, arguing with them as they left the clearing.

Once Ramaa understood what was happening, he hissed, "I do not know what you need, Mah. But I have promised, and am here for you." He started forward.

"No!" Odrak cried as he rushed over and pulled down

Mah's arm. "You would fight?" he asked, almost crying.

Mah snatched himself away, and speaking in the tongue of these people, he cried the word, "FOUR!! FOUR!!!" shocking this clan of nesters with how well he intoned their word.

The group let up a cheer that came even from the crowds that suddenly came out of their tree nests. The women started throwing leaves down and slapping their end-mounds. The two men slapped their thighs and cursed Mah, while someone handed the protector more stones.

"I think you need a keeper here, Mah," signed Ramaa as he stepped through the group to get Mah's stones.

The two men yelled and cursed Ramaa, but did not dare go near him. They called Uurxi over to make a fuss, yelling something about "matchless blood," "no doubt" and insisting that "the whole clan fight, if the giant fights."

Uurxi listened with only half an ear, looking back and forth between Ramaa and Mah, laughing to himself. He came over to Ramaa and pulled him down. "You have no spice seed, and your seed raised neither of these. If a woman has lied to you, it is no fault of my people."

Ramaa didn't understand, but he waited, keeping a close eye on the two men he would fight if they laid hands on Mah. He hoped for the first time that Mah would let Odrak fight, smiling because he knew either of these men could easily take Odrak and teach him a lesson.

Uurxi came back to Odrak and Mah and pushed them together, smiling slyly over his shoulder to his people. Speaking to Mah and Odrak he said, "Either of Geouu's fathers may take them from you," pointing to the protector and the men with him, "even if you win," he repeated over and over until both Odrak and Mah understood. "You," he pointed to Odrak, "knew the exact number. No one has ever known the highest number, but me. And you with the clouds in your hair, you have found lost seeds. The spice trees themselves have honored you. But neither of you have keepers here to build for you. Some of my people do not want either of you to have them, and others say it is fair. Two must fight, or all."

Odrak and Mah argued for a while, but Mah only became more determined and tried to pull away. "Umboi! Kangar!" Odrak called, while still holding on to Mah. "Between you, who is stronger?" he asked, pointing out the struggle between him and Mah to get them to understand. Mah spoke the proper words and

Umboi said with some surprise, "We will share a woman between us," and grabbed Kangar around his shoulders. "We will share even two women between us," joked Kangar.

"If they get another seed between them," smirked Uurxi.

Odrak understood and handed each one of them a seed. They whooped and jumped about, Umboi shouting "SIX!" and Kangar shouting "FIVE!" Uurxi looked at Odrak with watery eyes. He waved his hand in the air pointing, at the massive trees, then squeezed Odrak's arms and begged to see the remaining seed. He touched it once more, then folded it back into Odrak's hand and asked that he put it away.

Mah was fighting himself now. He wanted to be angry, because he wanted to fight. He felt the crowd open a space around them and saw three men come over to stand, one behind Kangar and two behind Umboi. Strong, tall men.

Odrak looked at Mah, imploring him to give up his anger, and maybe even some of his seeds. Mah looked at the four brownish seeds he had found many days ago while collecting food. He thought the stones were alive, because they had made themselves known to him. He meant to show them to Odrak long ago, but had forgotten about them, and now felt guilty that he had not shared this with Odrak. He forced himself to be calm and flushed the anger from his face. He pulled Odrak's hand up to his chest and laid it on his heart, then filled it, one at a time, with the spice seeds.

Odrak smiled, and this time he caught the stone heading for Mah. He turned an evil eye toward the one called Geouu, but managed to restrain his nature.

Kangar and Umboi angled around Geouu, after scooping up a handful of dirt and stones. They demanded his "fathers" step aside. When they would not, Umboi's and Kangar's keepers began accepting stones from others, and went to confront the men.

Geouu marched out into the open and cursed Kangar, who moved to attack. Umboi held him back and they turned to Odrak, who gathered them about him. He offered them each another seed, but they almost fell to their knees refusing. Their keepers rushed over, urging them to accept, but they refused. Uurxi came over and pushed the men away, shouting the number "SIX!," Umboi's cue to push all the others aside and throw his pebbles at Geouu.

Everyone began to sit around while the women threw leaves and slapped their end-mounds again. Only Umboi and

Geouu and their collection of keepers were standing. Kangar sat next to Odrak, begging him to put the spice seeds away. He showed Odrak how they were kept, between the seed bags and the pleasure stick. Odrak put two away after tying his cloth up tighter between his legs. Then he gave Mah back the remaining three and helped to tie them in place.

Just as the fight was getting underway, Odrak saw that most of the young protectors sitting near were looking at him and Mah with astonishment on their faces. Odrak slipped himself closer to Mah and rested an arm across his folded legs. Kangar was also looking at him oddly, and he wanted to asked Kangar what he thought, but a loud slap was heard and all turned to watch the fight.

Umboi and Geouu stood cheek to cheek, the side of their faces pressed together as they slapped and kicked each other until they both tumbled. The struggle was not a fight like one Odrak would be accustomed to; they pulled each other and got their bodies tied into knots more than they struck each other. Around and around they tossed over the ground. Whenever an arm or leg got free, the other flipped and they were tied in knots again. Umboi got an arm locked around Geouu's head and flipped him forward. Some of the crowd shouted for Umboi to finish with him, while others were shouting for Geouu to get up. Umboi was standing, but crouched over Geouu and waiting for him to make a move.

Odrak regretted turning this fight over to Umboi. He was thinking how simple it would be to finish Geouu now. As Geouu got into a bent position, standing on his hands and knees, Odrak spotted the place to land a kick that could easily take Geouu's life. Geouu started to get up and Umboi made his move, but Geouu spun around and flipped Umboi to the ground with a heavy thud.

Odrak jumped up and screamed at Umboi as he watched Geouu jump on Umboi with his knees. Umboi smacked Geouu hard across the chest and got an underhanded grip around his neck. Kangar and Mah pulled Odrak back down. Mah begged him to be still, and Kangar pleaded with him not to interfere.

Umboi now had both legs wrapped around Geouu's waist and an arm locked around his throat. He pulled back, ordering Geouu to yield. The crowd shouted for Umboi to finish, while Odrak cheered and wondered how much longer Geouu could hold out, now that he couldn't breathe, but Geouu tried to strike Umboi from behind, which only made it easier for Umboi to choke him harder. Geouu finally struck the ground and the crowd jumped to their feet. Uurxi shouted for Umboi to stop and pulled Geouu away, but only after Umboi had kicked Geouu in the face.

Odrak stood there wondering why Umboi had let Geouu go, but was confronted by all the other protectors trying to hand him and Mah stones. He watched as Umboi flung stones at Geouu, who was still trying to catch his breath. Odrak told himself he liked this part, and stepped up to face the fallen Geouu. Now he would finish Geouu like he wanted to.

Uurxi and another elder stepped in front of him and said something about not hitting Geouu in the head. Odrak protested, pointing to Mah and cursing Geouu by name. One of Geouu's keepers picked up a small pebble and threw it to the ground in front of Odrak, saying, "That is what he threw. No bigger."

Odrak dropped the larger stone and picked up the very pebble the man had thrown, but Uurxi stopped him and returned Odrak's original stone. He stared at Odrak with wide glaring eyes and huffed, "We do not take each other's lives. We are human. What are you?" Then he handed Odrak the stone.

Mah stepped in front of them and aimed his stone for Geouu's face to trick him, and managed to strike him in the crotch. The crowd laughed, and Geouu howled and twisted over the ground in pain.

Odrak moved the others away from him. He stepped back and threw the stone hard into Geouu's chest. Geouu fell back and cried out with both pains, but he was still alive, much to Odrak's displeasure.

Uurxi patted Odrak's arm and signaled the others to finish. Then Kangar and the others circled around Geouu, throwing small stones and pebbles. When they were done his keepers helped him up, and one carried him over his shoulder, leaving the clearing.

Kangar, Umboi and their friends surrounded Shhaha's apprentices, taking every liberty to feel them over and hear them speak. They uncovered their ears and delighted over the smooth unmarked skin they found.

"Uurxi says you go to the Temples of Light. There are five of you, and now you have just enough seeds to enter the gates. I did not want Geouu to take them from you," spoke Kangar, while playing with Mah's white hair.

"Kangar and I have seeds enough to trade for a woman

now," spoke Umboi, who turned to face his keepers.

"So that is what you wanted more than the spice seeds," laughed Uurxi, who Mah and Odrak were beginning to realize was like a blood keeper to his people. "Your new friend, Odrak, has the weapon of his people, and you want him to go with you. Tuk women will not have you trade for women in their presence. What makes you think Tuk men will be different?"

"I am no Tuk man. I am of the clan of the Tall Walkers," Odrak said, pointing to his clan relations standing off among the distant trees. "And if there are those who trade their women, why should I object?"

"Then you would come with us?" asked Umboi.

"It is a short but dangerous journey with so many finks [*man creatures*] and bears around. Women are too few in these lands. Umboi and I will need help to bring her back." Kangar looked about the clearing at those he knew were listening. "No man will come with us to the land of the Hoteps without a share of what we bring back."

Umboi came over and stood next to Kangar. He put an arm around his shoulders and said, "We are one, like you, Odrak, and you, Mah." He stumbled over Mah's name. "If you agree to let us have her first, then we will share the woman we get with you."

"Only because you know they will not be staying," smirked Uurxi. "Agree to share her with...."

Mah jumped in and said, "No need. We will both come...."

"No," spoke Shhaha, stepping into the group and surprising everyone with his presence. He shook his hands by his side and then his head from side to side in their custom, and then greeted Ramaa as he would his own people. Ramaa did not understand these body signs, but Shhaha was asking these people not to be angry with him for having taken them by surprise.

Shhaha handed his blood wand to Mah and turned back to the others, saying, "No. These two cannot go, but Ramaa and Keishlee," and signalling for her to join them, "they can go with you. In them you will find much protection and no need to share."

Kangar and Umboi looked back at Keishlee coming over and then up at Shhaha. "The Tuk woman will not kill us once we have traded for the woman?" asked Umboi. "The Tuk woman will let us trade for a woman?" asked Kangar, who tried to whisper as Keishlee approached.

"I am of the clan of the Tall Walkers," she spoke, as the group stepped away from her. "I am not a Tuk woman. You may look at me," she said, smiling now that she knew why they had all kept their distance from her.

Shhaha was speaking their words as if they were familiar to him. He repeated what Keishlee had said and they all turned and looked at her, moving their eyes and heads together in sic. Their eyes glistened over with desire for her. After not having dared to look her way, they stared at her now with budding lust, including one of Umboi's keepers. The man was nearly as tall as Keishlee, and his look was so imploring she was compelled to touch and comfort him.

His mate stepped up and pushed Keishlee off. She pulled a reed needle from her hair and called for other women to come and help her. She glared at Keishlee and said, "Challenge!"

Umboi pleaded with her and fell to his knees, while other women yelled down from the trees for Keishlee to leave.

"The long reed needles can hold enough poison to kill. One or both will surely die," whispered Uurxi to Shhaha.

The men were slowly dropping to the ground. Keishlee turned to the woman and dropped one knee. She was sure the woman knew what this meant, and when the yelling stopped, the woman reached out to help Keishlee up. They hugged each other and then the woman turned back to face Umboi. "You have ten?" she asked affectionately, but did not touch him. "You have ten between the two of you?" She looked over to Kangar.

Kangar nodded and then reached into his skins and showed her his five. Umboi pulled out the rest and showed her his six. Her eyes lit up at the sight of them. She rubbed a finger over each one and then in a rush of excitement, forced their hands to put the seeds back where they had been. "You will bring another woman, and not wine or sweet meats?"

"Yes, mother," Umboi spoke, cautiously caressing her arm, then watched her run off to tell the other women.

Shhaha had been whispering to Keishlee and Ramaa when the silence brought his attention back to Umboi and Kangar, who were looking hard at Keishlee.

When Keishlee looked at them they said, "If you are not a Tuk woman...," but before they could complete their words, Ramaa stepped forward and threw a hand down for them not to speak. He still did not understand their words, but the looks on their faces was something anyone would know. "We do not trade our people, and you are too young to mate one of our women," Ramaa huffed, knowing exactly what Shhaha would say.

Umboi looked up the long distance to Ramaa's face and hoped he had not insulted anyone.

"Can you run from now until high moon?" asked Kangar.

"Yes," huffed Ramaa, "but we can ride the tall walkers." He looked for the animals off in the distance. He smiled and pointed to them. They were being fed soft shoots and leaves by slaves and women in the trees. "The tall walkers appreciate your people," he said, resting a reassuring hand on Kangar's shoulder. "I will protect you both."

"We should leave now. It is a full night's run from here," spoke Umboi.

Keishlee and Ramaa said their parting words and followed Umboi and Kangar out to where the tall walkers were enjoying themselves. Shhaha gave Mah and Odrak a few more moments with their new friends, and then signed for them to prepare themselves for blood trancing.

▼▼▼▼▼

"What is it you do here?" Uurxi asked as Mah and Odrak were about to enter the tent.

Shhaha didn't want to explain, but said, "I must train my apprentices. If we may be alone for a time, until sunrise, you will have shown us a kindness."

"I do not know this sunrise, but you may do your blood magic here only if it does not anger our Great Mother."

Shhaha was impressed. He had guessed that the man was a blood keeper, and his knowing the correct form for the words 'blood magic' were a warning to Shhaha that he had some magic of his own. "I will not let my magic touch the spice trees."

Now it was Uurxi's turn to be impressed, but he was also frightened. There was a secret his people shared to know each other by, a thing kept secret even from their young, and this giant stranger alluded to knowing it already.

"You will do better than that," Uurxi grunted, more at Mah and Odrak, now angry with them for having earned the spice seeds. "You will not keep the spice seeds with you while you make this magic." He held out his hand to receive the seeds.

Shhaha signed for his apprentices to hand them over, but Odrak asked, "Will you return these same ones to us?"

Uurxi made a thin smile from a hard frown and said, "Yes. I will return them to you before you leave us."

Shhaha sensed a danger in these words, but said only, "My people and I are human and we mean you no harm. We will respect your dead and their spirits. We have made this camp well away from the older trees. Do not let others interrupt us while we are inside."

"They sense that you are like She Who Has No Name, and know how She would treat them. They will not dare," spoke one of the men with Uurxi.

Shhaha could see that Uurxi still needed assurances before he gave up. Shhaha said, "I already know where you bury your dead. No one else except my apprentices will know. I give you my blood in this."

The men crouched at Shhaha's feet, whispering so low that Mah wondered if they could hear themselves with their badly ruined ears. "She has sisters," "Some are deadly," "One can kill with a touch," "One is pure evil," "Another can lift you above the trees," "They will try to know what you know," "If not from you, from the young ones," "Like when we first came to meet," "What she did to him," "They will do worse to you."

Shhaha chanted against their fears and said, "They are only women, and we are only men, and all must be humble when they walk across the belly [*added from his trance with Swaahali*] of the Great Mother," using the magic of his voice to force them to sit against their will.

They could feel his magic around them and would not think to threaten him again. But once they recovered, Uurxi said, "Sometimes they hurt what the other one loves. She Who Has No Name loves us, and has given us life here for more than 40 generations." He openly revealed his blood knowledge.

Shhaha did not understand their numbers but was glad they kept pace with their blood. He sat on his heels and felt Uurxi's face, probing deep until he could feel the shape and strength of the muscles and bones. "Yes, your features are made by hand. It is something like the way one carves on wood, and it is done from birth over a great many seasons," he spoke, looking deep into his eyes.

He looked up to the trees and wondered how many slaves

were kept hidden there until they were considered well-formed enough to mix among the clan. "I will keep your secrets," Shhaha spoke again, having finally acquired their trust.

"And the young ones?" Uurxi asked.

Shhaha picked up his blood wand, saying, "You may trust them as well," and then sent them into the tent.

Uurxi called to someone quietly without looking, but Shhaha had noticed the protector making a fire near them and was not surprised that he would be needed here. The man came over with a large bundle of skins.

"Uurxi says you have few skins, and those only good to look at. Our skins are warm and clean. They are smoked, dried and stained with roots and salt to keep out bad magic and evil spirits," said the man with Uurxi.

Uurxi saw the look of determined refusal on Shhaha's face and said, "Our skins used to bring great trade before the desert came. Now most of the tribes are gone. Only the Hoteps and the Obies remain, and they say they no longer need our skins. But the air is cold here when darkness comes. My people sleep under a big skin at night."

Shhaha accepted the skins and waited for the men to leave before he headed for the tent. He forced his eyes to see past the lighted clearing to find Ramaa and Keishlee walking the tall walkers through the dark forest. He chanted a wordless call to the spirits of his kin, asking that they watch over them, and then entered the tent.

A bone pot stewed just outside the tent, and the smell of it was just beginning to waft its way inside. Shhaha could smell the blood, along with the faint and strange odor from a creature he did not know, and the crusty smell of burnt hair. He put his nose to the brew, getting most of the contents in the first whiff, and knew that Odrak had not made these preparations for their blood trance. There were things in the bone pot that Odrak would not have selected, and the water and herbs were mixed as if meant to eat. The fire was also very small, and Odrak would have made the fire hot, so that the brew might burn up before Shhaha could guess all its contents.

He crawled inside the tent and smiled at Mah, knowing Odrak had allowed him to prepare the test of smells. Odrak would never give up trying to trick him. His attempts were too good, but Shhaha had a nose and tongue that could not be fooled, even by things he might not know the name of. Before he finished locking his legs together to sit, he said, "A few strands of hair from one of these Kamituians, and the hair was first charred in here on the coals. A stone of yellow pepper and a bark of netted pine fur that was first dipped in palm oil. Something delicious, sweet herbs...no, I think small nubs of something, each cracked open to bring out more of its powerful scent. I hope you have more of this thing that grows in the ground and must be colored like the sun to have such a powerful smell. You should give some to these people to cover the awful smell of their cooking meats."

Odrak moved to sit with his back to the tent opening and turned to see the smoke and the fumes from the bone pot coming directly into the tent. He reached up and tore a few more holes in the top. "That was too easy. Even I can smell those things," he grinned at Mah.

Shhaha turned to Odrak and said, "He has mixed something never matched, and tries to confuse me with the powerful smell of this nub. Maybe you have used more or less of the nub, yes, less, and the rest of its tasty flavor comes from another part of the same thing, yes, a green part that must grow out of ground, filled with the juice of this nub. Aaah! oh aaah!" Shhaha sighed with surprise and delight. "Ants. Fat hairy ones!" He reached for Mah and pulled at his hair. The look on Mah's face told Odrak that Shhaha had gotten it right.

Mah pulled out the small nut shell to show him the ants still trapped inside. "Ants are good and powerful magic. They always have a powerful leader, and if you ever need a counter to a poison, kill some of her kin with it and give the dead back to her. She will eat them and change the poison in her body and then feed the cure to her kin. Gather enough of them to mix a potent and you will have a cure." Shhaha rewarded him with a powerful medicine.

"Also, you have made this brew to boil down to a thick salve, Mah. You have added some of the cleaning fluid and salt sands to purify it. To know more I would have to taste it, and I sense there is something more. Yes, something that considers blood. Wait. Something also hairy, bitter and has a poison. Something...a thing...yes, a spider. I don't smell any earthly thing, so this creature does not dig a hole. I smell tree bark, from these tall strange trees here, and silk webbing. This spider has a poison, a lot of poison for a creature its size. One of its legs or bellies is filled with poison. Is this a dangerous potent you make? No. Aaah!, the poison in their needles does not kill. It only makes one sleep...You hope to make a potent against sleeping."

"How can you know all this?" Mah looked up, dismayed.

"You have tried to make a potent?" Odrak asked.

"He *has* made a potent, Odrak. We will not let it boil to dry paste. I think if it is dried it will be too tempting. You should not make salves to taste and smell good. Let the ugly odors serve as a warning," Shhaha spoke, pulling his medicine bag over to him. "Here," he pulled out a small bladder with powder in it. "Add this. Just half a finger should do. It will increase the effects and keep the potent in the blood longer."

When Mah finished adding the new ingredient to the potent, they settled down to prepare for the trance. They began by forcing themselves closer to the ground, concentrating on each breath of air as it filled the tiny pockets of their lungs. Mah tried to see himself inside, as the air was changed and delivered to his blood and the blood rushed off to carry it to the rest of his body. Odrak centered himself on the beats of his heart, making himself aware of its weight and the hum-lump pounding of its opened walls.

Each began to see the flickering lights in his head, and took special pains to slow down the thrills rushing up their spines. Then they let their eyes roll back into their heads, since they were needed now in another world.

Shhaha felt closed in by the small space, as he watched Mah and Odrak take control of their breathing and the beating of their hearts. The air would become thin in here soon, once he dropped the herbs and roots onto the coals that glowed bright between them. Good, he thought. They would have to work quickly and their control would have to be firm, or they would choke from the lack of air. Shhaha hardened himself against them as he dropped in the herbs, and then pulled out the long, furry brown root his people called "she bleeds."

He looked over to Mah and wanted to hold him close. His stewing potent had been a challenge and a pleasant discovery, and there were still items he would not know without tasting. He opened the rip in the root by fingering it like one would a woman. It parted like a woman's pleasure bowl, and out dripped red drops into the fire.

To distract himself from the smoke, he recalled the dark

blue color of the Mah's brew, and knew that Mah had used up all his snake beetle wax, since nothing else could produce that color. He smiled, knowing Mah so well he knew if there had not been enough salt, Mah would have added some of his own sweat to rid the brew of the awful pasty taste of the wax. That was also why he added so much of the sweet-smelling nub he found. Shhaha was sure if he bit into this nub, it would open his eyes wide, and that was the effect Mah wanted, more than he wanted to fool Shhaha.

"You must always remember, the body does not belong to you. It is a mass of bits and pieces of all that exists, and if you look inside, it will show you what you have been, what your world is now, and what you may become," Shhaha chanted, while cutting his leg and letting the blood drip over the root. With the same small stone he reached over the coals and cut both Mah and Odrak on the thigh and mixed their blood with his. "Blood rushes through us all, and gives us life. This blood is us before we become ourselves. Like blood does, bringing all that is possible to make us, we shall use the blood to bring all that is to us." He finished mixing the blood and placed it over the hot coals.

The tent filled with smoke as the bloodied root burst open and the flames rose to consumed it. Shhaha rubbed a waxen leaf on each of their cuts to stop the bleeding. He recalled Uurxi's words and smiled, knowing that in the trance world he could protect himself and his apprentices from any evil magic. He let out a deep belly laugh as he could see them moving about in the trance world; Odrak slaying or making friends of evil spirits that came his way, and Mah quickly learning the tongues of the newly dead, and discovering their secret desires. A tear fell from his face as he thought about his own teacher, Shama. He hoped he had given Shama the pleasure these two gave him. He could die anytime now, like Swaahali had promised, because these two were already worthy to take his place. The ease of the thought snapped him into a trance, and his eyes rolled back into his head, while he began the wordless chant of spirits.

Belinda Coffy stepped onto the stage of the Ras Tafari Training Center Auditorium to cheers from the largest crowd ever gathered here. They shouted "Belinda! Belinda!" as she strutted across the stage and shouted, "They call us PAGAN WITCHES!" and did a little dance as she approached the podium. The crowd was screaming and yelling. If not for the mike she carried, nothing she said would have been heard. "They say we're just NEW NUNS! Bullshit!! BULLSHIT!! THOSE BITCHES GAVE UP THE POWER OF THEIR PUSSIES TO KEEP THE SANCTITY OF SOME DICK!!! Reverend Mother! Those women don't have babies! How dare they use the word among them!" she roared, looking out at the faces of all the lovely pledges. Maybe two in twenty would get accepted, and they would know the restrictions once she told them the World Consul had rejected their bid for a Mars colony. They had to understand that their first babies had to be born off-planet. This was to be their conditioning.

"That's okay. We don't have any more of 'em here," she said to a cheering crowd. "We have room now for all of you. You, the new generation of sisters. Sisters who will never forget their power. It is our power that has always been in control, but we had stopped using it. Let's put an end to the bad blood running this planet. The planet Earth!" she screamed at the rowdy female crowd. She continued talking but was thinking of Feegarmardar, who was handling the rejects.

Ebbie waited until the last of the pledges entered the room. She hadn't been told that these women were rejected from entering the Pagangenearchs, but she knew it from the looks on their faces and the fact that one of them was a known spy; another had to be a plant to assist her.

Feegarmardar entered the room in her usual stormy huff. To Ebbie's surprise, her teacher, Cleopatra Mandara a'La Hedrin, and two female troopers wearing Red Warrior arm bands, followed her in. Ebbie made quick introductions and planned to get out of the way this time. She didn't want to get another burn from the microwave laser guns when these troopers killed whomever they had come here for.

"Hello, ladies," spoke Feegarmardar with an unusually warm voice. "I am sorry to be the one to tell you, but none of you should have made it this far."

One of the women jumped up. "Why have I been rejected?"

Feegarmardar might have given this woman a taste of what she was capable of, had Cleopatra not been there, and Ebbie was grateful. She hated to see Feegarmardar brutalize people over some trifle.

Feegarmardar's look alone told the woman to sit back down. She smiled as she walked between the desks, and stopped at a beautiful, creamy brown woman with long relaxed hair, which covered half her face and fell over the back of her chair. Ebbie saw the look on the troopers' faces; even Cleopatra was staring at her. Ebbie cursed herself for picking a seat near this woman.

"Is there anyone here who considers this woman a friend?" Feegarmardar turned and asked the other women. No one stood up or spoke. Feegarmardar then offered the woman her hand and led her to the front of the room, near the desk where Cleopatra had taken a seat. The troopers repositioned themselves, one on each side of the room and Feegarmardar discreetly signaled for Ebbie to lock the door. Ebbie tried to be nonchalant, but some of the other women stirred and began asking Feegarmardar nervous questions.

Ebbie was heading for her seat when Cleopatra ordered the room to be silent. The chilling sound of her voice sent shivers up her spine. She seemed to awaken from a short dream to find herself sitting in her chair again, her eyes focusing on the face of the woman standing next to Feegarmardar.

Ebbie quickly pulled out the woman's folder. There was a collection of pictures on the cover, a montage of faces and places covering the last few years of this woman's life. Her name was Eden Elray and she was supposed to be a model, but she was really a corporate spy, working for Oshima Tong. There was also a notation on a report that suggested she also worked for the American CIA.

"Tell these women why you are being rejected," said Feegarmardar, after placing a hand on the woman's shoulder. "Your name is Eden Elray, correct?"

"Yes, but I don't...."

"Forget the formalities, Fee. I helped write the final report. She's being paid by the CIA to join us. Her modeling is just a cover. There's not a face or body in the business who knows her," spoke a trooper gruffly.

The woman didn't speak or move. She seemed well composed and only turned to smile at Feegarmardar, but a signal had been given, and the women nearest Ebbie ripped a small weapon out of her false breast. One of the troopers leaped on her. The lights flashed off and on and some of the women screamed, but their sounds did not muffle the explosion, which knocked Ebbie out of her chair.

Some of the women had seen it coming and scattered. Feegarmardar and Eden were still standing, poised and ready to attack each other, unmoved by the small explosion. The remaining trooper had her weapon aimed at the other women. Cleopatra came around to face Eden, and the move brought the room to silence. This time Ebbie blocked out the sound of Cleopatra's voice, and watched as the women were forced to return to their seats.

Ebbie stared in horror at the splattered flesh on the walls and desk, and the blood spreading over the floor. Neither woman had her head any longer and the trooper's body had been blown apart, her legs and torso were reduced to an oozing mess against one wall, her arm still clutching the dismantled body of the woman with the false tits. Something thudded to the floor and Ebbie didn't dare look at what she knew had to be the trooper's head. Instead she composed herself, and when Cleopatra turned an eye in her direction, she proceeded to gather up the loose files.

There was a banging at the door, and Feegarmardar was signalling the trooper to answer the call on her wrist radio, while the women watched Cleopatra pull Eden to the side. "If the sisterhood could trust you, your work could prove worthwhile and rewarding," Cleopatra spoke to Eden. "Do you really think we are an evil threat to women and humankind, or has the money made you not care?"

"I am an American, and a Catholic...."

Ebbie had stopped wiping blood off the folders and threw them down to the floor. She couldn't believe she had heard such a change in Cleopatra's voice. Feegarmardar hadn't said a word or moved, as if she had no intention of killing this woman. Ebbie refused believe what she was seeing or hearing, but it only got worse when Cleopatra started punching Eden in the face.

Everyone was in shock. Ebbie wanted to go to her, such exertion might kill the old woman, but Feegarmardar signaled Ebbie to continue picking up the files. Ebbie could hardly move. The two women were at it blow for blow, fighting like two rival lionesses. Some of the women were standing again, trying to get the trooper's attention. They wanted to leave, and so did Ebbie. The fight looked like some kind of bad joke, but when Cleopatra socked Eden with a roundhouse, knocking her to the other side of the room, everybody saw her jaw break, and knew that Cleopatra's hand and arm would be a long time in traction. Cleopatra fell to the floor and leaned on the desk to keep her head up.

"Grandmother!" Feegarmardar moaned as she helped Eden into a chair. "You mustn't kill her. We must send her back in one piece," she said, after making sure Eden was still alive.

Cleopatra picked herself up, looking and acting more like a woman her age. "Why must they always come to me with that same ol' bullshit!" she snapped, and struck the desk. "Can't they see how programmed they have become. 'I am an American, and a catholic, and I believe in only one god, and I work for the betterment of mankind'. Mankind!!" she mimicked and screamed at the women, "We Pagangenearchs are in service for *human* kind. Stupid bitch!" Cleopatra sneered and then creeped slowly back to her seat. "You are an evil thing among us. The women who failed us by letting you get this far will be disciplined."

"They will be severely disciplined," Feegarmardar slapped her hands together.

"You are a spy. You have nerve and strength, but the evil in you cannot be permitted among us," spoke Cleopatra, now with more calm in her voice.

"I challenge your right to breed," spoke Feegarmardar.

"I place myself against your blood if you will not share with us," spoke the trooper.

"I am the oldest woman alive, and I demand you turn your son and your daughter over to us. What has happened to you must not happen to them," spoke Cleopatra.

Ebbie didn't catch it then, but later she would recall these words and recognized the blood vows and hidden messages here. She looked at Eden, who was frantic to speak. Her jaw was already swelling and she was bleeding badly from the mouth, but she forced herself to turn to Ebbie and signaled for something to write with. Ebbie hurried paper and pen to her, then read the words she scribbled. "How do you know of my children? What have they to do with this, with you, or I?"

"When you can answer that, maybe you will have enough respect for us to join us. Not because we are your people, but because there are better uses for your blood and your skill." Cleopatra tried to smile. She turned to the rest of the women and said, "Now. Something is amiss here. If you have any idea at all, you may stay and join us."

"Otherwise, get the hell out right now!" snapped Feegarmardar, acting more like herself. She motioned for the trooper to open the door.

The room emptied so fast Ebbie didn't see the troopers come in to clean up the dead mess. Only two women stayed, a young black woman who was obviously another American, and an middle aged white woman with some gray at her temples. Ebbie couldn't guess where she was from, but she looked Polish.

The troopers had the room cleaned and smelling of fresh lemons before they left. Not a word was spoken, but Ebbie had previously witnessed other murders and was sure that by the time any acolyte passed into the sisterhood, they had seen or committed one. She turned to face Eden, who was distressed and shaking. She implored Ebbie with her eyes to help, and looked about the windowless room for some other way out.

Ebbie was suddenly filled with disgust for her. Eden felt no remorse for having caused two deaths, and now only considered herself. She had children, well, that was something. Ebbie continued to gather up all the files, putting them back in order with the folders for the remaining two women on top.

Cleopatra signaled to the white woman, who stood and introduced herself. Cleopatra then asked, "Tell me, what do you think is wrong here? Is there anything wrong?"

"Of course there is," spoke the white woman. "This woman is still alive. She is responsible for two deaths here, and must die," she continued with a heavy German accent. "But all the other women who saw have left, and now you have no witnesses to say that you didn't kill her, when you...."

"Enough," spoke Cleopatra, signaling the woman to leave. When the woman refused, she said, "The word of a Pagangenearch is our wealth. Eden Elray, this woman who sits here now, shall arrive back in America tomorrow night. Go."

"One more thing, please," the white woman begged. "As a pledge to the Pagangenearchs, I should have moved to help. We all saw some danger coming. I should forfeit my pledge. I have not proved worthy by my not even trying to help."

"Sit, down," spoke Cleopatra, looking the woman over again.

The other woman stood and waited for Cleopatra to acknowledge her. After giving her name and praising the time she had spent in the company of the sisterhood, she said, "I don't believe a person with a bomb could get into the acolyte quarters. If your security is good enough to have known about her, than I refuse to believe that anyone has actually died here," she pointed to the ruined chair. "I spotted those fake tits myself. You wouldn't take that kind of chance. Not with Belinda Coffy here. You two are my...."

"Enough. Sit, little sister." Cleopatra smiled broadly for the first time today.

Feegarmardar walked over to the side wall and tapped out a special knock. A door slid open and out stepped the trooper who they thought had been killed, along with the woman who had worn the false breast, now hanging loose from her ripped blouse. Two additional troopers brought in Eden's real backup. Eden nearly fell out of her seat, but sat there gagging on her own blood.

The two pledges jumped to their feet as Cleopatra and Feegarmardar came around to welcome them to the ranks of Pagangenearch acolytes. The room slowly filled with people. Techs came to rearrange the room and women began setting up new items Ebbie recognized as props. She was angry now. There were at least 1,800 pledges out in the auditorium. How many of these scenes would she have to go through?

Feegarmardar woke her from her reverie, saying, "Come now, you didn't do too badly. Just do your job and everything will be all right. Most of it comes as a surprise to us as well. This one had real people in it like Ms. Elray. The next few sets will all be makeups, but, you'd do better to figure them out as soon as you can."

It was night and the tall walkers were still fast walking, glad to be out of the heavy shade of giant spice trees and into clear moonlight. Some wandering beast men tried to attack them once, but Keishlee cut the head off one that got close and the others ran off. She had become one with the weapon and Ramaa knew he would not see her without it again. He realized that the Tuk women traveled the land, uncommon for women, but he was glad of it. Other small groups of creatures or men they passed saw her leather straps and the Tuk blade zipping through the air, and left them alone. He was happy for Keishlee, because she was happy, and it was the first time he could recall her being so. He only regretted her losing some of the tall walker saunter, which she didn't even seem to notice.

Kangar didn't like riding the tall walkers, but agreed their long legs covered a great deal of land very quickly, and with suitable night vision, their trek was faultless. He had been the one who couldn't stay on the tall walker without help, and had to ride with Ramaa, who could stay on without being roped. Umboi rode in front of Keishlee and tho he could keep his place, he was a sitting jitter, and occasionally wet himself. He couldn't believe Keishlee allowed him this closeness. Her pinning him down while she held fast to the creature's neck kept him in shivers and shakes.

When the curving walls of Hotep village came into view, the moon had just risen and was full again. Its light was bright and reflected off high rock walls and cone-shaped structures built into the winding stone walls. Small fires were glowing near the walls, and there were people and animals still about.

Umboi and Kangar wanted to dismount, which they did when they could see the people more clearly. The hungry tall walkers called out to the other creatures that might be around to get word on what was good to eat. There were herds of animals with bright white wings of fur on their rumps and long thin legs. It called back to the tall walkers as they came into the wide clearing. A large group of men came to greet Umboi, but they were more interested in the tall walkers and the giants dismounting them. None of their words were familiar to Ramaa and Keishlee, who let Umboi do all the talking. When they could see Keishlee more clearly by their torch fires, they bowed and backed away from her, offering to lead her somewhere.

"They wish to show you how well their women are kept," spoke Umboi, as they were led towards the village walls. "Before their trees were tall, a Tuk woman killed some of the men because one of them had broken his woman's arm. It was an accident, but the Tuk women took away half the women. The men live in fear that a Tuk woman will return to take the rest. One often comes as the long branches grow. Sometimes they bring a little woman and leave her to run with the deerfawn." He pointed to the large herd.

One of the men turned and smiled at Umboi, saying, "Our women are fast and strong. We are good to them. The Tuk women return some of the blood they took, to reward us for our goodness." He laughed and bowed repeatedly to Keishlee. Umboi translated for Ramaa and Keishlee and they followed.

Ramaa had been glad for the skins Umboi and Kangar had given him. The air had been too cool and rushed over him during the ride, chilling him to the bone. He had never known air that was cold and it reminded him of their travel across the escarpment. Now it was not so cold, and he removed the heavy fur wrap hanging over his shoulders and threw it over the back of a tall walker. Not liking the looks these people gave his clan relations, he ordered away the people coming near them, and sent the tall walkers off into the clearing. Some men followed the tall walkers, and Ramaa could only hope that these people did not have to lose their heads over them.

As Umboi led Ramaa and the others who followed, Ramaa found that the wall was not a continuous winding line, but that it turned into wide lanes with open shelters and tents, or even became the path they walked upon. Most of the village was sleeping, but many people were still about, tending small herds of a thing he would later learn was a pig-rabbit, and others watching over small groups of goats. They turned more walls and tall cones until they entered a large room, built into a section of wall atop large boulders, which they had to climb.

"This is the den of free women," Kangar said, grinning.

The room was much larger than Ramaa had expected and the floor was not a single flat plane. In some areas of the room it dropped to levels of rock that were not flat at all, but many of the various levels were of flat smooth rock with walls that curved around into darker rooms. Women sat about everywhere and were glad to see Keishlee among them. Some seemed frightened, but all greeted her with close hugs, and danced around to show themselves off to her. In this one room there were probably more women than in all the Kamitui tree village, and they were beautiful women. They wore a material over their bodies that covered all but their arms and faces, even their hair was slightly covered by hanging strings of feathers or white fur pieces, which they wore around their necks. On the higher levels the women worked on large pieces of the same material they wore, which also covered the floor were they sat, and was like the fur Umboi wore.

A few men came into the room, and they all tried to get Keishlee's attention, each showing her the furs on the floor, the women's clean, white teeth and their rich-smelling pots of food. They noted for her the cloth the women made, the piles of stored logs for their fires, the herds that could be seen from the chiseled windows, and especially the women's hands and feet.

Keishlee didn't know what to make of any of this, but after the men left, which they did in a hurry once they were sure

Keishlee was not angry with them, Umboi explained. She was laughing, as they all were, when a group of elder women came out of the dark corners, followed by small male slaves who brought piles of thick furs for them all to sit on. Women began to sit around the ledges of the different levels. Some continued their work, but all had their attention focused on the old woman who was speaking angrily to Umboi and trying to soften her words as she repeated them to Keishlee.

Umboi rushed to Keishlee, saying, "The den mother will not trade for women while a Tuk woman looks upon her."

All the women here used of the words of the Tuk women, which Keishlee had learned. They even changed the sound of their voices when they spoke to her, or to their men. Keishlee had understood the old woman and wanted to tell her the truth, but thought it would be better just to leave. She told the woman she would see the rest of the village, and left. Ramaa started to follow, but the women, especially the old woman, protested, assuring Ramaa that Keishlee would be all right.

A group of young women had gathered around Ramaa, and he could tell that they were growing fond of him, which surprised him, being unaccustomed to such attentions from young women. Most of the women his age sat on the upper ledges, and looked down on him with wide eyes. Some of them had removed a layer of cloth from off their shoulders, and he could almost see the small fullness of their feeder bags, which began to excite him.

They had never seen a man so tall before. Even sitting he towered over every human in the room, like a dark tree springing up between the boulders. He was blue-black, with rippling muscles over all of his body. His teeth were white and his breath was fresh, and the women gathered around to catch a smile.

No one had said why he was here, but they hoped he was here to trade for a woman. There was always too many women here and the majority of the men were either too young or too old. They turned from Ramaa and looked out over the clearing filled with deerfawn, jealous of their mating habits and their numbers. Why were they cursed to breed mostly women? Why didn't men ever come here to stay? They always came to trade for cloth, or skins, or food, or water for crossing the desert. Some wanderers had begun to come for deerfawn and even for their skins and fur. Of course there were the Kamituians, who sometimes came to visit, but who recently only came to trade for women.

The old woman chirped at the women, and they began to come down from the upper levels to line up behind her. Everyone tried to stand as near Ramaa as they could get, pushing all the youngest ones aside, or down to a lower level where they could not be seen.

"Why do you have these young ones speak for you?" the old woman asked Ramaa. "You, who bring two great and gentle beasts with beautiful hides for skinning. For these you can take your pick of five or six of our women."

Ramaa understood the Tuk words and almost fell off his furs. It was uncomfortable seating anyway, and so he slipped himself to the stone floor and watched as Kangar tried to explain to the woman. She laughed at them while looking them over. She said they were too young and should come back after there was some rain, which was an insult, since it never rained in these parts. The old woman laughed, and tried to find out what else the tall stranger might want to trade. She thought herself good at trading talk, and would settle him with a woman no matter what else he'd come for.

"We do not trade our clan relations," Ramaa was quick to answer. He stood up and the women cooed as he became a giant among them again. Some removed more of their cloths and skins, and Ramaa could see some feeder bags clearly now. They reminded him of the women of his clan, small and firm. How he missed his people and his mate. He smiled remembering Nuba. That's what he would call his mate when he could see her again. Nuba. He had liked the woman as well as her name. Ramaa recalled that some of these women would be descendants of Tuk women, which made him look around the rooms for Nuba's look, and he found one.

"We bring spice seeds," Umboi said, to stop the arguing with the woman.

This news brought a hush to the group, but the woman didn't believe them and laughed, saying, "If you have spice seeds enough, you can get your choice of a woman. One woman."

"They have ten, they have more than..." Ramaa was trying to recall the proper word for the numbers he had heard.

"Yes, we have ten!" Kangar snapped.

"Yes, we do have ten," Umboi shouted, and Ramaa got the hint.

"Really?" moaned the woman. "Stand up and let me count

for myself."

Umboi and Kangar stood together and each loosen their girdles of skin. The woman reached down their fronts and felt around, counting the seeds as she went. The youths were visibly and uncontrollably excited, and when she made a joke about "all the other fat parts down there," she had to clean the seed off her hands when at last they were removed.

"Your women are giving into their men this late in the season? You will be old and I will be dead when next fall the seeds of the living tree. How did you get so many?" asked another old woman.

"We have begun to hunt the finks, who sometimes kill our people. Sometimes we recover their spice seeds," replied Umboi. "Often the creatures eat them, as well as our people."

Some of the women gasped and men rushed into the room. They had stone weapons and sticks and looked about until the old woman told them, "Nothing is wrong here. This young one says the man creatures have taken to eating the spice seeds."

"My daughters!" some of the men cried.

"Even they used to know better," spoke another.

"I say again, we should leave these lands. Look what it comes to now," spoke another as they headed out of the room. "They would take away the little water left us."

Everyone whispered to each other for a moment, and then two young women were ordered to bring Umboi and Kangar some food. The older women scampered among themselves, bringing Ramaa a single piece of something to eat at a time. Ramaa tried not to let them see his disgust at the meat they offered him, but they caught on very quickly that he liked greens, fruits and nuts best of all.

Umboi and Kangar were quite relieved, now that they had finally let themselves go, especially Umboi. The ride with Keishlee had been unbearable. When they reached the walls of Hotep Village, he thought he might have to pull Kangar into the woods, or die of frustration. Once inside the den of women, it took all his strength to hold himself back. He was glad it was over and knew that Kangar felt the same.

Umboi refused the food, making the sign for selecting the trade space, which would be a spot between his furs and theirs. The old women smiled and shifted herself a little further away so that everyone would be able to see the trade items.

He pulled a single, somewhat slimy spice seed from his crotch. He made Kangar stop his eating and handed it to him. Kangar spoke to it and then placed it on the trade spot. One of the other old women quickly snatched it up and showed it to the others, turning it over and over, each looking at it from every angle to make sure it was real.

"Maybe you two *are* old enough," smiled the first old woman. "They call me, Faiyumbàtot'a. That seed looks good, but it will take the rest of my life to bring spice water up from the ground."

"If you do not plant it properly, it will take longer. But from it, something will always grow which is filled with water," said Umboi, shaking his head. "My brothers call me Umboi. This is Kangar, and we wish a woman to share between us." He smiled up at the women above, who were giving them a good looking over.

Another of the old women squinted at Umboi and said, "I am Ôltoganépt'manot. Why you come only for women now? Never you trade for anything else."

"Of course we bring buffalo skins," Umboi said, pointing to the skins he had placed on the floor, "...and reeds of spice gum, and a roll of buffalo butter." Umboi removed the packs they carried, and Kangar emptied their contents out near him. Some of the younger women came over to see.

"For the buffalo butter we give you deerfawn rings for your ears," spoke Faiyumbàtot'a. "But you may not get more from us if you do not show us more respect than this. One spice seed, and a small one at that. Hum."

Umboi gave Kangar a nudge and he quickly pulled out two seeds and handed them to Umboi, who laid them one on each side of the first one. The old women were about to snatch them up, but Umboi and Kangar stopped them, pointing to the second tier above them. "Let us see them. Just one or two," Umboi said, "to make sure there is still good blood among you."

The old women turned to each other and grunted. Faiyumbàtot'a kicked Umboi, and then called out to some of the darker women from the second level above. Brown skinned women, who knew they would not be selected, or who did not want to be selected, crowded around Ramaa. They were of many shades, but all were brown or black, the colors Ramaa knew. They were slight and small for women, he thought, but they looked healthy and bright, with white teeth and eyes, and hair much like his own. He wanted to touch them, but did not dare, and found himself looking away as their numbers grew around him. He peeked over and saw one that looked like Nuba and his heart almost stopped. He no longer saw the younger women. He saw Nuba, and the remembrance in her eyes told him that it was really her.

"All three of these you will find have the shape your people respect in a woman," spoke Faiyumbàtot'a, lifting the women's skins to show off their end-mounds.

One of the young women slapped her naked backside and Kangar let out a groan of delight. Umboi's mouth was clearly watering as he stumbled with another seed, which he sat next to the others. The three new seeds were picked up and each was passed back and forth between the women. Once they were certain that they were real, they placed them back with the others and whispered to the three women, who ran off into the darkness of an inner room. They soon returned with bladders and offered Kangar, Umboi and Ramaa a drink.

▼▼▼▼▼

Shhaha found a new kind of happiness, delicious and filling to all his senses, as he showed Mah and Odrak around the land of their blood memories. These were times long past, but which still lived in their blood. It came as no surprise to them that Mah had spent all his previous lives as a Great Mah. He last lived before the time of ice covers, which was why he knew their tongue from birth and had their smell. This would be his first time in life as a human, which brought him moments of regret and desperate longings, to know that he was not fully human. Odrak learned a new respect for the insects he'd eaten in his life. Even the rocks and pebbles had past lives that wandered the land of the dead.

During their wandering they passed the road Shhaha told him led to the Great Mother. Odrak and Shhaha would not step on the road, but it called to Mah with flashes of light, and darkness jumped out to pull him over. But Shhaha would not let him go, warning them that they were not ready. Demanding memory came to him, and he recalled a chant to quiet the road, then they moved away to visit the kin of the Kamituians, who started coming to them out of the sparkling light of trance.

Shhaha hid his fear from Odrak and Mah. They would not

consider it strange for people or things unrelated to them to come upon them in the land of blood memories, but Shhaha knew better. A Kamituian was touching one of them, and the memories of his blood came rushing in on them. They seemed friendly visits and their lives floated by like the breeze, so Shhaha let them come.

The Kamituians were trees in other lives. All kinds of trees, tall and short, wide and leafy, some that could be mated to a man or a woman, some that ate men and women, and others that were as tall as mountains, with frozen crystal leaves that took their nourishment from the clouds.

Shhaha showed them where the Kamituians buried their dead, under the roots of young spice trees, which needed blood, flesh and bones to grow fast and tall. These trees spread their roots far down into the earth, where they could always find water. They gave a special drink to humans, who they needed to take care of them. The trees needed the closeness of humans. They needed to feel their energy and it fed off their waste. To keep the people close, the trees rewarded them with a different kind of sight, the sight of senses. Not only could they feel, but they could also see what they felt, and did so as if each nerve had eyes. These people could feel movement many trees away, and could almost see what or who it was, but the spice water made them blind.

This made Odrak realize the advantage he had taken over the two sick protectors. Healthy Kamituians were only at a disadvantage close up, where their senses became overwhelmed with the presence of others.

Shhaha quickly stepped into his future and left Mah and Odrak behind, since they did not yet know how to follow. He wanted to give them some time alone here. He would be able to observe them, but there were things he wanted to know which his apprentices might not be ready to share. As he grew older he didn't often care to know such things himself, but tonight he did.

Keishlee found a group of young men and women running side by side with the herd of deerfawn. She watched with unbelieving eyes as the youths kept pace with these creatures, who ran as fast as collared minks [*lizard lions*], their thin legs darting out in leaps and bounds, which were almost invisible even in the bright, clear moonlight. The men and women kept to the rear of the animals, appearing like shadows against the white fur wings of the creatures' hides. The fastest humans Keishlee had ever seen were the Tuk women, who now looked slow by comparison.

Men were around, but she knew they would not come near unless she called. The air was cool, and she was glad for the skins she wore, as she quick-stepped around the open field, staring at the runners and wishing that her legs were not so long, and her body not so tall.

She walked right up to the herd, which she found friendly to her approach. They spoke to her and she tried to understand, proud of the blood that assured gentle creatures that she was safe to touch and taste. After she let them lick her face, she discovered the running group was standing around her. She tried not to appear too shocked at their heavily panting faces. Their chests moved in and out in great heaves, but they looked neither tired nor out of breath.

She introduced herself and was glad to see how totally naked they were. Tho these people were right to cover themselves in this land of cold nights, but fully clothed people made her uncomfortable, and filled her with distrust, since she knew now how weapons could be hidden in their folds.

▼▼▼▼▼

Shhaha could no longer see the visions of things yet to come. The visions had attacked and almost crippled him. Mah and Odrak held him to stop his falling into a another gap in time, and Shhaha moaned in pain and frustration, cursing himself and the journey they had undertaken.

Their trance world was cracking open with explosions of light and fire, leaving the startling smack of a void, devoid of energy or life. Odrak and Mah were surprised they could hold on to their calm. They had seen the faces, only for a moment, of the Kamituians standing all around them.

"Hold fast your places," warned Shhaha. "I feel we are not yet done here. Others are trying to reach us. I feel them coming," Shhaha spoke to their minds.

"You cannot leave the way you came," sounded the voice they all knew to be She Who Has No Name.

They were desperate to find her, as Shhaha led them away from past lives that came out to greet them. Their contact with them was slowing them down, separating them into running streams of sinew trying to detach itself from bones.

Shhaha had always been taught that nothing could harm him in the trance world, not even death of the body. To kill one trancing deeply gave him leave to take the flesh that touched him first, which is why a dead Keeper of the Blood was left to rot for 3 or 4 cycles of days before anyone would dare to touch him. Shhaha checked Mah, Odrak and then himself. There was an energy of protection all around them, but still he felt the danger, near and hot within his spirit senses.

There was a touch, but it was not human. The spice trees loomed up around them, their roots reaching up to greet them in some ancient custom long lost to time and knowledge. Next to the tree stood She Who Has No Name, and tho she was younger and her eyes were sighted and clear, it was her, and she beckoned them forward.

Odrak readied himself for attack, and his violent energy weakened his connection with the others. Shhaha and Mah had to chant him back into the world of trance.

"This one is in great danger," she spoke to Odrak's fleeting form, pointing to Mah. "Keep failing him and he will die this night."

Odrak took control of his heart beats. and using all his training, reentered the trance world to find himself pulling fire in behind him.

"Now you've done it," she screamed at Odrak. "They know where you are. They have a Gate Keeper, a slave forced to do their will by a curse placed upon his blood. Others can enter now, bringing those who would destroy us. Come," she pointed to the spice tree roots.

They ran each to a tree and pulled themselves up into the moving roots. She had not said what to do, and now She was gone. They looked to Shhaha who studied the air around him that began to glow dimly with a faraway light. It was coming closer. He turned to the tree and yelled out from the pain of a fire that was starting up around him. He calmed himself and then pulled himself up into the wide trunk of the tree.

Odrak was screaming and trying to get to Mah, who was being consumed by the fires as he held on to the tree. He could see the Kamituians gathered around them. He could hear them trying to put out the fires that were consuming the tent. He found that he was burning too and broke away from the clutching roots to get to Mah. The spice tree roots wrapped around them violently and strapped them to the base of the tree. They were screaming and ripping at the roots. Hands suddenly appeared around Mah's shoulders from within the tree and yanked him away from Odrak's crumpling embrace.

The sight of Mah's disappearance kicked a calm over Odrak's disintegrating form. He was on fire, being devoured by flames hot enough to crack opened his bones. He broke away from the tree and the reaching hands to see himself as if from all around, and found new senses with which to feel pain. He watched his eyes bubble and crust over in a bloodless ooze. They dripped down his face and were instantly burnt to a hissing twinkle of evaporating fumes. At the same time, he could also see all that was taking place around his burning body in the clearing of the Kamitui. Shhaha was trying to comfort Mah, who was screaming and pounding upon a nearby tree. All the Kamituians were standing around, transfixed with fear and awe, over the sudden appearance of She Who Has No Name, and the reappearance of a living Shhaha and Mah, and the way each of them glowed in the darkness of the night.

Mah was nearly insane, and this hurt Odrak with each beat of his heart. Terror throbbed throughout him, and the sound of Mah's pain filled the air around him.

Just then there was a little slave reaching for him, his light, pinkish-brown eyes tender and calling. It was someone he had never seen before, and of a color he did not consider natural. His hair was close to his head, short and kinky, but it was as white as his skin. He wanted to touch him, but the slave said, "Save me. Bring the other and save me."

Odrak was a raging cinder now and did not want to burn the slave with his touch. He fled further away at the sight of three women coming near. They too were more different than any he had ever known. One demanded, another coaxed and begged, while the other proved to be the source of all the fires.

The fires burning through him gave him speed and daring in his flight. He eluded the women, who screeched and made cries that tore at what remained of his burning form. But at every turn the little slave reached up to him with tears in his eyes, begging for him to come and save him.

He turned to see Shhaha forcing sticks into Mah's mouth. Mah was convulsing on the ground and thrashing about. Some of the Kamitui were holding Mah down, while Shhaha stopped him from biting off his tongue. She Who Has No Name was arguing with the elders, who were terrified and weeping, because she was asking for one of them to give up his life.

Odrak felt minds trying to probe him and knew at once that it was the three women still in pursuit of him. All that was left of him now were his bones, blackened by a fire without smoke. He closed the women off from him and found the action like a force slapping their faces. They caressed the small slave, who like always, was near enough to touch, and then they disappeared in a grisly, bristling light, one at a time, until there was nothing left but him and the slave, the darkness and the spice tree, still standing, but now so very far away.

"She can save him," spoke the little one as he looked out past the fires onto the real world and Mah. "She, who is the oldest, can give you back your human life. The other half of you can give you back your form. I am Farra. Remember me," he whispered to Odrak's mind, as his form fell away from what was real. His hand was the last to go and flickered out of sight, but the flicker became a glitter, and the glitter became a light, and the light opened up a hole, and in the hole Odrak could sense the nearness of true life, where he ran to the memories of all that he held dear.

▼▼▼▼▼

The Hoteps had long words which were really connected combinations of words Keishlee knew. It took a great deal of repeating and signing before she understood their meaning, but she figured out that her new friends wanted to take her somewhere, because of her name.

As they were moving back around the curving walls, Keishlee saw Ramaa with a woman she knew she had seen before. Ramaa was so absorbed he didn't see her. He and the woman were wrapped together like Tall Walkers, and she was leading him up into one of the stone cones built into the winding wall.

Keishlee tried to ignore them, but as the friendly group took her around and around the continuously twisting village wall, she found herself wanting to go back to Tuk Village. Until something in the entrance of the room took her breath away. The figure was completely covered, but Keishlee knew it was a woman.

She tore herself away from the talkative group and raced over to the figure, who was revealing a small string of bones around her ankle. The stones of the wall glowed an unnatural hue of reflected moonlight, which sent light into the narrow passageways between the twisting walls. Keishlee snatched the unresisting figure from the entrance and ripped loose the veils covering her face. It was hard for them to greet each other with all the grasping and touching, but Keishlee felt a joy she thought she'd never know again. Even cutting themselves on each other's weapons did not dull the pleasure.

▼▼▼▼▼

"Bring his body to me!" ordered the woman known to Shhaha as She Who Has No Name.

"What good can he be with his mind lost in torment?" roared Shhaha in another tongue that he was sure She would understand.

"Your belief in the blood of your own people is thin. How dim is your vision of this one's future," She replied in yet another tongue he had only recently learned. "But you do know how to look into the future. That is how they found you."

Her words stuck him like a knife. He wanted to cry as he pushed the others aside and carried Mah to her. He cursed her with his eyes, which he could not prevent from revealing that he had the power he needed to kill her. But that was why She had come. She had felt it. She knew what would happen now if She lost both their lives.

Laying Mah down in the space She made between the elderly Kamituians, he could feel the madness in Mah. He was biting the stick and his mouth was bleeding badly. Tears flowed from each eye, and yet his body was rigid with anger. Shhaha knew from the fading light around him that Mah was willing himself to die. This was the promise of blood he and Odrak shared. He might have been able to do it if not for the trance knowledge being forced on him now. There had been no time to warn them that this would happen, even he suffered from it now. But Mah was fighting it in order to free his will to end his life, and the battle taking place inside was consuming his soul.

People were bringing Shhaha his belongings and he sat among them, glad that they had not been destroyed. He proceeded to chant for the return of wandering spirits, throwing off some of the powerful bones of his ancestors, which were now ruined from the fire. He rubbed a spot clean on the silver ring, surprised to see it still intact. Only the tall walker hair that had been attached to the ring, and all the skins he wore, were gone. He sat naked among his things and began to make a potent that only now started forming in his mind.

She Who Has No Name was speaking with the Kamitui, who were now humbled on the ground all over the clearing. Shhaha had not guessed there were so many, and did not imagine that She had such total control here. He knew what She planned, and tho he wanted Odrak back, he would never be able to take the life of one of these people to do it.

One of the old men screamed. He stood immobile, muttering words Shhaha did not understand. He stumbled over and reached out to the strange woman, who looked at him with bright clear eyes that sat on a face Shhaha was sure looked younger than before. She hopped around him, screaming and calling out the names of ancestors. Others started moaning and she ordered them to silence. She walked around the old man, and when she touched him, they both let out a scream and jumped away.

"Something keeps him here. He is still alive. He is strong and near, I tell you!" She cried, stepping quickly over to Shhaha. "Do whatever you can to clear this one's mind, and tell him there is need for his memory of the other," She pleaded with Shhaha. "I know you cannot do what needs to be done, but he can."

"Aaah!" Shhaha spoke in the absolute affirmative of his people. "Of course. There is much love between them."

"Good! Good!" She scampered about and ran her hand across the naked body of Mah. "This one is new to the world of humans. He is a blood keeper with relations whose spirits now roam in other worlds," She spoke, and the strange light glowing from her grew brighter. "He shall be ours!"

The last thing She said Shhaha did not understand, because she started speaking in a tongue he did not know. As She chanted, he committed to memory her every move, the words She spoke, the tongue of the words and the looks upon her face.

Only the chant of the dreaded moan would do, and he called to Mah to let him know that Odrak was still alive and in need of him.

Out of nowhere, She Who Has No Name pulled out a wooden knife and cut Mah across his chest. Shhaha had known some blood would be needed and did not fear the sight of it. A breeze fluttered through the trees and began to blow up dust, as She smeared the blood over her face and slowly approached the old man, demanding him to give up his life to save his people.

"I may return to make the spice?" the old man used up all his strength to ask.

Holding his head up, She said, "It is a painful way to die, but your doing so will not be forgotten. May I never bleed again if you do not return to rise up over the Kamitui clearing."

Shhaha saw the old man smile, and heard the women slapping hands and the men clacking their bone dangles. She Who Has No Name held him close and whispered something in his ear which gave him the strength to stand. He managed to loosen the skin wraps around his waist, and all the young slaves and protectors scurried over to guard the spice seeds that fell.

Shhaha now understood the pride of their burial custom. The old man had more than 20 seeds, root-locked together in groups of threes and fours. A single seed could produce a giant Kamitui spice tree. The seed-locked groups would produce a faster growing spice tree, one that would produce spice water within a single turn of seasons. The spice water meant life to a people who were cursed to be born completely blind. It gave their senses sight and kept their secret safe from outsiders. Shhaha smiled, knowing that in death this man could look forward to helping his people survive.

So many things fell into place about these people now. With perfect hearing, their constant yelling was a ploy to fool outsiders or to block out all the distant sounds that they could also hear. They molded their features because in the light of day human auras were less clear. Their physical sameness allowed them to know with a single touch who was really near. And tho the taking of human life was the greatest thing for them to fear, being buried with their spice seeds was something they all held dear.

Odrak saw himself as small charred bones being protected by spice tree wood, which refused to be consumed by the unnatural fire. Spice tree wood resisted fire over long periods, but time was a concept he did not really understand and could not think to trust it now.

Reaching into the odd black hole of strange lights was an act of desperation, but the hole left by the colorless slave had a force that compelled him to enter. Odrak couldn't believe he still knew himself or had control over what was left of his form. But

Mah was alive, and that gave him hope. If Mah could not join him here, then he would not die this way. He would not be left alone and lost in this trance world.

He endured being slowly drawn into the small opening in the void around him. Wanting to erase his fear he tried to laugh, but he was now something other than human, and his reactions did not fit such concepts. He could see the sticks of spice wood and feel the raging fires that still burned around his bones. As he was sucked deeper into the hole, there was a sound like tittered wailing, crackling around the fire. Odrak realized it was the chanting voice of his comfort and joy. He would be with Mah again, and called out to him, and to Shhaha, and to She Who Has No Name, and to Keishlee and Ramaa, and to Zambe, and to Uurxi, Kangar and Bellar....

▼▼▼▼▼

Shhaha was wrapping slender strips of skins around the new loincloth at his waist, all the while he chanted and kept an eye on Mah. She ordered fires made on either side of Shhaha, which was done quickly, and then he began to dance between the soaring flames. He took no notice as She had men climb the trees that bordered the clearing. He didn't see her grubbing through the remains of the tent and the ashes that should have included all their bones. But he heard Odrak calling as She brought his bones near.

"Humans are an easy bundle when reduced to this," She groaned, and threw the charred bones down at Mah's feet.

Mah sat up and stared directly at her, shocking her so much that She jumped away. Soundlessly he reached for the bones and smiled when he found them all there. She returned without her fear and rolled up her sleeves for the old man to see the claws now fisted to her hands. He signaled for two protectors to take his spice seeds, which they did with great haste. The instant the last seed was removed, She clawed the old man's face down to his chest, and still caught him before he could fall.

She looked down at the bones and then up to Mah, and said, "IF YOU CARE FOR THE OTHER, SAVE HIM NOW WITH THIS LIFE!"

"IF? IF! You dare!!" Mah roared, jumping up with arm and legs bones in both hands. He ran over to the man, and the crowd grew frightened. The dying man looked at him, and for an instant, Mah could not find the strength to do the deed.

"In my time I have seen many little trees rot and fall. The spice trees live forever. Make a spice tree of me," whispered the man with his dying breath.

Before She Who Has No Name could scream that the time was lost, Mah plunged the bones into the man and drove him from her arms to the ground. He retrieved the other bones and laid them out in the flowing blood, and then made everyone moan when he kissed the old man's face. The man was blind and could not cry and that had given Mah strength.

The fires were cracking and sparking, and their lights glowed around the clearing like wild twilight near the end of day. Mah's body was shadowed by their light, but as he and She Who Has No Name touched the old man, he was illuminated by an eerie glow.

People were kneeling and crouching nearer, murmuring to each other about the water that fell from Mah's eyes like rain, and glistened down his face like a coating of clear wax. They had never seen tears before or they were just rare and hard to sense, but as they bounced and dripped over the man, the Kamituians cooed and called his name.

She Who Has No Name screeched a curdling cry and pushed Mah away as the man burst into flames, unnatural flames that filtered up white and purple smoke. Shhaha stopped his dancing, but continued his chanting as he watched the old man's body melt into a murky goo of mucous and bloody flesh.

Mah seemed to know that when the man's fire turned blue, to reach into the fire and call Odrak's name. And tho the fires were painful, he reached down into the icky goo, and everywhere he touched, a human body appeared.

"This one shall bring the other back!" She yelled out to her people. "This one knows everything about his flesh!" She spoke, prancing around the fires and making sure the people kept their distance. "Use the senses your ancestors have given you. Remember this night, always."

Mah was frantic now, but used each finger with meticulous care, allowing only his passion to touch him here or there. He caressed the chest and bore the pain of ghostly flames to listen to its heart. He tore away for a moment, but rushed back to give shape to arms and legs. Even his tears helped to give moisture to all the parts. Mah felt over the chest again to replace the marks of the crackhorn rambull, and took great care to mold and reshape Odrak's long face and ears. In the excitement of his recreating, Mah reshaped Odrak's lips to something like his own, but knew he wanted nothing of Odrak changed. He brushed in hair and then rushed to remold Odrak's fingers and toes. Mah rolled him on his side and continued giving Odrak back his sinewy shape. He slipped his arms under and around him, to make him a man again, and then snatched him up into his arms to hold and kiss him while he awaited some sign of life.

She Who Has No Name pushed Mah aside once more and threw a dry potent over Odrak, which opened up his eyes. He moaned a little, but She began to scream and sign for Mah to remove Odrak from the spirit fires.

When Odrak was once again alive and in his arms, they rubbed their heads together and entwined all their limbs. They chanted the welcome of those returned and were checking their private signals, when Shhaha roughly pulled them apart.

Mah hadn't noticed that they were brightly glowing and that She Who Has No Name's lights were now dimming. She was staring hard at Shhaha and the look appeared frightened and lost. The light of the spirit fire was caving in upon itself and her light was being drained away with it.

Shhaha took control of the clearing and ordered the two protectors to give Odrak the dead elder's seeds. He slapped his thigh as a signal for the others to gather the remains of his membrane-covered bones and flesh, and followed as they carried the dwindling spirit fire light out of the clearing. Mah moved in his tracks, pulling Odrak along as he helped him hold the spice seeds in place, not even noticing that She Who Has No Name was collapsing as the light diminished around her.

The trance memories were upon him now, but Odrak kept enough control to keet pace with what was going on around him. Men had dug a large hole into which they placed what remained of the old man. Then Odrak took almost half the seeds and pushed them into an opening Uurxi made in the dead man's chest. He gave Uurxi the seeds that remained, and then chanted the planting call while the eerie light in the hole grew dim. Demanding memory rushed in on him, and before Odrak knew what he was doing, he had cut himself with a stone Uurxi had given him. He let the blood drip over the spot where the seeds were hidden, until the dead man was covered with his blood.

People shouted and slapped their bodies, while another elder squeezed Odrak's arm to stop the flow of blood. Shhaha licked the wound and covered it with an ointment that stopped the bleeding. Small slaves were permitted to cover the hole, and men rushed about collecting rocks and stones to build a mount over the spot.

"With this seeding, this man can now give birth, and like the mother, become the father to those he leaves behind. Rise again, elder Ankh, and may your branches be many and strong," spoke Uurxi.

The spirit light from the mound faded entirely and put the area in darkness. Only the women carried torches, but Mah was not surprised; he knew now that only the women needed light to see. Mah's own good night vision allowed him to find Odrak, who was weakening from the lost of blood and the onslaught of trance memories. He held Odrak up and led him back to the clearing. Shhaha stayed to watch the people dance their slow, fumbling, hop-step, running jump-step dance, which took great courage for a people who were blind.

It was too dark to see clearly, but Shhaha knew there were many close trees in this section of the forest. They were another kind of tree, which would be devoured by the spice tree during its first stage of growth, and Odrak had assured them that this new spice tree would be a huge thing in only a short period of time. They would have a great tree among them, a place to bury many dead and a source for keeping many others alive. There would be spice waters enough for even the slaves to drink, and a home for many new nests.

Shhaha found Mah and Odrak back in the clearing, but could not find She Who Has No Name. She had dragged her weakened body off and wanted no one to follow. Mah was trying to comfort Odrak, who was going through the mental torture of forced memory storing, worse than demanding memory because it compelled one to some action. Mah rocked Odrak in his arms and chanted the call for welcoming close kin home.

Shhaha looked at them and smiled because they were better prepared against evil magic than he had ever been, and he was pleased again that he had taken them on this journey.

Ebbie was tired from all the pledging activities. She was

angry with Feegarmardar and even with Cleopatra for having rejected so many women. These women had come so close and from so far, willingly. They cried when they headed back to their dormitories, knowing they would have to leave the country without the film-dress or the red universal passport of the Pagangenearchs. Some had left already in frustration or despair. Others barracaded themselves in their rooms, refusing to leave, or fought with standing pledges like herself and made threats against the sisterhood, or attacked Command Sisters like Feegarmardar or Teresa Eckers. Of course Feegarmardar was merciless and brutal, and all Ebbie could do was watch and record.

The Pagangenearch Ras Tafari Training Campus was in turmoil. Red Warriors had to be called in to assist with removing the rejected pledges. Those who refused to leave and were steadfast or good fighters, would find rewards and be given another way to serve the sisterhood, but all those who had drawn blood or swore some revenge on the Pagangenearchs, would find an enemy among all its sisters.

Teresa Eckers and Cleopatra Mandara a'La Hedrin sat before her now, making small talk of the wealth of new sisters who had made it into their ranks. Nobody was like Feegarmardar, but Teresa was something made from the same material: tall, powerful, commanding, and beautiful by any standard. She wore long, thick braids encrusted with jewels and gold band, her physical appearance serving only as a disguise, hiding the brutality that lay in wait within. With them was a very dark man two Red Warriors had brought in.

"You performed well all summer," Teresa smiled and spoke as if she were a meek woman. "A trooper informed me that you saved her life without giving the test away. You have earned an honor guard. I have assigned a woman to you I trained myself. She will protect you well."

"That's not necessary...."

"If you wish to insult...."

"If she wishes...."

"She has already chosen," Cleopatra huffed.

"This is Terry Clauds," Teresa introduced the truly black man sitting next to her.

He stood and smiled down at Ebbie. She could see that he was very tall with long arms and broad shoulders. He placed a light blue flower in her lap and took a seat next to her.

"He will be your mate for awhile, unless you find him unworthy, or unable," spoke Teresa.

"You will not find him lacking or tampered with. He is from a Mandarian Den," Cleopatra noted with pride, "the best breeding stock in all of Africa. He is from a long line of ancient warriors, re-hybrid for love and loyalty since the sixteenth century. There are only a few pure Zumas left in all the world. You should not refuse. He can no longer hold himself and needs a mate. Since you have no mother, I have chosen him for you."

Ebbie wanted to faint. She was too tired and nothing had prepared her for this. Was this a test? Why was this necessary? She kept her emotions to herself and looked over to Terry and into his shocking gray eyes. He looked like some kind of African freak, with those light eyes sitting in what was the blackest face she'd ever seen. She came from a long line of near-white-looking African Americans. She took a lot of pride in being black, but had never gone to bed with a man half as dark as this one. Her vagina was dry as bone and sealing itself permanently shut.

"What is your real name?" she managed to ask him, without any distaste showing in her voice.

"Tercouta'acu. But Americans cannot say it...."

"Te-rye'co-u-taaa A-cu," Ebbie repeated perfectly. "From your accent I suspect you're originally from the same country as Fedora Kylie. Your last name, your blood name is shared by the Claukens...."

"They are close kin to my family, yes," he spoke neatly, taking her hand in his and smiling handsomely over to Cleopatra. He nodded slightly, affirming a question she asked with her eyes.

"What happens if I fail to become a truthsayers? I'll be...."

"Ebbie, please," Cleopatra warned her to silence with her gentle tone. "There are no more tests for you. There is nothing to fail, and you have all your life not to do so. You will have to spend the next few years honing your skills. What better time to take to have your children?" she continued and then threw a chain of thick gold covered with long white teeth into Ebbie's lap. "This is one of the many gifts his mother sends you. We have prepared a chest for you to fill and return to his family with his sisters. They wait in your rooms to be served."

No, nothing had prepared her for this, and once again she was not being given a choice, not really. She could refuse, but this could prove to be a nice distraction from the constant routine of study and the technical work she now had to do in the waste chemicals reemployment lab.

"Will there be legal obligations?" Ebbie asked and then turned to give Terry another look.

"Mate, not marriage as you know it. The only obligation you need consider should be to your children, if you are so blessed," spoke Teresa, a little condescending.

"Only consider him as a father to your children. That would be important to him," Cleopatra injected.

Teresa said, "No law binds you, and he will not hold you against your will. One child will make you a mother among us, only one, and then you may do as you please."

"Trust me in this, my child," Cleopatra implored. "I shall stand as your mother with his people. There shall be a mating feast in three weeks...."

Ebbie was no longer listening with all her awareness. She watched Terry's teeth gleam at her as he smiled and helped to put the golden gift around her neck. "This is ivory from an bull who died two years ago, at 62. Sixty-two, and we still have three others that are older," she heard him say, but continued to observe him as he moved nearer and rested both his hands in her lap. She knew he wanted her to kiss him; it was something important connected to an old custom she knew nothing about, but she knew better than to do it, even tho she would hate to see the disappointment on his face or the catty smile Teresa would give her.

She suddenly hated the power that was working its way into her system and her life. All it took was a close look and she could almost read minds. She saw clearly the reactions to her every move. Understanding the people involved, she could foretell the future of a moment waiting to spring into life before her.

She gave Terry back all her attention. He was dressed for a private rendezvous, and smelled of sweet oils and the freshly made linen he wore. He waited for some words from her which she had to give, but had not been told what they were. Cleopatra was still talking about a feast to be given in honor of the pledges and the couples to be mated.

"Your father will be present," Ebbie managed to hear Cleopatra's words.

Of course that was the final touch Ebbie needed. She turned to Terry and picked up both his hands and held them to her breast. She moved his fingers so that he could feel her through the deceptive material of the film dress. "I shall give you a child," she spoke without thinking or worrying about the effects of her words. She knew from the first syllables what to expect.

"And I shall keep your child and make him or her my own," he replied, almost in chant as he went to his knees.

"This child will then be our child, and in this child we shall be one," she almost blurted and cursed herself for still not being able to chant properly.

"Then it is done," he replied.

Cleopatra chuckled and said, "I still like the longer one, when she says, 'I shall give you many children'."

"I'm afraid that is quite out of fashion these days, Cleo," laughed Teresa, as she watched Terry place his head in Ebbie's lap and Ebbie sprinkle the petals of the blue flower over his head.

▼▼▼▼▼

Ramaa, Umboi, Kangar and a strange young woman had returned. The sun had been rising for some time, but Shhaha did not want to wake his apprentices. He had been most of the night with the Kamituians, who were still celebrating the death and rebirth of one of their own. They were drunk on a special wine made from the spice waters and the spice tree spider's poison, which they also used for their reed darts.

The woman Umboi and Kangar had traded for came willingly and was pleasing to the eye, but she was already drunk with the other women, who had forced themselves upon her. All the women wanted to greet their new sister, even tho they could hardly stand. Umboi and Kangar sat near Shhaha and were treated to every kindness the other protectors could bestow upon them. Even their enemies looked at them with new respect, and spoke heartfelt words when sharing their spider wine.

Ramaa told Shhaha that Keishlee was waiting with the tall walkers just outside the forest, and he knew it was because his clan relations refused to enter the tall forest again. He was prepared and ready to leave, but wished to be a little while longer among these people, and to give Mah and Odrak a bit more rest. These were a people a Blood Keeper could be proud of, and he found himself feeling jealous of She Who Has No Name, because they belonged to her. These people did not balk at giving up their life for a greater purpose, and did not regret the loss of a loved one for themselves, instead, they rejoiced for having had the soul among them, and for the many memories he left behind. But their true joy came when they spoke of the tree that the old man, Ankh, would soon become.

Occasionally they came near to caress the sleeping Mah and Odrak, and even drunk, managed to make new sets of skins for them to wear. The men made sure they were warm and strong and the women chose only those made most perfectly, and brought down hidden stores of special foods that would keep well on their journey.

Out of respect, Shhaha ate some of everything, except the meats, and packed the rest away for their journey. He took pause with a substance that he knew came from an animal, but it was not flesh, so he tried it. It was a thick and creamy blood-filled substance that was sweet and rich. It gave him new energy and his body accepted it. It reminded him of the blood thickener he had used on Medra, only it was tastier. He packed a good deal of this away in his empty bladder sacks, and smiled back at the people, who were glad he was doing so.

From the look on Ramaa's face, Shhaha knew that he had enjoyed his visit with the Hoteps. It was likely that these people had many free women in need of relief, or that they had simply been very good to him, allowing him to forget the dangers he had suffered. Ramaa seemed in no rush to get back to Keishlee. Maybe others had followed them back part way and were now looking after her, but he was sure she had her Tuk blade, and so he let Mah and Odrak continue to sleep, and enjoyed himself at the feast.

▼▼▼▼▼

Ebbie walked down the aisle arm in arm with Cleopatra and Terry's mother, Erfout Clauds, a lovely, stout woman in her early fifties. Before and after her walked many other acolyte sisters and their mothers and mothers-in-blood.

In a huge cluster of men dressed in everything from expensive suits to elaborate chammies, stood her father, Rockmon Farmer, whom she had not seen for almost five years. He was talking with Terry as if they were old friends. She wanted to run into his arms, but there were customs to be observed here, and she would not be able to touch him until after her mate had reintroduced her to the crowd.

Once each couple met in the center of the dining hall, which had been specially decorated for this occasion, they performed a little dance, first the woman and then the man. Then the man lead the woman to her seat at a long semicircular table across from a long straight one where the men sat.

The dances were mostly short performances, but of course there were those who stretched out their time with turns and spins, leaps and jumps, made to let others know that they were professional dancers, or just better than the rest. At each place setting there were tiny little bells next to water glasses, and when a pair finished dancing, their guests would ring the bells in their section of the dining hall. Whenever someone did something especially nice, all the bells tinkled through the air like angels flying overhead. It gave Ebbie sensual shivers while she waited to take her turns on the marble floor.

Ebbie made her dance very short and simple, even tho she could dance well. But in honor of Terry's sisters, Otbarou and Necoufa'oo who were great dancers, she engineered a beautiful swirl of silk streamers into a flower around her as she came to a stop, and waited for Terry to approach. She knew she had gotten this trick Mageeta had showed her down just right when the air filled with the twinkle of singing stars. The flutter of dancing, cream-colored silks was lapping all around her as Terry was compelled to move towards her. Each step he took was strong and bold, but she could see that he was not a dancer. Yet he was elegant, and his clothes moved about him in a regal manner that gave her some respect for him.

The artfully falling silks that were part of her dance were also part of her dress. At the end she would do the quick turn step to snap the silks into flowing streamers behind her, as an added special exit effect. Terry would do his dance and then greet her at the table, but she could see that he didn't want her to move, and she kept wiggling the silks to keep the flower shape a little longer. He ran and leaped over her, and then around and around her, whipping the air and the silks into a slightly different shape. He slid into a back looping dive and wrapped himself around her feet.

The sound of bells gave her shivers and made the silks shudder against her will. Later Ebbie would remember the painting called "coelogyne cristata," but now she was only half aware of the compulsion that made her snap the silks out over Terry. She was really angry with him for spoiling her effect, but when she reached for him, he took one arm and pulled her close, and they became the orchid that hung over the water in the center of that picture. Everyone saw it and knew it was the picture hanging in the main lobby of Wind Limited. They stood and rang the bells until Rockmon Farmer, President of Wind Limited, helped Terry and Ebbie up and sent them to their seats. Ebbie was flustered, but Terry seemed unaware of the adulation surrounding them. He pushed her chair in behind her and took his kiss before she could protest.

▼▼▼▼▼

Odrak was glad to see Keishlee and the tall walkers. He didn't like walking with the spice seeds between his legs, and he hated the skins tied around his body even more. The sun was falling low and it was hot. After tying their packs up on the shoulders of the male, he and Mah took off the skins and tried to find another way of keeping the seeds in place so that they wouldn't ruin everything else that was there.

Keishlee was glad to see everyone, but Shhaha could tell that she had grown sad again, like she had after leaving Tuk Village. She had seen her friend again, just as Ramaa had seen the woman called Nuba again. Shhaha suspected that Hotep Village was a breeding place for the Tuk women. If they went on that way they might run into many traveling Tuk women, which he did not want to do. Keishlee was yearning too much for her friend, and Ramaa was committing himself to more than just relief with this woman, Nuba, when they had no more time to lose and didn't need to get sidetracked by these longings.

"Has your friend gone back to her village?" Shhaha asked Keishlee, while she made string for Odrak and Mah.

Trying not to be surprised, she said, "Yes."

Shhaha turned his vision inward and then said, "She will never forget you, nor you her. But her people are coming into difficult times and she will need to forget you to go on."

Everyone trusted Shhaha's wisdom and his visions, but there was no need for them this time. She and Adah had already said their goodbyes, and Keishlee knew they final ones.

"Come, we have rested and eaten enough. Let us make good time," spoke Shhaha, as he watched Mah tie a piece of pocketed skin around Odrak's waist and up between his legs. When Odrak had done the same to Mah, they were off again, heading away from the slopes of the Hoteps, and the receding mountains.

They cleared the forest grounds just before sunset, where they all began to notice the land sloping steadily downward. They could see for countless trees in all directions, except for the land that swung up behind them, and the sight of the enormous trees reaching up from the center of the forest and poking into the sky. The trees swept up into the sky beyond the clouds, and in the fading light the clouds glowed like a ring of white silver. Shhaha rubbed his silver ring, and knew then that it was created for this journey alone.

Ramaa and Keishlee were taken back by the sight. "It's a gift from the Great Mother," moaned Ramaa.

"The Kamituians are the descendants of the spice tree," spoke Mah solemnly, "and the trees are older than the Tall Walkers, and all human life. Their size cannot be appreciated up close. One must run the long distance."

"The sun makes its run to rest, but the trees will greet it before it rises," spoke Odrak.

"They look taller than the mountains," sighed Keishlee.

"The one Odrak planted will be," Shhaha smiled down at his apprentices, knowing that he could now finally start working his own magic on them.

Belinda Coffy speaking to the International Sappho Commission: "My sister's favorite line is 'There's power in the boo-tae', and as usual she's right. The first egoist was a woman, and it was her 'boo-tae' that allowed her to be one. Her identity and the proof of her power was the miracle of childbirth. Prehistoric women were worshiped because of this power, and it is this power alone that makes the whole world go round. Somewhere back in time men decided that the struggle of their seed was more important than our months of labor. If there is an original sin, it happened when the first woman told some man how babies were really born, and taking this apple from her, he has managed to rule the lives of women ever since. If we lose the right to control our own bodies, it'll be like telling the gods that we are not worthy to control the power they gave us."

"The Pleasure and Delight"

Shhaha and his people traveled for 2 cycles of days on downward sloping land. The view ahead lost its lush greenery and the land became dryer around them, while the distant view behind them disappeared under low-lying clouds or misty covered hills. Whenever they could, they gathered greens and herbs for boiling or roasting, and collected tree bark for seasoning and chewing. They dug for nuts and gathered berries to make food paste, and saved all edible insects and roots for the harder part of the journey Shhaha warned was still to come.

They had traveled for 7 moons already and did not look at three more as much travel, but Shhaha was being grave and deciphering omens aloud, which meant that danger was near. There was a new star in the sky at night, which Shhaha said pointed back to their people. He wanted to return home, and even suggested they visit the Valley of Names another time. The others protested; having come this far they would not turn back now. Ramaa tied most of the bundles around the shoulders of the male tall walker to make their stepping lighter, and took the lead to keep them at a good pace. He was fearless and considered any danger Shhaha felt, only the complaints of his old bones.

Ramaa and Keishlee had seen two colliding stars the night the new star was made. They watched the brilliant show of lights together with the young Kamituians, who considered it a good omen for their trade. They had rushed back to the land of the giant spice trees under the glow of the star's clear light, and had not thought of it as a bad omen.

But now as they traveled, they did come upon some strange and scary things: creatures that were not snakes but who slithered, oversized animals that ran about screaming as if in pain, and others that made them wait before they could pass. Soon they were all feeling Shhaha's tension, but the tall walkers' instincts were good and clear. They saw no real danger coming near or far, and had found many new friends among the creatures of this land, where everything here ran or hopped about. Their running was the only thing to give weight to Shhaha's fears, as if everyone should run from danger here.

One night while the moon waned, the air became thick with fog and mists, a thing seldom seen in their land but of which there were many stories. Ramaa walked ahead with Odrak's blood wand and a Tuk blade in hand, since a fog was a thing from which an evil could spring, or one could walk right into a waiting death. Still, they walked most of the night, not wanting to sleep on the damp ground. Ramaa kept the Tuk blade ready, and used the blood wand to make sure every step was placed on solid ground.

They walked until the sun was up and there was more light, but still they could not see further than a hand away. They feared losing each other if they did not keep close, so Ramaa chanted a low call for them to follow as he continued pushing them on. Shunning his fear, he stepped into thick, bellowing vapors and warm steam that rose up from the ground. They listened closely to each other's steps, following Ramaa as the land began to slope upwards. They had to coax the tall walkers along each footfall, because their clan relations could not see any better than they. The incline became more steep as the ground turned to rock beneath them, while a dirt and rock wall started to form on one side, growing taller and taller as the day wore on. Soon they were tired from the climb and their lack of sleep, but Ramaa had gotten further ahead and was still chanting for them to follow. Shhaha gave each of them a taste of the potent Mah had made at the clearing of the Kamituians, and they found strength to move on.

Suddenly the tall walkers started to bleat, smacking their

lips together as they walked past the others. Shhaha ordered Keishlee to make them silent, while he and Mah listened for Ramaa, who was no longer chanting off in the distance. Odrak marched off ahead trying to locate him, but there was only silence, except for the flapping of wings high above, and the occasional tumble of rocks below.

"Stay to the rock wall," Shhaha ordered as he suddenly realized they had climbed a mountain side.

Even the tall walkers seem to understand, and now walked closer to the mountain's wall of rock and dark stones.

Keishlee picked up a pebble and tossed it to one side. It landed quickly. She tossed another further off and it too landed quickly on solid ground. Mah threw the next much further off, and they listened and waited. Their hearts almost stopped as reason failed to perceive the height to which they had climbed. They waited longer, in silence more impassive than before, but the stone still did not make a sound, as they felt the mountain press quieter around them.

"Odrak!" Mah called, but there was no reply.

Keishlee took Shhaha's hand and they followed Mah and the tall walkers up the mountain. Sound came back to them, but it was mostly wind and the sound of a mountain growing ever so slowly. Keishlee screamed as a bird came from nowhere and attacked her. The snake leather strappings around her arms were all that saved her face. Mah beat the bird back with his blood wand, then Keishlee took her Tuk blade and sliced off part of a wing. As it fell to the ground, Mah tried to speak with the bird, Keishlee did too, but it only screamed and lunged for him as tho it might jump up in his face and kill him.

"Run!!" Shhaha screamed as he heard the warning "moo" of the tall walkers. They had dashed off ahead, an inelegant move for tall walkers running up hill, but a trusted sign of coming danger.

Keishlee followed Shhaha, slicing at the air above as the sound of many wings descended upon them. They ran pass the crash of birds smashing against the mountain wall, while others screeched a promise of more attacks. They were like flying eyes coming out of the sky and mist. Luckily they were not very good flyers, and even Shhaha fought them off easily, but their numbers were too great.

They ran faster, trying to stay close to the tall walkers, who were crying from the birds' attacks. The clatter of their running became the only sound as the mist started to clear around them and they left the attacking birds behind.

They could smell the fear the tall walkers felt at the narrowing of the path ahead. The path twisted and turned around the mountain that rose above them, into a mist more like clouds than fog. The tall walkers would not move now, and in their lazy stubborn way, laid on their legs to tend to their wounds.

Keishlee took the cleaning fluid from Shhaha and helped clean their cuts. Mah went to the edge of the path to see the sun starting its descent, and the fog that covered all the land. They were standing atop the tallest of a collection of many mountains, all with similar paths. Mah walked further along the path and could see it turn into other paths, or become linked with other mountain cliffs, or turn around a bend and disappear. He called Shhaha over to see the thing that connected this mountain with the next one.

Shhaha saw the hanging walkway connecting the mountain peaks, but noted more the bubbling mist below. It was something he had seen before, but only in an amount that would not have made this difference to the surrounding air. This fog was mixed with steam that came up from deep cracks in the earth. The smell here was sulfur, well mixed with earth blood, running into a river or stream somewhere far below. This place was part of the danger he had felt, and the fog was the reason he had not seen it clearly.

Shhaha felt the stone ground and listened closely to the sound of moving fog. Off in the distance he saw the big-eyed birds still flying in and out of the mist below. "There," Shhaha said, pointing Mah to an upward billow of smoky steam. "There you will find Odrak. Go silently, Mah, and come back quickly."

Mah quickly looked around and understood. There were paths below just like these above. Odrak must be trapped on one down there. "What of Ramaa?" he asked, heading down.

"We will not find him until later. He is well. Go now. Silently, or Odrak might fall."

Keishlee watched Mah quick-step down into the mist, and turned a fretful look on Shhaha. He signaled her not to worry, but she could find no comfort as she watched the birds flying in and out of the mist around them.

Mah was careful as he reentered the thick gray air. He was a little startled by the number of dead birds he found. He hated to see all the blood that was so easily spilled by the Tuk blades. His was still strapped to his side, along with some of the small bundles. He didn't like using it any longer, and often wished it would break. He recalled the lizard that had crawled against it, a friendly, talkative creature that had died in agony from the blade's poison. In five days the tiny lizard was a gob of moldy flesh, good now only for growing grass. He had begun to use the weapon less and less since then, and now turned to it hardly at all. He carried the blood wand more often now and was pleased that it offered more choices than death. He picked one of the dead birds up and found it cut clean through. Its guts slipped out and Mah let it fall back to the ground.

He made himself small against the wall as a bird swooped down near him. Mah held his breath and tried to stop his heart as he watched the bird hover and then fly away. Sitting there with the mists pressing in on him, he could sense the other creatures that lived here: eye birds, large snakes, and rambull goats. Mah got to his feet, realizing how strong his powers were getting. He saw things that had touched a place he touched, and it was getting to be a frightening experience. The vision had come to him because he wasn't really frightened at all, which meant he needed to be.

He continued down the path, trying to understand what the danger could be. He stepped off to the side and discovered a path that went down and then turned up into another path. The cover of the mist was disorienting, and he slowed his pace. He found a peacefulness in this moment alone, and realized he was glad for it. Being alone drove away the feeling of danger that had suddenly surrounded him.

He reached out and found ropes, thick, coarse ropes leading out into the darkening mists, that began to tied together in a pattern like a mat. Mah felt around and found ropes on the other side of him, and they too turned into knots and matting that climbed along the edge of a rock wall.

Suddenly mist bellowed up into his face, and in another step the wall was gone and the ground shaking beneath him.

"Why do you close yourself to me?" came a voice Mah knew better than his own.

It broke his fear and Mah realized he was standing on one of those things he'd seen earlier, hanging between two cliff sides. "Why do you stay here waiting for rescue?" replied Mah, trying to see Odrak through the thick fog.

"Come a few steps forward and look down."

Mah did so and saw the gap in the boards of the skywalk. As he watched, sometimes the air would clear and he could see the great distance and the rocks below. Fear ate away at his self confidence and he felt the wind blow around him. Wind shook the skywalk and for a moment he could see Odrak, clinging to both sides of the roped walkway with a look of terror on his face.

"The boards broke behind me and they are broken in front of me as well," spoke Odrak.

"Come," Mah said, stepping back on the solid rock of the cliff side. "I will hold the ropes. Stick your toes in the holes and climb over."

Odrak had been waiting for one of them to come and do just that. He was terrified of such heights, and his time with the Great Mahs had helped only a little. The skywalk had felt insecure, and the side Mah was now holding was partly frayed. He feared the next breeze might lose him to the air and dared to move without assistance, but he wished it had been Keishlee who had come to help.

"You were right to wait," Mah warned as Odrak raced across the ropes. "Hurry, the ropes are slipping."

Mah had been pulled to the very edge of the cliff by the time Odrak made it over. Odrak fell on him and they tumbled down the path as the skywalk fell away and into the mist. It could hardly be heard as it smacked against the unseen mountain on the other side. They did not greet each other, or even look to see that the other was well. Mah gave Odrak the warning of silence Shhaha had given him, and they proceeded down the path and then up the connecting slope.

Odrak quickly realized his mistake and walked past Mah up the slight slope. Mah was glad Odrak was safe, but he would think no more of danger. Odrak was sure to face many dangers; he was so full of ready fire, so quick to anger, and these traits were attractive to any danger. Of course it would find him.

Odrak turned to see only the fog around him and the comfort of it. The solid ground beneath his feet gave him a pleasant pause. The silence of the fog pacified him as Mah passed, and he was glad for this moment to clear the fear from his mind. Why did Mah have to come to rescue him, again? It was unbearable to see his own reflection in Mah's eyes, and worse not to be allowed inside, inside Mah's heart, mind and body as he had always been. But since the blood trance, all the usual doors were closed to him. He suspected his own were closed as well, but could not think of that. The trance had taught him the necessity of it, and he had doubts that he would open his mind again for anyone. Even Shhaha would find it difficult to enter there again, but there were other places within him that refused to stay closed. He caught the smell of Great Mah oil and Mah filtering down to him in the mists, and wished he didn't like the smell of it and him so much.

He thought his eyes were playing tricks on him when the mists cleared and he saw Keishlee, resting with her head on one of the tall walkers. She was looking at him with suspicion, which he could not bear. He walked over to her and made himself happy, and then, without realizing, he used some of his power to clear her mind.

"I have searched my memories and this place is not among them," said Shhaha, pulling Mah closer to the edge of the mountain path.

"I feared that we were lost," replied Mah, daring to stand with his toes overhanging the very edge of the cliff.

"Not lost," Shhaha smiled. "We were brought here without our knowing. Our way was clear, and so I let Ramaa lead us. Something here directed him here. He is with it now. It has control of him."

"It?" Mah asked and tried to feel out a presence.

Shhaha walked over to the high rock wall of the mountain and rubbed clean a dark collection of glittering stones there. "These are ox stones," he whispered.

Mah instantly recalled the tale of a great blood keeper called Ishaha, whose power did not die with him and caused fires and floods where he was buried. A black ox stone came down the mountains and fell on the place where he lay, and his power was forever sealed at the spot.

"Ox stone can block your power, even from yourself. It can take an entire life to pass through its depths, or add power to your touch and rush it on before the thought is done. A blood keeper to learn a quick path through one would be powerful, indeed," whispered Shhaha.

"You have touched it," Mah spoke, showing his fear and protectiveness.

"It knows we are near already. It has Ramaa."

"Ramaa has a strong will. He would not tell...."

Shhaha raised the finger he touched the stone with and placed it at Mah's forehead. "An ox stone placed here makes thoughts easy to see for one with the training."

Mah stepped away from the wall and turned his eyes upward so that he could close any entrance to his thoughts from there. He began to chip away stones from the wall, and by the time he got one loose, Odrak was there to pick it up.

Shhaha wanted to warn him of it, but it was too late, and the stone was glowing dark in his hand. Shhaha placed a hand on each side of Odrak's head and instantly the glowing and the pain in Odrak's hand stopped. Keishlee shuddered as she saw his eyes turn black and their whites disappear. Shhaha chanted the call of warning, and Mah echoed his tones.

"I see them. I see Ramaa!" Odrak shouted.

"Your mind has linked with them, but they know you not. I shall let them see you, Keishlee," Shhaha called.

Keishlee stretched out her hand and watched Shhaha's face for signs of what to do. Mah understood the signal and placed her hand on the stone, quickly snatching his own away.

"Good. Good, Mah." Shhaha smiled, trying to keep his concentration on Odrak.

Keishlee didn't feel pain or see anything, but moaned of an odd taste in her mouth and a strange smell. Odrak twisted about and Shhaha hissed. Shhaha knocked the stone from their hands and pulled Odrak to him, asking, "Where are they? How many are they?"

"Many," Keishlee said, without having really seen them.

"A great many," added Odrak.

Keishlee looked down at the stone and said, "It...."

"You said IT as well," wondered Mah, trying to understand the words on her face and in her eyes. "Are they not human?"

"I don't know, but they are many. Blood keepers all and all powerful," spoke Odrak.

"No blood keepers. Only powerful beings. Creatures unlike any you have ever seen before," Shhaha corrected.

Once again Shhaha sat down to trance, but did not sit close to the rock floor. Odrak made a small fire and Keishlee prepared a meal of fruit and boiled leaves dipped in lemon juice and rolled in insect paste.

With Shhaha trancing there was nothing for them to do but wait, and they fell asleep, resting on the tall walkers, who had partaken of the meal with them. Mah was resting on the female with his head on her belly, and he dreamt of the little walker she would bear, a long-legged pup, tied to the head of a giant fish moving on top of the water.

A cool breeze woke him up, and he found the moon rising overhead and everything still about him. Shhaha and Keishlee were rising and Odrak was tending a small fire. Mah removed two torches from the fire and went to Shhaha, who had been keeping the watch. He was staring at the moonlight being reflected off the mountains and the mists. When everyone was ready, he cautiously led them along the mountain paths.

There was a blossom that came out in the moonlight, growing in cracks along the walkways they passed. They glowed from the moonlight like markers, directing the group along the paths. Keishlee collected some of the petals and Mah stored them in his packs.

The moon was high when they reached a wide stone walkway. They had come quite a way up the mountain, but had yet to see the tops of any of those they'd climbed. Across the stone walkway they could look down on the tops of smaller mountains and were surprised to find the land still covered with fog and mist. There were some openings in the fog where they could see fields and trees, and the sparkle of a narrow, rapid-flowing river. It seemed impossibly far away from the land below, but it was not cold as one would expect, nor was it devoid of life. They could see many flying birds making their way out into the moonlight, leaving a seasoned smell on the breeze and a tiny screech in the air.

There was a large entrance on the other side of the stone walkway, with fire coming out of stone-carved pillars. Someone was standing in the entrance, whose face and hands were completely hidden from view. The moon was high and shining down on the stone walkway like an invitation, but the figure standing on the other side stood there like a warning.

Keishlee took hold of Mah, protecting him from the thought of crossing, and looked at Shhaha as if she dared him to do it. Odrak walked up to Shhaha and waited for his signal, while Shhaha studied the figure and the stone pillars at its sides. It raised one of its cloaked arms and the tall walkers meandered across the walkway, whistling as if they had seen an old friend.

Ebbie reluctantly said goodbye to Terry's sisters. She had been enjoying their company and was not ready to be alone with Terry in their new rooms. But there was no sense in putting it off. Terry had been walking around with a soft erection all day, thoroughly embarrassing them all.

Ebbie undressed while Terry put out the lights. He opened the drapes in their bedroom and the room shimmered with moonlight. All she could think about was how much her bald head was probably shining in the light, and how she hated not wearing her film dress and not feeling the strength it gave her.

She realized her back was to him when he came over and took her hand, and waited. She almost wished he was the type of man who would take her and get his pleasure over with, but she knew she would have to kiss him before he ever got inside.

They walked up the steps to the large bed-pile, and stared out the large windows onto the moonlit fields. Two giraffes drifted by, strutting in single file as was their custom. They were so in tune with each other, she thought, and such beautiful creatures to watch.

Terry turned her around and she found him beautiful in the dim light, with his eyes and teeth glowing in the dark of his face, his face shining blue in the light. She ran her fingers over his hair, feeling the soft length of tight curls, which were much longer than they appeared. He pulled her close with his large firm hands and kissed her neck, while she reached down and satisfied the curiosity that had been building for three weeks.

"I like this animal, this giraffe," he said, looking out the wide windows, past the tall trees where the giraffes were disappearing. "We have nothing like them in our country."

"They're almost sacred to the sisterhood. They mean to make it possible for them to live in the cities among people." She smiled while feeling his readiness, and was completely satisfied with what he was about to offer her.

The cave reminded Mah of the citadels of the Great Mahs, except they did not smell as pretty. Along the walls were holes in which burned a white oil, and everywhere there were figures in stone. Most were of men with tiny private parts and small shapely eyes. Many were creatures with so much flesh they looked more like waterhorses on two legs than humans, but all of them had comely faces, and beautiful delicate hands. Mah could hardly resist touching the lifelike carvings of lizards and birds.

They were taken to a chamber, where they were relieved to find Ramaa. Once inside, a stone was quickly moved over the opening, and all they could see of the creature that had led them here was its cloaks fluttering by as it passed a section of holes in the wall.

Ramaa was sitting still as stone and hardly seemed to breathe. Mah and Keishlee sat on the stone floor and rubbed his legs, while Shhaha rubbed his head and checked his eyes.

"Shhaha!" Ramaa called out, not aware of where he was.

"You have been dreaming soft dreams," Shhaha spoke to him quietly. "They have fed you rest and food with their minds. Now you must eat with your mouth." He pointed out a pile of food waiting on stone shelves on the opposite side of the room.

Of course he knew. Without looking, Mah could smell it too. "Roots, and ground foods and fruits," he whispered.

Odrak was lighting an oil bowl near the entrance with his torch, and without looking he said, "No flesh, but separate vials of blood. Some is human, and some of it is not."

"You are right," Keishlee mumbled as she picked up one of the many bowls of thick blood. They were being warmed by small fires coming out of white sticks placed under the stone shelves.

"They think because we are Blood Keepers, we live off blood," Shhaha laughed with his apprentices.

Shhaha went over and tasted each of them slowly, one at a time, giving himself time to check for poisons or the blood of beasts. Keishlee checked the food placed nearby and then fed Ramaa, who was almost too weak to move. She helped him to place his back against a wall and then tasted each item before allowing him to eat.

When his head was clear and Ramaa saw the room around him, and Keishlee sitting on her heels in front of him, he pulled her forward and rubbed their heads and arms together.

After tasting all of the blood bowls, Shhaha picked out the ones he wanted Mah and Odrak to taste. There was not much blood to a bowl, so Shhaha let them drink all that was left. He did not need much to know from what it had come, or its full contents, if other than blood was present. He would trance with the blood still in his belly to learn about these people and the generations that had made them.

"These people have only just learned of blood keeping from Ramaa, and fear what we do with it. Treat each drop with respect," Shhaha warned.

Shhaha sat on his heels and started a small moss fire, and the others knew that he was going to blood trance again. Keishlee protested, having heard what had happened back at the Kamituians' clearing. Ramaa had gone to sleep and she wanted to enlist his aid, but Mah and Odrak refused to listen, wanting instead to join Shhaha.

"Come," Shhaha warned, "and follow close. Nothing else will follow us this time, but keep close so that none will hear," Shhaha said and took the small cutting stone from Odrak and made a small slice on Mah's thigh. He scooped up the blood and let it drip into the fire. Odrak cut his own arm, and seeing the other marks, realized that once he had enough cuts on that arm, he would need the string of bones to keep his skin from reopening, each bone carefully aligned across the length of each cut, and strings of bones all the way up to his shoulder, like Shhaha.

Keishlee watched them in silence for a long while, keeping time with the torches and the slowly burning white sticks, and avoiding the thickly fragrant smoke that came from the moss fire. Ramaa was sleeping peacefully, but Shhaha, Mah and Odrak looked like the living dead. Sometimes their eyes opened and she could see only the whites. Their heads shook and their skins moved over their bones as if something alive was underneath. More surprising was the small moss fire, which should have burned out by now. It made her nervous and she paced about. She even tried to move the stone, but it felt locked in place and would give in no direction. Through the small holes in the wall, she sometimes saw a light go by, but never saw its carrier, only the fully cloaked creature that stood silent on the other side of the stone, its face hidden by a hood of cloth.

Keishlee wanted to leave, or scream. She hated traveling with blood keepers, which she now also considered Mah and Odrak, since they too practiced the act of blood trancing. She thought it such a waste of a man to become a Keeper of the Blood.

A man could run all his life, come and go when he pleased, enjoy the pleasure of his body without labor or burden, and was more often stronger. "He could move this stone and be gone from here," she whispered to herself, angry with her body and her efforts with the stone.

"No man could move that stone," moaned Ramaa, lying on his side. "Come, sister. Calm yourself."

"Every time he does that he changes my water. My blood flows whenever it pleases these days."

"We are always glad to have you to drink from." Ramaa smiled, motioning for her to come over.

"It is all right for you, but I cannot keep track of my days. I might be all right if I were on the other side of that wall, but here we share the same air."

"You are feeling ready to mate then?" Ramaa asked, sitting up with his back against the wall.

Keishlee had a moment of silence that disturbed her, but she said, "Yes."

"Good. The women of our clearing will be pleased. I shall pick him out for you, if no one comes to dance."

"You!" Keishlee laughed. "You are close to no man. If it were not for this journey, you would be spending all your time with Maum."

"Yes, the honey bee's delight. I miss her much," Ramaa said, pulling Keishlee close.

"I feel close to you, Ramaa, because of this journey. I thank the journey for that, and for allowing me to become close to Mah and Odrak," she said, holding Ramaa's hand over her heart. "Did you know Odrak's keeper?"

"I knew the one they whisper about. The one they say might be his keeper. The one from the clan of black cats? Yes I knew him. We were young, but I knew him close. Only once. We picked many yams together."

Keishlee stretched her neck around to see Ramaa's face. She was surprised. "You have been close to another man?"

"Stop calling me a man," Ramaa laughed. "I have only three slaves in my keep, and I have no hair on my face as yet." He paused to pinch a peck of sand off the floor and flick it in her face. "It does not matter to slaves as long as they can be close. You think I learned late? Like you?"

Keishlee braced herself. There was no way to explain to Ramaa what it was like before she knew how to be friends. She was like wind that could not be touched, and lived with a pain that could not be healed. Anger filled her heart and there was no room for others to enter. All she ever wanted was to be a breeze, and went from moment to moment filled with anxiety and loss. Riding had been her only close pleasure and the wind her only friend. Walking across the escarpment had erased her comfort with the wind. It too had turned bitter and cold, and could smell bad for no reason, and worse, the loneliness of it threatened to rip her mind apart. Yes, she learned late and it was the journey that had forced her to change.

Ramaa pulled her back to him, glad that he could now claim to know something of her touch. It gladdened his heart, since she used to avoid him. "I am happy for you. I wish you many mouths to feed," Ramaa whispered, and rubbed his head against hers. "Let Odrak pick for you then."

"No. Mah shall pick for me, and Odrak can judge his dance, or I shall wait and visit the land of tall grasses when we return."

"Yes, Odrak has a good dance. The elders say he has the step of the oodda."

"I should have mated...."

"If so, you would have missed this journey, and you would not have earned your Tuk blade." Ramaa pointed to the pile of weapons behind Shhaha.

"I wouldn't be locked in this room either." She pointed to the stone, but was looking at the blades she'd wrapped together and placed behind Shhaha for safekeeping. "And Mah and Odrak would still be close!"

"They are past not being close. Forever will they remain as one. They have much need for each other. Someone, a young protector maybe, will try to come between them, or try to harm one of them, and he will suffer a great deal to heal the strange hurt between them."

"Someone comes," Keishlee whispered and pointed to the faint light coming through the wall holes.

"Maybe now we can leave," hoped Ramaa.

"Be still," spoke Shhaha, shocking Ramaa and Keishlee by being near them, with Mah and Odrak standing at his sides.

Keishlee and Ramaa jumped to their feet as the stone was rolled aside. A tall, fully robed figure stepped in and pointed three fingers, one each at Mah, Shhaha and Odrak. Two small figures rushed in and went for Keishlee, who rushed to her weapon. She was stopped by Shhaha's voice, but Ramaa had caught hold to one of the dust-covered men and accidentally broke his arm. The taller one came for him, but was stopped by Shhaha calling out a name.

"Zen, begotten of Bio."

The figure stopped in mid-step and clapped its hands together. The remaining dust-covered figure took hold of the injured one and dragged him from the room. Someone standing outside helped carry him away, and all of this happened almost too quickly for Keishlee to realize what had taken place.

"Why have you brought us here?" Shhaha asked softly and gestured for the tall figure to come closer.

It snapped itself erect while throwing off its hood. It glared about the room, studying the contents and then the people, leaving Keishlee as the last to be looked upon.

She had not seen the faces of the other two, and thought them just covered with the dust that was everywhere here, but this creature was indeed the color of dust, almost gray, and slightly pink around the eyes. Its eyes looked black and the whites were bloody red. It was a human face, but it had the likeness of a lizard about it. It smiled at her, and she could see that its teeth were green, to match the almost greenish brown color of its hair. The sight almost made her sick. Ramaa was also filled with disgust, but he knew now that Shhaha had come to heal these creatures, and he wanted Shhaha to go to it.

"So, you do not need the stone to see. Yes, I know your words. We are Tututs. We want to go with you to the Great Sharing. We shall trade with you. One of the smaller males for one of our Aphros," it spoke, but its voice was pitched so they could not tell if it was male or female.

Shhaha tried to hold back his laughter, but it stumbled out and his people became unsettled. Keishlee pulled both apprentices near her, while Ramaa moved to block anyone from getting near Shhaha.

"Your offer is not fair. Aphros are common among you. You are an Aphro yourself," laughed Shhaha.

The creature, which had been standing tall, seemed to sink within its robes, its long nailed hands disappearing inside the armholes of its cloak.

"Do not tease," it screeched. "None of your people have ever seen an Aphro, and still you say you would not like one of us among you? Then you are not wise enough to go to the Great Sharing. You are not wise enough to take one of us with you," it rattled and then turned to leave.

"You may come with us without a trade," Shhaha offered.

"You lie," it snapped around and hissed.

The move was vicious, and all smiles were gone except for Shhaha's. Its moves were like the slithers of a snake, and this only made Shhaha smile more, but the others backed away, as it stared at them from behind a mask of eyes of fire.

Ramaa remembered himself and stepped between the creature and Shhaha, saying, "What is that? Whatever it is, we do not do it!"

The creature moved its hand and Ramaa was compelled to step aside. Shhaha's stance told them not to worry, but Keishlee kept looking towards the weapons, and Ramaa located the blood wands, standing opposite the entrance.

"Maybe not," the creature stood erect again and faced Shhaha. "You are something different, indeed," it squealed with mild delight. "I saw you looking, and you," it said, pointing to Odrak. "You dare think you know your way through the temple stones," it smirked and then laughed through its nose. "A tiny one can offer you a journey longer than the one you've traveled already, and also one more deadly," it spoke slowly for the first time.

"Enough!" Shhaha demanded. "You know what you can offer us. The three of us."

"One."

"All."

"One."

"Show us now!" Shhaha ordered.

Zen clapped its hands together and another creature covered in stone dust rushed into the room. He was as tall as Keishlee, taller than Odrak and thicker than both of them. He had knotted hair of many textures, along with a matt of hair on his chest. Ramaa did not want to consider it so, but he was human, or near-human at the least.

He bowed to Zen, and in that moment was flipped on his

back while his body rose slowly into the air. It was done with only two moves of the taller creature's hand, then as the hand moved over the man, he rose higher into the air until he reached Shhaha's waist. Mah rushed to one end of the floating man and Odrak to the other.

"You are unaffected!!" screamed Zen.

The floating man fell to the floor. Mah and Odrak performed the bow for the creature, but it was furious and ran from the room. Mah and Odrak helped the man up and he too left the room after a quick look round.

Shhaha was laughing silently, pleased with the whole affair. Ramaa and Keishlee took deep breaths and were glad they could move of their own accord. Keishlee quickly strapped a Tuk blade to her side, while Ramaa handed Odrak and Shhaha their blood wands. He kept Mah's stick but nodded to him for his approval.

"We shall carry the wands out of respect for these people," spoke Shhaha, signing for Ramaa to turn the blood wand over to Mah. "Keishlee," he called to stop her from handing out the Tuk blades. "Whatever happens, you are not to use that blade to kill, no matter."

Ramaa took the blade and wondered why Shhaha's words were for her alone. He watched Mah and Odrak each repack a large bundle and carry it over to Shhaha, who was preparing to leave. He strapped the blade to his back, out of sight, but he had every intention of using it if anyone touched his Blood Keepers out of hand. "Nothing out of hand," he whispered, but his blood chilled as he remembered the floating man.

The apprentices signaled that they were ready, and followed Shhaha out into the dark corridor. The creature standing there pointed them in a direction deeper into the mountain cave. It called another creature over out of the darkness, and it replaced him as the guard to their room. It then led the way and all of Shhaha's people followed. Ramaa took the last position, and was not happy to feel the heavy cover of shadows following him at a distance.

Ebbie awoke to the rising sun splashing down on her from the floor to ceiling windows. Her first impulse was to cover them. She never kept her drapes open in her old room, but then she didn't have this view before. The land was lush and full of life. There were greens and blues she had never seen before, making the air sparkle bright and clear. She felt new with the sun warming her naked body.

"AnRam," Terry moaned the name he called her during the long night. "AnRam," he whispered a kiss.

Ebbie could now laugh at his mispronunciation. Last night he got so carried away she had struck him, thinking he dared to call her by some other woman's name, but he read her body perfectly and made her forget his words. She pulled back the sheet to see his body again and was glad a man his color had been responsible for making her feel this good. Once again her father had proven himself right after all. After all the years of running down men for the wrong reason, there was something to having a mate chosen for you. For the very first time in her life she had six different kinds of orgasms in one night, and with the same man: the one a woman gets for providing good service, and the one she gets for being good; then the ones that are achieved when affection can make the body wet again, and the mind no longer cares about the burden of being pregnant; and the ones that come from the satisfaction of pure lust.

Still, she felt that particular woman's kind of jealousy, when a man appears to have had the greater pleasure and leaves you wanting more, even when no more could have been endured. She was sure he had reached his climax twice, before she ever got started.

"What did they do, tie your hands behind your back all your life?" she whispered into his ear and kissed his face before she got up to shower.

Shhaha found himself standing before a mass of heavily cloaked figures. He and Ramaa were by far the tallest beings in the room, but these creatures stood tall and daring in their robes of green and gold. One of them shuddered forth like bones on strings. It should have given up walking long ago, but it crept forth and only looked up when it came near Keishlee.

Mah wanted to touch these people. He wanted to smell and taste them like he would any new people. These people meant them no harm. If it were not for the Great Sharing, they would have put Ramaa to shame with their dancing by now. But he had to wait. He had to allow these Tututs to find out for themselves if Shhaha and his people could be trusted. Mah moved his head and arms, just a little, to show them that their combined power still had no effect on him.

Odrak stepped closer to Shhaha, letting them know that he too was unaffected. He turned from the cloaked figures and stared at the other faces assembled here. He considered each one here an "it," as he looked deep into their eyes and saw the mix of man and woman resting there; their shapely faces, full and laced with care; their heads, covered with oddly textured hair, on bodies forged from something to which he had nothing to compare.

And yet among these there were clusters of another group of people here. They were nearly naked and colored gray-brown, which was kinder to the eye, but their hair stood about their heads like giant cotton flowers. The hair on their faces told Odrak that these were protectors. They carried weapons and wore bands of dark feathers and girdles of yellow cloth. Their cleanness, more than the order of their dress, seemed to signify that they held a place of respect among these people. And in their light honey-colored eyes, Odrak could see a lust that could not be hidden, tho lacking some degree of thrust, it was a lust that kept them dripping as they waited to be touched.

Odrak could not bear the separation that loomed between him and all these people. Who could not care for the tender likes of these? Who would not want to see their dancing and learn from them a step or two? A little longer at the trancing, and he would have had a step to relish, one that he could embellish with his own. But they had started coming, and a touch by any of these might have brought on something worse than what had happened at the Kamituians' clearing.

Keishlee and Ramaa found their bodies useless. The feebleness of it almost made Ramaa cry. They had to be helped to the floor and even to sit erect. His skin crawled as the creatures touched him. He did not consider any of them human. He still had the Tuk blade in his hand, but it did not cause the slightest notice. The most deadly weapon he had ever seen was being removed and laid aside as if it was a stick for tossing. He was almost twice the size of the tallest creature in the room, yet his body was now like that of a tiny slave, and he had to suffer being propped up by young sand-colored creatures, who he could not tell were protectors or feeders. Even their touch was confusing, their bodies strange and deceptive. Their skin color was disgusting to look at, and their smiles were a queasy horror.

"Do not struggle so, Ramaa," Keishlee whispered as three brown protectors sat her up close to him.

Ramaa felt her touch against him like a shock wave running up his arm. The contact made her shiver and she put her hands to her face to calm herself.

She could move, Ramaa realized. He could feel her weapon still strapped to her side, which only frustrated him more. He strained to try and speak to her with his eyes, but she would not look. She touched the face of one of the protectors seating her, and something wet shot across Ramaa's face.

Ramaa forced his eyes to move to where the liquid had come from, and then up to the face of the young protector who had lost control of his seed. Ramaa's blood was boiling as he saw the carnal lust embedded in the youth's face. Drool poured down his chin, and Ramaa wanted to kick him for the taste running over his mouth.

Why had Shhaha allowed him to be subdued like this? What had these creatures to offer in blood that was worth suffering the horror of their presence.

Keishlee wanted to cry. She could not stop the feelings that bombarded her from these creatures. Helpless to see beyond the confusion of their appearance, she fought against committing herself to their comfort. She found some stability in the power of her blood keepers, a thing real enough to touch, yet a torment to her limbs, as she saw they were free to move about.

She wanted to leave. She could not stand to look at the faces here. The well-defined bones and lips gave her shivers. The blood-shot eyes of many colors blinded her to what she knew she saw: thin skin, the color of sunburnt soil, on limbs in so many shapes it caused the mind to swim. She saw bodies with single feeder bags covered with animal fur, and milk-filled feeder bags on creatures who looked more like men. There were men with hairy chests and arms who had blood wounds between their legs, and yet almost all had delicate hands and feet that danced as they moved. Their feelings and the smell of them was everywhere, a smell of blood and seed, mixed for an eternity with sand and stone.

If she could just stop their eyes alone, she might find some comfort. They all looked at her with desire and hunger, and she wondered if they would be satisfied with her flesh alone, the flesh that crawled over her as if it wanted to be taken. Her feeder bags were taut and tender, and the blood wound between her legs was moist and inflamed, even tho it sat flush against a cold stone floor.

There were lighted sticks all around the massive room, and stone carvings everywhere. Some were replicas of the very people here. Most were lifelike enough to move, while others kept their beginnings in a place too hard to find, and their endings to themselves. The place was filled with a golden glow and the robed figures stood haloed by its light. They did a little spin around stones hidden by their flowing cloaks, and then sat down like falling leaves.

The one called Zen threw back its hood as it stood off to one side. It did a quick step past Odrak and Shhaha to stop and stare at Mah. It quick stepped over to one of the others, who then rose and stepped past Mah and Shhaha over to Odrak. It snatched back its hood to reveal a long thin face of pale gray skin and a head of coarse curled hair. Its eyes were large and almost clear with only specks of red, beautiful round eyes that reminded Shhaha of the birds that had attacked them, but its nose was too long for the delicate features, and its lips were thin enough to slide off its face.

"I am Tehuti," spoke the long-nosed creature, standing close enough for its nose to touch Odrak's cheek. "Do you like this cloak I wear? I will trade you it for the other." It ripped a finger through the air toward Mah.

"I am Zen, as you know, but I am not an Aphro," spoke the one facing Mah. "Do you like these?" It revealed two hands filled with shiny gems. "If you like, I would trade you these for him." It smiled and jerked its head toward Odrak.

"If you insult my apprentices again, we will leave!" roared Shhaha over the steady flapping tongues.

There was a quiet hush that moved around the room. The others began to sit themselves over the stone figures or on the floor. Each move was like a slow dance that pulled at Keishlee's heart, because she could not always tell if it was the people or the stone figures moving. They seemed connected and alive in some unseen way, and yet all could be just as still and lifeless as stone.

"Young men are common among us," spoke Zen, squeezing out the words.

"I meant no offense," hissed Tehuti with a smile.

Zen let the gems drop to the floor and removed a long stick from inside one of its cloak sleeves. It fanned the thing out to reveal lovely white and brown feathers, with which it stroked the air in front of Mah.

The room had been growing steamy and warm from all the close bodies, but now the air that passed over Mah was cool and fresh. Mah smiled at it, and then the other seated figures began to move about. One pointed to the sack Mah held and another pointed to his blood wand.

Tehuti pulled a bird out from another sleeve. It was small and black with a brightly colored beak. It let the bird walk across its hands and then helped it up onto its shoulder. It fed the bird something and then the bird said, "Tehuti is the best. Tehuti is the best."

Mah was jealous of the offer made to Odrak. The bird was pure delight. He was willing to give up even his blood wand just to hear the bird speak again. Shhaha's body began to hum, and this gave Mah pause, sealing his desire just below the skin.

Zen would not be outdone. Zen twirled and fanned the feathers so that it danced over its hands, around its arms and up over its head, where it wrapped and fixed the feathers together so that it sat atop its head and feathered out like a river goose crown. Zen then produced a stone bird from inside the belly of its cloak. Zen stroked the stone figure and rubbed it to its chest, and then each time Zen ran its hand over the figure and let it fly, a tiny white and yellow bird flew out its hand and up into the crown. Zen did this over and over until the crown had to be filled, and then Zen smashed the stone bird on the ground, reached up into the crown and pulled out a small black cat.

Keishlee heard the kitten cry out and tried to tear herself from the ground. She had to move slowly, and tho the people seemed surprised that she could move, a path was cleared for her. She turned around to look at Ramaa, and found the spot she'd left being licked clean by all those who were near.

She went to Odrak's side, where she could see the one called Zen trying to hand Mah the kitten. It was small enough to have just been born, but clean and friendly. Her mind screamed out for them to offer it to Odrak. She wanted to speak, but Shhaha gave her a look, and she knew better than to try.

Tehuti pulled a long-stemmed flower from a hidden fold within its cloak. It was a large black blossom with bright red and green veins. Tehuti danced over to Shhaha to let him catch its scent. It passed the flower under Mah's nose, then returned to dance the flower around Odrak's head. Odrak took a deep breath and Tehuti stepped back, waved a hand over the blossom and the petals began to fall away. The center crown swelled and then opened to reveal its seeds.

"That is enough!" Shhaha snapped, "We must be on our way."

One of the seated figures jumped up into Shhaha's face. It snatched back its hood and in a slithering voice said, "Then, we will, we'll keep, you here, here with us, us...."

"Then before, before you kill us, us...I, I will let, let Ramaa loose, loose among you, you, Delta...." Shhaha mimicked, using the creature's own voice.

Speaking the creature's name without having been introduced brought a silence to the room that had not been heard before. Even the stone figures seem to turn to face the cloaked ones, and everyone waited for a response.

The old one that had paced the room earlier, waved a bony hand up at the others and the other Tututs returned to their stone seats. The elder threw back its hood and signaled for Zen to speak.

"This is our way. We have made generous offers to your...to your apprentices. They still offer us nothing. Nothing," spoke Zen sorrowfully.

Shhaha nodded to Zen and Tehuti and then the others. He reached out a hand to Mah, who filled it with a small necklace of Great Mah feathers. Shhaha waved it in the air for all to see the play it made of light. Without looking, he took the spice tree seed from Odrak, and all the cloaked figures were standing before he could even display it as he had planned.

"No one has ever offered either of these," spoke one of them as it removed its hood.

They all removed their hoods and whispered among themselves. The result was a little ghastly, with their big eyes and thin faces glowing in the light. Only a few of them were brown. The others were all gray, like sandy water or uk milk covered in dust.

They all wanted to see the Great Mah feathers up close, and the elders had to bring order to the group. The eldest one signaled for Zen to speak and it said, "We trance like you. We trance deep into the salty waters or high into the freezing sky. We have seen this bird fly by, but only for a moment."

"My name is Shhaha. This is Mah and Odrak, whom you

know already," he spoke to all and smiled at Zen. "We offer you this to wear. We offer you this seed to plant."

Another stood and said, "My name is Thoth. Will you tell us how to plant it properly?" Mah could see that this one knew they kept a secret about the seed. "Will you show us how it's done?"

"Finally," Shhaha sighed to himself. "Only if you teach us your skill with the stones." He pointed to the figures that were all around them.

"This is not enough," spoke someone.

Then all eyes turned to Keishlee.

"Let us all trance together so that we may know your people," spoke Shhaha, avoiding what might next be said.

"You ask too much," spoke the wrinkled elder.

"You know too much of us already," spoke Thoth.

"Teach us then how to move through the ox stones you wear." Shhaha made his final offer.

"What you offer are prizes indeed, but if you would ask this for these, then what will you ask for your protection, and company to the Temples of Light?" asked Zen.

Shhaha turned to Mah and Odrak and felt ashamed to continue with their plan of trade. These people were not willing to ask such a thing from strangers and had planned on keeping Shhaha and his people here for many days in order to know them first. Shhaha said, "Nothing. We give you that freely, since all humans are kin who are descendants of the Seven Sisters."

There was much whispering again as some began to smile. Hands were clapped and movement started all around them. Stones were being placed around the room and long stone slabs were laid flat on top of them. The robed figures moved and a long stone slab was lowered over their seats. They signalled for Shhaha and his people to sit on the floor around the stone, while others brought in piles of food and drink.

It was quickly done, and Shhaha and his people were sitting across from the elders, who explained everything placed before them. There were eggs of many colors and sizes, which Shhaha and Mah refused to eat. Odrak and Ramaa made a feast of them, while Keishlee found the sweet and sour herbs better tasting on her fingers. A large stone bowl filled with honeyed peach and lily blossoms sat filling the air with sweetness, each pedal puffed up from being roasted in the misty air under the hot sun. Green tender leaves, salted and filled with a single large hairpiece [*butterfly*], were devoured by all. Shhaha unrolled one and found it almost too beautiful to eat, but this was his favorite insect, and he would not pass it up.

There were smaller bowls filled with all kinds of spice paste in which to dip long shoots of roasted bamboo or thick chucks of black spores. One of the nutty paste dips Shhaha found especially delicious. There were all kinds of fruits and vegetables which none of them had seen before, but they found the thing they called bread the most tasty, filling thing of all. It was like pounder, which Shhaha's women made, but was thicker by a hand and filled with tasty bits of soft salted roots.

The Tututs, as they were generally called, did more drinking than eating. Before the meal, they drank a stone goblet full of dew water, collected from the fog and mists. Then they ate a little and drank some river water. They did most of their solid food eating after that, and long after the meal was finished they continued with goblets of fruit wine or salted sour drip [*thinned doe's milk strained over a salt net and then mixed with palm sap*].

More wax sticks were lit as others asked to speak to Keishlee before they left. Everyone begged a touch or to be allowed to say a few kind words. As Keishlee expected, neither she nor Ramaa understood any of their words. They were totally different from those used between Shhaha and these elders. Ramaa and Keishlee had to respect Shhaha and his apprentices for what it took to know a people's words without ever having known the people.

"Who are they?" Ramaa pointed to the well-defined, light brown-skinned men standing about with weapons. They were the only ones with human color he had seen in the mountain.

The elder, whose name was Ibis, smiled broadly and said, "They are also Tututs, but they are the descendants of Aphro. They keep the sacred Waters of Aphro."

"May we see these waters?" asked Mah.

"They find you beautiful. All of them are willing to show you," spoke Zen. "But I think not."

Mah did not understand, but Shhaha stopped him from inquiring further. Tehuti and some of the others clapped their hands together and young creatures rushed about clearing away what remained of the food. The slab they had been eating from rose into a darkened place in the ceiling and soon only the robed creatures were left. The long slabs and sitting stones were gone and the room was brighter without so many people.

Zen and Thoth signaled for some of the others to leave, and greeted each by running dancing figures down each other's arms. Those that were leaving quickly covered their heads and faces, and left the room so fast, Ramaa tired from jerking himself around to see where they had gone.

Ibis and Tehuti moved closer to Zen to observe the strangers. Shhaha ordered Keishlee and Ramaa to seat themselves back in the larger room, away from them, while Mah and Odrak sat at his sides. Thoth then spoke quietly with the others.

Odrak found the sign words of the Tututs very complicated; the word sequences required only the arms, and the descriptive sense of each was given with the fingers. He enjoyed the flinging motions of their signs and decided to make this his major study among them.

The Tututs were fascinating to Mah in every respect. He had listened hard to the leave-takings and had gotten the taste of a few words. As always, it was his duty to learn strangers' words quickly and then pass them on to Shhaha and Odrak. Their words had high-low intonations which he sensed made drastic changes to the meaning of the words, but the sound of their voices and the way they used their tongues would be the hardest parts to learn. He did not think he'd ever be able to move his tongue as fast. His own mind kept pace with their meaning when they used words common to his people, but when they spoke only their words among themselves, it was like falling into a bright, sunlit well; he could see the words go by, and even grasp some of their meaning, but he would have to reach the bottom before he understood.

Shhaha watched Ramaa reluctantly remove himself from the sitting stone. He was walking closer to Keishlee than Shhaha had seen him do before. It worried him slightly, and he sealed Ramaa from the others with a mental potent. He wanted to be the first to sense Ramaa moving towards some danger, for it would be a grievous thing if Ramaa picked up his weapon now.

The section of the room Shhaha sat in was a small enclave within the larger room, but it too was filled with stone carvings. Most were near-human creatures like the Tututs. The carving styles were widely varied, but all were done in gray-colored stones, with drawn-out features: long arms, fingers and toes, and thin lips, large eyes and long noses. There were distinct blood lines kept here, even tho they kept no more history of their ancestors than a wandering tribe. Yet the walls and floor alone spoke of the uncountable lifetime of living already finished here.

Ibis was an elder over the line that produced the light-brown Aphros. It was also the oldest creature here and as such, held a high degree of respect and power over all the others. Tehuti was much younger, about as many seasons as Keishlee, but was wiser and older in its blood than Ramaa and Keishlee together. There seemed to be no elder over it here, and it was allowed free speech by all. The one called Thoth had many close kin among the elders. Their faces were pouty and fleshy, with slight traces of hair around their mouths and under their necks. They were distinguished mostly by large floppy ears and tightly knotted gray-white hair. Another one called TasiSabl, also had elders here, but had the look of one whose blood is used like spice for the blood of others. It was shorter and slightly heavier, but was the palest of them all, shaded the exact dust-gray color of the dying, with features in its face that looked like it might be so. TasiSabl was a source of frustration for Shhaha. Only its clear light voice assured him that it was truly alive. In his vision he had not seen it, nor was he aware of its presence here, and TasiSabl was the only one who dared to look Shhaha deeply eye to eye.

Zen was the speaker for these people, and it was the one who had been speaking while Shhaha observed their faces and the still and silent way they sat. Zen was younger than Tehuti, only seasons older than Odrak, with the same look of all the others, as of being older and taller than it was, as if its skin tired and grew older than its muscles. It was the past of what these people had been. It had the purest blood from fruit long fallen from the tree that gave these creatures life. It alone most resembled the faces of the carved figures around him.

While speaking it had lifted a sky-blue stone from the belly of a stone figure near the entrance to the enclave. A wall began to slide around behind it, and the floor moved, slowly turning around. Mah and Odrak had jumped to their feet, but not out of fear. An amazing thing was happening, something that confounded the mind, but like good blood apprentices, they were not filled with fear; instead, they were filled with admiration and curiosity.

Shhaha stretched his senses out to Ramaa. He knew he

was making another way for these creatures to enter him by showing them how he entered others, but he did not want to battle with these people, nor did he want to lose the life of one of his own. He awakened Ramaa to his memory of entering this place and how he should return. This would comfort him and Keishlee, as they were dumbfounded by the slowly moving wall, a wall of thinly carved serpents and leafy tendrils climbing around stone pillars, overlaid with figures of birds. When the room had ceased its moving, Shhaha was grateful that Ramaa continued to sit and Keishlee only to stare, and that the Tututs had not had to use their power on either of them.

An ornate spindle stone rose from the center of the floor when the room came to a stop. The Tututs sat in an semicircle around the room facing Shhaha. Mah and Odrak were still standing by his sides when Zen came over, walking slowly for the first time, as if it carried a heavy weight in its hands. Zen placed the blue stone atop the spindle point, and as he backed away the stone began to glow.

"You are the first outsiders to know this much of us in 3 rings [*apprx. 300 years*]. We are the Tututs, and we welcome you to our Mansion Management," Zen greeted Shhaha in its most formal manner and then did so again to his apprentices. "We have brought you here because you know how to bring your flesh to the Temples of Light, and because you possess clear memories of times none of you can claim you spied with either eye. And you," it flashed a palm down at Shhaha. "You see things before they happen, and know of many things that were not always dust. This is unknown to us. Even the powerless one..." it turned slightly toward Ramaa, "has misty memories of Great Sharings long since shared by all. By all except these people." It pointed to the others around the room. "We have never shared outside these mansion walls. In this ring of time, we received a summons to cross the sandy falls and enter the Temples of Light." Zen pointed to the blue stone.

Inside the blue circular stone appeared a crystal white light. From that they all received the vision of the place Shhaha knew as the Valley of Names. Its high white walls gleamed bright with reflected sunlight, but was shaded by tall spice trees and giant palms.

The vision vanished, and the elder Tututs slumped on their sitting stones as if all their strength was gone. Ramaa leaped up and rushed to the pillars of the wall that separated him from the others, calling for Shhaha to leave.

"Stop using your power on him," Shhaha demanded of the elders. "Age has made you bullies when there is no need."

"I shall determine what is needed," snapped Ibis weakly. "I shall determine the need."

The younger ones threw off their cloaks, spread their legs apart and clasped their hands together so that all their fingertips touched. They all gave Shhaha angry looks and then looked up to Ibis and Zen.

"No power is known to us that can breach these walls. No creature, living or dead, can make a way through their ox stones without our help, and no life form known to a Great Parent can make the soothstone sing!" roared Zen.

"It spoke to you?" asked Mah, attempting to use their words, and pointing to the blue stone.

"Not with words like you or I," replied Thoth.

"But a voice to our ears nevertheless. It came from this our sacred jewel, in this very enclave when all were at their rest. Everyone from this management heard the call, and came to see the soothstone singing still," spoke Zen with the memory of it fresh in its mind.

"Then you will go with us?" Shhaha offered again.

"Over there rests a polish of my parent, surrounded by the spindles of its womb," came the voice of Ibis to crack the silence. It pointed to Mah. "Move it a step or two."

Mah gave Shhaha a quick look and moved to head for the tall gray and black stone carving. Shhaha stayed Mah's feet with a single motion of his hand and Odrak ran over to the stone instead. He had taken notice of this figure many times during the meal. Its shiny smooth surface made a sheen of eerie shadows in this corner. It often made him think the figure had moved. Close up he could see that it was a naked feeder with strong arms, stringing together cloud ferns for making lace. She was surrounded by small slaves trying to climb up into her lap, their bodies were delicately formed and carved in great lifelike detail.

Odrak braced himself for the weight of the stone, since it appeared more massive than the others. He had no fear to touch it since it was not ox stone, so he pushed it from one side of the room to the other. Pushing it gave him a closer look, and he laughed to himself for having thought their work too great for comment. But someone had made a mistake in their carving between the legs of one of the slaves. It was obviously a male from the shape of the hands and toes, and the veined erection of his rod was clear. Yet the figure had one leg up, giving a full view of the other thing between his legs, a thing only female slaves have. A thing men call a blood wound, or which protectors call a pleasure bowl.

Odrak could not stop his eyes from checking all the others, and yes, some hint of it was there with all. His eyes followed the fingers twitching cloud fern leaves into strings, down to where the strings had been thickened and shaped, to rest upon the lifelike pile of lace in her lap that had been pulled moss thin. Just under the lace, between the feeder's open legs, laid something limp that should not have been there.

"You see, your people have the strength of body. It would take five of my people to move that figure a few steps. One of your young has moved it more than twenty stones," blurted Thoth.

"We would live in constant peril outside these mansion walls, which are the source of our power and our protection. Here nothing can harm us," spoke Zen dejectedly.

Shhaha studied Ramaa's face as he stood at the pillar wall holding stone snakes in each hand. He looked frightened, like a small slave, and would not stop the flow of his intent from reaching Shhaha's senses. He had to know the others here felt his fear as well.

"You are all filled with fear from your summons," Shhaha spoke, trying to keep a smile upon his face. "The summons is a reward for all the descendants of the Seven Sisters. It is a moment laid down in time, an order for all blood kin to share. A time of abundant touches, and for all to know that the Great Mother is alive and that she cares. She needs us to know this, and to know one another."

"We know your words because of this one," spoke the one called TasiSabl, pointing to Ramaa. "But we do not understand all their meaning. We know of the life you call the Great Mother, but it will not shield us from the harshness of the sun, or protect us from the creatures that would kill and eat us."

"You want blood promises for trade!" Mah said, astonished that someone would ask for such a thing as yet undeserved.

"You would have the power of the journey stone," huffed

Zen, against the harsh looks of Shhaha and Mah.

"No." Shhaha said flatly. "I want only the knowledge to use and keep the ox stone among my tools. If not for me, then for my apprentices."

"And these we will not accept in trade for our lives," groaned Mah. "To do so would give you a magic over us, and our people that I could not bear to live with."

Shhaha signaled for silence, sensing that Odrak and Ramaa were also about to speak. He watched as the elders opened their robes and began to fondle their necklaces of ox stones. When the blue soothstone glowed dimly, Shhaha tapped his blood wand three times on the floor. Mah and Odrak produced small ox stones from their waist sacks. Ibis' eyes brightened, but as Mah and Odrak held the stones out in its direction, they did not glow or burn their hands.

Shhaha tapped his blood wand once and then once again. Mah and Odrak picked up their blood wands, and still holding the ox stones, tapped the stones against the carved heads of Puutha at the top of their sticks, and began to chant the call of blessings.

"We are blood keepers from a river of blood so deep that we can never be removed from life. We keep our people's blood out of the mud and are human, as you can see," Shhaha began.

The elders began to twist about as the tall walkers called from somewhere nearby, while Ramaa and Keishlee echoed his chant with wordless calls.

"We keep to blood for healing and for keeping our people human. The Power in the blood makes for magic that is more than soothing, for potents that are powerful and for seeing into things yet to come. Run with us, but run of your own accord. Follow our lead as we follow the air...."

Shhaha was speaking the words for a runner's protection, but he was chanting the tones of his most powerful healing spell. Odrak and Mah touched his head with the ox stones and then went to do the same to the others. Mah got to Zen first and touched it with the stone. Zen let out a frightful screech. It whirled around almost knocking the orb soothstone from the spindle point. Odrak steadied Zen, but backed away as it began to remove its cloak and robes.

"You are a feeder," whispered Odrak, on seeing the small but fully formed feeder bags.

Some of the elders twirled around excitedly, while others

brought over wet lace for sponging Zen's face and arms. Shhaha was still chanting when they removed the rest of Zen's robes and laid him down on the cool stone floor. Mah almost dropped his stone and stepped back in disbelief. Zen had a lengthy pleasure stick, which was now dipped in the blood that ran down its legs.

Ibis was slowly making its way over to Shhaha. Others were already sitting at his feet. Some were cleaning the blood from Zen's legs and robes, while Mah and Odrak studied its body from a distance. Ramaa and Keishlee were both standing at the pillar wall trying to see what was going on.

"Shhaha. Mah! Odrak!" Ramaa cried softly, trying to get someone to tell him that Shhaha was all right.

"Zen is healed!" spoke Tehuti and TasiSabl, astonished.

"It is Shhaha's strongest magic. It flushes the body of tainted blood." Mah stumbled over his words, mixing them with those of the Tututs.

Odrak tried to remove the shock from his face before he spoke, but it came out when he said, "Simple body magic will he heal now, if you allow."

All the younger Tututs were now kneeling before Mah and Odrak. They even left Zen to bleed on the floor. Mah went about touching stone to heads after watching them undress. Each time he and Odrak had to be reminded of what they were set to do, as the surprise of seeing the mixed private parts together in one place unnerved them, and for a moment made it difficult to move.

After they recovered from the spell Shhaha had placed on them and the stones, Mah and Odrak helped to clean the others. Much blood was being wasted and Mah and Odrak could not stop themselves from getting sick. Shhaha moved into a full trance with all the blood surrounding him, and the elder Tututs rushed to use all that was left of their power to follow him. While Mah and Odrak were sick, the still bleeding Tututs took advantage of this moment and touched them, hoping to know them better.

In return, Odrak began cleaning away the blood from TasiSabl. He cleaned completely in order to investigate thoroughly, and found the seed bags as the upper most part of the blood wound folds. While cleaning each strand of hair, he parted the folds and found nothing lacking in its look or smell. He lifted a leg to clean a cheek, just to see if the other hole was there. He touched the pleasure stick as he put the leg back down, and was frightened away when it moved.

Mah's investigation included the feeder bags, which he was sure could produce some milk. They were small but firm, with large peaks, which were the darkest parts of their all too light colored bodies. When he finished, Mah was so embarrassed to see Ramaa and Keishlee staring at him and the creature beneath him, that he ran over and took his place back next to Shhaha. Odrak returned and they began the chant for new life, and Shhaha's eyes came back around. Shhaha looked down at the drained elders and laughed.

Some of them almost broke Shhaha's strings of bones trying to touch the skin of his legs, but all of them were too weak now and were falling quickly off to sleep.

"When they awake, we each shall have a string of ox stones more powerful than Keishlee's Tuk blade," smiled Shhaha, who then lowered his head to rest.

Ebbie sat before the Command Council of the Red Warriors. She had been called before them for an interview before leaving to join her new mate in his offices at the Imperial Towers, headquarters for Wind Limited. Feegarmardar had warned her that they would refuse her application for employment, which they did, but they were keeping her longer than she expected and she wasn't sure why.

Seven large, muscled men sat before her in the library of the Pagangenearchs acolyte training center, each a different shade of brown or black, and dressed in the black and red of their rank. They were studying her every move, watching her words and listening to her body. She had already been with them an hour, but they continued to question her about her father, her mother, her dead brothers and sister, the other men who knew her mind or body, her experiences in New York, her job at New York University, her reason for becoming a librarian, her relationships with the few political figures she knew, why she wanted a job in the public relations department of Wind Limited when she had no prior training, and why didn't she apply for a job in research like Mageeta Sparrow or Michael Blackamoor, the other two research trainees?

Ebbie was tired of the all the flashing questions, but did not let it show. She managed to be pleasant and even to flirt with one of the men she suspected of not being a Red Warrior at all. She watched them go over and over the massive materials that made up her personal file, listening to them speak highly of her father and of their loyalty to the sisterhood. Not having been prepared by Feegarmardar or Teresa Eckers (who was beginning to oversee her training more, now that Feegarmardar prepared to leave for Japan), Ebbie wasn't sure what these men really wanted of her.

Louis Bogdan, who she only knew from a file she had seen, was a General in the Red Warriors. He was pleasant enough, but unable to hide his dislike of her bald head. He stared at her between questions as if he were trying to use some power to grow her hair back. Failing, he snapped another question at her with the hope of startling some reaction from her. But Ebbie was getting the best training in personal control she had ever known. She had already judged them unable to force reactions from her without using physical force. These were men used to playing war games, unlike the command forces of the Red Warriors, who actually fight battles. This would only be a game, and for her to win, she only had to keep cool.

"Woman Farmer," Louis Bogdan addressed her formally. "You understand the necessity for this interrogation. Ethiopia has many enemies and Wind Limited has many more. If we were not...."

"I am a Pagan...."

"Not yet," snapped the man Ebbie suspected of not really belonging to the ranks of the Red Warriors. "You have not presented a testing. You have not even been asked to kill anyone yet."

"I may not be, yet. But why do you say such stupid things to me about the sisterhood? I can no longer be moved against my sisters. Please do not try that again," Ebbie spoke, sliding all her controlled anger out under her words. She already had her hand on the microwave laser gun hidden in her bag. Smiling at them still, she was prepared to kill Louis first, if anyone of them directly slandered the sisterhood again.

"We are Red Warriors!" Louis rose from his seat and made a gesture that would signal any minor Red Warrior to his aid. "There is no need for your temper, or your ready hostility." His eyes moved down to Ebbie's hidden hand. "We assume the sisterhood has tested you and has approved of you, and that is enough. There is simply no position available for you at this time, and without qualifications, your motivations must be double checked. Remember that."

"If you are so determined to work for Wind Limited, why not get your father to intercede?" spoke another man, who smiled at her snidely.

Ebbie had had enough. She rose, slowly but with finality. Only an order would seat her again. Silence bristled around the room and Louis said goodbye to her and she left, bowing to each of them before she actually closed the door behind her.

Louis was still standing when another Red Warrior, a Command Chief, entered and silently signaled to Louis that the woman Ebbie Farmer was out of the building.

"She is the best of the lot," spoke Theacknar Kamsa to Louis. "She understands loyalty." He smiled, remembering her subtle move toward some hidden weapon in the folds of her bag. "She has the highest ratings, has outperformed all others in memory training, and has the look of the panther in her blood line. I vote for her over the others."

"Michael Blackamoor has a photographic memory," spoke another man trying to get closer to Theacknar and the file he was still going over.

"Romie Beldesech's ratings were just as high," interjected another.

"But," Theacknar silenced the others about to speak, "Miss Farmer's abilities are dialectically profound. The man Blackamoor hides his ability from us, further compounding his weaknesses. And, she is the daughter of the father."

"No man can say," grunted Louis.

"The mother was a priestess for the American order of the Oracles of the Eastern Star," suggested another.

"But it looks like favoritism," snapped another.

"Again. More favoritism they'll say," spoke Louis.

"Out of 12 world oracle organizations, 40 different religious interviews and 8 business seminars, the woman Farmer was the only one to gain acceptance into all their minor orders. I vote for her as well," spoke the highest ranking officer in the room.

There was a grumble around the room, but all the others finally agreed with him.

"But why must the new Minister of Justice be American? Why? Why? Why?" shouted Louis.

"We've gone over this," spoke Theacknar, rising to

confront Louis. "Only the blood of a African-American will seal the breach. Only once they are returned to their rightful places among our people, will we see an end to turmoil between ourselves, and our lands undivided. The wound must be healed and the curse lifted."

"You and your talk of curses and blood," snapped Louis at Theacknar. "Training! That's the key. Look at me. Training put me here, nothing else."

"We have our two," spoke another, "and we also have the French one in reserve if Blackamoor and Beldesech fail the testing. Let the women have their two. They won't try anything against us. There's too much at stake. They need us more than we do them."

"You're wrong about that," said Louis, turning his eyes around for thought. "But we do have Blackamoor, and they say he has been some help in the research labs."

"Yes, Blackamoor has come a long way. He is good," spoke another man.

"Yes, but the woman Farmer is better. She predicted the attack on the synfuels lab in Debow. They say she is pregnant already, and Blackamoor still refuses to plant his seed."

Odrak and Mah sat on each side of Shhaha, while he and the elder Tututs slept on the sitting stones. Zen and Tehuti took care to clean and redress the others. Ramaa and Keishlee sat just on the other side of the pillar wall in silence, watching the moving Tututs with awe and suspicion. Nothing was said for a long time, but there was a sound like humming coming from out in the corridors and halls that surrounded their rooms. It was a dim sound, but it vibrated the floor and walls, making the air tingle around them with the sensation of waiting, like a heartbeat almost stilled and trembling to beat on.

Neither Mah or Odrak looked at each other, nor did they share the shock or frustration of what they felt. All their attention was spent on watching the air around Shhaha and keeping themselves tuned to the younger Tututs among them. Ibis was the only one Mah felt was not truly sleeping. The others were off into a sleep so deep, that if not for their eyes rolling around their head, they might have been mistaken for dead, but even under the cascade of folds from their robes, Odrak sensed the greedy breathing and the involuntary muscle movement, as the sleep unwound the tensions within.

Zen began preparing something with small stones that he removed from each of the stone figures in the room. Tehuti, Delta and TasiSabl moved the elders back against the sitting stones, which took all their effort and quite some time, but neither Mah nor Odrak made any move to assist or question them.

Mah checked himself to get some sense of the time of day or night. He listened for calls from the tall walkers, which he knew were nearby. He opened his mouth and used the high-head, soundless calls to speak with them, but the thoughts did not travel far between these thick walls.

The tall walkers would have called to Keishlee if they were in need, but she sat quietly watching Tehuti and the one called Tut, who looked like very close kin. She should have sensed Mah's call, but Tut had her eyes and Tehuti had her mind. As Mah looked closer at the expression on Keishlee's face, something about it shocked him. She snapped around and peered behind one of the pillars towards him. He turned his eyes away, now embarrassed at having used his power to see past the columns into her, and what she was just beginning to understand of what she felt. Turning away, he saw his own expression on Odrak's face.

Mah suddenly felt the slip of his hold on the space around him. He jerked up to see Tehuti looking at him with dismay and longing, his eyes pleading with him to say some words that he might understand. Tehuti looked around the columns to sneak a peak at Keishlee, to which Ramaa took offense. Zen clapped his hands together many times, in such a fashion that Odrak could sense the words within the slapping sounds of flesh.

Mah already had his eyes on the entrances when groups of Aphros came into the larger cavern. They were carrying sticks with fanged teeth for weapons, and motioning for Ramaa and Keishlee to come with them. Ramaa and Keishlee stood but looked over to Mah and Odrak for some word. They in turn looked to Shhaha, while Zen called two of the taller Aphros over and spoke to them through the snake-covered pillars.

Shhaha struggled a bit, as if with his sleep, and Ibis fell over on himself near one of the stone figures. Thoth and some of the others rushed to him and sat him back against the stone. Mah went over to the end of the pillars where Keishlee and Ramaa were now standing. "Look," he whispered and pointed to Odrak attending Shhaha and mixing powders from Shhaha's ankle bones.

"Odrak prepares the black salt. None here will harm us. Go with them."

Ramaa heard the sizzle of the salt turning black and noted the special bladder always used to carry it. He turned and smiled at the approaching Aphros and their simple weapons. The slightest suggestion of danger to Shhaha's person would bring these Tututs to a horrible death. He almost felt sorry for the creatures in the room with Odrak. Odrak was quick to anger, and having had no comfort for more than a moon would make him a ready taker of life. He saw no change or understanding of what Odrak had done on their faces, and held a hand out to the Aphros to hold and lead him away. They would not touch him or Keishlee, but as they left he could see them all beginning to notice the changed person standing guard over Shhaha, and he was glad of it. Black salt was a horrible death, and no human, or whatever these creatures were, should have to suffer it without a warning.

"I give you the warning," Mah slapped his hand against his chest and pointed to Odrak. "No harm must come to Shhaha from any of you, or your people. No harm must fall on our kin, Ramaa and Keishlee...."

"Keishlee?" someone repeated to Zen. "Keishlee? That is the name for the only woman?"

Zen ignored the words and the others trying to get its attention. It walked slowly over to Mah and its eyes were on fire. As Zen stood before him, Mah was surprised, but glad Odrak hadn't dashed some of the black salt on it already. In the past, the danger in Zen's eyes alone would have been enough.

"You who know not the secrets of life, dare, you dare to think of us as shallow creatures of mud. We are Tututs!!" Zen almost shouted, pulling back the opening to its robes to reveal the chain of ox stones around its neck. "Life is sacred to us," it continued, as it looked hard to the spot where Keishlee had left water stains on the floor. "All life is sacred to us. We are human, like yourselves. We think and care for our suckles as you do."

Mah did not understand all of what Zen was trying to say, but he got the meaning and it hit him like a slap in the face. Odrak might kill him soon, and the black salt had only been made as a warning to them and a comfort for Ramaa.

After signaling for Odrak to keep his place, Mah said, "Our Keeper of the Blood and your...your elder are trance raiding each other."

The Tututs turned to Ibis and each touched the hidden ox stones around their necks. Mah could see the larger center stone on Zen's neck, shaped in the likeness of a human figure, with head, arms and legs. He admired the detailed workmanship of the small black stone, but quickly turned his attention back to Shhaha and Odrak, neither of whom had moved.

"Our Ibis is with your old one?" asked Tut as it came forward. "I cannot see them."

"I cannot see them either," came a rush of voices. Thoth held them back as some made moves toward Shhaha.

"Do not touch Ibis again," ordered Zen to someone approaching. "And do not go near their old one." His voice became a whisper as he glimpsed Odrak move into his stance of attack. There was no doubting that all the Tututs standing near were in mortal danger.

"Be still, Odrak," spoke Mah plainly. "We have come to you in peace, but will do much damage here if any lay bold hands on our Keeper of the Blood."

"His move is something used to kill," moaned someone Mah could not see.

"There is great speed in his step," suggested another.

"What strength of body," cried yet another.

"Will he kill our Ibis?" asked Tut.

Both Thoth and TasiSabl moved closer to Tut, flashing desperate looks toward Zen. The room was silent except for the crisp of burning light from the waxen sticks.

"Aaah! it is done. Aaah," came a voice that was not Shhaha's. "Beautifully done."

"Whose beauty?!" replied Zen, as if in echo to a chant.

"An older one than stones can remember," came the voice again, and Mah knew it was the elder Ibis.

"In truth?!" came the question like a reply by all.

Odrak was just to the side of Shhaha and already on his knees. The sacred Aaah! had been used and Mah too should be on his knees, or at least sitting on his heels, but he waited instead to hear the word from Shhaha, who was just beginning to open his eyes, a broad smile beginning to beam out over his face. When his eyes rolled back and Mah could see them clear and bright, and looking directly at him, he slowly fell to his knees, motioning the others to follow his lead.

"Do so, and sit as they. It will do your body good to fold it closer to the stones that have become our...like our, our kin, or clan relation. The friend to our clan. For we are a clan. True, Shhaha? True?" rattled Ibis, struggling to pick itself up off the floor.

Everyone was sitting in some fashion closer to the floor when Ibis reached Shhaha, still rattling about truth and being related to stone.

"We cannot touch him," started Zen when Ibis reached out to touch Shhaha.

Ibis snapped its frail body around and the quickness of it brought silence to Zen. "Do not speak until the Keeper of the Blood has accepted you in his presence. He has just come back from a visit with the great force within. I have been with him, and we together have laid hands on that which is all there is. This is simply a respect he must insist on. I need a moment myself, but I am too filled to ever rest again. I want to thank the elder loves." It waved a hand in the direction of the sleeping elders. "I have used up all their strength just to keep pace with Shhaha on this journey. A good use of strength. A beautiful resource of time. Time, is there one among you who understands time?" it seemed to ask the group, but Mah knew better than to speak. "Time is something we lost within the power of the journey stone. They call it an ox stone. It is very rare in their lands and they knew not the power." It turned back to Shhaha and clasped its hands together.

Shhaha moved a hand in front of Odrak as Zen and some of the others rushed about the room performing some private task. Mah had eyes everywhere. He hardly understood any of what Ibis was talking about, and Shhaha had yet to even speak to his mind. He stared at Odrak for a moment and saw the confusion on his face as well, but made no sign to speak to him with his eyes. Instead he watched Zen remove the large blue stone, holding itself against the spin of the room, as Ibis moved toward the disappearing pillar wall.

Ibis signaled again with hand claps, and a path opened between the poorly seated group of Tututs. Shhaha rose and walked beside Thoth, while the others wiped the floor clean before them.

Once on the other side of where the pillar wall had been, Shhaha turned around, and Mah felt for the first time the immensity of the rooms. Shhaha's power was all around him, like the first time he felt Shhaha spell casting. Shhaha deserved his name, "magic voice," and he used it now, ordering Mah and Odrak to follow him.

"Leave these," Ibis laughed at Zen, who was collecting the pieces of ox stone it had piled at the base of the spindle stone. "Rubble, all of it." Ibis kicked the stones, which had fallen into a pile when the spindle stone went back into the floor. "Come all to the hall of past journeys. Come see why their elder has such a name. Come and I will tell you of our ancient loves, lost to time and that which makes all things crumble to dust. We shall gladly share what we have with those who can give us back those lost loves. Come see!"

Shhaha followed Ibis out into the dark corridor, with Odrak following after. Mah and Zen were near a state of shock, and did not understand any of what Ibis was saying. All the others looked to Zen for understanding. Mah signaled them to follow, but none would move until Zen headed out. Mah was the last to enter the dark unlit corridor, leaving the other elder Tututs still sleeping on the cool stone floor. Only the sound of their footsteps made clear in which direction he should go.

The floor was smooth and well worn by use. They descended the dark, down-sloped ledges into other corridors before they saw torch-light. Mah had heard the silent breathing and was not surprised to see the walls lined with people, sitting on stones or standing, all robed so that their faces and hands could not be seen.

They entered another well-lit room, passing Aphro guards, who humbled themselves and bowed as Ibis passed. Mah was the last to enter and was glad to see that most of them were as tall as he, broad-chested and trim. But they had hair so short he found it hard to think of them as older than himself.

Mah was staring at the round-eyed Aphros and trying his best to think of them as human. They were exactly the same from one to the other. In their groups there was not even a smile that was different between them.

A moan lit up the silence around Mah like fired torches. Everyone was looking at small snakes, newly hatched from red and green shells. They had gathered at the base of a towering structure in the center of the room. Shhaha was signaling Mah over. Ibis was still talking, brightly and with great affection, but in the words of his people, which bounced off Mah's ears like hairpieces off water. As he approached the thing built up from a well in the ground, Mah was baffled by the crude objects before him. A high stone thing that could only be considered a wall rose up from the ground in various levels, altered, it seemed, for the purpose of actually climbing up to the peak where tall ox stone figures stood. The stone figures were now only silhouettes of what they used to be. Having been chipped away or diminished by time, their features were rendered impossible to comprehend.

"These our ancient loves, were polished for hand use," Ibis was saying as it removed small round stone balls from different levels of the altered wall. "Listen," Ibis hearkened, striking the balls together.

The room glistened with a sound new to the clan of the Tall Walkers. Mah rushed to Shhaha's side, looking closely at the round stones being tapped together in Ibis' hands. "Chock-ting, chock-ting," went the crisp clash of stone. The sound vibrated throughout the room and up the altered wall, and Odrak gasped as the small snakes began to stand at attention.

"Fear not the serpent of the ancient loves," Ibis said quickly to stop its people from rushing from the room. "It is the savior, the blessing of our people. Oh! Oh, what beauty it has when it is fully grown," it continued and stuck its hand out to one of the standing snakes.

Of course it bit Ibis. Odrak raised the sack of black salt but was stopped by Shhaha, who only smiled and signaled for him to step aside. He too now allowed the snake to bite him and then sucked dry the spot of blood it made. Ibis began tapping the stone balls together again, saying, "There is so much I shall tell you, my loves, and I know I shall have the time needed to do the deed. Come, gather round the altar of the serpent's nest. Take your places upon the steps of...."

"There is no time, our Ibis love," spoke Shhaha using the words of the Tututs. He then sorted through the other stones on the altered wall until he found a stone like the ones Ibis was tapping together. He twisted gently and to the surprise of all, except Ibis, it came apart in two halves. He held one half opened for Ibis to see. Ibis smiled and laughed and then tasted the powder that lay inside. Shhaha emptied the dry contents and held it over to Odrak who stared at it, not understanding what Shhaha intended.

Carefully, Mah removed the black salt sack from Odrak's

hands and poured the entire contents into the ball. Shhaha sealed the halves of the stone together again with a twist. He gave Ibis a look and waited for him to stop the stone tapping. The snakes began to slither about the levels again, and Shhaha signaled Mah to place the ball on a spot high up the altered wall.

There was some hesitation, but Mah complied. Odrak watched as the snakes sensed his movement. Some slithered away, but others came to greet him, hissing their tongues at him as he climbed up the wall. Odrak looked up at Shhaha, but turned away before anything was said with his eyes.

"Remember the spot. Remember the polish our Shhaha has filled for us. It is powerful magic," he said as he signaled Zen to take another path up the altered wall.

Odrak was suddenly jealous. The small surprised cries Mah made from the snake bites no longer reached his ears. Something was being offered here and he was not to be included. He watched Mah return and saw the tiny blood spots on his legs and arm, but Odrak's eyes were comfortless. He turned to see Zen reaching the top of the wall, where two tall ox stone figures had been carved countless generations ago. He put to memory every move Zen made and the look of the place. He earmarked the silent hand signals from Ibis, which told Zen to chip away the fingers and return the pieces to him. All the while the room grew more silent as hostility brewed among the Tututs over what Ibis had decided to do.

When Zen returned, Ibis spoke with some of his people and they carried the many pieces away. Zen was furious, but did not speak. When Shhaha removed one of the snakes from the wall, Zen shook with violent hatred and turned to the other Tututs, who now stared at Ibis as if it had lost its mind.

"See, I warned you not to allow this filth into our management," snorted the Tutut called Opetimem.

"Why have they even been allowed to see the sacred icon?" shouted Zen.

Ibis laughed at them. "It will take much time, but all will be clear. Trust me," it said, using words Odrak and Mah understood. "Yes, trust me. Yes, trust Shhaha and listen."

Shhaha was tending Mah's snake bites, and listening to the silence return to the room. He had given Odrak a snake to bag, and as he did so, he could hear the hearts of the Tututs beating defiantly, angry now with the visitors they had agreed to bring in among them.

A space was slowly opening between the Tututs and the people of the Tall Walkers as Shhaha continued to lick clean the blood from Mah's wounds. When he was done, he sat Mah down at the base of the altered wall near the opening to the well below. He signaled for Odrak to begin an echo chant and then looked hard at the Tututs and said, "Humans of the mix, endeavor to make a pick of tooling stone and bone to fix a polish of a finished life. With your hands you do as we do, and create a thing of chanting, bringing to your people a planting of stone; the heart of your home, as we leave you here alone. Then visit the way before us, go on journey both day and night in trust, that we will do as we can, for those who are both a woman and a man, to live and learn from the greatest sharing yet to come, where we all shall stand as one."

Shhaha spoke their words even with their lilt of tone and accent. He repeated the chant over again in words Odrak would better understand. Odrak then took up the echo in earnest, still only calling out the even tones of sound. The cavern filled with the ringing of words that now bounced off the walls exactly as the tapping stones had done. It was a very different chant for Shhaha, but his voice began to have its effect on the Tututs, and even Ibis danced about in place, unaware that he even moved at all. Odrak watched Shhaha as he threw his voice over the altered wall and brought the snakes back out from their hiding places to stand erect again.

"Crawling up and over walls there is a creature known to all. It bites and leaves a patch but brings no harm you thought to last. Now listen as I say, kill this thing that truly makes you ill. Your bodies over time have lost their strength, their colors, and are pale. Clear your management of this filth, and watch no more your bodies wilt. Over time you may once again dare to roam the land, and touch the places of your mind's eye with the heart of your hand."

Later, Mah would place this chant in memory as a call to duty. For now he began to hear the words as if slowly going into trance. He felt the poison of the yellow snakes heat up his blood and cause his muscles to flex without control. The Tututs were searching the cavern halls now and stomping crawling insects that were everywhere about. Ibis followed after them, repeating some of the chant and then leading some of its people to the altered wall, where it held out their arms to be bitten by the snakes, only once, and then returned them to be moved by the power of Shhaha's voice.

When all was done, they sat on the floor holding each other, exhausted from their romp. It was obvious now that Zen and Mah, having gotten an extra dose of the poison, were both suffering from its effect. Zen was doubled over on itself and being supported by two Aphros, who came to help kill off the hard shelled insects.

The Tututs who had left with the finger pieces returned, followed by many of their people, who seemed forbidden to enter the cavern chamber. They presented the stones to Ibis, who turned them over, checking the workmanship with its hands and the quality of the stone under the light of the torches. Ibis smiled approvingly at the Tututs and touched their faces, then presented the stones to Shhaha, who was once again tending Mah.

"There is no time to teach you the way through these journey stones now, my apprentice. There is a better place where you both shall learn," said Shhaha, signalling Odrak over to receive the first string of stones.

Odrak felt their smoothness and coolness as they laid across his chest. Strings of them hung down behind and he felt them resting on his back. He helped Shhaha hold Mah steady, who was beginning to suffer violently. But Mah accepted the matching string of stones with a forced smile. Shhaha took the last of the strings, a bare thing with only one journey stone, a solid end finger pointing up and held in place by two other tiny stones. They were attached to a string of knotted fibers like dried animal skin, tough and leathery. The others looked on in their weariness and Odrak could see that they were beginning to comprehend the worthiness of this trade.

Shhaha spoke their words freely, more slowly so that Odrak and Mah might understand, but with the ease that comes with something familiar to the tongue. He called over each Tutut by name, his voice compelling them to movement.

They knew what had to be done, but did not expect him to know as well. "Beautifully done!" came their remark as each touched the stones and then the faces of Shhaha and his apprentices. Each attempted to linger with Mah, whose guard was weakened, but Ibis moved them on.

"Whose beauty?" came the chant-like response.

"By those who save their polish for the journey stone

alone," replied the voices moving about the room.

"Are they beautiful?" came the voices of those gathered out in the corridor.

"No pain," replied each as they left Mah or Odrak.

Even Zen was brought over in its weakened state, its eyes red and its face darkened from an inner pain. It struggled with the words and groped to use the power of its own hand to touch the stones, but had to be helped. When it was done they led it away, and sat it near Ibis to be held up by the Aphros standing near, waiting to assist.

"We must leave you now," spoke Shhaha.

"I regret that we have not the proper robes for such a journey, but we shall make them for the day when you shall return to us," spoke Ibis for all to hear.

Shhaha looked up at Ibis sorrowfully, saying, "You know we shall not return this way. You have seen."

"We may hope," Ibis said and lowered its eyes.

"Have you made your selections?" Shhaha asked Ibis.

"Yes," it replied and turned to the Tututs now standing around him. "You, our TasiSabl and our Tehuti, shall make the journey with them to the Great Sharing. Bring with you fresh robes from the elder stores and select two strong Aphros to assist you each. Bring also the carry stones of your elder loves. Only the best polishes should be taken, as many as you can carry in your robes, and also, fence a toot to bring as an offering for the Hall of Names."

Zen was struggling, obviously upset with the selection. Odrak too had thought it would have been one of those selected to join them, but if they were to leave now, it was in no condition to make the journey. However, neither was Mah.

Ibis led Odrak and Shhaha, who carried Mah out of the cavern, leaving the others behind. The Aphros, who seemed to need no word, followed as well, and they were led through many turns and up and out into a mountain field full of growing foods, small animals and bright moonlight. Ramaa and Keishlee were being tended by a few of their people, and the tall walkers were nearby, drinking from a fall of water from a higher mountainside.

They had passed the day away enclosed inside a cavernous mountain. Odrak was surprised that the tall walkers took to walking through the dark and low ceiling corridors so well, but as he could see, the Tututs had made friends with them. It was a rare thing for people outside their clan, but he realized that it was their mix of natures which made them an easy people to be near.

Odrak greeted Keishlee and Ramaa and did not watch or help as Shhaha laid Mah in Keishlee's arms. Instead he helped the Tututs, who were bringing over their belongings, and called over the tall walkers to repack them for the continued journey. He remembered the words he needed to tell the Tututs to gather food and water, and watched as they packed a feast into the sack made of the Great Mah feathered cape.

Keishlee was glad to be with her people again and tended Mah as if he were a slave. Ramaa was glad to see that Odrak had separated himself from Mah, but it was an unhealthy thing for him to be willing to allow Mah to suffer. He knew the kind of man a broken-hearted protector grew into, and he hoped Odrak was not going to have that flaw in his nature.

The moon moving high in the night sky only served to remind Shhaha that they had to leave the mountains of the Tututs before daybreak. Contact with the Tututs had given him many visions, not all of them pleasant, but he had been casting a spell around his apprentices since the journey began, and they were almost ready to come into their full powers, and, to take the Test of Blood. Just thinking of it gave him shivers, as he looked back into the vision he held of the great halls and temples they would find in the Valley of Names. Contact with all the people there would serve to prepare his people for the future he saw before them. No cost was too great to see Mah and Odrak standing on the peaks of the mountain temple. Their lives and powers would be a thing of legend, of great storytelling for generations upon generations to come.

Ramaa helped Odrak pack the tall walkers with Tehuti's belongings. There was not much, but as he looked upon the slope of the tall walker's back, it was hard to believe they had collected so much. It had to be roped to the front legs of the tall walker so that nothing would slide off. There were so many gifts—those from the Great Mahs, and the furs from the Kamituians. The cloth from the Hoteps and the Tuk women alone made a bundle big enough for a woman to carry. With all these sacks and bladders of food and drink only one tall walker would be available for riding.

Ibis was as happy as a slave after the rainy season. It talked to its people nonstop as they were led down from the mountain garden back into the mist and fog. Many followed, including some of the elders who had risen from their sleep, surprised that Ibis had the strength to join them for the long walk down.

Ramaa carried Mah until the mist started to clear and Ibis said they would have to leave them. They said their goodbyes and took leave of Tehuti and TasiSabl after wrapping their arms around each other and squeezing tightly. They begged Keishlee with wanting looks and she allowed them all to embrace her. There was something she would later call lust in the way they did so, but Keishlee was not offended and looked after them as they disappeared into the mists.

"Be kind and look after our loves," Ibis asked Shhaha as they embraced. "They must reach the Valley of Names in good health."

"I know the cost your people will pay otherwise. I have seen as well as you. They will be safe with us," spoke Shhaha as he pulled the cloak hood up over Ibis' head.

Suddenly Ibis seemed tired and drained, as if its age had caught back up to it. Two Aphros had to assist him back up the misty mountain path. Shhaha looked over the group and was glad to see Ramaa walking once again with only the blood wand in hand. The Tuk weapons were hidden in their bundles packed on the tall walker, and only Keishlee had hers strapped to her side. Mah was being carried by two of the Aphros, while Ramaa took the lead next to Tehuti, who would show them the way out of their swamp lands.

Odrak had been bringing up the rear and was just passing someone in the fog when he heard Ibis say, "Speak of our Shhaha love with more respect. He is only a man, but a creature that would give up his life in this journey to save his people. Such a one is better than the Aphros among us. Our loves will return to us, when he will not return to his."

Belinda Coffy speaking at the International Convention of Women Philanthropists: "...I say men are only the reflections of women's desires, or worse, what women have left over for them to be. Women stay virgins, while men are whores. Men remain caretakers in their homes, while women continue to make the word "mother" meaningful. If a woman takes up a needle and thread then it becomes a woman's thing. If a man takes up a hammer and nail, it becomes a man's thing, and to keep our identities, we rarely cross over those invisible lines. Over time the war of the sexes has grown like a disease, spreading over into race relations, where as if whites do it, then blacks don't...."

"Of Life and Death and Joy and Strife"

The Tututs were tireless walkers. Used to stone floors, they found the wet swamp lands a splendid sensation and the soft grasslands a pleasure to endure. Everything was a delight to them, even the many flying and biting insects that were everywhere here. They praised the warmth of the days walking in light, and kept their robes off to be touched by the sun. Half naked, they were burnt badly time and time again, but refused to be stopped by these troubles, forcing Shhaha to take serious notice of their resilient skin.

Like Keishlee, they cleaned themselves in water and collected new types of food, but they also copied Ramaa and Odrak, and dug for roots and ground foods and learned to release their waters while standing. Sleeping on soft ground was an enormous joy, and tho they did not sleep long, they slept like the dead and began to enjoy their dreaming. Hard ground bruised them so badly, Shhaha often had to tend to them, but they healed faster than his own people.

The songs of new birds were a thing to make them cry sweet tears, and seeing Keishlee speak with animals without touching them made them fall at her feet with praise. They missed the sunrise view from their mountain management and the reflected colors over their misty peaks, but enjoyed the sight of flat lands stretching out in all directions, and could not believe the land had no edge to fall off from.

The larger animals gave them some terror at times, like the large flesh-eating creatures they all had to run from, or the giant hawks they saw ripping a lone bush horse to pieces. The Tututs ate some animal flesh, but found it a horror that animals ate each other with such frequency and ferociousness. They cried with Ramaa when they could not rescue a colorful squawk from the clutches of a wild wolf hound, and helped to kill the creature when it threatened to climb the tree and finish off the squawk's mate and young.

Watching the Tututs fight, Shhaha's people began to have their first doubts about bringing these Tututs along. All the Tututs were uncommonly weak, but they were thoughtless killers, especially the Aphros, who, when caught without weapons, would use their mouths to rip a creature to bits, even to biting at the vines of the heart to pull it out. Great enthusiasm was their greeting to everything they saw, but a lust for life as well as death, was the dreaded mark they wore. With the Tuk blades and the Aphros keeping pace with Ramaa at the lead, more killing was done in a day than would have been done in a moon's span without them. But Shhaha was in a hurry, and having to be sidetracked by savage creatures made them all kill quickly.

When Shhaha considered the original plans of the Tutut elders, and their wanting to send the hateful Opetimem and the mindless Delta, he was glad that only these had come. But the Tututs did have many fine qualities. Tehuti was a marvel at getting others to like it. When it touched gentle animals it was a better translator than Keishlee or Shhaha. It became quickly adept at calling the tall walkers, and even learned how to stay astride and ride. Ramaa found its company pleasing, and took it on raids against packs of horned boar. But it was TasiSabl's company he enjoyed the most whenever he needed comfort. It picked splinters from his feet, and gave Ramaa body rubs that always put him straight to sleep.

TasiSabl taught Keishlee new ways of preparing food, using only preheated stones, or stewing ground foods [*peas & beans*] in preboiled seasoned water while they walked. Keishlee was also grateful for the use of its chipping tool, which could be used to hollow out stones very quickly, for making stewing pots or drinking bowls.

Shhaha's only complaint was that the Aphros pressed

themselves on the Tututs every night for relief. From the first night Shhaha argued with them, insisting that they refrain from the possibility of having to make this journey rooted. The Aphros promised to spill their seed elsewhere, but Shhaha continued to argue with them, until Tehuti told him that the Aphros had the right and could not be refused, since neither of them was mate-locked [*mated*].

Allowing them their customs, Shhaha spent his nights away from the sounds of their coupling, and to his surprise, Ramaa and Keishlee both slept near him. They too did not want to hear the unusual and harsh talk the Tututs and Aphros made during the night.

Most of Shhaha's time was spent with Odrak, going over the teachings necessary for him to be a true Blood Keeper. They went over lessons of blood rites and practiced new spell chants and calls for spirit healing. Shhaha taught Odrak the low-voice calls of the Waterhorse clan, an almost soundless voice like that of the tall walkers, except that it was all lower range belly tones, instead of the high tones from the head. They studied the new words they had learned on this journey and made healing potents. Odrak went over and over all the lines of blood from his clan and stored in memory the details of Shhaha's trance with Swaahali.

Odrak described to Shhaha, again, the elements of his trance state back with the Kamituians, and the visitation by the three women and the skinless slave that spoke to him. Shhaha taught him to care for the yellow snake they carried and how to collect the poison from its fangs, which could cure many sicknesses from insect bites. They practiced thought sharing and light trancing for visions, and ended each day by studying the parts of the human body.

The journey seemed to move along more quickly and with more enthusiasm than before. Shhaha found everyone in better cheer for the new company—except Odrak, who, outside his training sessions with Shhaha, fought back worry and frustration over Mah's continued sickness.

Most of the time Mah was carried by the Aphros, who were glad of it. Shhaha gave them a potent to feed him at sunrise each day, which they never failed to do just as the sun was breaking. They took turns carrying him between them. They helped him relieve himself of body waste and kept him clean and groomed, even making sure to clean and replace the spice seeds whenever he soiled himself.

For 8 days and nights Mah was unconscious. He burned with fever and had to be dried often, and seasoned to keep out evil spirits. When they walked and the Aphros were busy with the noisy toot they carried, Mah was tied to the back of the free tall walker and allowed to moan in agony while the animal fed itself. He spoke while sleeping and could not keep down solid food when fed. Keishlee wanted to tend him herself, but Shhaha wanted her to hold the lead with Ramaa since she was the fastest runner next to Odrak.

Odrak could not bring himself to touch Mah, and Shhaha seemed not to consider him. When they rested and he was not teaching Odrak, he tranced and left Mah's tending to the Aphros. Once Keishlee commented that she thought Mah was losing his scent to the funk of the fever. Odrak's only response was to hand her some of the Great Mah oil, and then returned to his meditations.

Mah managed to get better without Shhaha's care, which was what Shhaha wanted to see. When he was finally able to walk on his own, the Aphros still insisted on carrying him. They alone talked with him that day, and all could overhear their possessiveness towards him, each grunting at the other when it was time to switch, or whenever he accepted food from another. One night the Aphros accepted the refusal of the Tututs to couple for relief, and at sunrise Shhaha found them sleeping near Mah and the tall walkers.

The land grew harsh as they traveled and all at once they found themselves in a vast, open and barren plain. Once again they turned to eating most of their meals from their stores. For countless trees there was nothing but burnt grass or dry soil on the horizon before them. The Tututs seemed not to mind, but the others grew restless and weary of the hot sun beaming down on them; and as the heat can do, it made them careless with one another.

Mah was much better now and feeling glad to be alive. The heat of the sun seemed cool in comparison to the heat of his past fever. It warmed his stiff and aching muscles and kept him filled with pleasing words, which helped to calm the growing tensions between them all. The Aphros fawned over him, attracted to any kindness, since the Tututs had begun to ignore them after their first night of being left alone. It seemed their only joy in life, to be allowed to serve others. Like slaves they attended Mah's every move, and learned to speak his words to assure him that he could do no wrong by them.

At twilight, in the grayness of the dry, burnt land, Mah sang the call to the Great Mahs, and put the Tututs and the Aphros under a spell. They had never heard a human creature sing, and the tenor of Mah's voice filled them with whirling emotions. They cried, they laughed, they danced around, unaware of the convolutions of their bodies, then sat unmoving in the deathlike silence they did so well, and which made them look like stones.

When the singing was done, the Aphros threw themselves at him. He had not seen their close greeting before and took it as an attack. Ramaa dashed over to stop them, and bashed the Aphros upside their heads. They already knew who was the stronger between them, and did not dare to strike him back, but their looks were filled with curses, and even the Tututs camped away from them when it came time to sleep. That night the Aphros tried to sing, but it was an eerie thing they did, and gave the others nightmares, in which they realized the song was a warning.

Ramaa could not believe that Odrak ignored all this. Keishlee treated him sourly and took to feeding and keeping company with Mah herself. Fearful and more careful with her, the Aphros kept their distance. She was an "only woman," to be treated with much respect. Also, they had seen what was possible with the Tuk blade and did not dare to anger her.

They traveled for two more days in silence over the deserted land, with the Tututs forcing Ramaa to a near run to keep his lead of the pack. The land was once again running downhill, which put them all at a faster pace.

The tall walkers sounded their cry of ready thirst, and even the Tututs knew they had spotted water and trees. They traveled through the night, having walked parched land for three cycles of days, they would not stop now that they knew food and water was near.

During the night the faint smells of other humans kept them alert and moving. They were attacked by a troop of stalking stone-jaw hounds, but Ramaa only had to hurt one of them with the blood wand for the others to flee. Soon after they all caught a strong whiff of women, and all their moods were changed. Even Odrak stayed with the lead, leaving Shhaha and Mah trailing far behind. Keishlee was confirmed in the ways of the Tuk women, but spoke of the comforting scent of other women being near, and they all quickened their pace to be near the smells of fresh food and new company.

The glitter of sitting fires off in the distance put them in a run. They could hear the relief cries of the tall walkers, who were already drinking. A shriek broke out and then the cry of a wounded tall walker. Ramaa and Keishlee were off like sparks in the direction of the cry. Shhaha pulled Mah off in another direction to get the moonlight off their faces. Odrak raced towards the fires with the fighting end of his blood wand ahead of him, leaving the fast running Aphros and the slower strutting Tututs far behind.

The dirt under their feet began to mix with softer sand when they saw the light of torches coming towards them. Keishlee called out warnings in the different tongues she had learned, but it was not until her weapon sparkled in the torchlight that the approaching group stopped and took heed.

Even tho Keishlee kept her body covered in leather straps, it was clear to any who saw that she was a woman, especially when standing next to the towering Ramaa. To her alone they seemed to bow and titter their bodies, as if attempting to make this sign their words. Ramaa stepped forward and they growled and threw stones, then dashed about while swinging sticks and torches at him.

Keishlee cursed and flashed her weapon again, almost cutting one of the men just as the light of the moon showered down upon them. Now they could see Keishlee's face and form in full. Still swinging their weapons at Ramaa, they could not stop themselves from smiling at her, revealing full lips and bright teeth. They could also see Ramaa now, who shocked them with his height and build. They looked back and forth between Ramaa and Keishlee, and slowly lowered their weapons as awe began to mark their faces.

Ramaa slapped one of the stumbling men. He struck his blood wand hard across his palm so they could hear its sturdiness against his hardened flesh.

"We are humans of the clan of the Tall Walkers," Keishlee spoke slowly, hoping they might understand.

They only grunted and patted their chests. Some made low screeching sounds that sounded familiar to Ramaa's ears. Then Ramaa pounded his chest, and began his squawking call for respect for his size and the might of his arms.

"Yes. They are a clan related to squawks," spoke Shhaha

calmly, from just behind the group of surprised men.

Ramaa continued to pound his chest and his shadow loomed out behind him like a mountain. Keishlee saw no real danger here and ran off to find the tall walkers. Mah tried body signs and hand signals to speak with the strangers. They took note of him, and some smiled, but they did not understand. Shhaha tried many words, some of which they knew, but they were more taken with the sound of his voice than with what Shhaha was trying to say.

They gave Shhaha and his people a sturdy sniffing, and then signaled for them to follow. They passed a narrow spring shining in the moonlight, where Keishlee was tending the male tall walker. Knowing the kick he could deliver, Shhaha's eyes moved through the dark to where a body was lying, and then off in the direction to where the head had gone. It had been a woman's scream, but a grown man had been killed, to Shhaha's relief. He listened for the breathing of one in shock, and found the woman huddled near a small bush.

The men watched Shhaha more closely than the others. Some ran to the spot were he had last rested his eyes, while others began to mourn the lost of their friend. Ramaa made the sign they had developed for Tuk blade, which meant that he was not going to leave Shhaha's side. Mah offered to find the Aphros, and Keishlee signed that she would stay to tend the tall walkers. "I could not bear it if they took sick," she moaned.

The men returned with the woman and the dead man's body, grieving loudly as they headed towards their camp. Others stared at Ramaa as if he were to blame. They demanded to have the head back, cursing Ramaa with harsh grunts and spitting in his direction.

The air here was desperately dry. The only thing saving this small spring was the odd collection of rising boulders and trees that gave shade to the ground here. It seemed unreasonable that dry land peoples would spit at their enemies, wasting water in such a way.

"Where are the lands of your people?" Shhaha asked in the same manner he would address slaves. He repeated it in other tongues and signaled for Mah to sign.

The men turned to each other for a moment, and then one signed to say it was in the same direction they had come.

"We are Timbutikata, this was...."

"TIMBUTIKATAS!" Ramaa shouted, crouching with an arm outstretched and his hand pointing down, and then touching it repeatedly to his forehead. "I am Ramaa. We are the people of the clan of the Tall Walkers," Ramaa said proudly, using some of their words he only now remembered. "They are from beyond the range mountains and the lake of flying fish," he repeated to Shhaha.

Shhaha and Mah copied the greeting sign, and watched as memory and smiles began to take the place of angry frowns. "Shama," spoke the man holding the dead body. "Cleesha," spoke another, and "Jerruut," spoke another, calling out tall walker names they knew. They all crouched a little and made the greeting sign, then made a set of signal calls over to their camp, which were returned.

When they spoke again, Ramaa remembered enough of their words to translate. They did not speak many words, but Ramaa was pleased to have come upon them. He took great pains expressing his regret for their lost friend, assuring them that all his people would help with their respects for the dead. While they spoke, Mah had collected the dead man's missing head and returned it to the men. They continued on towards their camp, but the men were surprised that Ramaa would leave his woman behind, and offered to wait for her. With stern words and a harsh rap on his chest, Ramaa said, "Leave her! She is a free woman, and she can kill a man."

At first they thought it was a joke. Ramaa gave Shhaha a worried look, but he was already signing for the men to lose their smiles. "In truth, she can kill a man. In truth, she can kill many men," Shhaha said, his voice being better trained to place truth in the heart.

At the camp site there were many people gathered near a fire. Odrak was holding a man to the ground with his blood wand and kicking others who tried to attack him. Others were holding two of the Aphros. One was pinned to the ground and bleeding badly from the mouth. At the sight of the dead man's head rolling across the sandy dirt, they quieted, but continued to hold their captives.

Shhaha ordered Odrak to let the man go. When he did, he was attacked by three others. Shhaha called for them to be still, while Odrak freed himself, kicking one of the men into the fire. The man jumped out and was hardly burned, but he ran off into the trees as if he had been set ablaze.

"Let our people go!" Shhaha spoke, using the full power of his voice. Mah and Odrak would realize much later that his use of this much magic early on was a warning to them that much more magic would be used here.

The people almost fell to the ground as they found themselves without the will to stand. The Aphros were free, but they also could not move. The dead man slipped from the grip of those holding him, and Ramaa had to assist them.

Someone shouted, "Timbuk! Timbuk!!" and the call was soon picked up by all. Others moved the dead man near Shhaha's feet, and someone offered the head to Shhaha. Soon all the strangers were sitting on their heels with an arm outstretched.

Odrak could not stop himself from saying, "I am glad our clan relation has taught us graceful body words."

Shhaha gave him a rough look, but turned a smile out to the people and signaled them to stand.

"You must touch each of their hands, or their heads, or they will not move. They will sit like this through the night," whispered Ramaa.

Mah was only a small slave when it happened, but he remembered the raiding party that took some of the protectors from their clearing for many moons. They had returned with many stories of the Timbutikata and their Kong [*the biggest one*], who was to be given the same respects as a Keeper of the Blood. Mah had hoped someday to meet the Great Kong, and hoped the man had not died during his journey here.

Shhaha greeted each of the Timbutikatas, as was necessary, and made Ramaa proud of his Keeper of the Blood. Shhaha had made them acknowledge and respect him at their first meeting, just like their Kong had done to him and Cleesha when he was younger.

Some of them Shhaha shunned, but when the people grunted their approval, Ramaa also fell on his heels to honor the great Shhaha. He had remembered all the tales of their customs and would walk among these people as if he were their Kong. Ramaa relaxed, knowing that Shhaha would now be able to control any trouble here, and he was glad, because these people could be very cruel.

"Let us respect the night and the dead, while the moon is still high and blood still drips," spoke the man who carried the dead man's head. "My people call me Ulongtim, and this is Timbuk."

Weariness had finally caught up with him, and it was all Shhaha could do to chant a few words, while the people built up a blazing fire away from the trees, in preparation for some elaborate burial, Shhaha thought. He looked forward to seeing how the Timbutikata gave respects to their dead, but when they threw the body into the fire, and ran around it screaming with the dead head, Shhaha did not speak again until the next day's midday meal.

Just before the crack of dawn, Mah was awakened by a large group of rowdy protectors. Some were digging at his white streaks of hair while others rubbed his smooth, hairless face and chest. All of them were older and bigger, and for the first time since the start of this journey, Mah felt his true count of seasons. Suddenly it seemed he was back at his own clearing, and here were protectors ready to make raids on some creature digging up their fields. Stretching himself, he counted 20 and 2, and all of them were trying to pull at him.

Shhaha bristled at the sight of the youths mauling Mah. They had the look of trouble, but the one from his vision was not among them, so he relaxed and thought no more about it and went off to perform his morning chants.

Ramaa had gone to the stream to find Keishlee already stoning ground foods and boiling greens. There was a new smell in the air, and he liked the sensation it made as it cleared his nostrils and made his mouth water. He stepped out from the shade of the camp and allowed the sun to cover him, but when his eyes adjusted to the spark of first light, he was chilled to the bone by the sight of the vast, empty desert.

A tall walker stood large in the streaming light, staring out into the desert's loneliness. Shhaha moved towards the sun, waving at its light, and Ramaa knew Shhaha was chanting the morning call. Colors streaked out over the butter-brown sands that glowed like fluffs of yellow feathers. With Shhaha standing next to the tall walker, and them both echo-chanting the call to morning light, Ramaa could almost think the sight of them and the desert beautiful. But as he turned to see the darker browns and blacks of the dirt sweeping up into the camp grounds, and saw the trees, tall and varied, lush and plentiful, stretching out along the desert's edge and up into a cove of small hills and thick forest, he hoped they were going to continue in that direction instead.

Odrak was surprised to find Mah without sleep in his eyes. The sun had not yet crept into the camp, but there he sat on the ground showing a group of youths and protectors his blood wand. He looked pleased with the Timbutikatas heel-sitting all around him. Odrak knew the stories Mah could weave along the blood lines of the wand. Mah could hold them fast from now until sunset.

Odrak turned his head to see one of the Aphros rising from the base of a tree, moaning with the pain of the sun crawling over his face. The Aphros did not like the sun as much as the Tututs. Odrak knew he would be cursing it and hoped Shhaha would not hear. He then left to find Keishlee.

"He will be better, but he must rest for a day, I think. Nothing is broken, Shhaha says," Keishlee explained to Ramaa, but she knew he was not listening as he stared out over the camp grounds.

The tall walkers had told her about the desert last night, saying it felt like three seasons' crossing. She was rested, but had not really slept all night, dreading that they would have to cross it. The tall walkers would not mind so much, but all her people would. Closeness to the living and the touches of life were like blood to her people, especially to Shhaha. It was said that if a people wanted to keep their blood keepers healthy, they would never leave them alone for long. Having to cross the emptiness of desert would be like slow death to Shhaha, and she wondered what it would do to Odrak, as she saw him coming near.

The trees thinned at this edge of camp and the ground was sandy, but Odrak felt the desert more than he saw it. As it became clear to him between the trees, he knew it was not like any desert he had ever heard of. It was motionless as far as the eye could see, and lifeless as far as his senses could reach. Here one could see further than was normal and yet not see a bird flying anywhere. That meant that even they did not dare to cross this bleak terrain. Odrak finally understood why there was a place the Great Mahs did not go, why even they did not fly over this tract of wilderness.

"Maybe Shhaha has forgotten the way?" Odrak hoped, while looking at the dry flatness everywhere, like unmoving yellow water. "Maybe that is not the way," he whispered to Ramaa.

Ramaa pulled him towards a tree where he could see

Shhaha and the tall walker standing bare to get the morning light. Odrak did not look. He had felt Shhaha there and knew which direction the stars had pointed the night before. For the first time in many days, he used his inner sense to locate Mah. The shock of Mah staring back at him from where he sat threatened to cause a knocking in his head.

Ramaa saw the strange looks they gave one another and said, "Go tell him about the dry sands."

Keishlee saw the desperate look on Odrak's face, and went to him to be tender in contrast to Ramaa. She gripped him by the shoulders and said, "Give him some warning before Shhaha returns. Shhaha need not see our fear of this."

Odrak turned again to Mah, who turned away. He tore himself from Keishlee and said, "He knows of the desert already. The Timbutikata have just told him."

"Words are never like the things one sees with eyes," huffed Ramaa getting angry with Odrak. "You have not spoken words to him since we left the Kamitui. Why curse him so?"

"I have seen two of my people catch their first sight of this," Keishlee paused to stop a tremble, "...this desert. I would not want Shhaha to see that look on my face. The fear on our faces would...."

"Mah knows! Mah knows everything I feel. He knows what I have seen and what it makes me feel, as I know everything of him. Everything! All of him is inside, with me now, always!" seethed Odrak, straining to hold back words that were finding relief in their overdue release.

Everyone heard it. None except Keishlee and Ramaa could begin to understand it, but as they saw Mah dash away from the group of protectors, it was obvious that the wrong between them was something neither of them could control. It was something neither of them wanted, but could find no way to heal. Worse, Odrak had used the power of his voice on them to drive the feeling to heart. The pain that was inside him embarrassed Keishlee, and made her turn away, while Ramaa stood dumbfounded, unable to speak.

The Timbutikatas began to gather around Odrak, affected by his voice, but too amused by his size and hairlessness to give him the respects due one having such power. They taunted him and pushed him about. They were angry with him for stopping the storytelling, and for running off the one with the hair of elders.

They were forcing themselves on him now, and these were a people who grew to their fullest while still young. They were all brutish looking, hairy and large boned, with big hands and feet. They smacked their hands across their chests, calling on Odrak to justify his mocking their Kong by using such a powerful voice around them. For a moment, Odrak stood there and took it, but one of them smacked him in the face, and Odrak ripped into him, looking for a death.

Suddenly Shhaha was standing right next to Ramaa, signaling him to stop the scuffle. Odrak already had blood on his fists and was digging his fingers into another youth's neck. The others had jumped on Odrak before Ramaa could reach him, and Ramaa had to throw them off. Keishlee stepped back, since between her own people women did not stand near when men fought, but when one of the protectors inadvertently elbowed her, she slapped him to the ground.

"Woman," he whispered, seeing her for the first time. "Woman. Giant woman," he continued and was slowly joined by the others. The fighting quickly broke itself up, and they all rushed over.

"I am Keishlee," she introduced herself to the young protector she had struck.

Ramaa pulled two youths from Odrak and then yanked him up from the ground. He started to help dust him off, but Odrak snatched himself away. Rage flooded over Ramaa. This would be the last time Odrak would turn his back on him without word or cause. Ramaa had him by the arm and was about to give him a good knocking, when Shhaha stayed his hand.

"Let him go," Shhaha ordered, and watched as Odrak shook himself free and ran away.

"He has forgotten himself," snapped Ramaa.

Shhaha turned watery eyes to him and said, "No. No, my friend. He is trying to learn who he is now."

Ramaa did not understand. He stomped off in the direction of the camp of the Timbutikatas, and only calmed himself when he caught a whiff of the women's clearing, and saw the enclosure built for them. He wanted to clear his head of Odrak, and Mah, and the desert, but as usual Shhaha's words would not leave him unaffected.

He turned back to see Odrak sitting under a tree with his head between his legs, his body heaving, heavy with grief and some inner pain. He looked around at the group of young protectors; although they were older, they should have treated Odrak with more respect. He was an apprentice to Shhaha, and soon to be a full Blood Keeper. But he need not consider that. If Odrak was who he knew him to be, he would make them all understand that they had wronged him. He would have their respect by the right of it, if not by some force, because Odrak was not the forgiving kind.

Ramaa had worried over Odrak for one reason or another all during this journey, but now he considered how Odrak had become a protector without his clan and friends or the life normal to his people. He had no keeper or feeder most of his life, only Mah; and now all things were changed around him. He was probably in a growing stage and would soon drastically change in size as well, and all before having to cross that desert.

"I would forget myself as well," he grunted to himself, as he approached the open clearing.

Ramaa peeked over the smaller trees and watched the sun light up the yellow sands. He chanted to himself the call of welcome for the rising sun, and hoped his blood kin were looking after his three slaves, and his mate. "Maum," he whispered her name, but thought of her now as Nuba, a name he cherished, for a woman he would not forget. After seeing her in the walled habits of the Hoteps, he had begun to look for her around bushes, near gullies and behind trees.

He thought of Maum and wished he could touch her, and share the things he had learned. He recalled a tasty memory of the specialties she could make, which contrasted sharply against the thin soups and paste Keishlee prepared. How he missed her chewy pudding, and roasted hoppers baked inside palm nuts. His mouth watered for steamed pepper grass, mixed with tender mud-greens.

"Has your Kong put a spell on you?" came a voice as if from another time. "It is I, Ulongtim."

Ramaa's eyes focused on the man and he managed to say, "I know," and started to walk away, until he saw the group of men and women coming towards him.

Keishlee couldn't believe these protectors were as young as their hands and feet revealed. Some were almost as tall as she, with wide, broad shoulders. Her own people seemed unconcerned for food, even Shhaha, which upset her a little. But now she had these youths to feed. They had surrounded her small fire and were sniffing at her bowls.

She gave the sick tall walker a taste first, and then turned the bowls over to the naked youths. They attacked the bowls and each other, threatening to disturb the tall walker, until she shooed them away. They left immediately and seemed full of regret that they had done something to irk her. They all made hand signs to show her their goodwill before leaving. After they left, she stalked off toward Shhaha, who was talking with an Aphro. She looked around for the others, and realized she had not seen them or the Tututs since they entered the camp.

"You must bring them now," Shhaha was saying to the lone Aphro. "The Timbutikata must see them with my people, or I may not speak for them later."

"They will not come," spoke the Aphro.

"You must make them come. I may not leave the camp except to enter the desert," replied Shhaha as Keishlee approached. "Go, and tell them there will be trouble for them if they do not come now."

The Aphro ran off around the trees, back towards the dry grass lands. "I shall make them come, if necessary," said Shhaha, in answer to Keishlee's unspoken words.

"They fear these people?" she asked, feeling the question a bit silly. These people seemed gentle to her.

"With reason," Shhaha smiled at her. "These people would kill them if they were seen fully naked. They fear all things different, or things not approved by their Kong. Try to remember the moment you first truly knew them. You made water on the floor to curse them...."

"But I do not...."

"Not now. But first, you cursed them," declared Shhaha, and then he walked away.

It had only been a little water she had forced out. How could Shhaha have known, she wondered?

"I am Shhaha, Keeper of the Blood for the clan of the Tall Walkers, who are humans one and all. Born in the line of Axum, of the Seven Sisters, from the Great Mother Puutha, mother of all human life. From blood of Cush and Kukh we come, and are what is gracefully placed upon the land. For the good we are endowed with powers never before known to any clan, and can count feeders and slaves on many hands...." roared Shhaha the chant of the blessing, mixed with the chant of clan blood, as he headed back to the desert.

He might as well have slapped her across the face. If he turned around she would fall on her knees to beg a word of kindness from him. As it was, she was grateful no one else was around, and walked off to hide her shame. She reached down to feel the weapon strapped to her side, and the comfort of it told her that she had become too bold with her own resources. She had dared to think something would be unknown to Shhaha, and worse, she had tried to deny what was true.

She looked back out towards the desert and felt less awed by it, with Shhaha looming in her mind like a creature too big to be born of any woman. He was Shhaha, the magic voice, and he was her Keeper of the Blood. He had the right to strike her down if she mated disaster to the clan. She went to find Mah, and promised herself that she should never make that mistake with him again.

Deeper into the camp, near the enclosure built for the women, a man ran over to Ulongtim with word that the one called Shhaha was once again standing on the desert sands. Ulongtim was making a show of the women of his tribe, who had insisted that Ramaa be presented to them.

Ramaa had not seen any of their women before, and was astonished that he had been taken to them, and then even more so at the size of some of them. They were large, thick women. Some of them were bigger around than Waterhorse women. The very large ones wore leaves woven into wrapping banners. The others, like the men, wore netted grass, or straw tied into short hanging skirts. There were only a few who wore their feeder bags bare, a comforting sight to Ramaa after the small things the Tututs carried, and Keishlee, who never went bare any more. They all looked at him with pleasure, and some coveted him. As they stepped up closer and smiled, men grouped around him with sour looks, and he knew that none of these women were supposed to be free.

Mah had walked off into a cluster of trees towards the covered hills. He wanted to be alone with his thoughts and the peace of this small jungle around him. He had seen himself in the vastness of an empty yellow land some time ago, and was unhappy that they had reached it so soon. He had seen death in that place in his dream. Shhaha always said that to dream of death did not always mean that someone would die. It could also mean that something or someone would change, but somehow he knew that human blood would be spilled, and it would be from their group that it would flow. He had kept it to himself, not wanting to worry anyone, and understood now why Shhaha did not always tell all he knew. But he kept it from Odrak, and he had never kept anything from Odrak before. And this was added to the many things that had recently come between them.

It had become an unbearable thing to have someone know his motivations and his mind in the same instant he did himself. And then there was the steady increase of his blood powers. From the sound alone he knew the truth of what was said by anyone who spoke. There were no words for this, and he had yet to discuss this with Shhaha, who allowed him to frustrate over this, and with Odrak always looking into his thoughts, it ripped at Mah's bones to have Odrak confuse his frustration with what he really felt.

"How dare he doubt my love! How dare he take all that has gone on before and mix it up with what is happening now! How dare he do this while he alone has Shhaha's counsel, who has not counseled me for many days," Mah cried to himself.

Kneeling under a tree, he forced himself to collect the fungus growth there for what might be a meal, or medicine. He tried not to touch the tree, but as usual now, he was compelled to it, and slipped off some of the leafy bark with his nails. "Did you feel that as well Odrak?" he asked aloud.

He talked to trees often now that he could sense the activity of their life, but did not have to deal with the slightest intrusion of another's mind. Since his contact with the spice trees, he had begun to realize that plants and trees were creatures that lived as well as any life. It pleased him to know that one day he might discover a way to speak with them, but it frustrated him not to know what he should eat any more.

He pinched a piece of the soft green-brown bark and sucked on the seasoning and the sticky sap that clung to his fingers. Immediately he knew a healthy wine could be made from its juices, and that its fruit would be soft and only partially sweet. He looked up to see the bunches of long green fruit hanging low from the many thick overhanging branches. This thing was a thick collection of trees instead of one solid trunk of life. It was as old as some of the spice trees, and heavy with ripening fruit, which ripped at his nose with a stingy scent.

"No eat! No touch!" came the clatter of shaky voices repeating some warning they'd been given.

Pointing to the fruit, Mah said, "It is safe to eat. It will not harm...."

"No. No touch! No eat!" ordered one of the young protectors coming near.

Mah reached up to pull one of the fruits free, and was yanked hard to the ground and stepped on. He swung around and kicked the legs heading for him and up turned their owners. The shorter ones screamed at him while the taller ones tried to jump on him. Mah rolled across the massive root legs of the tree and leaped to his feet. "Stop! Stop!" he yelled.

"You are cursed!" someone screamed.

"The Kong take life!" spoke another.

"No touch! No eat!" repeated the others.

"The fruit here is safe to eat!" Mah yelled back. "Your Kong has lied to you!"

They did not know his words, but all at once they understood his meaning. Only agitated and annoyed with him before, they were frustrated and furious with him now. They surrounded him, but would not touch him, while some were sent to bring others.

Mah stared at the young protectors, most of them older than he, and all of them more broadly built. He would have a rough time of it in a fight, but perhaps they would not be prepared for his kick if he had to use it. They made menacing sounds and gave him deadly looks. The tallest one had to hold some of the others back, while he bared his teeth and hissed at Mah with wild eyes. The smell of hate was all around him. Mah knew then that he had spoken a mighty curse, and that it would not easily be healed between them.

"WHO DARES?!! Who dares?!" roared a grown protector running toward Mah.

"I only wished to...."

Mah was knocked to the ground by a backhand to the head, and then stomped upon by the younger ones. Two older protectors dragged him back to their camp, cursing and yelling for the others to come. The younger ones kicked him as they went. Curses were flying from all directions, and the group around him got larger and larger.

When they released him, Ramaa was standing near, just outside the female enclosure. Everyone was standing around and Mah got his first look at the heavy Timbutikata women. Their feeder bags were the size of a man's head, and their wide round bodies were wrapped tight with leaf bands, or swinging heavy with straw skirts. Everyone was screaming at once, and Ramaa was trying to get Ulongtim to tell him what they said. He demanded that the people be silent, but the noise continued until a group of women stepped up and signaled for the men to move away from Mah's beaten body.

"You have said a mighty, evil thing," spoke one of the women, leaning over into Mah's face.

Mah was terror-stricken and unable to speak.

"You have sworn yourself to the death of Kong. You have cursed his blood. You have said the Kong knows only lies," snapped another woman looking down at him.

"No. No. I only meant...."

"He said it. He said it!" screamed some of the youths. "He say Kong lie! And those who lie are dead!! So what you say is Kong must die!!!" came the words like a deadly chant.

"Kong lie?! Kong die?!" howled the women standing over Mah. She snorted hard and ripped open her chest covering, revealing her weighty feeder bags. They came down at him suddenly, flying toward his face like giant palm nuts.

Fearful of the dark nuts about to crush him, he twisted free from under someone's foot and rolled off to one side. The heavy feeder hit the ground and screamed. Men stepped in, trying to kick Mah. More women moved in, yelling, "He curse Kong?! He curse Kong?!" while pulling loose their head wraps and exposing long flatly matted hair. They stood over his body and the men backed away, saying, "He dare! He say Kong lie. He dare!"

Another woman leaped over Mah while another tried to hold him down. He slipped from their sweaty, yet strong hands, and his ability to do so made him smile up in their faces. They screamed at him, and all the women joined in to stomp him or jump on him, while tearing at their hair and body wraps. There were too many of them, but Mah could not be moved to strike a woman, especially large feeders like these. Even now they filled him with a hunger to touch their round fleshy faces, or to pull at the many extra folds of skin. All he could do was roll back and fourth across the ground, outwitting their attacks with his speed.

Someone had picked up Mah's blood wand back at the tree, and now held it over his head, ready to crush his skull. Ramaa tore through the crowd and picked the grown protector up into the air and held him above the crowd, roaring, "If you spill his blood, rivers of Timbutikata blood will flow!" Then he threw the man to the ground at the feet of the stomping women, who then cowered under Ramaa's great size.

"You must give us our time with him," ordered one of the braver women.

"Woman must draw first blood," yelled some of the men.

"He has cursed us!" roared some of the women. "He has cursed the Great Kong," hollered the men. "No protection must you give him!" screamed the heavy women, rubbing their sore spots.

"He is an apprentice to our Keeper of the Blood. If he has wronged you, than he shall mend the wound and heal it, but none of you will see his blood," spoke Ramaa clearly.

Mah snatched the fallen blood wane to him and pulled himself near Ramaa's legs, watching his back as the men moved in closer. Now Mah prepared to fight and protect himself. Ramaa had his Tuk blade, and he did not want him rampaging against these people.

Just then Mah realized that they were both caught up in the power of a few misplaced words. He could see the error of them clearly, and thought of Odrak. The noise around them was increasing, and their hostility reddened every eye. Even the youngest ones, those closest to Mah in seasons, were cursing and yelling at them. Mah could see that they were trying to build up their courage. Soon they would attack, no matter.

He caught sight of the one called Ulongtim. He and another man were the only ones not shouting. They looked at Ramaa with anger, but they were more disturbed with something else going on here that Mah could not guess. Mah rose slowly, hunching forward on his toes, knowing that this would increase their anger. He quickly called to Ulongtim with his eyes and spoke to his mind: ""Come. Protect your people."

Something began to spin up Mah's spine, shooting severe pains into his head. Mah jumped to his feet, screaming.

"Protect your own people! Protect your people, as well as those you have insulted with your truth!" was the command ringing above his eyes and around his ears, like stones pounding at his flesh. Mah fell back on Ramaa, who tried to hold him up, but Mah broke away, stumbling over the legs of the man Ramaa had thrown to the ground.

The people quieted. They did not understand what had happened, but Shhaha, who was a Kong to them, was among them, and they knew his power was ruling here. Odrak and Keishlee were also coming towards the group, and Keishlee had her weapon drawn.

Forced into a slight trance, Mah could see the awful future of his people and those around him. Keishlee had become a creature used to the raid and the sight of blood. With the power of the Tuk blade in hand, she and Ramaa would not hesitate to kill these people if his blood was spilled. These people were the pure blood of Oro and were in great numbers in their land. Many Waterhorse clans had blood related to them. Once word of this reached their people, it would not be long before they came in search of his people. Then their would be blood fighting between all their peoples.

All at once Bellar seemed a feeble thing to leave behind in Shhaha's place. His people were without a proper "speaker," and would be subject to the whim of any elder blood keeper. Mah had to mend things himself, so that Shhaha need not interfere, and that no one's blood was spilled here.

There was no time to waste. "I give myself for punishment. I have offended the Great Kong!" Mah repeated, until he was sure the people understood. Turning himself over would show these people that he truly did not mean to offend, and by their own standards, no blood would then need to be spilled.

The clearing settled, and for the first time in many days, Odrak smiled, but only until he remembered what a punishment was. Mah had remembered this thing, which Cleesha had witnessed among these people. It was natural for Mah not to forget things, but as he recalled the details of the punishment, he wished he had.

Mah handed the blood wand to Ramaa, who stood there bewildered that Mah was turning himself over to these people. Didn't he remember the stories told about these people, and of how cruel they were? Ramaa grunted, but it did not matter; his own resolve was firm. If they drew one drop of Mah's blood, Ramaa would slaughter all those who stood near. He would kill those who drew the blood, as well as any who watched it fall.

Ramaa smiled over to Keishlee, who stood guard over the group. These people looked at her only as a woman to be given the general respect; they had no idea that she was capable of covering herself with their blood. He let out a slow grinding laugh as a warning to those who cursed and gathered closer to Mah.

Mah fell to his knees and crunched himself against the ground. He looked up to see a strange look on Ulongtim's face, a thing of fear mixed with something akin to wonderment. When their eyes met, Mah noted the heavy brows and deep brown eyes, and was slightly comforted by the small smile he tried to make of his hairy face.

Ulongtim shoved someone's head toward Mah, grunting something which Mah remembered had something to do with food. Then they all began to sniff him. But others pushed them aside and freed themselves from their wraps. Mah closed his eyes and tried to cover his face, but hands reached out and snatched them away. Then streams of waste, piss water and partially digested foods began to pour over him.

He could hear Ramaa and Keishlee cursing them, but no blood was being spilled, so there was nothing for them to do. The smell was awful, but all Mah could think about was that some of them were sick. One of them was moaning as his waters flowed, and the smell of blood was unmistakable to a blood apprentice. Mah peeked out from the slime and marked the face, but the human waste threatened to blind him. He could smell the heavy, sticky scent of feeders squatting over him, their mucky matter descending about his head and ears. The smell alone was enough to sicken a man for many days. Mah could not bear the thought of being stricken with sickness again, but he forced himself closer to the ground and stood the weight of it all. They cursed him, but none of them would touch him now, and when the sounds of hissing water ceased, he heard only the disgusting grunts and farts of strained bodies and emptied bellies.

There was a long pause, but soon he heard the familiar pace of Keishlee coming near. The smell was unbearable to one whose sensibilities had turned towards all things fresh and clear, but she stood over him and called for him to raise himself. "I will help you if you need it."

"No!" Mah demanded she keep her place. "I am not hurt," he protested, then rose and tried not to slip back into the muck that was all around him. "See. I can stand." He reached for the spot where Odrak should have been, and snatched his hand back when he felt Keishlee move there. It was a crushing blow. Somehow he had thought Odrak would take mercy on him, but he knew if he opened his eyes he would no longer find Odrak in the clearing. He had gone back to the woods to see the tree that had caused the fuss. Without anyone looking, he would even eat the fruit and then bring the knowledge of it to Shhaha. They would sit and study what they had learnt, and Odrak would turn his mind away from Mah, completely.

Keishlee would not let anyone abuse Mah further, and threatened a woman who started to spit, by slicing a log in two. All the women ran away, then she called for Mah to follow her out towards the dry sands, which might prove a good duster for his cleaning.

With Keishlee to assist Mah, Ramaa turned to Ulongtim and another man who had stayed behind. "Must move camp because of this. You help?" Ulongtim asked Ramaa meekly.

Ramaa looked down at the big leathery man and almost laughed at what he saw there in his eyes. He had seen it many times in his own clearing, when those in need of relief caught a whiff of Mah's scent close up. It was an odor pleasing to all the senses, bracing and fresh, like a field of ready blossoms, or the den of a creature with a special musk. He had finally succumbed to the scent with Nuba. It was difficult not to want Mah for quick relief.

"I will help," Ramaa smiled and greeted him with a touch of his back hand to the man's face, a special greeting of friendship among these people.

Ulongtim introduced the other man as Augklac, and they all turned away from their anger, and forgot the trouble that had interrupted their day. As Ramaa left the clearing with the men, he saw a group of women staring after Keishlee and Mah. He was not sure what they thought, but it was obvious they were not pleased with Keishlee for helping the punished one.

After rolling and dusting himself for most of the day, Mah sat naked on the hot sands letting his body sweat. The sun seemed to leave them too quickly here, and the female tall walker was angry with the desert as if it were to blame. Keishlee had sat with Mah for awhile, sharing Ada's last words with him, and telling him about the Tututs in hiding. Keishlee made him laugh when she told him about the men and women of Hotep village, and of the spice seed settlement made by Umboi and Kangar for the dark beauty. Mah was glad to hear that they had gotten her for less than 10 spice seeds, but nothing distracted him for long from the sight of the far-reaching desert.

"It will swallow us alive," he had whispered between Keishlee's words.

She did not want to think about it, and after sitting most of the day, gave up trying to cheer him.

Mah was fairly clean, but he feared the smell would never leave him. He was thankful the tall walker did not shun him, and knew she felt his embarrassment and shame. He had forgotten about consequences, the first teachings to a blood apprentice. All day he hoped that Shhaha would come and counsel him, or even scold him for his foolish pride. It made him weep that Odrak would not come to comfort him, and he sat upon the desert feeling as small as the grains of sand.

The tall walker left to feed herself on the taller trees of the camp. Mah sang softly to himself, and found that sound did not carry far in this land, a thing that would weaken his and Shhaha's best talents. The sands were devoid of life as far as he could see, and to be so next to a fruitful camp meant that it was worse further on. Heat vapors and hot air filled with sand made it difficult to see clear shapes out past the horizon. It made the mind form images of its own, and he dreaded the visions this brought him, but he kept fast to the sands, continuing to dust his naked body, and holding the spice seeds close.

Odrak watched the all-too-quickly descending sun and it gave him chills, as he considered the long days of darkness crossing the desert. Mah was calling to him with his mind, unwillingly, but in dire need of what only his touch could give. Odrak blocked it out defiantly, still angry with what he considered the great lies between them.

The young protectors of the Timbutikata were playing a rough game that reminded him of the fighting style of the Kamituians. They were demanding that he join in, but Odrak let them know that none who played so far were good enough to beat him. They continued up the ranks of their play, while Odrak fought back his desire to run to the desert, and Mah.

Odrak was angry over so many things that his mind could not sort them out. He was furious that Mah only pretended to enjoy holding him between his legs. True, there had never been another, nor had Mah thought of anyone even in passing, but Odrak saw it as a failure all his own, and wanted to give Mah room to find another. He also took the lie of mock pleasure as an ability to deceive, and he had not thought Mah capable of such a thing.

He had continued to think of Mah as the little slave who clung to him and followed him wherever he went. Now Odrak saw that *he* was the one who followed, like a constant shadow, who was only thought about when Mah thought of himself or was in need. Odrak cursed aloud and the others took it as a sign that he was ready to match his strength against the winner. As a distraction, Odrak threw himself into the taller broader youth as he had seen the others do. He was wrapped around the protector's legs, with his face pinned to the ground, before anyone else had moved.

The agility of the cat was in Odrak's every step. Two others tried but neither could force him to loose his balance, or be thrown, or pulled to the ground. A much older protector decided to take on the wily stranger and declared to all that this would be the time for his fall. All the youths were gathered here, as well as some of the women. They wanted the young ones to make room for the older men to play, but the men had just moved camp and were glad for the entertainment.

Odrak had a much harder time of it. This protector was broad with short heavy arms which Odrak found nearly impossible to move; but move him he did, as he jumped on the youth's chest and threw him off balance with a kick to the head. He hit the ground hard, and liking that, they women howled with pleasure. This brought over more men, who were just coming back from hunting for animal flesh.

Odrak walked with the pride of the tall walker around the ring they made. The youths taunted him for his 'unnatural walk', and a few stood to show him how the winner should step around the ring, swinging their arms wildly in the air. Odrak laughed and showed them the quickness of his legs, by lock-tripping each of the protectors to the ground.

The women screamed with laughter and signaled insults to the young protectors. Some of the older protectors stood up, and those who had keepers here were flanked and pushed forward to confront Odrak for another match. Odrak tried to refuse politely, but was insulted by one of the leading women, and the silence that followed told Odrak that the words were meant to wound him. He would have to take another match for the "tumble down" in order to gain their respect again.

Ramaa was standing next to Ulongtim and began to cheer Odrak on. The others called for a youth named Omolungway to take the challenge. He was one of the standing favorites. Closer to Keishlee's count of seasons, he had hair growing on his face and chest, and stood tall and broad like the rest of his people. His arms were slightly longer, and were thick and heavy. He stepped forward and the crowd sat back on their heels to watch.

Odrak moved his spice seeds into a better position, then made a show of taking a sniff of Omolungway's scent, and the horror he found in it. Of course this brought back all the former yelps and jeers, and Omolungway lunged for him with a wide spread of arms.

This was too easy, Ramaa thought, as he watched Odrak dash-step off the ground out of reach. Omolungway plowed into the ground face first.

"No win!! No win!!!" Omolungway roared.

Odrak laughed while Omolungway prepared himself, this time knowing better than to charge at him again. Two men came over and forced them to grip each other's arms. Odrak could feel Omolungway's strength, and knew that he planned to throw him over his shoulder. Odrak was too light to stop the move and did go flying off, but like the cat, he landed with his feet firmly placed, standing fully erect.

Omolungway was blinded by his own fury and charged Odrak over and over again until he was caught. They pounded each other with their fists, and Omolungway managed to get an arm around Odrak's throat. Choking his breath away, Omolungway began to force Odrak's head to the ground. Odrak kicked and pounded Omolungway's legs and face, but his strength was nothing compared to the taller youth, who seemed fortified against harsh blows.

The women were squealing with delight, and pushing the younger protectors about. The men were kicking dirt and sand into the ringed area and shouting for Omolungway to finish and win. Omolungway had one of Odrak's legs bent and his face almost in the dirt when Odrak kicked him away. Odrak was struggling for breath when Omolungway kicked him in the chest and knocked him into a group of men. They pushed him back into the ring, and Omolungway pounded both fists into Odrak's back, bringing him to his knees. Smiling, he reached from behind towards Odrak's untied hair, but Odrak had timed a back kick, and placed it firmly in Omolungway's gut. Still trying to catch his breath and clear his head, he was almost up from the ground when Omolungway's dead weight fell on him, forcing him to the ground.

The crowd jumped up with shouts and screams, bouncing about while someone revived Omolungway. Odrak had expected the body to fall the opposite way, but did not take the losing badly. He pounded both hands on the ground as he had seen the others do, and waited for Omolungway to move his heavy body. But Omolungway was still angry and slammed his head against Odrak's face. Odrak reached up and took hold of the large moving knot of Omolungway's throat. This peculiar sensation told Omolungway that his life was in danger, and he stopped moving. Still holding his neck, Odrak rose with him from the ground and punched him between the eyes to blind him, while he placed himself for the kick. Then, with his left foot, he sent Omolungway flying into the silent crowd.

Twilight had been upon them for much too long, Odrak thought, as he accepted a smile from Ramaa. People were shouting at him, but most were shouting at Omolungway and the man helping him, who was probably his keeper. After much taunting, and fussing, and pushing about, it was decided that Omolungway had won the tumble down but had lost the fight, which made them all laugh. Odrak didn't care any more. He thought these people's play too rough and would not get involved again, even at the cost of his pride.

Twilight and the sheen of the night about to come were still glowing when the Timbutikatas finished preparing their foods. They had slaughtered two speckled-colored creatures they called a "bleat," because of the sound it made. Its smell filled the clearing, and Odrak learned that the oils from its body could be used to make bowls of fire for the night. They prepared lots of greens and roasted large orange ground nuts that were plentiful here. Most of them were not fond of animal flesh, but had been here for five moons, and had learnt to eat many things along the way.

"Kong take Eserol. Kong take Cheetong. Kong take Squeceebuk into desert, during night. Kong order Timbutikatas to stay. We wait," spoke the man called Timbuk, who was sharing his meal with Ramaa.

"Where your Kong?" asked Augklac.

"No see Kong whole day. Kong go to desert? Kong leave people to wait?" asked a young man called Glyph.

"Our Kong makes magic before going into the desert. He is still here with us," replied Ramaa.

The men moaned with surprise and looked about, as if Shhaha had made himself invisible and was floating through the air. They stared at the ground, checking foot prints and feeling the air next to them to make sure nothing was there.

Odrak wanted to laugh at their silliness, but thought better of it as he remembered the sensation of being pulled from the thick wet mud that had refused to let him go. He wondered if the memory would ever leave him.

"Young timbu remembers powerful spell of his Kong? Young timbu learns from Kong? Young timbu will be Kong?" Ulongtim spoke to Odrak, understanding what had passed over his face.

"Ulongtim will be Kong someday," Odrak replied to the wanting in Ulongtim's eyes.

A quiet hiss ran over the clearing as those who had heard the words and understood, passed them along to others. Some of the men patted Ulongtim across the back and lowered their eyes and head.

"Truth. Truth," smiled Ulongtim. "The Great Kong has spoken."

"Is there another among you who might also be Kong one day?" Ramaa asked.

"No," spoke Augklac. "Only Ulongtim read bones. Only Ulongtim know to make magic here."

"There is another to take your place?" asked Ulongtim slyly, revealing a touch of malice. "The one with the signs of wisdom in his hair," he suggested, and then remembered how his people had soiled him. "He will be Kong?!" Ulongtim waved a hand over Odrak's face.

Odrak saw the sign of visions cross Ulongtim's eyes. "Two Kongs! No. Three Kongs? No!"

Ramaa laughed and said, "They are both apprentices to our Kong, our Keeper of the Blood. Odrak will lead a new clan of our people someday. We will keep them close, Shhaha says."

"Only one Kong," Ulongtim snapped. "Others must die," he said flatly, as if it were a natural fact. "They are still small for your people, yes? There is much time."

Odrak saw the regret in his eyes, and knew that Ulongtim sided with Mah for a killing. Others were giving him the shine of their teeth, and he knew that they had sided with him, but thought him weak-looking for the part. Odrak smiled back at them, glad that his people were different from these. The look on Ramaa's face told him he felt the same, and they continued their meal and listened to the tales of the Timbutikata's journey here.

With the coming of night, Odrak had made a few friends among these people. Two of them had been constant losers to Omolungway at the tumble down, and were glad of the company to one who had come close to winning. Odrak didn't consider it a loss any more. He had carefully looked Omolungway over during the long twilight, and was sure that he was a bully and a fool, an easy target for manipulation. He laughed with his new friends and when night finally fell, he showed them how his people made fire with the tools from his stone-sack.

An elder protector who knew of the Waterhorse and Tall Walker clans was aware they all carried the bag of stones around their waists, and was glad to know the reason. But they all dashed away in fear of the scratching pop. When they returned to see the fire starting, Odrak laughed heartily at them, especially at the two fully grown men.

Ramaa and Ulongtim gathered others for the night raid to warn off the animals around them. Ramaa was glad for a custom he understood, and rallied with the men. He surprised them by making dress preparations and chanting a version of the call to blood, which he had heard these people do. The Timbutikata did not dress for a raid, but Ramaa demanded that they do so, because it would show respect to the Great Mother if they had to kill one of her creatures. Ulongtim thought it a foolish idea, but when he saw Ramaa tying large comely salad leaves around his legs, he realized the true value of the dress.

"Creatures will not go near salad again!" Ulongtim roared to his men and shook Ramaa's leg. He understood how frightened the creatures would be to see the food moving.

Ulongtim shoved his men about, and made them gather only what was plentiful and tasty. Some of them didn't understand, and Ulongtim told them their sweat would make the food taste better. Of course that made some of the men cut up some meat and wear that as well. It was fully dark when they were all dressed and ready to raid. They shouted their raid cries and screamed for the night spirits to stay clear of their camp, which was now filled with torch lights and the fettered screams of women and young protectors. Ramaa and Ulongtim raced around for all to see, winding themselves through the camp and then into the jungle behind them.

Night came so totally there was a moment of temporary blindness when darkness finally came. If not for the Tuk blade at her side, Keishlee would have been frightened by it. She had cleaned and dried Mah's loin cloth and walking carry sack, and was carrying these to him when night fell.

He greeted her warmly when she found him and waited for him to dress. His body was hot, yet her touch did not pain him. They went back to the camp in silence and she wondered if anything could take his scent away. He was almost as fresh smelling as always, except for his hair, which would require water washing. There was hardly any trace of the horror that he had been. She entwined her arms around his and held him to her tight and close. They were at the edge of the camp when she felt his need come to her through the darkness.

"Bird of many colors, speak to me and share what keeps you far away." She let her words caress him.

Mah could not tell her of the many bits of unclear visions he had seen across the desert sands. He had changed his mind about this strange expanse of land, which was a remarkable place for training the inner eye. But as it was so often, there were no words to describe this to anyone unless they understood Great Mah bird song. Only Shhaha, Bellar and Odrak could even begin to understand what he felt. Human words could not express all of what a heart could feel.

He turned around to the darkened desert, which he could still see clearly, and there it was, the glitter of sparkling sands, giving off something to the night which had been given to it from the day. "I have been destroy and reborn all in one day." He turned Keishlee around to see the desert again.

She saw the infinitesimal glitters covering the sands and it renewed her spirit. Mah wanted to pull her away. It was a beautiful sight, but he feared she would lose her night vision to it, as he was losing his. But they both looked until their sight was gone. Night blinded by the lights, Mah smiled and led her back in the direction of the tall walkers.

"He is better," Mah spoke softly, rubbing his hip.

"She says he is just being lazy. He does not want to look at the sands," said Keishlee.

"The blood of the tall walkers was created on desert sands," Mah offered. "She has a memory of other kin here."

"Oh. So that is what she said," Keishlee groaned and took hold of the resting female. "No you must not, you must not, no matter your dream," she shouted at the female and rubbed her head up along her neck. "Look at this place. It is too lean of life. What a place to think of such a thing."

Mah chuckled and said, "There are women here who have."

"She did not tell you that," Keishlee snapped, knowing he could not speak to the tall walkers as well as a woman could.

"She will hardly speak to me at all, but there is a new sound to her call, and she coddles him now. Look at him. Look at how content he is, when he has been sour all during the journey."

"You think she has done it already?"

"I think she will tell you when it is done."

Calling them by the names she'd given them after leaving Tuk Village, she said, "Feathertip, do not do it here." She stroked the female. "You hold yourself back, Lightstep," she begged jokingly, but was hoping desperately that they had not done it already.

Mah's vision was slowly returning to him. He could almost see beyond the fire's light. He gathered up some of the food Keishlee had prepared, and filled the space within that had grown impatient.

"You have not said anything, Mah. Neither has Odrak. He and Ramaa have been with the Timbutikata, but you have been alone. As you know I have. Shhaha...."

"He has eaten and he is well. I will know otherwise, and when it is his time to die, I will know that as well. Then I will sleep for many days and nights, so I may get the final lesson from him. We have been connected for some time now. Odrak as well."

"Mah, are you and Odrak Blood Keepers now?"

"No," Mah said, knowing the awful truth of it, and wondering what he would be like when he was. "No. Not yet."

That night they laid awake for a long time, waiting for the moon to rise to make their chants. Keishlee was asleep before it did, and when Mah finally saw it, and was sure it was the one he knew, he too fell fast into slumber.

Odrak stayed awake most of the night. He had grown accustomed to it during the journey. The four young friends he'd made kept him near their camp, telling stories of their village above the high stock kernel [*kind of corn*] plains, a well known rich and expansive feeding ground. A place where a human could walk next to a killing beast and be offered food by it, and a moment to sit down and talk with it.

They told him that in this land the moon was seen for only short periods, even tho the sky was always clear. Odrak had expected as much, considering the shortness of the day. It was the long twilight that still fascinated him most. It was said that twilight was the best time for the dead to make their way back to the Great Mother. It was also the time they used to find other spirits with which to walk the night. The long twilight made Odrak wonder why the dead here needed so much time to prepare, but thinking of the desert, he wondered if it was the amount of dead that needed preparing.

After the moon had risen, Odrak heard confusing cries of pleasure and pain. There was the sound of someone being dragged off, and then the distant pleas of quiet torment. Odrak rose to investigate, but was stopped by Cheemaxs, one of his new friends, who said, "Omolungway takes his prize for tumble down. I say you won. You may shitty me as prize."

Odrak was stricken. From the words he used, Cheemaxs was offering himself to be brutally beaten. "I don't want to fight you," Odrak replied and laid back down next to Cheemaxs. Cheemaxs then tried to force Odrak to strike him, but Odrak still did not understand. Cheemaxs would not let him sleep now, and seemed in need of both fighting and relief.

"I go to release my waters," Odrak said, trying to be kind as he hurried away.

Cheemaxs knew he would not come back, but for a time he sat up and waited, listening to the sounds of Omolungway and someone else wrestling in the sand.

Odrak came out from between the trees, where he could see the desert glittering from the moonlight. He wished he had not come this way, but the sounds both repelled and attracted him. He could see them, their naked bodies shining with reflected beads of sweat. Omolungway was beating some poor soul into submission. Odrak didn't really mean to watch them bucking in the sand. He really didn't want to sit there fuming over the blood that would be spilled from forced entry. He had only wished not to fight Cheemaxs, and was now glad of it if this was what was expected.

Once Omolungway finished finding pleasure for himself, the other one ran back into the trees, away from the camp. Odrak waited to clear his head, but finally could not stop his legs from moving. He found himself crouched over Omolungway, ready to kick or claw if the need arose. To his surprise, Omolungway was rubbing himself in the dirt, moaning with some pain. But Odrak did not care about his pain; he would give this one the warning as it should be done.

"It is you," Omolungway spoke, when his eyes could see Odrak's face. "Come to give me what is mine. I do not want you, but in a moment...."

"How dare you!! You filth!!" screamed Odrak, trying to hold back his voice.

Omolungway shot up and stood over Odrak to remind him of his size and might. "Should have been you. They say my winning not fully won. They say your Kong may curse us. I do not care!! There are no little women here for us. I will have my pleasure!"

Odrak stood up slowly. The movement alone warned of the danger. He dug one foot into the sand and poised himself to kill. "You shall never do this to me. Not by surprise, or will, or might. Do not call me to the tumble down again. Try not to look my way. And if for any reason you lay a hand on me, I shall kill you. In truth! Remember this and believe what I say."

Odrak did not have the power of voice that Shhaha and Mah shared, but the point was clearly made, and Omolungway could feel the truth of it. When Odrak turned his back to him, Omolungway was furious beyond all reason, but did not dare to speak or move. He watched Odrak go back into the darkened trees and hoped no one had seen or heard. Odrak was small-framed compared to him, but he had felt the bones in his chest come near to breaking when kicked, and Odrak had done that with a smile. Anger made one more powerful. He would remember what was said.

Odrak slept that night by himself, near a tree exactly like

the forbidden one. Not even the night insects crawled. It seemed the raid had been successful. He stared at the speckles of stars and marked the ones that pointed back to his people. It had been a long journey, and they still had some distance to go. He looked forward to leaving this place and these people, even to crossing the desert to do it. He dreaded the sunrise, when he was sure there would be other tumble downs, and more winners in search of a prize. He hoped the elders played for a different gain. He was unsettled by so many different people and customs. Shhaha had told him that when they left the Valley of Names, they would return by another way. He fell asleep worrying that they would have to do this all over again, with all new people.

Keishlee had gone into the stores of food they carried and was preparing a small feast for the morning meal. The female tall walker had brought back some interesting nest remains, along with large red and yellow leaves from a tree that was not among those she could see. She had tasted them and found them very pleasing. She covered them with fruit and nut paste and rolled them up with beans to bake in the hot rock hole she'd made.

Hoping to make everyone happy, she pulled out one of the small salt sacks and salted the nests, then placed them on top of the hot rocks, pouring drops of water over them for steam. In the ground underneath she had placed an assortment of ground foods to bake, and on top she was mixing a special mush for dipping and finger licking, which she had not made during the entire journey.

Mah awoke to the smell of the mush, a brew of strong beetle bellies and various animal eyes and skull matter [*brains*], which she had collected before the break of day. It was a special mush usually prepared only for a feast. Mah sat by the large stone bowl, unraveling the contents with his nose. He knew better than to steal a taste until Keishlee was done, but as she added another touch of salt to the mix, he could not hold back, and begged her for a finger full.

She denied him any, but smiled at the water about his mouth. She sent him off to gather more ground sponges, which could be found under rocks near the banks of the stream.

"Did you bury the creatures?" Mah asked, sneaking one of the empty beetles into his hand.

"No," she replied, intent on her stirring and watching the

eyes in her mush change color.

"You did not make a beggar pile here?!" He stopped and turned around to see Keishlee pull out a leaf net full of large black and red beetles. They had white stripes down their legs and were still alive. "There is enough muscle mush here for all our people. Beggars will cry all day!"

"No. I placed them at the entrance to the feeder enclosure of the Timbutikata. Aaah, they eat flesh."

"Yes they do, Aaah!" Mah said, remembering the smell of animal flesh when they first came upon the camp. He turned away from the sight of the beetles that were making his belly rumble, and ran off into the trees.

Soon Odrak followed the smell of the special mush and ran over to Keishlee, demanding a taste. It was the best thing she had made all journey, and he knew it was good for the heart, and other muscles, which was why it was so named. But she denied him any as well. Odrak decided to sit in front of the bowl and wait, and warned her to give him the first taste or he would upturn the bowl.

Keishlee was beaming with pride. They had not praised her womanly abilities before, and she had only hoped to make a good enough meal to bring Shhaha out of hiding. She added a little more water and salt for the smell to rise, then pulled on Odrak's loose hair to let him know how pleased she was.

Mah had thought to go around the waking camp of the Timbutikata, but saw Ramaa trying to get away from a group of people and decided to see what was going on. A woman was speaking to Ramaa and holding two of the slaughtered creatures Keishlee had used to make the mush. Some of the men had the others, and a small group of women had the rest.

"I do not know who she killed them for. Take them as a gift. Separate them among your people," Ramaa was saying.

"I saw," one of the women said. "Your woman put here for us!" she growled and pointed to the other women.

"Women no hunt food!" bellowed the men.

"She hunt. Giant woman hunt!" roared the woman.

"Your woman hunt?" asked the man Mah remembered as Augklac. "Your woman hunt for you, yes?"

"No!" Ramaa grunted with distaste. "My people do not eat flesh," Ramaa shouted as he saw Mah come closer.

Some of the women began throwing sticks and sand

pebbles at Mah. When he would not go back they cursed him and turned their backs to him, kicking dirt and sand back up at him with their feet.

Mah understood now that he was to be shunned as well, but did not care. He looked at Ramaa and said, "Do you smell it?"

"I have been trying to get away. She has made the muscle brew. I did not know she could. The muscle brew...."

"No speak with filth," whispered Glyph. He turned to Mah and kicked loose dirt at him and said, "Filth! Filth!"

Mah smiled at Ramaa, who was looking ruefully down at these people. He signaled Mah off and watched after him as he made his way out of the clearing. Then he roared at the people for silence, as the fuss began to start up again. "I will bring her here!"

"No. We go!"

"No!" Ramaa demanded, knowing that some of the men had also smelled the muscle brew. He could see their mouths watering even tho their eyes were on the flesh the women carried. "No. I shall bring her here. Stay!" he ordered, and then stalked off.

When he reached Keishlee, she already had a taste for him on her finger and he lapped it up without a word of greeting. His eyes beamed with joy that she had done a special mush. He almost picked her up from the ground as he greeted her, begging for another taste. She denied him and made him sit, which he did to get a good look at the brew. Odrak was sitting across from him, hot-tempered over the slight. He would guard the mush now even from Ramaa.

After getting his nose full of the rich and spicy aroma, Ramaa told Keishlee about the squabble over the animal flesh. She huffed at the silliness, but agreed to go settle matters. For a taste, she bribed Odrak into a promise to watch over the mush without tasting more. He did not want to make such a promise, but would not think of leaving it unguarded. He watched Keishlee and Ramaa walk through the trees over to the main camp and braced himself for the torture of having to wait until her return. Then he saw the pile of empty beetle shells and made haste to lick each one clean.

At the feeder enclosure, Ramaa and Keishlee found two men beating one of the women. He was trying to take her animals away. Keishlee did not hesitate to draw her weapon. Ramaa tried to speak against it, but knew his words were wasted.

Everyone saw her quick move and held their places as they

stared at the weapon. Keishlee called out the words to bring forth the women, but none responded. Ramaa repeated and emphasized the necessity for a Timbutikata woman to speak. Only the one still holding her two dead tree moles stepped over and greeted her.

"Weapon?" the woman asked, pointing at the Tuk blade.

"Death for one or two," Keishlee replied then pointed to the two men who had beaten her.

"Woman can kill a man?" the woman asked.

"He has spilled your blood. Yes, if either one is your mate, and you wish it because you cannot," Keishlee replied.

"I can kill a man," another woman laughed and pulled out a small stone knife. "Kill men," she ordered.

Other women were coming over to the group, some at a run. Men were gathering about and when they understood Keishlee's intent, they made moves towards her as a warning, some even making blood threats. Ramaa had a respected place among them now, and a leading group had begun to gather at his legs, awaiting his words.

Keishlee strode forward, knowing it would be an easy feat, but Ramaa held her back, asking quickly, "Are they your mates?" He repeated it so both women would understand.

The woman with the tree moles looked at the men and then at Keishlee and said, "No. But kill him."

Keishlee looked up at Ramaa and then back at the other women.

"Have you mates?" Ramaa asked the men, signaling them to be quick with answers.

Everyone became agitated, and the other women began to call out words of respect for the men, but for all the men, as if they belonged to them all. Some women began to show their power over the men, and ordered them about, or made them sit, or made them fetch drinks and such. Three strong looking women came over to the men Keishlee threatened and explained to them Keishlee's full intent. They stomped about, shouting and throwing harsh looks and signs. The three women then came over to Keishlee like a thick wall. They were staring at her weapon, and everything about them told Keishlee that they were about to make an attack.

Ramaa tried to warn the women away, but they attacked. Keishlee broke two of their legs with kicks before they could get another punch in her face. The look in her eyes told Ramaa that she would use her weapon if they tried again.

The men were silent now and signaling for the woman holding the dead moles to speak.

"We do not understand 'mate'. Any woman may take a man. Any man may take a woman," spoke the woman.

Keishlee understood. She looked down at the moaning women at her feet and then up at the one still standing ready for attack. "You wish to save these men?" she spoke to the woman standing in front of her.

"There will be no more talk of taking life!" came the force of a powerful voice. Everyone, including Keishlee and Ramaa, were bowed with bent knees. "We are strangers to these people and they know not our ways. They were here first, and we must not interfere with their customs."

It was a lesson for slaves, taught by every keeper in their clan, but Shhaha gave it the force of something to be revered. Keishlee felt ashamed, and looked at her weapon as if it were responsible for how she felt. She placed it back in the hang net on her leg but was then knocked down by the woman. Before she could get up the woman ran back to the men, who grunted at Keishlee, then returned to their humble attitudes to greet Shhaha as he entered the clearing.

The Tututs and the guarding Aphros following him were causing much disturbance. Having had plenty sun, they were yellow-brown now, but they still did not look human. Their chest and arms were bare, but their long skirts made the sand and dust of the clearing dance around them as they moved.

Ramaa saw the danger here and knew that he would never be relieved of duty. He would have to guard the Tututs with his life to stop these people from removing those skirts.

Keishlee was agitated anew: someone was bringing the special mush closer. She could smell it coming through the trees and knew that Odrak was carrying it. She looked at Ramaa and saw that he already had his eyes on the bowl as Odrak came into the clearing. The young protectors stepped in front, their mouths watering and their eyes glued to the source of the delicious aroma. Even the Tututs and Aphros were looking at the large bowl with pleasure.

Shhaha walked over to Keishlee and greeted her in the custom of their people. With this done and the look he gave her after, she knew he was not disrespecting her by giving her special mush away to these people, but he would put her in a position to do a kindness.

Angry, she ordered Ramaa to build another small fire. When the men saw what she wanted they ordered her away, insisting that she do her cooking among the women. Keishlee agreed to be moved, but demanded that all the women tend to their own bowls and cooking fires, or she would make enemies among those that kept eyes on her. The women got her meaning, and for the first time, Keishlee felt the links that told her these people were human, such as the things that can be know between women without words or signs, things common to a woman's nature.

Keishlee laughed when she heard the women begin their farting as they walked by her cooking fire. Odrak guarded the special mush. He had it sitting on rocks, waiting for the fire to get hot while slowly adding more water to the brew. One look from him told the other youths not to approach. They grunted at him and ran off towards the stream as it disappeared into the trees.

Even cool, the special mush filled the clearing with succulent scents and kept some of the men hovering nearby. The sun was full around them now, and Shhaha was allowing some of the people to touch the Tututs and greet the Aphros. The women were cautious of the strange looking Tututs and called them "strange blood," but they liked the Aphros with their lusty smiles, and their ability to look at Shhaha without fear.

Soon the small clearing outside the feeder enclosure was filled with small cooking fires and men and women trying to prepare special foods. Keishlee ended the continuing dispute over the dead animals by slicing the entire lot to bits and handing out the pieces. She was glad to see that only a few would eat the flesh raw, and that most of them used it only to season other foods. A women brought Keishlee a taste of the long green fruit that she had been roasting. Keishlee thought the first taste too bitter and chewy and suggested the woman remove the skin from the fruit, and act that would later make her Keishlee's name sacred among these people.

Mah returned with his arms full of fungi and salt straw, which Keishlee was overjoyed to see. She hadn't hoped to find any in this dry land, but then she searched for the curl ferns and milk weeds which always grew near salt straw, and found them among the items being offered by the two youths with Mah. Now she could make other special foods her feeder had taught her to make, and knowing what the want of tasting them could make people do, she turned a wicked smile on the other women who thought they could cook.

She greeted Mah with a kiss as she dusted a spot for him to set them down. She called Ramaa over and asked that he and Odrak join the hunting party just starting to enter the thicker woods. She offered them three fingers each of the special mush and they left in a hurry to return for more.

As Odrak was leaving he began to notice that the women were beginning to shun Keishlee again, because Mah was near. A space had formed between her and the others, and tho Keishlee would prefer it, Odrak did not want her to lose the friendly company just yet. He called Mah over to join him, ignoring the slight everyone gave him as Mah came near.

As always, Mah was fresh-smelling and free of the usual dirt so easily gathered by those who sleep on the ground. It was painful and pleasing to have him close again, but still he could not look him directly eye to eye. Instead he turned his attention to the group of angry protectors, who watched Mah like lizards stalking prey. Among them was Omolungway and another protector, looking at Mah hungrily.

Among the Tall Walkers there could be no feast without the entertainment of a great tale, and so Shhaha gathered the people around him with his voice and his dance. Using all his powers to bring to life, Timbu and Tikata, the ancient elders of these people. Timbuk and Glyph, who stayed in the clearing to be near the smell of the special mush, were amazed that he knew any of the tale. It was a sacred thing among their people. Only the Great Kong knew all the words. They shouted at each mention of the mother of their clan, Kata-Tikata, and stomped and screeched at the mention of Timbuka. Shhaha sat on his heels, knocking knee bones together in echo to the tale, and the people held fast to every word and gesture, as Shhaha recalled how Timbu and Tikata were brought together by the giant squawks, who saved them from great quakes.

Once Mah was gone, the women showered their favors on Keishlee in exchange for a taste of the now steaming special mush. One woman brought her a large empty shell which Keishlee had admired. It was as large as the stone bowls the Tututs made, which they always had to leave behind, except it was lighter and allowed food to cook more quickly. She could not tell if it was some creature's egg or the hull of some giant fruit, but it smelled nice and felt sturdy. She thanked the woman for the shell with a handful of the mush.

She regretted not having had time to learn more from her feeder, but this was a brew no one ever turned away from. She saw the delight in the woman as she moved it back and forth in her mouth in order to keep the taste there longer, daring the others to come near her while she ate. When the woman left she was smiling and trying to imitate the tall walker saunter.

Keishlee kept her fire at a spark. The air was too hot for flames, and most of the women laid their seasoned piles in the open sun. Later when the men returned, they all had something for what was now sure to be a great feast, but the clearing quickly grew too steamed and crowded for easy company.

Seeing the need, Shhaha ordered the sitting group around him to move to the edge of the camp onto the sands, where he would tell them another tale about their people, one which they might not know. From an outsider, this seemed almost an insult, but in the silence Shhaha whispered the name, "Etutilare," and watched as their angry pride turned to wonder and dismay.

Etutilare was the blood that held them together as a people. It was the name given to their Kongs from the roar of the great squawks living in their land. It was a secret name among the Timbutikata. Only those old enough, or worthy enough would know. This was an ancient custom, and Shhaha had no way to know it was still used, but as usual he had guessed correctly. Some would hate Shhaha for knowing it, while others would respect and revere him for the power and kinship in his knowing.

"Etutilare-Kong," came the quiet whisper in response to the name. "Shhaha-Kong!" they spoke more loudly to offer him their respect. "Man of many words," added Timbuk, whose words told Shhaha that he knew this tale. They would follow him now. They would sit near and attend his needs, as his own people did, and they would allow him to do his magic among them, and heed his words.

There was much word sharing and many names remembered as they moved to the sands, leaving most of the women and some of the men to finish with the feast making. The day had somehow become special, like the foods they prepared, and everyone made themselves busy with the necessities for such an occasion. The youths downed branches, separating the bark and gathering the edible leaves. Older protectors made splinter piles of the fallen wood for fires and cleared the area around the enclosure of waste, which they threw into holes where there had once been trees. Women gathered water and men skinned and cut dead animals into pieces, which they cooked on seasoned leaves covered with the new salt grass.

But Keishlee also had rock salt, which the Timbutikata had never seen. They found it a marvel to eat by itself, and considered it a magic for what it did to food. Even the men, who only cooked animal flesh, begged some salt from Keishlee by showing her some extra kindness. When the two she would have killed returned, carrying a large horned creature between them, they made a presentation of one of the useful horns to her in order to get a piece. By then everyone had given Keishlee the eyes and skull matter of their slain animals, and now she had the large shell filled with the special mush.

Mah and Odrak would not kill any animals; instead they went to the stream, and after making a leaf net, caught many fish for Keishlee to bake with her roots and herb greens. Others had come to the stream to watch them, and were soon trying to catch fish themselves. They had seen fish before, but had never thought to eat any. Now they trusted the ways of Shhaha's people and were disappointed when they had to return empty handed. Yet they would not approach Odrak, who sat next to Mah, to ask his help.

Two protectors had been following Mah around all day. He had told them that he was no longer soiled, but they still would not get too close, fearing the curse they said he now carried. The youths held back for most of the day, doing what he asked from a distance, but when the tall walkers entered the clearing and greeted Mah, they rushed over and begged Mah for use of his leaf net.

The youths were bright and endearing when they tried to use Tall Walker words, and did not realize that they touched, picked and licked their lips while they spoke. To Odrak they were a nuisance, appearing slightly dimwitted, since they were seasons older than he.

Mah showed them how to hold the net between them, and explained how to walk the lake silently so not to frighten the fish away. He laughed at their calling the fish "swimming food," and watched them race by the tall walkers back towards the lake. It was then that Mah and Odrak noticed that the clearing was empty except for Keishlee and the tall walkers. Mah called to Keishlee, who was busy removing the eyes from the fish, and she saw the empty clearing and laughed.

She scolded the tall walkers for frightening the Timbutikatas. "You would do better to make friends of these people. They might spare you some of their leaf pile."

Odrak saw the women cowering behind trees and inside the leafy enclosure. This is why no one came back to their end of the camp, he thought. Odrak signaled for the men he saw to come from behind the trees, while begging the limping tall walker to rest himself. No one dared to move out from hiding until both tall walkers had their legs folded under them. Keishlee was scratching their necks and giving them a taste of the fresh salt grass dipped in the sweet palm oil. She didn't really like having them here, since it meant that no one was guarding their packs.

Odrak saw the worried look on her face and the direction of her attention, but before he left he said to Mah, "These people have a thing they call tumble down. It can be a pleasure, but you must not join in with them."

Mah looked at Odrak as if he had cursed him. These were the first words Odrak had spoken to him in many days, but they were not the words he wanted to hear. "They shun me. Who would ask me to join in their play?"

"Those two," Odrak huffed.

"Cheemaxs and Oulaboul?" Mah questioned, showing off the fact that he knew their names. "You care for me no more. I should be an unnatural thing if no one cared for me. Would you have me be unnatural as well as brokenhearted?" Mah spoke the words he had not really wanted to say.

Odrak kicked the fish towards him and stalked out of the clearing, telling himself that Mah no longer cared for him. The proof of it was that he sat considering others. "Let them try for him!" Odrak warned the trees as he rushed by. "I will spoil it for them."

Odrak ran past the trees to their end of camp, where their food was still baking in the ground, and their packs were heaped together in a pile near the tall walkers resting place. He spotted the Great Mah feather cape that was filled with the gifts from the birds. This end of the camp was bare except for a few trees. As he came closer to the piles, he saw the desert with the sun bouncing off the yellow sands, and he cried, dry tears stinging his eyes, because they would not fall. He chanted to himself the call against evil, and demanded that the evil spirits coming for him find another one to bother. He would not let evil take him. He would not give into his jealousy. He would allow Mah to find another if that was what he wanted.

He cleared his thoughts and covered their packs with the leaf pile Keishlee used to feed the tall walkers. Seeing no one around, he went to find Shhaha and hear the tales he was recalling for the others.

Keishlee could hear the shouts of the group gathered around Shhaha on the other side of the trees. It made her proud to know that Shhaha was such a worthy blood keeper. In a sun shift he had gained loyalty and trust from these people. He mixed their words with his own as if they were always spoken together. Even Ramaa stumbled over their words, and for her it was a constant struggle. She smiled at the women that braved getting close to the tall walkers. They would get used to the tall walkers, and she would get used to them.

Mah's two new friends came back, proud of their small catch of medium-sized fish. They paraded them in front of the women, but would not allow any of them to be touched, except by Mah, who showed them how to remove the scales, which they could not eat. The protectors then made a small fire over which they held the fish on long sticks. The women teased them about not having the salt, and kicked dirt at them for speaking with the "filthy one."

Keishlee gave Mah a look, then he took a pile of the salt grasses, wrapped each fish with the thick soft stalks, and then sprinkled them with water. Now the fish dripped oil that sparked in the fire, and Mah showed them how to turn the fish to keep the oils from dripping too freely. Soon even they could smell that this made the fish better. But as Mah was leaving them, the women threw small stones and sand at him, and cursed. It didn't really hurt, and so Mah ignored it.

When the sun started its quick descent, the tall walkers went off to get their own meal. Shhaha went out to the desert to stretch himself, and the men and women returned in readiness for a feast. They made a circle of themselves and talked up their best tumble downers in order to get them going. In no time at all they were rallied around their favorites, shouting at the first two men to bring one or the other down. The women explained to Keishlee that the winners would be the first to eat, which made the first few rounds go by quickly. Everyone played with great enthusiasm.

Ramaa was more than hungry, and joined the group with Ulongtim and Augklac. When it came his turn to take the center no one wanted to challenge him. Ramaa was starving and offered to take on any three men to even up the match. No one stepped forward, but the people shouted for "Eblickibutea," who jumped up and pulled another man in with him.

They feared Ramaa's great size, and did not make much effort, until Ramaa signaled another man over from one of the standing groups. With their best three fighters in the ring, the people howled for Koro, Eblickibutea and the new man, Urang, who quickly had one of Ramaa's long arms pinned behind his back, but they could not bring him down. The Timbutikata had good balance, but the thing a Tall Walker could do best was keep his feet on solid ground. A stumbling Tall Walker was unheard of.

Once Ramaa tried of playing, he threw one man back into the crowd and leaped on the other two, pinning them flat on their backs in clouds of dust. Ramaa's name filled the clearing, while two of the most corpulent Timbutikata women offered themselves to him, along with some of their food. Ramaa assured them he would have everything offered, but he was going to swallow his food first.

Keishlee sat the original bowl of special mush in front of him, and chuckled as he scooped out a handful to feed himself and the women sitting at his side. The other winners sitting near protested and threw Keishlee jealous, pouting looks. Ramaa laughed and scooped out another handful, then gave the bowl to the man nearest him to pass it to those who had already played.

Now the clearing was full of wild calls and screams as the tumble downs continued with rapid speed. Two men tried to pound each other into the dirt, without a single knee actually touching the ground. To cheer them on, the previous winners shouted that the food of the Tall Walker woman was too great a prize, and should not be given to losers.

There was some protesting at first, but then Shhaha came over and said, "Yes! Only the winners should be allowed the muscle brew," then he stepped into the empty center ground and called for the strongest man to come forth.

Everyone went silent. Shhaha was a Great Kong to them,

and someone not to be touched out of hand. But like their Kong, he was willing to stand the tumble down, even tho he was much too old to stand any chance of winning.

The standing groups sat down to watch, whispering among themselves and wondering if this Kong would curse them like their own did when he lost. It was common knowledge among them that whenever the Great Kong lost, the winner would be found dead the day following the next full moon. No one wanted to die, but there were many days and nights before the next full moon, during which the winner would be treated to every kindness from his people, because they knew he would soon be dead.

The people looked first to Ramaa and Keishlee for their approval. Ramaa only laughed and declared Shhaha the winner. With good cheer, the women howled at him and then screeched at their men to stand the challenge. The men praised Shhaha for being a true Great Kong, while the women called forth those who were good, but whom they would not mind living without.

Ramaa gave Eblickibutea a warm smile and signaled for him to take the challenge. When he stood up he was pouring sweat from the heat of the day, but he gritted his teeth and rushed forward, wanting only to get it over quickly. Shhaha made a quick move as if to brace himself against the weight, then fell to his hands and swung his body around to trip the younger man up. Eblickibutea fell on his face like a cut tree.

The entire clearing was a hush of heartbeats and then a roar of delight. Women rushed to Shhaha and fell at his feet. Others ran to their food piles and made him offers. Even the men made offers of their drinks, hoping that he would grace them with a touch of his hand.

Shhaha signaled them away and called for another match. "I want the other cooking shell placed before me." He smiled at Keishlee so that all would honor her with another round of screams for her special mush.

Three men rushed over to Keishlee and offered to bring the heavy shell to where Shhaha would sit. When it was put in place, another man jumped into the center ring, screaming to gather his courage, and then began his attack.

Ramaa and Keishlee were filled with shame, but could not stop themselves from laughing, as Shhaha made haste with a quick step and side kick that made the man trip over his own feet and fall on his back. These were tricks Shhaha was using, well-known to anyone from their clan. He would not have dared to use these among any Tall Walkers. But the Timbutikata were gaped and astounded. They rushed to where Shhaha was to sit, setting up piles of food to honor him. Two others followed in quick defeat before Shhaha stepped regally around the ring, and then took his place behind the huge shell of muscle mush.

Now the tumble downs proceeded in earnest. Hard knocks were taken, and the next two losers had to be dragged out of the ring. They all could see that Shhaha was taking his fill of the special mush and that he only gave out small portions to the winners. Soon only losers were playing again, but a new distraction seized the crowd once the winners had filled themselves. They wanted their normal prize, and now that they had three new feeders among them, they wanted to taste these as well.

The Tututs, who had stayed near Shhaha, pulled up the backs of their robes to hide their feeder bags and crept closer to Keishlee and her weapon. The men were pleading with Ramaa and Shhaha that it was their custom, and that they had the right, but the Aphros would not allow them near enough to touch the Tututs. Even the women became angry with the Tututs, whom they thought too skinny and unattractive to be rejecting their men.

The tumble downs continued amidst this quiet fuss, as the young protectors rushed to get their meals before all the best foods were gone. Odrak was one of the first to join a standing group. Omolungway was the first to play and win, but when he went for his handful of the special mush, Odrak insisted that he be next. He could not stand to see Omolungway eat before him, so he wasted no time with the youth who challenged him. Shhaha rewarded him with two handfuls, which he went without thought to share with Mah.

The tumble downs were going by very quickly since the youths were hungry and not serious about fighting. When Odrak approached, there was a swirl of agitation among the people as he made an offer to Mah of the special mush. Mah looked up at him, and for the first time he felt hurt by their shuns and curses. He turned a harsh eye over the group, but only Ramaa and Keishlee did not turn away from him. He slipped from under Odrak and stepped into the suddenly empty ring. Mah seethed as people began throwing dirt at him.

Odrak ate his mush, trying not to think about what was going on. It was still warm and so full of flavor that it kept him distracted against his will.

Shhaha was looking only at Mah, spell-casting with his narrow leering eyes.

Ramaa was tired of the slight they gave Mah, and Keishlee hated them throwing things at him. She jumped to her feet and slowly caught the attention of the other women with her stance, which said there would be trouble if they continue in this way. Ramaa too would not allowing Mah to continue suffering like this. He turned a cold glare on Shhaha, then suddenly realized that it was he who had been making Mah suffer all along.

Shhaha knew that vibes were a force of energy that all life forms produced. Humans with strong energy could produce vibes that are as clear as words. This is what is looked for in a slave chosen to be an apprentice to the Keeper of the Blood. With Mah it was always believed that his smell overshadowed what vibes he really had, especially after the Great Mahs took him to sleep with in the open fields. But even these people could see now that Mah did not need to speak to impress his presence and feelings upon them. This is what is needed to be a good teacher and a Keeper of the Blood.

The clearing was suddenly quiet and Odrak was leaping away with tears in his eyes. Everyone was staring at Mah as if he had told them some sad tale, yet he did not move or speak. He was not even looking at them, only at Shhaha, who seemed to be holding him still with some invisible power.

"Do you find me such a horror that I may not be relieved of your curses?" Mah turned and spoke to the crowd.

The people looked at him uneasily. They had not known any one to recover from the curse of the filth pile. Most would grow feeble and die after a long illness. But this one no longer even had the smell about him, and there was no sign of sickness about his eyes.

"You have insulted our Great Kong!!" spoke the heavy woman, who never hesitated to speak for these people.

"Your Great Kong had a reason for telling you not to touch the tree, and to frighten you against it," Mah spoke carefully, already knowing all their words; they had so few.

A silent cry went up from their hearts. Somehow they had known this. The fruit from that tree was no different from the many smaller ones around them?

"You claim the power of the Kong?" blurted someone.

"No," Mah spoke, knowing the truth of it. "Look at the fine and loyal people he has to follow him. Our Shhaha, who I will say has greater power than your Kong, is jealous of your love for him. You give your blood to him without words. You would stay here and die waiting for him. Our people did not think to give our Shhaha the kind of protection this group can offer, and for this journey it was, and may still be needed."

The Timbutikata did not understand all his words, but hearts went out to him. He had praised them and their Kong, and still kept faith with Shhaha.

"I do claim some of the wisdom of your Kong," Mah continued, through only minor objections. "This tree is more fruitful than any I have ever seen, and does not grow in the lands of the Kong, or the lands of the Tall Walkers. I believe he wishes to take the whole tree and all its fruit, since it has no seeds, back with you to your people. He wanted to keep the tree safe until his return."

"There is always fruit on these trees," grunted the woman. "Yes. Yes," agreed the others.

"This is why your Kong wishes this tree to grow among his people. Think of the dry seasons that come over the land, when all people must wander away from the safety of their clearing to find fresh water and food to feed themselves. It is the wisdom of your Great Kong that I did not consider before I spoke."

Shhaha rose in one quick motion. It was a shock to see such old bones move so quickly, such a move demanded attention and respect. Most people never saw elders with this many seasons, much less see them move about with vigor. Mah fell to his knees and bowed himself to the ground with his face in the dirt. Keishlee and Ramaa did so as well, causing the others much consternation as they tried to get into the position of humility known to the clan of the Tall Walkers.

"All things in their time," Shhaha spoke to all the people and then bid them to listen. "Trust that I am worthy and that what I say is truth." He paused to give them time to pass around his words and to prepare themselves for the dread within them. "Etutilare-Kong shall not return to you here." He paused again to wait for them to settle down. "I can speak no more of him, but you must not fear the tree. You must learn to care for it and then leave this land, taking the tree, all its roots, and its fruit with you. This," Shhaha received a wilted plant from Tehuti, handing it to him on cue, "...is the plant you must gather and keep safe until you return to your own lands."

Shhaha allowed the plant to be passed among the people. The heavy woman took the plant and not only looked at it closely, but smelled it and rubbed it into her face. Then she passed it to another and went up to face Shhaha, crouching in the accepted form for addressing a Great Kong. "We have been here many moons now. We fear what you say, but hear the truth in your words. We believe you know the ways of the Kong, and we will do as you say," she said, then managed to make the move she saw Mah and the others do, but then needed help to get herself up from the ground.

There was a peace settling over the clearing. Keishlee heard the tall walkers passing through the trees on their way back to their camp and answered their soundless tones to tell them that all was well. Odrak stood off near the trees with the look of wanting all over him. Ramaa had already gone to greet Mah, and was holding him close, rubbing their heads together like two youths renewing their friendship. Shhaha went back to making a hearty meal of the special mush, and finally accepted some of the offerings from the other women.

"I will make you tumble," shouted one of the youths that had braved his company earlier. "No, I!" shouted another.

Soon the women were roaring again for the tumble downs to continue. There was much pushing about for placement in the standing order, but the one called Oulaboul got to the center first, and he and Mah greeted each other before going at the play in earnest.

As the young will do, Oulaboul had learned the stepping tricks of the people of the tall walkers just by watching Shhaha, and tried to use them on Mah, who played with him at first. But Oulaboul was serious. He wanted to win and tried using his larger build and stronger arms to force Mah down. Mah might have been a bird in another life, but he was a Tall Walker now, and could not be put off balance. They threw each other and stumbled around the clearing to the shouts of the crowd, but Mah would not go down. Oulaboul pounded Mah across the chest and kicked at his legs. Mah used Oulaboul's own weight against him and managed a body twist to get Oulaboul down to one knee. They could not continue like they were, so they started over.

Odrak had run over to Ramaa's side and was sent into a rage every time Mah was struck. Ramaa was shouting for Mah to win, but did not look assured of the outcome. The other youths were all gathered at one end now, screaming for Oulaboul and grunting the wordless calls of the tumble down. They were pushing and shoving each other for new standing when the one called Omolungway knocked some of them down and took the lead. Odrak stepped into the ring just as Mah was bringing Oulaboul down. The crowd hooted and yelled, calling Mah's name as he was pushed back into the ring to take his walk around. When he reached Shhaha, he dipped both hands into the shell and pulled out a thick heap of the special mush, which he ate lustily while still standing. Keishlee took the bowl from between Ramaa's legs and went over and sat Mah down with the bowl in front of him. Mah pulled her down to him and held her close, thanking her and kissing her face. She felt the tears, and knew he did not want the others to see. She rubbed her face and hair against him to wipe them away, and then kissed his face again.

When she was gone and the tumble downs had continued, Mah motioned for Odrak to come over. "Share with me," he said, reaching for Odrak's hand. The darkness of night was just about to drop over them and the sky was twinkling as patches of light disappeared.

"It was hard won," Odrak suggested. "Maybe you might have need of me still."

"Why do you think otherwise?" Mah whispered.

"You do not really need me. I know you now, and you know how well I do."

"As I do you. Since the Kamituians I...."

"You have not wanted me, nor do you dare to look at me without hating me. Hating me," Odrak groaned.

Mah could not deny it, but it was not how he felt.

"I have never hated you. Even when you seek to be with another," Odrak said and without looking, pointed to Cheemaxs and Oulaboul, who were sitting across from them. Oulaboul was staring hard at Mah, and at where the tears had been.

"Never. I do not care for relief as often as others do. I do not think of it unless I think of you. I do not believe I could enjoy another. I do not believe I could be moved to try," Mah insisted, pulling Odrak back to him.

The truth of it was so clear Odrak felt foolish for having had the doubt. Unlike himself, Mah had never been with another. "You know my heart." Odrak mellowed and turned his coarse and hurt voice closer to Mah's ear. "But you think always of death and of me. You wish me dead, I think," Odrak finally worded his torment.

Mah was crushed. He had closed himself to Odrak so that he wouldn't see these things. Yet while they touched, everything they knew or thought was known to the other. It started the night he remade Odrak in the Kamitui clearing. It was too frightening to know that he could not have lived if Odrak died. His own grief would have killed him, as it did to Keishlee's feeder when she thought her mate had died, as it might have done to Pison when he found out that she was dead. Leaving the clan of the Tall Walkers and not having Keishlee around to remind him had saved him. Mah could think of nothing to save him when the duty to his clan would not, and he would have to live with this knowledge as long as he lived.

It had been unbearable for a while. He only wished to shut it out until he could think more clearly. It wasn't until he saw the desert, stretching out vast and enormous before him, that he remembered a lesson Shhaha gave him when his own feeder died. "Death only changes things for a little while. So do not look for reasons why. There is no reason why to die, when life is only given order by those who live."

Mah had come to terms with his own mortality out there on the desert, which had knotted his mind with fear. Mah had had to face his own death. The fact that he would died one day became real, and he hated Odrak for that. Death was always around, near enough to know whenever needed, but he had been a slave and death had been something for the old to consider. Now he knew death was a long chant, of which he was only a constant echo, and it recolored his whole world.

"I hate your having *taught* me death. But I do not hate YOU! I will always have need of you, Oodda," Mah broke down and called him by his secret name, the name of the clan the feeders whispered when speaking of Odrak's keeper.

Mah's face became a stream of water, and Odrak pulled him close and rubbed their heads and faces together. Odrak had his arms wrapped around his shoulders like the Aphros did, and he could feel the bruised skin and tightly knotted muscles. He pulled the bowl closer between them and ran a hand into Mah's walking carry sack. He found the assurance he wanted and needed, and then whispered to Mah that he would return with an oil node to rub his bruises. Odrak then dashed off towards the trees.

"It is my turn and I challenge you!" yelled Omolungway.

Mah had been sitting there for some time recovering himself. He hadn't noticed when the crowd thinned and all of the women were hustled away. Only one of the Tututs and two of the Aphros remained. Ulongtim and some of the other elder protectors stood near one of the fires, and only the youngest protectors sat about to continue the tumble down. Darkness was already around them, and Mah was taken by surprise. He jumped to his feet after Omolungway kicked dirt in his face.

Mah tried to calm himself and to refuse the fight, but Omolungway would not have it. The other youths were shouting for Omolungway, and Mah could see that Oulaboul had been badly beaten about the face.

Omolungway tried to pull Mah into what remained of the ring. They attacked each other, but as Mah was about to try and trip Omolungway up, he remembered that this was the one whose water had been filled with blood. The distraction caused him to lose his grip and Omolungway took the advantage. He picked Mah up and threw his weight over him to the ground. It knocked the wind out of Mah and he lay there unconscious, while Omolungway jumped around the clearing, declaring himself the winner.

Suddenly Omolungway pummel Mah in the face, then tried to drag him from the clearing. TasiSabl signaled to one of the Aphros, who did not hesitate to attack Omolungway.

The Aphro leaped on him and knocked him in his head. Omolungway managed to get on top to start pounding the Aphro's chest. The remaining Aphro jumped in, along with three other Timbutikatas. Timbuk bashed one of the Aphros in the head with a stick, demanding that they allow Omolungway his prize. Now the other Timbutikatas could hold back the remaining Aphro, who tried to yelled for assistance from the Aphros in the enclosure. They broke a stick over his head. and in the silence, allowed Omolungway to drag the unconscious Mah out of the clearing.

Ulongtim was angry with his people and cursed them for forcing their customs on the strangers. He warned them that death would come for them if the youth's blood was spilled and then stormed off towards the enclosure, unable to bring himself to stop Omolungway, or to find Ramaa or Keishlee, who would. He told himself that once Mah was made ready, maybe he would accept

Ulongtim, and then he would offer Mah all the protection he would need. Even against his people. "Yes. Better this way," he told himself aloud, as he entered the enclosure to find a willing female.

When Odrak returned he found the clearing almost empty except for a few of the youths. TasiSabl tending the wounded Aphros. Odrak was all smiles and pleased that the cover of night had come. He would take Mah out to the desert and lose himself in Mah's arms. They would cover each other with sand and heal the wounds they had made inside, and once again they would be one and whole.

"He is not here," TasiSabl answered the look on Odrak's face. "He...he," TasiSabl tried, but did not wish to be the one to tell him. Tonight was the first time it had seen these two close together. It had thought them enemies to one another, but in their touching it saw a closeness even the Tututs lacked. They were one person. After all the time spent apart, now that they were close again someone would die if Mah was harmed, and TasiSabl knew that Odrak had the power.

"He has gone back to the camp to find me?" Odrak bent down to help tend the bleeding Aphro.

"No, Odrak," moaned the Aphro.

Odrak had been walking on air when he came into the clearing, but the look in the Aphro's eyes, the changing expression on TasiSabl's face, and a young protector's swollen lips, dropped him to the ground. The oil nodes and body paints slipped from his hands as he jumped up to stretch out his senses. He knew Mah was hurting, and was somewhere on the other side of the lake.

"Omolungway," was all the Aphro needed to say.

Odrak leaped over the young protectors, and before they could turn around, he was in the darkness of the trees, carrying only the insanity of his mind.

ProCord Publications

9 Heckman Drive, Suite 1B, Jersey City, NJ 07305
(201) 435-7816

DATE: ______________

NO.: ______________

NAME: ____

COMPANY: ____

ADDRESS: ____

CITY, STATE & ZIP: ____

PHONE: ____

QUANTITY: ______________ @ 19.95 ea. TOTAL: ______________

Special Delivery: ☐ add $4.05 pp   Regular Mail: ☐ add $2.05 pp

(2 TO 3 WEEKS FOR DELIVERY)

- -

TITLES:

COMMENTS: ____

Words In The Wind ☐

____

In Their Whispers There Is Sin ☐

____

The New Slave Market ☐

____

Slipping Through The Blood of Our Lovers ☐

____

Upon The Breeze Their Power Bends ☐

______________________________ REP: ....

RECEIPT: ____________ × ____________ = ____________

Price*   Quantity   Total Amount

* Must include delivery.

ProCord Publications

9 Heckman Drive, Suite 1B, Jersey City, NJ 07305
(201) 435-7816

DATE: ______________

NO.: ______________

NAME: ______________________________

COMPANY: ______________________________

ADDRESS: ______________________________

CITY, STATE & ZIP: ______________________________

PHONE: ______________________________

QUANTITY: __________ @ 19.95 ea. TOTAL: __________

Special Delivery: ☐ add $4.05 pp Regular Mail: ☐ add $2.05 pp

(2 TO 3 WEEKS FOR DELIVERY)

- -

TITLES:

COMMENTS: ______________________________

Words In The Wind ☐

____

In Their Whispers There Is Sin ☐

____

The New Slave Market ☐

____

Slipping Through The Blood of Our Lovers ☐

____

Upon The Breeze Their Power Bends ☐

______________________________ REP: ....

RECEIPT: __________ × __________ = ______________

Price* Quantity Total Amount

* Must include delivery.